Years later Cameron would regret having bullied his sister into hiding her grief. Hiding things, after all, had been part of the problem. Years later he would learn, too, that even tragedy has its flip side and that there are, indeed, lots of bright colors in the box of crayons. But that summer, when he was fourteen, when he left the garage with Lauren and looked into his father's stunned face, that was the moment when he learned what the worst thing was, the worst thing of all.

THE PUMPKIN-SHELL WIFE

"Hooray for the return of the four
over-the-hill sleuths
McShea introduced
in *HOMETOWN HEROES*! . . .
THE PUMPKIN-SHELL WIFE
blends old fashioned who-done-it
with humor and wonderful characters."

Annette Meyers, author of *The Deadliest Option*

"Will delight readers who like mystery
served up with character"

Publishers Weekly

Other Avon Books by
Susanna Hofmann McShea

HOMETOWN HEROES

Avon Books are available at special quantity discounts for bulk purchases for sales promotions, premiums, fund raising or educational use. Special books, or book excerpts, can also be created to fit specific needs.

For details write or telephone the office of the Director of Special Markets, Avon Books, Dept. FP, 1350 Avenue of the Americas, New York, New York 10019, 1-800-238-0658.

THE PUMPKIN-SHELL WIFE

A Hometown Heroes Mystery

SUSANNA
HOFMANN McSHEA

AVON BOOKS ◆ NEW YORK

This is a work of fiction. The events described are imaginary and the characters are fictitious and not intended to represent specific living persons.

HEART AND SOUL by Frank Loesser and Hoagy Carmichael. Copyright © 1938 by Famous Music Corporation. Copyright renewed 1965 by Famous Music Corporation.

AVON BOOKS
A division of
The Hearst Corporation
1350 Avenue of the Americas
New York, New York 10019

First Avon Books Printing: August 1993

AVON TRADEMARK REG. U.S. PAT. OFF. AND IN OTHER COUNTRIES, MARCA REGISTRADA. HECHO EN U.S.A.

Printed in the U.S.A.

RA 10 9 8 7 6 5 4 3 2 1

For my father, Charles B. Hofmann,
with love and respect.

Acknowledgments

Special thanks to Jay Calvert, Ph.D., for the advice on genetics, to Ruth Cavin, an editor ever gracious and supportive, and to my agent, Jane Cushman, who believed in my writing and offered helpful suggestions.

For each ecstatic instant
We must an anguish pay. . . .
                    —*Emily Dickinson*

1 In a darkened hotel room on Manhattan's West Side, a woman awakened and reached for the bedside lamp. She squinted through myopic eyes at a Tiffany travel clock nested on the bureau among prismed perfumes, jars of makeup and ropes of pearls. She groped for a pair of sensible brown plastic eyeglasses and tried again. With the help of the thick corrective lenses she could just make out the numbers. Eight-fifteen.

The woman didn't know it, but the remainder of her life amounted to twelve minutes.

Scolding herself for having dozed off, she lifted her large-boned frame from the rumpled bedspread. She smoothed the threadbare fabric. She grabbed a plastic wand and pulled back stained brocade drapes, then yanked a soiled cord to withdraw inner ones gray with soot and grime. She gazed into the blackness of a night pockmarked by flashing neon and yellow postage stamps of light.

The room smelled of ammonia and sweat. The shag carpet was littered with bits of lint and yellowed toenail clippings. The faded wallpaper was streaked in places where previous tenants had hurled drinks or, worse, relieved themselves. An ancient air conditioner provided a whisper of a breeze more frustrating than refreshing in a losing battle against heat and humidity.

The occupant next door flushed something, possibly a rat, down the toilet. Pipes rattled. The emergency bell in the elevator down the hall screamed once again. A baby cried. The woman heard a sharp smack and winced.

As was her habit, the woman tried to ignore the sights, sounds, and the smells of the St. James Hotel. She turned her mind away from the shabbiness of the surroundings and to the promise of the evening that lay ahead.

Quickly she double-checked the room to make sure everything was perfect . . . the scented candles strategically placed to cast romantic light . . . the bottle of Dom Perignon chilling in the plastic ice bucket . . . the bedside radio tuned to a station featuring soft sentimental music.

With trembling fingers she untied the turquoise Japanese silk robe and let it fall to her ankles. She stepped out of it and hung it neatly in the closet. Momentarily she surveyed the wardrobe inside . . . the white raw silk suit by de la Renta, the demure flowered Laura Ashley cotton dress trimmed in antique lace, the sheer lounging pajamas belted with a ribbon of pink satin, and, finally, a red sequined polyester see-through blouse with accompanying black vinyl miniskirt discovered at Job Lot Pushcart over on Eighth Avenue.

The last gave her pause. She shook her head distractedly and poured yet another iceless drink into her plastic glass, telling herself it was worth it. When you're in love, anything is worth it. She snapped the louvered doors shut and tried not to worry about possible disappointment. Tonight would be different, she told herself. Tonight everything would be perfect.

She went into the bathroom, turned on the water full force into the claw-foot tub, tore open a packet of Piquant Passion bath salts and sprinkled them into the churning water. An overpowering scent of roses filled the steamy white-tiled room. She had purchased these bath salts, along with Vaseline Intensive Care, a new toothbrush, Summer's Eve douche and a month's supply of calcium supplements, just this afternoon at a Duane Reade drugstore on East Forty-second Street.

It gave her a thrill to perform these mundane tasks anonymously in the city. It made her feel alive and alluring. Like she was worth something. Like she was desirable. She gazed into the bathroom mirror. The face that looked back was plain, somewhat puffy, and forty-three years old. Its expression was rather sad.

Most people thought she was plain, but in reality it was her bearing that caused them to think so. Her features were fine and strong, her large body statuesque and well proportioned, her eyes gentle and kind. If someone had told her these things she would not have believed them. Except here. Here everything changed.

The face in the mirror froze. An old nursery rhyme popped into her head and gave her a chill. *Ashes, ashes, we all fall down.*

I could stop if I wanted to. Any time.

Sure.

Once on one of her furtive trips to the city, she had wandered into Bloomingdale's. A smartly dressed woman in the cosmetics department cornered her with the offer of a free facial makeover. Appalled by the suggestion, she backed away clumsily into a nearby jewelry display. To her horror a revolving Lucite case tipped to the floor where it shattered as though it were a land mine, spewing shrapnel of glittering rhinestone earrings.

Frantic to make amends, she crouched and skittered across the floor like an ungainly crab in an effort to retrieve the scattered merchandise. Her face flamed. She felt pinpricks of sweat under her arms. She heard the crunch of jewelry underfoot as other shoppers walked by. No one so much as looked at her. Yet deftly, almost imperceptibly, each shopper in turn altered direction ever so slightly, guided by the internal radar peculiar to New Yorkers.

Burning with embarrassment, she struggled to her feet. She handed the saleslady a fistful of glass shards and clasps. She wondered if she should tell the woman that she had an IQ of 145. That she had four lovely children and a husband who was a doctor. That she had a home on five acres in Connecticut with a swimming pool and tennis court. She wondered if the woman would care.

To make amends she bought two hundred and fifty dollars worth of Clinique cosmetics, waving her credit card like a white flag.

"You have marvelous bone structure," said the woman as she slipped the purchases into a Bloomie's bag. "High cheekbones, clear skin, expressive eyes . . ."

The compliments hit her like fists.

She returned to the house with the swimming pool and tennis court, locked the bedroom door, and tried on the makeup. It was then that she discovered she could be prettier than people had led her to believe.

That had been the start of it.

I could give it up. I could.

Sure.

Distractedly she ran a hand through mouse-brown hair, destroying the dowdy suburban hairdo Michelle at Charles of the Ritz had labored to create just that morning. This gesture of defiance gave her a surge of satisfaction.

She turned her back on herself and gazed out the bathroom window into the wall of the office building across the alley. She could barely make it out through the flat blackness of the soot-spattered windowpane. Behind her the roar of running water filled the room. Suddenly her eyes shifted and focused on a window one flight up. She felt her heart quicken, her breath catch. There he was. Again.

The man up there was looking down at her naked body. Just as she knew he would be.

The man did not smile. His steady gaze and vacant expression never wavered. He made not the slightest move to acknowledge her existence.

Yet instinctively she knew what he wanted. She lifted her drink to him in a timid salute. She swallowed what was left of the scotch and set the glass on the radiator. Slowly, tentatively, her hands wandered to her breasts.

She toyed with the nipples, delicately allowing them to harden under her fingertips.

She could not believe she was doing this, but the urge to continue was irresistible. She started a slow dance with herself, twisting and turning before the sooty window, moving to a rhythm only she could hear. She closed her eyes and lost herself to the music. He was watching, she knew it. Watching and admiring. It was their private moment. *I love you,* she told him. *This is our secret.*

In her mind, she heard him cry her name.

Suddenly she remembered the time. Her eyes snapped open and she looked up at the man who was no more than a shadow trapped in his own pane of glass. *I have to go,* she told him silently. *I'm sorry.*

Minutes later there was a knock at the door.

Oh God, she thought, he's early. Early, and I am totally unprepared. I want it to be perfect. I want it to be—

Hastily she grabbed a towel and cinched it tightly around her chest. She ran a comb through her hair, flattening the hated hairdo as best she could.

The knock came again, a sharp rap this time. Insistent. Demanding.

"Just a minute," she said breathlessly. She ran to the bedroom bureau, plucked a garish red wig from its Styrofoam head and placed it on her own. Jerkily she began applying makeup.

"Open up," demanded a muffled voice from the hall.

It was no use. There was simply not enough time. Almost weeping in frustration, she flung down a tube of mascara and crept to the door.

"I'm not ready," she whimpered.

"Open up," the voice demanded once again, louder this time. "Hotel Security." It sounded as though his lips were pressed right against the wood. The voice was artificially gruff and guttural yet somehow intimately familiar. She felt a ripple of excitement.

Despite her cheap costume and veneer of hardened sophistication, she was a country girl playing a dangerous city game. In one thoughtless moment, she unlatched the chain and opened the door.

She stared at her visitor in disbelief. "Oh baby—"

They were the last words she would ever speak. Before she could reach out to reassure her loved one, she heard an inhuman whispered cry of disgust followed by a blur of motion. The broad side of a hammer came from nowhere, crashing into her face, shattering forehead and cheekbone with one deft killing blow, ravaging her almost pretty face, driving fragments of bone into her brain.

No, you don't understand! She gulped air convulsively as her throat and nose filled with blood. *Please!*

In the instant of consciousness that remained, she thought of her childhood, her children, and of things as yet undone. She was a woman who apologized compulsively, and now, as she floated backward into a sea of black, the words she wanted to say most of all were *I'm sorry.*

She reached out, clutching blindly at the blood-spattered arm. Then she staggered back, red wig tilting crazily, mascaraless eyes locked in apology and death.

2 Former Raven's Wing police chief Forrest T. Haggarty lay sacked out like a bag of bones in a green plaid hammock. His white hair lay plastered on his scalp. His beaked nose protruded skyward. His sinewy arms dangled lazily to the grass. One forearm displayed an elaborate heart-shaped tattoo in blurred hues of emerald, turquoise and rose. The center of the heart bore the name TARA, an indelible reference to a long lost love that never failed to drive Irene, his live-in companion, crazy with jealousy.

He sighed contentedly. The rush of the wind through the trees, the soothing drone of cicadas, and the hum of faraway lawn mowers made him drowsy. Through lids of closed eyes he could see the orange glow of the noonday sun.

Suddenly Forrest felt a shadow. "Reenie?" he said before opening one eye. It was her habit to creep up on him this way, a habit she had adopted ever since his supposed heart attack last fall. Sometimes he half expected her to hold a mirror under his nose, searching for signs of life. In the past he had gleefully taken advantage of Irene's anxiety, holding himself still as stone without breathing, then exploding with laughter just as the poor woman started to fall apart. She made him promise not to do that anymore, so this time he decided he wouldn't. He murmured her name softly and hitched up one eye.

As it turned out, the person hovering over him was not Irene Purdy. It was a strange creature, an embryonic bloodless semblance of a human being. In his semisomnolent state, it gave Forrest a terrible start. A boy, it was. An albino sort of boy with blond spiky hair bleached so white it blazed like fire in the noonday sun. A boy with pale unnaturally blue eyes magnified enormously behind lenses thick as prisms. A boy with a red runny nose that twitched this way and that like some kind of laboratory rabbit. A boy with big teeth that glinted behind a latticework of steel braces.

"Christ!" snapped Forrest. "You shouldn't oughta creep up on a man like that!"

"Sorry." The boy stepped back a pace.

"Could give a body a heart attack, creeping that way."

"You were sleeping," the boy explained. "I didn't want to wake you." He stood up straighter now, as though determined not to cower.

Forrest studied the boy closely. He looked about twelve, maybe thirteen, all arms and legs, ready to shoot up when

zits and pubic hair took hold. His crew cut was definitely not the kind kids were wearing today, not the kind
cropped short on top and long down the back. No, his
hair was chopped unfashionably short all over. Looked
like someone with Parkinson's had taken a lawn mower
to his scalp with the blade positioned too low. Naked pink
ears stuck out like flags.

"How old are you?" demanded Forrest.

"Fourteen."

Jesus, thought Forrest. "What's your name?"

"Cameron."

"Cameron?" Forrest looked at the boy hard. A strange
name for a strange boy.

"Maine. Cameron Maine."

"You don't say. Doc Maine's boy?"

"Yes."

Of course nobody called Cameron's father "Doc Maine."
Jonathan Maine wasn't a real doctor like Forrest's friend
Trevor. Not a GP. He was some sort of candy-ass doctor
who fixed faces. A plastic surgeon was what they called
him. A man who straightened bent noses and filled in
facial craters and sucked away globs of excess fat for a
living.

The mere thought disgusted Forrest. After all, wrinkles
were something you wore proudly, like army stripes, and
fat was something you didn't develop in the first place if
you lived right.

Yet over the years he had come to accept and even
like Jonathan Maine. For a plastic surgeon, and a well-
to-do one at that, Jonathan Maine didn't put on airs.
He had the demeanor of a basset hound and the placid
temperament to match. Jonathan Maine was a thoughtful
sentimental sort of man, the type who choked up at old
movies and escorted his little girl proudly to the town's
annual father-daughter square dance. He drove an old
blue Buick with a Save-the-Whales sticker on the back,
wore suits off the rack from Allen's Men's Shop on
Main Street, and taught Sunday school at St. Mary's.

He walked around with his socks sometimes drooping to his ankles, wore heavy glasses that slipped down the bridge of his nose, and invariably fumbled the ball when he participated in townie softball games. He'd been that way even as a kid in high school, Forrest recalled. A likeable fumbler.

Forrest winced at the thought of Jonathan wielding a scalpel.

Yet wield it he did, with renowned success. Forrest saw an article once in *The New York Times*. People came from as far away as Europe and Asia to seek the deft hand and famed artistry of Jonathan Prescott Maine. He was a maestro when a knife graced his hand, it said. His practice in Manhattan had a year-long waiting list. His ability with especially tragic and challenging cases was legend. He delegated routine surgery to other physicians in his employ and devoted himself to the most difficult, most grisly cases, often performing his skills without charge. Forrest suspected Jonathan would have been able to handle cases such as the brutally beaten Central Park jogger, the fashion model who was horribly slashed by a spurned would-be suitor, and a burned Harlem toddler whose face was a bubbled mass of blisters and melted flesh. His hands were magic, the article pronounced.

But there was more. In addition to his success as a surgeon, Jonathan was a sculptor of some repute. His smooth, elegantly simple marble carvings were represented by the prestigious Pennington Gallery in Manhattan and sought after by an increasing number of astute collectors.

Jonathan himself was humble about it all, both amazed and repelled by such worldly recognition. He had never sought it and certainly never wanted it. It was embarrassing, he once confided to Forrest. Those people at the gallery were a bunch of phonies. He refused to go to any of his openings or their artsy-fartsy parties. Refused also to be interviewed by *Vanity Fair* for a profile. Refused to play their pretentious games. The artist-doctor indeed.

Nonsense, he told Forrest. It's what I do. It's a gift from God, not something to be flaunted with arrogance.

That was another thing about Jonathan. His religion. He was Catholic, very much so. Forrest, who had drifted away from organized religion years before, tried not to hold it against him.

Forrest decided Jonathan Maine was sort of like those Hebrew National franks advertised on TV. He answered to a higher authority. True, he could be a little pompous sometimes, a little stiff-necked, but that was okay. At least he had values. So many folks today didn't.

"I know your father. Haven't seen him around lately though." Forrest said the words without thinking. An odd look—almost a wince—crossed Cameron's face. It was a look that didn't belong on a child.

Suddenly Forrest remembered. Esther Maine. Why, of course. Jonathan's wife. A quiet, beige sort of woman. Heavyset. Kept to herself. Forrest tried to remember exactly what the woman looked like but couldn't.

"I was sorry to hear about your mother, boy."

Cameron Maine pulled himself in tighter and said nothing. Like all Maines, he was reserved and unfailingly polite. He gave no indication of the courage it had taken to venture into this yard, his sweaty hands stuffed in his pockets, his dry tongue stuck to the roof of his mouth like a piece of cardboard. He dragged a sneakered toe across a patch of dirt.

Forrest had meant to stop by to see Jonathan, meant to offer his respects, maybe take one of Irene's rhubarb pies or something. But somehow time had slipped by and he never had. Besides, what could he have said, with her dying the way she did under such strange circumstances? He felt guilty and at the same time annoyed that he should feel so.

"Shouldn't you be in school, young fella?" asked Forrest pointedly, wanting to return to his nap now that these minimal obligatory condolences were out of the way.

"It's summer," said the boy to his feet. "We have vacation."

"Oh." Forrest waited but the boy made no move to leave.

"I saw you on *Twenty/Twenty*," blurted the boy. He looked down into Forrest's face with those unnerving Coke-bottle eyes.

"Yeah," said Forrest, like it was nothing.

"Saw how you solved those serial murders, caught that guy right here in Raven's Wing. The one who killed all those ladies."

"It took a long time," grunted Forrest. "Years an' years. And in the end I didn't do it by myself. I had help."

"I know. I read the story in *People* too." He reached into the back pocket of his raggedy cutoff jeans and extracted a rumpled packet of papers. They were limp from humidity and constant handling. Carefully, almost reverently, he unfolded the sheets. He held out the first page and showed Forrest a black-and-white picture of himself along with Irene Purdy, Trevor Bradford, and Mildred Bennett. "They called you hometown heroes."

"Folks called us a lot of things," said Forrest grumpily, "some of them not fit to print."

"Look," said the boy, "I was thinking . . ." He pushed the glasses up the slick bridge of his nose.

"Oh you were?" said Forrest warily.

"Maybe you could find out what happened to my mother."

"There's nothing to find out. The way I hear tell, it was an accident."

"That's what they're saying, but it isn't true."

"She slipped in the bathtub," said Forrest shortly. "Took one helluva brodie. Terrible thing, but it happens every day. People die from that. Slipping."

"In a strange hotel room?" The boy's voice was a mixture of anger and disbelief. "Registered under another name? With clothes and stuff in the closet that weren't even hers—"

"Listen," interrupted Forrest as kindly as he could. He looked at the boy and drew a blank. "What'd you say your name was?"

"Cameron."

"Right. Listen, Cameron, I don't know rightly how to say this. It's a long time since I had boys of my own; longer since I've been one myself . . ."

"Uh huh." Cameron Maine braced himself for an inevitable adult lecture.

" . . . but grown-ups sometimes have secrets. Not that that's bad, mind you. We *all* got secrets, see? And that's the way it should be. We all got a private place inside that's ours alone. Understand?"

"I guess," said Cameron politely.

"Your mother was your mother, sure. But she was a person too. A person with her own private place. So she took a day off, took a little vacation maybe. You got brothers and sisters?"

"A brother and a sister. Two and twelve. And another sister." He added the last almost as an afterthought. "Claudia. She's nineteen."

"There!" said Forrest. "You see? That's a handful. Plus taking care of the house and all."

"We have a lady who cleans."

Forrest ignored this offhand remark born of an easy privilege. "So she took herself a little vacation. Rented herself a nice quiet hotel room, and planned to have herself a nice relaxing time."

It was the kindest way Forrest could think to put it. If the truth be told, Esther Maine was probably seeing someone on the side. It happened all the time. Forrest called it the "Bored Housewife Syndrome," although it was far less common now, what with so many women working at full-time careers and finding partners to screw at the office. But Esther Maine had no career. She was your typical Raven's Wing corporate type wife. Not so pretty and on the quiet side maybe, but who knows what was smoldering underneath? A woman with time and money on her hands.

The way Forrest had it figured, Esther Maine went to New York City to shack up, with someone out of her social circle most likely, and had the misfortune to slip in the bathtub. A similar incident happened twenty years back when the pastor from St. Mary's in Raven's Wing was found dead in a New York City hotel bathtub. Also under an assumed name. Turned out the cleric was homosexual and had gone to the city to indulge his proclivities under a cloak of anonymity peculiar to Manhattan. It wasn't a crime, but there he was just the same: dead and exposed for all the world to see. Of course, Forrest told Cameron Maine none of this.

Cameron looked away, disgusted with the pitter-patter of politeness. He'd expected better from this man. He said the words before he could stop himself. "You think she was fooling around."

"Hush your mouth!" Forrest almost fell from the hammock. The very idea, a boy talking like that about his own mother. "I'll take you over my knee, don't think I can't."

"That's what people think," the boy shot back, "I can tell. And so do you. Well it's a lie. A dirty, rotten, disgusting lie."

"Of course it is," said Forrest quickly. All at once he was flustered. Damn this boy anyway. Who did he think he was?

"It just doesn't make sense."

"Why the hell not?" said Forrest. He wanted to resume his nap, to drift off to sweet dreams. Never mind death and adultery. Never mind a pain-in-the-ass kid who didn't know better than to rattle his elders with blurted statements about delicate subjects better left unmentioned. He closed his eyes in exasperation and willed the boy to be gone.

"It doesn't make sense because she never took showers."

"Huh?" said Forrest, not sure he'd heard correctly.

"My mother. She never took showers. She only took baths." Cameron Maine knew this for a fact because throughout his childhood he'd been lulled to sleep by the soothing sound of water running for his mother's nightly bath.

Forrest opened his eyes but didn't look at the boy. It was a small point, of course. Probably nothing. Still, it was just the sort of small point, just the sort of discrepancy, on which cases are made. He could feel himself being drawn in. Shit, he told himself, I don't need this.

"The police," recited the boy doggedly as though speaking to a dull-witted child, "told my father she slipped in the bathtub. During a shower. The shower was still running, that's what they told us. And I'm telling you my mother never took showers."

"Maybe she did this time," said Forrest with false indifference. He felt the skin on the back of his neck prickle. Stop, he told himself. Just quit it. You can't afford to get involved.

"Maybe nothing!" said the boy angrily. He threw back his head and closed his eyes in frustration. . . .

How could he tell this man the truth? It was his mother. Suddenly the world had turned upside down and inside out, turned into a nightmare worse than he ever imagined. Yet, amazingly, no one seemed to care.

Oh, people were ever so polite with their tears and hugs and well-intentioned words of comfort. Sympathy was a hat they put on for special occasions. They came to the funeral and said how sorry they were. But inside he knew what they really felt. They felt relief. Relief that it wasn't them, or someone close to them, lying in that casket. Inside they thanked their lucky stars that it wasn't them with the rouged cheeks, formaldehyde veins, and lips sewn tightly together with twine.

Not me, thank God. Not me that kicked the bucket. Not me that bought the farm. Not me that cashed in my chips. I've got my chips right here, see? Yes indeed. Lots and lots and lots of chips.

No, it wasn't any of them. It was his mother. Esther Jamison Maine. And they were sorry.

Well wasn't that fine.

Monsignor McLaughlin had taken hold of Cameron's inert hand. The priest sought out his averted eyes. They faced one another beside a pile of dirt covered with a green blanket that was supposed to look like grass but didn't. The words were practiced and automatic and predictable: "I'm so sorry."

Sure, Cameron wanted to say. You're sorry. Bullshit! To a priest, a monsignor, no less. But his manners took hold and he pulled himself in tighter and all he said was "Thank you."

His mother would have been proud.

Everyone drifted away from the cemetery leaving Cameron with his broken father and motherless siblings, wondering what to do next.

Of course there was no one to ask and no one to help either. Turning to his father was out of the question. His father, who had always been a rock, had cracked. His Grandma Lucille was a spiteful old bitch, eaten away by years of bitterness and recrimination. His sister and brother, Lauren and Timmy, were too young. And his older sister Claudia? Well, you couldn't count on Claudia for anything.

It had been Cameron who had taken charge. Cameron who called the relatives. Cameron who picked out the headstone. Cameron who insisted on a closed casket. Cameron who threatened not to go at all if that casket wasn't closed. Cameron who veered his face away when they tried to make him look. *Say goodbye,* they said. *You'll regret it later if you don't.*

But he couldn't. Wouldn't. Didn't.

No!

Don't look, Dad. We'll just pretend it never happened.

But later at the cemetery the truth came to him with a force that made him shrivel up inside. Even as part of him denied what had happened, he knew they would have to learn to accept it. His mother had died but their family still numbered six: Jonathan, Claudia, Cameron, Lauren, Timothy, and another. A stranger. An unwelcome visitor called death.

Cameron had known it would come one day. He'd understood that early on. He'd tried to plan for it even, tried to get a head start. Even so, his mother's leaving caught him off guard. He tried not to blame himself. After all, no amount of foresight could prepare you for something this fucked up.

The search had begun almost as soon as he could talk, a game of sorts in which Cameron would pose grotesque questions to anyone who would indulge him with answers.

"Which would you choose: to go blind or to lose one of your legs?"

"I'd choose neither, Cameron. Neither appeals to me."

"But if you had to choose. If you had had *to."*

Finally his father or big sister or whoever it was would relent. "Well then, I suppose I'd lose the leg."

"Would you rather be blind or deaf?"

"For heaven's sake, I'd rather be neither."

"But if," Cameron would press, "you had to choose."

"I don't think we should encourage him by answering those questions," said his mother. "It's not normal."

"Nothing about Cameron," replied his father proudly, "is normal."

By the age of three Cameron was cursed or blessed (depending on your point of view) with a sensitivity that made daily life difficult for those around him. Although he would realize that the questions were upsetting his mother, he could not resist. Reluctantly he would put them aside for a while. But only for a while. The morbid game would invariably resume another day. It was as though he were flipping through a monumental mental Rolodex of tragic possibilities, asking, sorting, prioritizing, in a futile effort to determine the very worst thing that could befall a human being.

"Why do you ask such questions?" asked his mother.

"I don't know," he replied. But this was not entirely true. He had a feeling, that was why. A bad feeling. Because even then Cameron Maine suspected that the world could be a dangerous place. There were things you should look out for. Things to avoid. He had to figure it out and there wasn't much time.

"I'm worried about him," said Esther Maine one day. "He talks to himself."

"I know," said Cameron's father without concern. Cameron's father was the ways and means of the Maine family. He was strong. He was a rock. He knew how things were supposed to be, and when they weren't he made them so.

"He has imaginary friends. He says they live under a manhole and they're named Gleeglas and Glas. He talks to himself. All the time."

Jonathan Maine set down his cup of herb tea or his American Medical Journal or the plastic sack of dried pitted prunes that helped him stay regular. "He has an active imagination, Esther. It runs in the family. Didn't you have imaginary friends at his age? Didn't you tell me so yourself?"

Esther's face became pained. "Well," she said uneasily, "I . . ."

"What, honey?"

"I don't want him to be like me."

"Now, now," Cameron's father would scoff. "What a thing to say. He's shy, that's all. All Maines are shy. It's in the genes."

"I'd feel better if he stopped going into corners talking to himself."

"Take him to the doctor if it will make you feel better."

"Could you take him?"

"Esther, we've discussed this before."

"You know I get tongue-tied with strangers."

"Well you'll just have to get over it. For heaven's sake, you don't stutter here with the family, do you? Of course not. If you set your mind to it you won't stutter outside either. You're making such progress. You can't hide in the house forever."

"I know," she agreed.

So Esther Maine took Cameron to the doctor herself, and the doctor confirmed what Jonathan had said. *He has a vivid imagination. Don't tell him not to talk to these friends. He will lose them soon enough.*

And sure enough, Cameron did lose them. He lost them and never really made any others. He lost them round about the time he went to kindergarten. He went off to school that first day, carrying the empty cigar box the teacher told the children to bring for pencils and crayons. He walked off in brand new unscuffed orthopedically correct Stride Rite shoes, wearing brown wool pants that itched and a new plaid shirt Grandmother Maine had sewn by hand with needlework initials embroidered on the pocket.

"Look at this, Jon," Cameron's mother said after only two weeks.

"It's very nice," replied Jonathan Maine absently.

"It's all in black. He only uses black. Forty-eight colors in the box of Crayolas, and Cameron only uses black."

"Give him time. He'll get to the other colors."

"The teacher doesn't like it."

"Tell the teacher," Jonathan replied, *"to take a flying leap."*

"Shhhhhhhh! He'll hear you. It's his teacher, Jon."

"So the boy has a mind of his own. Cameron is special, Esther. We've always known it. He's better than the rest." Just like me, that's what the words implied, and Cameron was proud.

"The teacher says this drawing is morbid."

"No it's not. Look there . . . He drew flowers. A field of flowers. In great detail too, I might add. Look at that sun on the horizon. That sense of perspective is remarkable for

a five-year-old." Being a plastic surgeon, Jonathan Maine was proud of his artistic eye. He knew about things like perspective and detail.

Esther took a deep breath. "The teacher says he's pre-occupied with punishment. The concept of punishment."

"Oh for heaven's sake."

"I asked him why he only uses black. You know what he said? He said black is real. What a strange thing for a child to say."

Jonathan Maine chuckled. "You worry too much."

The next day in school Sister Bernadette announced that they would all draw pictures on the blackboard. Did she smile at Cameron in a superior way, knowing that he couldn't use black crayon on a blackboard? Knowing he would have to use white chalk? Or did he just imagine it?

He went gamely to the board with all the others and clutched the chalk in a sweaty palm. He had no idea what to draw. Other children were drawing stick men and grotesque ballooning animals. Suddenly, frantically, his mind seized on an idea. In an uncharacteristic fit of enthusiasm, he drew sweeping, uninhibited chalk lines.

Cameron finished first and sat down before all the others. After a while they sat down too.

"Who drew this?" Sister's voice demanded. The voice was not happy, not happy at all. Flushed with shame, Cameron saw that she was pointing to his drawing.

He had drawn Christ on a cross. In great detail. He had drawn him as best he could, and he had drawn him smiling. The people around him were having a party. Eating, drinking, making merry. It wasn't morbid. There was no punishment. Wasn't this what everyone wanted?

Apparently it was not.

"I did." He stood up as he said it, and it came out more defiant than fearful. This surprised Cameron. His voice dared her to say something.

She didn't say anything, though. She just looked at him, looked at him in a way that said You're-a-strange-child. You will never fit in.

She was right, Cameron realized later. According to the school psychologist he never "made the preschool transition from personal isolation to social integration." Cameron had seen it written in his file. But as he matured he accepted it. It was simply the way he was.

Nine years later it was summer in Connecticut and he was fourteen. Nothing had changed and yet everything had.

He had been playing "Heart and Soul" on the piano. Helga was singing in the kitchen, preparing lunch for Timmy, who slammed his spoon loudly on the tray of his high chair. Lauren was packing her trunk for summer camp. Every summer Lauren and Cameron were sent to Our Lady of the Lake Camp in the Berkshires for six weeks. His father told them it was to build self-reliance, but Cameron suspected it was really to get them out of the house.

Cameron loved his mother, but for as long as he could remember she had been what they called "delicate." She had trouble coping with things. Once someone told him his mother had a nervous condition. He also heard the word "unstable." He wondered what, exactly, that meant. He wondered if it, too, ran in the family.

Everything was the same, and yet it was not. His mother was not there. His mother had disappeared. Nobody said so straight out either. Everybody pretended everything was fine. It was like she was on vacation or something. He had a feeling he would not be going to Lady of the Lake this year. He had a feeling everything was about to fall apart.

His fingers tapped the keys nervously. Heart and soul, I fell in love with you. Heart and soul, a love that was so true. Maaaaaaadly . . .

All at once out of the corner of his eye he saw his father coming up the flagstone steps, black bag in hand, hunched forward as though he were heading into a storm. And Cameron knew. His father would never come home from New York at 11:30 in the morning unless something was horribly wrong.

His stomach clenched. He thought he might throw up. He pictured piano keys flooded with vomit.

His father grabbed him by the shoulder and called Lauren. "Kids," he said, "I want you to go out in the garage." Cameron and Lauren looked at each other, eyes full of fear. Helga plucked Timmy from his high chair and fled.

For the rest of his life Cameron would remember that garage . . . the cleanly swept concrete floor, the rows of mason jars filled with nuts and bolts, all precisely grouped according to size, the paint brushes pegged on the wall, the smell of turpentine. Lauren ran to the far corner, leaned against the wall on one arm, and stared at the tops of her white Nikes. Her frizzed hair looked as if she'd set it with jumper cables. Suddenly he felt a wave of sadness for her.

He remembered the planking on the wall, the grain of the wood, some putty in a crack. His ear was plastered to that wall.

He could hear his father making a phone call in his study. Making a long distance phone call to Europe where Cameron's Grandmother Jamison was on vacation with a group off friends from her Boca Shores senior citizens complex.

"Lucille," he said finally, "I have bad news." A moment of silence followed during which Cameron stopped breathing altogether. "There's been an accident. A bad one, I'm afraid. Very bad . . ." His voice cracked but did not break. "Esther is dead." Loud and clear, Cameron heard those words. He would never forget the snap, the finality, of the last one.

He turned away from the wall. Sick at heart and angry too, he spat out the words. "Mother's dead."

"I can't stand it," Lauren cried. She crumpled to the floor and buried her face in her hands.

He ran to her and almost whacked her. "Yes you can," he said. "You can and you must. We must. For Dad's

*sake. Because as hard as it is for us, it's worse for him.
Remember that."*

*She swiped away her tears, and together they went to
face their father.*

*Years later Cameron would regret having bullied his
sister into hiding her grief. Hiding things, after all, had
been part of the problem. Years later he would learn,
too, that even tragedy has its flip side and that there
are, indeed, lots of bright colors in the box of crayons.
But that summer when he was fourteen, when he left the
garage with Lauren and looked into his father's stunned
face, that was the moment he learned what the worst thing
was, the worst thing of all.*

3 "What is it boy?"
"I can't . . ." *breathe! Oh God, I can't—*

Forrest twisted out of the hammock. "Good Lord, you're
turning blue."

"Asthma," he gasped.

"Christ, I'll call a doctor!"

He shook off Forrest's hand. "No." He yanked an inhalator from his back pocket and sucked on it. His breathing came in harsh rasps. "I'll be okay . . . It happens . . .
sometimes."

"Jesus."

Forrest watched worriedly until the boy's breathing
came easier and his color returned.

Cameron stuffed the inhalator back in his pocket.

"Jesus," repeated Forrest. "You gave me a scare there."

The boy ignored him and returned to the subject of his mother. "She never hurt anyone. She didn't deserve to die." He turned to leave this useless old man.

"Hey, don't run off."

The boy stopped in his tracks.

"Maybe we could continue this conversation."

"You mean you'll help?"

"I didn't say that. I mean I'll think about it."

The boy considered this for a moment. It was better than nothing.

"Why don't you stay for lunch?"

Cameron pictured a tray of old people's food. Mashed potatoes. Macaroni. Tapioca. Everything bland and white and oozing. He fought a wave of queasiness. "Okay."

"Good."

No sooner had they approached the weather-beaten picnic table than a short, squash-shaped woman named Irene Purdy trundled out with a towering platter of sandwiches and a pitcher of lemonade. Cameron had heard about Irene but never seen her in the flesh. She was considered an eccentric. For years she lived in the woods in a log cabin she'd built herself. With her husband dead and no children, she turned to wildlife for companionship. She fed deer and raccoons and beaver. She paid no mind to the rabies epidemic spreading up from New Jersey. In fact, she paid no mind to anybody and always did exactly as she pleased. Then last year she came to live on High Ridge with Forrest, and people in town buzzed about it. She was crazy, some said. And just watch. She'll bring in all kinds of vermin. Cameron hadn't seen any vermin yet but was hopeful.

Irene commenced to shuttle back and forth for plates, cutlery, glasses, potato salad, pickles and chips, with Cameron Maine trailing in her wake. And the moment the words "Let me help you" crossed his lips, Cameron Maine was on Irene Purdy's hit parade.

"Cameron here is certainly a gentleman," said Irene as they seated themselves. "Which is more than I can say for some people." She shot a pointed glance at Forrest.

"Irene's my partner," explained Forrest. "We're taking care of this house for our friend Mildred Bennett, who lives in New York City."

Irene paused in mid-chew and pressed two words through a mouthful of tuna: "Separate bedrooms."

"Reenie, for God's sake."

Irene forced the contents of her mouth down her throat and chased it with a healthy slug of lemonade. "I don't want to give Cameron here the wrong impression. We're not living in sin, after all. You can tell the rest of the neighbors that too."

Cameron didn't believe that for a moment. He knew the sap still flowed in old trees. But he blinked twice behind his glasses and nodded. He pried open his sandwich and peered inside. "Would it be all right if I ate just the cheese?"

"Don't you like bologna?" asked Irene. "I never knew a boy didn't like bologna."

"I'm allergic," he said apologetically.

"Don't eat it then," said Forrest, not wanting to witness another attack.

"Allergic to bologna?" said Irene. "Why, I never heard of such a thing." She leaned over and whispered to Forrest. "No wonder he's so skinny."

At the end of the meal, Irene passed around a cut glass bowl with candy in it. "I hope you like M and Ms."

Cameron's face lit up like a small child. "I like the red ones," he said, and proceeded to pick them out.

Forrest took a handful. "So Cameron, tell Irene what you told me."

Cameron Maine chewed on an M&M thoughtfully. He folded his napkin and proceeded to tell Irene his story.

"There's not much to go on," commented Irene after he finished, "but there are certainly a lot of unanswered questions, I'll grant you that." She looked at Forrest hard and then at Cameron sympathetically. "Honey," she said gently, "Forrest here is supposed to be retired."

"Now Reenie, don't start with that."

"Well you are!" She turned to Cameron. "He had a heart attack last fall."

"A moment of indigestion," protested Forrest. "A minor blip in my circulatory system."

"An earthquake."

"A minor tremor!"

"An eight on the Cardiac Richter Scale!"

"Oh hush up!"

"He's supposed to take it easy," persisted Irene. "Supposed to *relax*."

"Christ on a crutch, Reenie, relaxing in that hammock is what's going to kill me. You'll relax me to death, mark my words." He turned to Cameron. "Did you notice how she wouldn't let me have any of them chips? How she managed to keep them just out of reach and snatched them away every time I made a grab? Well, did you?"

"No," mumbled Cameron, not wanting to take sides.

"Cholesterol," barked Irene. "They're loaded with fat."

"And cigars. I can't have any of them neither. And bourbon, oh how could I forget that? She took my bourbon away. A case—an *entire* case—a rare custom-blend—a gift from Millie—collecting dust in the basement. It makes a grown man want to cry."

"It's for your own good, Forrest."

"Next thing you know sex will be out the window."

"Forrest!" Irene turned to Cameron. "Sometimes he talks downright crazy."

"Maybe a diversion would do him good," offered Cameron, deftly changing the subject to his advantage.

"The boy's got a point, Reenie. A diversion, yes indeed. He's a bright boy, Cameron is."

"Oh, I don't know," said Irene reluctantly. "We're not even talking Raven's Wing this time. We're talking New York City. That's a whole 'nother ball game." Her mind filled with scenes of garbage-strewn streets, phlegmy vendors hawking stolen merchandise in broad daylight, homeless people urinating in gutters, and sticky-fingered pickpockets reaching brazenly into her brassiere for spare change. "Lordy," she said out loud.

"Millie's got a place in New York," said Forrest quickly. "She said we could stay there any time. And she'll want to be involved anyway. She'd be hurt if we didn't ask her. *Hurt* if we pass up this opportunity, Irene."

"I'd love to see more of Millie, that's true." Irene smiled as visions of city streets were replaced by the comforting memory of her good friend.

"And Trevor would come along, don't forget," said Forrest. He turned to Cameron. "Trevor's a doctor."

"I know," said Cameron. "I read the article, remember?"

"Well," said Irene, "I don't know. I have to think on it awhile."

"I'd promise to go slow," Forrest put in quickly. "I sure as hell promise that." But as he looked at Cameron Maine sitting there in his Ocean Pacific T-shirt with his hands folded on the table and an open, hopeful expression on his face, a dark thought crossed his mind: Maybe we shouldn't do this. Some things are best left alone. He forced himself to make one last effort to save this boy a lot of grief.

"Look, Cameron, maybe you want to think about this first."

"I already have," said Cameron simply. "I've thought about it a lot."

"No you haven't, boy. Not by a long shot. You think knowing what happened is going to make you feel better?"

"Yes."

"It won't," said Forrest flatly. "Mark my words. It never does. It'll make you feel worse."

"That's okay," said Cameron with the blessed ignorance of youth. "I can deal with it."

"Maybe you can," said Forrest thoughtfully. "Yes. I believe you just might be able to. But what about your family? What about them?"

"I don't see—"

"What about those sisters of yours and your baby brother? What about your dad?"

"My father . . ." began the boy. Without warning, tears stung his eyes. He blinked them back and forced himself to continue. "Nothing can make my father any sadder than he is now. Nothing."

Ah, thought Forrest, that's where you're wrong. You think you've seen grief. You think you've plumbed its depths? You've put a toe in the water, that's all.

"My father has fallen apart," explained Cameron. "He's drinking too much. He cries all the time. He takes the train to his practice in the city, and that's what he does—he stands between the cars and cries. Or at the back of the train watching the tracks go by. He told me so."

"Yeah," said Forrest, thinking that violence sucked. Literally. It bled the life from more than one victim.

"I don't think he believes it was an accident either. And sometimes I'm afraid he might jump from that train."

"What we find out might push him," said Forrest bluntly. "Think about that."

"Nothing can be any worse than it is now," said Cameron doggedly. "Not knowing is worst of all."

"They teach you that in school?" asked Forrest cynically.

"Father Healy taught me that. At Canterbury."

Canterbury. A fancy boarding school. A Catholic prep school that ranked with WASP enclaves such as Groton, Exeter, and Choate. Mildred would have known that, but it didn't mean diddly to Forrest or Irene or even to Cameron.

"He taught me that the truth matters. Nothing else."

"Oh boy," sighed Forrest, "I wish it were that simple."

4 Forrest took a shower after dinner that night. He put on a pair of freshly pressed khaki pants, a blue checked cotton shirt, and a pair of white deck shoes. With Mildred's fashion suggestions and Irene's meticulous ironing, he was turning into a regular peacock. Forrest made a face. Next thing you know I'll be wearing pastel golf pants and white loafers with tassels. He resolved to keep an eye on Irene, lest she creep up on him and further fancify his wardrobe.

Every evening after dinner Forrest took his evening constitutional, only tonight he took his walk in a different direction. He avoided the sidewalk along High Ridge Avenue and headed instead through a mustard-colored meadow that lay behind the house. It was dusk and fireflies blinked around him. Soon burrs clung to the cuffs of his pants and his deck shoes were wet with dew. He inhaled the clean cool air deeply, almost forgetting his yearning for a good cigar.

Without warning his foot broke through something soft and crumbly. Thrown off balance, he collapsed to the ground as one leg dangled into an unexpected void and the other curled painfully beneath him. "What the!" he cried.

For some moments he remained motionless, half squatting in the wet hay, one knee to his chin, wondering what the hell had happened.

"Jesus H!" Stiffly he hoisted himself up. He brushed away damp bits of straw and twigs, smoothed back white

Brillo hair gone wild, and looked down to see a gaping black hole where his leg had been.

"Of all the mother eff-ing dumbass things! A body could kill himself!" He looked closely. The hole appeared to be some sort of abandoned well, covered decades ago, now overgrown and hidden with brambles like one of those Vietnam booby traps. Waiting for some innocent victim out on a nightly stroll to fall and crack his skull wide open.

Muttering to himself, Forrest dug his fingers into what was left of the rotten planked cover and lifted, exposing a perfectly round stone-lined opening, about eighteen inches across give or take. Forgetting his errand for the moment, he grabbed a pebble and chucked it down, waiting for the telltale "plunk" to help him gauge the depth. When there wasn't any, he reassured himself the well was dry. At least, he told himself, a dry well isn't so dangerous as a watery one. And it's too narrow for a body to fall down in any which way.

He replaced the crumbly lid and reminded himself to cover it with something more substantial tomorrow, lest some unsuspecting rabbit or possum fall into its depths.

Forrest approached the Maine house from the rear and studied it silently. The sprawling stone and glass monstrosity was the very picture of American success . . . a shimmering turquoise pool . . . a pristine white cabana with a life preserver hung precisely in place along one wall . . . an enormous flagstone patio with built-in gas-fired barbecue and enough color-coordinated lawn furniture to accommodate a football team.

With admiration, he surveyed several strategically lit statues carved from what appeared to be white marble. Their beauty took his breath away. A Canada goose in flight . . . a silver fox . . . a doe with a fawn.

The house wrapped around this playground, with multiple glass doors leading to various rooms inside. Behind the center door he saw an expansive ultramodern kitchen. Forrest squinted his eyes. A willowy blonde in a white uniform moved about efficiently. He heard the clatter of dishes.

It was like several hundred other houses in Raven's Wing on a sultry summer evening. And at the same time it was like one of those puzzles in a kiddie magazine: Can you see what's wrong in this picture? Forrest knew what was wrong. Someone was missing. Someone was dead. Maybe the reason why was simple, but then again, maybe it wasn't.

All at once he realized there was a person sitting by the pool. In the moonless night Forrest could make out the silhouette of a solitary figure—a man, it looked like. He was at one of those round tables with an umbrella stuck through a hole in the center. Cold blue light from a nearby electric bug zapper gave him an unhealthy glow. Indeed, as he sat there stone still he appeared carved from a block of phosphorescent ice, his hands folded and his head bowed as though praying. Forrest backed away a step. Then, breaking the spell, Jonathan Maine raised a glass to his mouth, emptied the contents, reached under his chair for a bottle and poured himself a hefty refill.

Forrest coughed deliberately and moved forward. "Jonathan?"

"Huh?"

Forrest couldn't see him too well in the darkness, and he was glad for that. After all, when a man is grieving, some shred of privacy should be preserved. But Jonathan Maine swung his head around and his face was exposed in that cold blue light, a face etched in abject misery. A damp splotched face with watery brown eyes. It was a round soft face, not very attractive, framed by a receding hairline inadequately camouflaged with a few pathetic strands of limp hair. Forrest couldn't help but think that here was a man who could use some of his own plastic surgery.

"Jonny boy," said Forrest with forced cheer, "how are you, fella?" He grabbed Maine's shoulder and gave it a squeeze.

"Oh," replied Maine woodenly, "all right, I guess. Considering."

"I meant to stop by before," Forrest apologized, "but somehow things got away from me."

"It's okay, Forrest. I've been, keeping to myself. I've been . . ."—his voice drifted into a sigh—". . . ah, I don't know what I've been."

"I'm sorry about Esther, Jon. Real sorry."

Jonathan looked at him bleakly. Several yards away an unfortunate bug crackled in the zapper. "Ah," he sighed, "yes."

For a moment Forrest feared Jonathan Maine might actually succumb to tears. His face seemed to crumple, but he managed to pull himself back from the brink with obvious effort.

"It's kind of you to visit, Forrest. Sit down. Please." He gestured to another chair at the table.

"Well," said Forrest, "maybe for a minute." He noticed an ashtray brimming with ashes and half-smoked cigarettes. Then he noticed a second whiskey glass. "Looks like you knew I was coming."

A startled look on Jonathan's face turned to embarrassment. "Oh," he stammered. "That. Well, it was part of our evening ritual—Esther's and mine. We'd sit by the pool for a nightcap. Just a glass of sherry. We weren't really drinkers . . ." His voice trailed off. "I brought the second glass . . ." He coughed awkwardly. "Force of habit, I guess."

"No need to explain," said Forrest quickly. "When I lost Queenie I did things like that. You wouldn't believe some of the things I did."

"Like what?" asked Jonathan. The man sounded desperate for a kindred spirit.

"Oh . . ." Forrest turned his mind back in time. ". . . things like not letting anyone sit in her favorite chair. Like keeping an old sweater because it still smelled of her lavender soap. Like only sleeping on my side of the bed, pretending she was there next to me. Things like that."

"I see." He took a big slug of his whiskey. "Would you care to join me in a drink, Forrest?"

"I'd care to, but I can't. I'm supposed to stay away from the sauce." He tapped his chest. "They tell me my ticker isn't what it used to be. What do doctors know, right? Still, better safe than sorry I always say." He paused, considering. "Listen, I know it seems bad now and I guess folks have told you this before, but . . ."

Jonathan looked at him expectantly, as though his friend Forrest Haggarty were about to impart some universal truth that would magically release him from his anguish.

". . . things will get better—"

"—in time," Jonathan finished hollowly.

"Yeah," said Forrest, realizing how feeble the words sounded. "In time. Right."

"She was the center of my life, Forrest. I know people say that about each other all the time, and it sounds so trite. But with us it was true."

"It's rough losing a spouse," Forrest commiserated. "The roughest."

"No," said Jonathan, swinging his head from side to side. "You don't understand." He stopped, getting his bearings. "No one can understand how it was with us. Esther was my life. People thought she was a burden because she had a few problems. But I didn't care. I loved her just the way she was. Everything I did, I did for her. Everything I am is because of her. Everything." He set down his drink and gripped the aluminum arms of the chair. "I tried to protect her, and I failed. Sometimes I don't think I can go on."

Forrest knew what he meant. "You've got your children," he said sharply. Contemplating suicide, even in the face of tremendous grief, was out of the question as far as Forrest was concerned. "You owe it to them to get hold of yourself."

But Jonathan Maine, an inexperienced drinker who had drowned his sorrow in more than a few shots of Canadian Club, went on as though Forrest hadn't spoken. He opened his hands, framing his portly shape. "I was—am—a plain man at best." Forrest started to protest, but Jonathan waved him off. "Don't think I don't know it. I never was what you'd call a lady's man. I have an eye for beauty, that much is true. Beauty is my business. I used to joke about that. But I myself am plain and make no apologies for it. I've always been a bit of a square."

It was true. Forrest and his old-time Raven's Wing cronies joked among themselves about stodgy Jonathan Maine. He was a man who never in his life owned a pair of dungarees. A man who sorted his socks in the drawer according to colors of brown, navy, gray, and black. A man who wore galoshes when it rained and carried an umbrella no matter what the weather. A man who played by the rules. A belt-and-suspenders man if ever there was one.

"Cameron, God help him, is turning out just like me."

"That Cameron's okay," protested Forrest in the boy's defense.

"Anyway, there I was, unathletic and overweight even at twenty-eight, looking at the world through thick horn-rimmed glasses."

"Oh no," protested Forrest. "Why I remember back then. You were a bright young fella. Had your head screwed on straight. We all knew you'd accomplish great things."

"I had just finished my residency and was starting the practice, drowning in a sea of debts." He looked at the luxury that surrounded them as though noticing it for the first time. "It seems hard to believe now.

"In any event, I met Esther at a party. A *party* for goodness sake. I wasn't very social and I never went to parties. But for some reason I went to that one. It was over in Greenwich. Plastic surgery was just starting to come into vogue. There were supposed to be a lot of fashion people there, people in entertainment too. I'm far better at surgery than I am at socializing, but I forced myself to go because it would be good for business.

"Once I got there, I fled to a corner with my glass of ginger ale. And there she was—wearing a black dress with white lace apron, carrying a tray of canapés—scared stiff. The poor girl was totally overwhelmed by her surroundings. Of course I was overwhelmed too but didn't say so. I tried to talk to her, tried to put her at ease."

"Sounds like you were a regular Prince Charming."

"Esther thought so. Oh, she was meek as a mouse, scarcely said two words, but I could tell right away she was a person of quality. Nothing flashy or pretentious, but refined, you know? I made small talk, babbled like an idiot I suppose. I fully expected her to make a polite excuse, then bolt at the first opportune moment. But she didn't." A look of amazement crossed Jonathan's face at the vivid memory, and he took another gulp from his glass.

"She was a treasure, Forrest. She was *innocent*. Untouched. A solid old-fashioned girl, a girl with traditional values, in the midst of all that phoniness and glitz."

"And you got married?"

"We did. My family wasn't thrilled because Esther was poor and her family lived . . . well, you know the area over there by the lumber yard. But she was the best choice I could have made. Selfless and caring. She devoted herself to me and the children. She was a thoughtful person. A loving person." He stopped abruptly. "Forgive me, I'm running off at the mouth."

Forrest nodded sympathetically. "You know," he said carefully, "Cameron came to see me this afternoon."

"Oh?" Jonathan's face took on a look of concern.

"Yeah. I guess because I used to be police chief around here."

"Of course," said Jonathan. "A fine job you did too."

"Yeah," said Forrest, brushing off the compliment. "Anyway, Cameron thinks his mother's death might not have been accidental."

"What?" Jonathan's head swiveled toward Forrest.

"Well it was an accident, wasn't it? I mean, that's what folks are saying."

"Yes," said Jonathan quickly. "Of course."

"You don't sound real convinced."

"I am. It was an accident."

"Come on, Jon. You're a lousy liar. Tell me."

"There's nothing to tell. Cameron should leave it alone. For his sake, for everyone's sake, he should leave it—"

Forrest felt a prickle of annoyance. "You want me to call the city police? Is that what you want?"

"No."

"Look, Jonathan, Cameron asked us—"

"I know what Cameron asked you!"

Jonathan Maine shifted uncomfortably in his chair. "All right," he said at last. "It may not have been an accident. It just seemed, well, for the sake of the children, it seemed best that that's what I said it was."

"You mean it wasn't?"

"They're not sure. Entirely."

"What's that sposed to mean?"

Jonathan Maine took a deep breath. "As you probably know, Forrest, there are four ways the medical examiner can rule on a death. Natural, accidental, suicide, and . . ."

"Cause of death unknown pending investigation," finished Forrest. "That's what they said?"

"Yes," replied Jonathan bitterly. "Pending investigation. An investigation that in all likelihood will never happen."

"Why the hell not?"

"Because . . . because . . . because I don't know! Because they're overworked and understaffed. Because there was no trace of physical evidence at the scene. Because . . ." His face contorted with pain. His voice dropped to a whisper. "Because they don't think she's worth it."

"Not worth it? Sweet Jesus."

"They never said so in so many words. But that's the impression I got. They found her in a disreputable hotel, under an assumed name. They seem to think . . . seem to be treating her . . . God, Forrest, they act like she was a prostitute or something."

"Lord," murmured Forrest.

"So you can also understand why I'm telling the children and people in town it was an accident."

"Sure. But Cameron isn't buying it. He's a smart boy. And he knows you're not buying it either."

"He never mentioned anything about this to me." Jonathan stopped for a moment, then looked at Forrest guiltily. "But then I haven't really been listening to him lately."

"Anyway," Forrest went on, "the boy's so upset—"

"He's not your average boy," Jonathan interrupted. "Some call him strange. He keeps to himself. Marches to his own drummer. Hasn't eaten meat since he was six, did you know that?"

"He said he was allergic to bologna."

"True, but it's probably psychosomatic. He developed a physical aversion to meat because he believes animals have souls." Jonathan read Forrest's skeptical look. "Well, who's to say he's wrong? We're a religious family, Forrest. The church has given us tremendous strength and our faith will sustain us through this. Cameron takes his religion very much to heart, even more so than the rest of us. He talks of becoming a priest."

Forrest pictured skinny jug-eared Cameron Maine wearing a Roman collar and swinging a set of clickety-clack rosary beads. Pictured him saying to a congregation not only can't you eat meat on Friday like in the old days, you can forget it the other six days too—because animals have *souls*.

"Well," offered Forrest with characteristic lack of tact, "I guess it's good you know about it now so you can stop him before it's too late."

"We'd be proud, Forrest. Proud if Cameron were called. Esther and I used to pray that one of our children would hear the calling. It would be a blessing in this day and age."

"Humph," grunted Forrest. Some blessing, but he didn't say that. "I thought," he continued, "it wouldn't hurt if I looked into Esther's death just a little bit. You know, talk to the police. Make sure they've got their facts straight."

"Oh," said Jonathan disparagingly, "you won't get anywhere with them. I tried, believe me. I wandered from station to station day after day before Esther was found—and then became a veritable fixture at the Midtown Precinct after she was. The place was a madhouse." He shuddered at the memory.

"I pleaded with them to tell me anything they knew. Anything at all. They shunted me from one officer to the next to the next. They gave me watery cups of coffee. They tried to refer me to some sort of pathetic support group." He looked at Forrest incredulously. "Me—sharing this, this . . . *outrage* with a group of strangers."

"Well," said Forrest, "I might have better luck with the police, having been in law enforcement myself."

"Finally they told me to stop harassing them. That was the word they used. 'Harassing.' They told me it would be duly investigated. Told me they'd call. And that," said Jonathan Maine shortly, "was that." He fished a bent filterless Camel from a crumpled pack and lit it with a shaky hand. "I gave these things up twenty years ago." He sighed, exhaling a stream of blue smoke.

Forrest suspected that Jonathan Maine was at this moment among the world's loneliest men. "Look Jonathan, maybe I can help. No promises now, but who knows?"

Jonathan Maine sat silently for some moments, smoking, thinking. "It's not a good idea. We have to put this behind us. The children don't need—"

"That's the whole point," Forrest pressed. "It would be better for us to investigate than the police because we'd keep things private, see?"

"We?"

"Yeah. There are four of us. Irene Purdy, Trevor Bradford, Mildred Bennett and me. But we'd be discreet. There wouldn't be any ugly publicity."

"I see," said Jonathan thoughtfully.

"And Cameron's mighty set on having us take a look-see."

Jonathan looked at Forrest with agonized eyes. "Cameron," he said numbly. "Ah, yes. I wish he would let it go. But his mind . . . I don't know. He has nightmares. Visions." He seemed to stop himself short. "When he's set on something, there's no dissuading him."

"Exactly," said Forrest. "And left to his own devices, the boy's liable to get himself into trouble. Run off to New York or something crazy like that."

"Something crazy . . ." repeated Jonathan in a daze. "Yes. Well, perhaps some sort of preliminary investigation would be all right," Jonathan said at last. "Lord knows, Esther's mother is so distraught about this she mentioned hiring a private investigator—and Lucille doesn't have two nickels to spare for that kind of thing. No. Your way would be better, I guess. It would spare her both trauma and expense. And your point about the publicity is well taken."

"Good. It's settled then."

"Under one condition."

"What's that?"

"That you come to me with your findings. Or with your suspicions."

"Of course," replied Forrest. "That goes without saying."

"Good. When will you start?"

"Tomorrow."

"I want to help."

"The best thing you can do, Jonathan, is to sit tight."

"You'll need spending money. For cabs, telephone calls—"

"No," protested Forrest.

"—payments for information," Jonathan continued. "You might have to do some of that, mightn't you? It might be a nasty business."

"We'll manage all right," said Forrest, though he wondered how, remembering his meager pension.

Jonathan held up his hand like a traffic cop. "I insist." Taking charge seemed to infuse him with energy. He withdrew a checkbook, scribbled quickly, and pressed the piece of paper into Forrest's clenched fist.

Forrest had trouble reading the scrawl in the light of the zapper, but when he did he whistled softly. "This," he said in disbelief, "is for ten thousand dollars, Jonathan."

"Let me know if you need more."

"It's far more than we'll ever need."

"Then bring back what you don't use. If you insist. Or give it to charity. I really don't care, Forrest. Money seems rather worthless now. In any event, hold on to it. I'll feel better knowing I'm helping in some small way."

"This isn't small. Not by a long shot."

Jonathan took a long drag on the Camel and stared at the stars. Then he crushed out the cigarette and looked at Forrest with bleak eyes. "That money doesn't seem enough. All the money in the world doesn't. I keep thinking if I'd been a better husband, a better father, none of this would have happened."

"Don't go blaming yourself."

"I'll do anything I can to help you, Forrest. Anything. Just name it."

"Well," said Forrest thoughtfully, "we might need information. We might want to ask you some questions—"

"Whatever," said Jonathan.

"—and the children too. We'll be gentle, of course."

As if on cue, a sandy-haired toddler clad in blue pajamas with rubberized feet bolted onto the flagstone patio and headed straight for the pool. Reflexively Forrest reached out and grabbed the child as he streaked by.

"Whoa there, young fella!"

The child's legs continued to move, pummelling Forrest like pistons. "Whoa, there! By golly," laughed Forrest, "I got a live one here."

"Helga!" barked Jonathan. "Helga!"

"I am here, Dr. Maine!" She swept onto the patio, her long blond hair trailing down the back of her spotless white uniform. Forrest caught a tantalizing scent of perfume. Her flawless face was pinched with worry, yet breathtakingly pretty even without makeup save for a touch of gloss on full, sensuous lips. Before Forrest could introduce himself, the young woman snatched the squirming Timothy Ryan Maine from his hands.

"For God's sake, Helga, he almost made it to the pool this time."

"I'm sorry, Dr. Maine."

"I don't want to lose another member of this family."

"Dr. Maine," gasped the woman with the hint of a Polish accent, "I would sooner lose my own life than lose this beloved child."

"Spare me the melodrama. If we hadn't been here—"

"I know, I know," she interrupted, trying to defend herself. "But he doesn't mind. He runs from me. I try to teach him no. I spank him—"

"I told you not to spank," interrupted Jonathan angrily. "I won't abide violence in this house."

"Bah," she said, dismissing his words. "Children. A firm hand now and then doesn't hurt. It shows that someone cares, no?" She looked at Forrest for support, then turned back to her employer. "But this running, it is only a game, you see. And sometimes . . ." she paused for breath " . . . sometimes I cannot catch him."

"Well try harder," said Jonathan shortly. "Timothy should have been in bed hours ago."

"Ya, ya," she replied. "And he was, Dr. Maine. I had him all tucked in and I read him a story and teach him his prayers and say goodnight according to your instructions. I follow the routine you specified. And the minute I turn my back, he is off. When I went to check on him, when I went to kiss my Timothy goodnight one last time, he was gone."

"Yes, yes," said Jonathan, waving her off. "Just put him back to bed. And ask Grandma Lucille to keep an eye on him. At least she's reliable."

At the mention of the interloper Lucille, Helga's jaw set defiantly. "My Timothy does not sleep. He needs his mother." She hurled out the last word angrily, like a curse.

"Jonathan," said Forrest softly, "don't you think you're being a little hard on young Helga here?"

At Forrest's words of support, Helga's eyes flashed. She turned and stalked out with Timothy clutched to her breast.

"I don't know," muttered Jonathan distractedly. "Maybe." He fingered his glass and looked at Forrest. "Where were we?"

"Talking next steps," Forrest reminded him. "I might need to look through some of Esther's personal effects. You still have them?"

"Yes," replied Jonathan, sinking into his former gloom. "I can't bring myself to throw anything away."

"Don't," said Forrest. "Tell you what. It's getting late. Why don't I come back tomorrow? I'll ask you some routine questions, and I'll take a look at Esther's things. What do you say?"

"Yes," replied Jonathan. "Maybe you should do that. There's more, Forrest. More I have to tell you."

Forrest almost pressed him, but then forced himself to get up. There would be time enough tomorrow to find out what Jonathan meant. As for now, he was getting tired. Much as he hated to admit it, he had to pace himself.

"It'll be okay." He placed a hand on Jonathan's shoulder.

"My family," said Jonathan hollowly, "is destroyed."

"No it's not."

"Yes it is. I'm going to rebuild it, but it will never be the same."

Forrest winced inside. Jonathan's bitter tone pained him. So much for answering to a higher authority. Now it sounded as though the good doctor had developed a sense of revenge.

5 Irene Purdy busied herself with the dinner dishes, simultaneously keeping an eye on a smiling feminine face that filled the screen of a little countertop television at her elbow.

". . . A lovers' quarrel? Or was it murder for money? Only the victim knows for sure." Dramatic pause. "Hello everyone! I'm Maureen O'Boyle, and this is *A Current Affair!*"

The show made her want to throw up. She hated herself for watching. But every night, right as rain, when Forrest took his after-dinner constitutional, Irene found herself glued to Channel 5, voyeuristically anticipating yet another lurid tale of infidelity, murder, and assorted deviant behavior. It was like some kind of insidious addiction. It was the *National Inquirer* of the air, that's what, and it was hateful. Sinful almost. The word Irene was looking for was *prurient* but she didn't know it.

Mildred would have known, of course. Mildred knew such things. Mildred was educated. Mildred was rich. Mildred was a woman of refinement and high class.

And Mildred is my friend, thought Irene. Fancy that. Mildred, of course, would never watch *A Current Affair.* Irene knew that too.

Irene's strong blunt fingers worked steadily at the crusted grill with a Brillo pad. Warm soapy water sloshed up her ample arms. She blinked through her bifocals at the sea of suds and considered the dilemma at hand.

On the one hand, Forrest's health wasn't A-1, and they probably shouldn't become involved in what could turn out to be another demanding case. On the other hand, she would dearly love to spend some time with Mildred. Forrest was a good companion, to be sure, but she sorely missed the comfort of easy woman-to-woman chitchat. On still another hand, New York City was a pit, a place to be avoided at all costs, there was no denying it. Irene had spent more horrified hours than she could count watching stories about death and destruction on *Live at Five* with Sue Simmons and Tony Guida.

Sometimes infuriating snippets of local news were inserted without warning into regular prime time programs. Like the time Sue Simmons beamed from the picture tube and announced "Baby thrown from rooftop. At eleven." Then she winked at Irene and vanished without further explanation.

That particular snippet almost drove Irene crazy. She never stayed up until eleven, but that night, after hearing about that poor baby, she worried herself sick. She paced the living room and waited up, then hovered over the tube clear through the eleven o'clock news, not even going to the bathroom during commercials. And guess what. They didn't tell any story about any baby thrown from any rooftop! There were stories about drug busts, Mafia slaughter, and gang rape in Central Park. Horrible stories. But no baby.

Perhaps the baby was preempted by the rape. Perhaps the news people made the whole thing up. Perhaps it was a monstrous mistake. Irene went wild with speculation and called the station direct, demanding an explanation, putting a toll call on Mildred's number in the process—something she hated, absolutely hated, to do.

But no one could tell her about any baby. They acted like she was crazy. They told her to call back the next day. As if a toll call was nothing.

In some ways I was better off living on the mountain without electricity and without television, she reminded herself for the umpteenth time. Better off with my raccoons and possums and birds. Better off without modern contraptions. Look at me now—using a gas-fired barbecue grill, mastering the art of cooking by Cuisinart, soaking every night under the stars in that decadent hot tub, bare-ass naked. Where will it end?

Sometimes she feared she might lose touch with the simple things, might lose sight of what's important, might indeed become dependent on air conditioning, central heating, and flush toilets.

These disconcerting thoughts were interrupted by a knock at the screen door. She wiped her hands on her apron and snapped off Maureen.

"Coming!" She wondered who would come to the back instead of the front. When she got there and squinted through the screen, she saw Lenny Pulaski, chief of the Raven's Wing Police Department, standing there awkwardly, shifting from foot to foot. He was out of uniform, wearing enormous ballooning red bermuda shorts, Dock-Siders with yellow socks, and a blue knit shirt. The outfit made Irene's teeth hurt. Some men, she thought to herself, never learn how to dress.

She opened the door and grinned. "Lenny, what a nice surprise."

The barest look of discomfort flickered across Chief Pulaski's face. "Evening, Reenie."

"Forrest's not here," said Irene, "but he should be back any time. He's taking his evening constitutional."

"Actually, Reenie, it's not Forrest I'm here to see."

"Oh?" Something was up, Irene could see it written all over Lenny's face. "Well sit yourself down." She motioned to the planked kitchen table. "I've got coffee and fresh blueberry pie."

"That's nice, Irene." Lenny eased his ample girth onto a ladderback chair and waited while Irene fetched dessert.

"It's decaf," she said, setting down steaming mugs. "Brewed decaf. Ground the beans myself with that there grinder."

"Fine," said Lenny.

"Trevor says decaf is better for Forrest than regular."

"Right," said Lenny.

"Trevor says Forrest is doing real fine."

"That's great," said Lenny, biding his time, chewing a mouthful of pie until it was puree.

They sat in silence for some moments.

"I wanted to ask you about something, Irene."

"Sure. Ask away."

"I got a call today from the people over at West Mountain Game Park."

"Oh?" said Irene. Now she saw the light. Carefully she cut a corner from her pie. She eased it delicately up on the fork with her thumb. She raised the fork to her lips.

"I think you know what they told me, Irene."

She chewed slowly, steadily, savoring the tart blueberries. Irene loved her pie sour and put in only a fraction of the sugar the recipe called for.

"Nope," she said, avoiding Lenny's gaze. "I haven't got a clue."

"They told me someone went over there last night with a pair of wire cutters."

"Goodness." She took a sip of coffee, keeping her cool.

"Yes indeed. Someone took those wire cutters and let out all the animals."

"You don't say!" exclaimed Irene, with the best indignation she could muster.

"Someone not only opened the cages—let out raccoons, possums, skunks, pheasants, Canada geese, porcupines, deer, and—God help us—a black bear—"

"All indigenous to this area," Irene interrupted. "All from West Mountain originally or kin of those stolen in years gone by."

"True. In any event, someone not only cut open the cages, they cut sizeable holes in the chain link fence that surrounds the entire park." It was a feat Lenny Pulaski found truly amazing, considering the strength of the chain link. He surveyed Irene's muscular arms with new respect.

"If that don't beat all," said Irene, allowing a glimmer of satisfaction to break through her nervousness.

"I don't think it's funny, Irene. Not one bit, I don't."

"Oh come on, Lenny. Those animals were in miserable small cages with people gawking at them and no place to hide. The Fish and Game folks have been trying to shut that place down for years."

"They have a valid permit. A legal permit. They were operating within the law, which is more than I can say for some people." He looked pointedly at Irene.

"Well," she sniffed, "I'm sure I don't know about that."

"One of the employees was there," said Lenny. "Sleeping off a drunk. Or, who knows, maybe dealing drugs. I've been hearing stories . . ."

"Oh?" Irene hoped Lenny would go off on one of his drug tangents. If there was one thing Lenny had no patience for it was drugs.

"In any event, he saw a car."

"Oh," said Irene, feeling her stomach do a flip-flop.

"Yes. An old green Volkswagen Beetle. The real old kind with the little window in back and itty bitty taillights. He remembers that clearly. You don't see many of them nowadays, after all."

"No," agreed Irene wretchedly.

"What he doesn't remember is the license number."

"Thank God," blurted Irene.

"I told the owner of the park—you know, George Sparkes—I'd look into it. Sniff around. After all, how many old green Volkswagens can there be?"

"Not a whole lot, I guess." Irene looked at Lenny with worried eyes.

Lenny studied his coffee cup. "As I understand it," he said carefully, "your particular vehicle—your old green Volkswagen Beetle—has been out of commission for the last two weeks."

"Huh?"

"Inoperable," he went on. "For ten days or so. Totally undrivable, Irene. Isn't that right." It was not a question.

"Oh," she said quickly, "right. The darn thing died on me right out there in Millie's driveway."

Each looked the other in the eye without blinking.

"Irene," said Lenny finally, "I'll help you this time as best I can. But I want you to know I don't like it."

"I know." Her cheeks flushed with embarrassment.

"I don't like lying. And I don't like breaking the law."

"Even when the law is wrong?"

"Even then."

"Jeesum, Lenny, you're just like the church, telling me to obey rules that don't make sense just 'cause the pope says so."

"Irene, don't push me on this. I'm offering a favor here. For old time's sake."

Irene was an independent sort who found it difficult to accept help from other people under the best of circumstances. Lenny's gesture and her dependence on it pained her greatly. "Well, I appreciate it, Lenny," she said at last. "I really do."

"Like I said, I'll do my best. But you should know that George Sparkes is awful pissed. And when he's pissed, he's like a terrier with a bone, take my word for it. He won't let this thing die so easy."

"He won't?"

"No. He'll snoop around and fuss and fume. He's liable to become obsessed. He's that type."

She repeated the word, testing it. "Obsessed." It had a frightening hiss.

"He might even hire a lawyer or private investigator."

"Oh dear." Irene's world was going to hell in a handbasket on greased skids, that was for sure.

"So I recommend you don't drive around town for a while. Better yet, I recommend you take yourself a little vacation till this thing blows over."

"A vacation?" she repeated as though the word were totally alien to her, which indeed it was.

"Sure. You and Forrest. Go off somewhere. Just for a couple of weeks."

"Where on earth would we go?"

Even as she spoke the answer came to her: They'd go to Mildred's. There it was, just like that. She was trapped. Trapped into agreeing. Trapped into going to Mildred's. Trapped into getting involved in a new case in a strange place.

She clicked her dentures and tried to be optimistic. After all, things could be worse.

Having completed his business, Lenny Pulaski gulped the last slug of coffee from his mug, thanked Irene for her hospitality, and pushed his girth through the screen door.

"Lenny?"

He stopped in midstep. "What, Reenie?"

"You heard anything about the Maine woman?"

"You mean your neighbor? The lady who died?"

"Yeah. Esther."

Lenny shook his head. "Terrible thing, just terrible, a nice lady like that. I called the New York City police, just to find out what was going on. They don't have any leads. 'Sides, they say it was an accident, probably."

"But maybe not, huh?"

"I got the feeling it wasn't, but they're cutting their losses. That's between you and me. You know how it is in the City. Any given precinct has more homicides in a month than a small country does in a year." He stopped short and looked at her keenly. "You folks aren't thinking of messing around in this, are you Reenie?"

"Us?" She arched her eyebrows innocently. "Why, of course not. For heaven's sake, Lenny."

6 Trevor Bradford gazed morosely out the window. His mother had had a word for what he was doing. Glutzing. Surveying the scenery when you're down in the dumps, and Trevor most certainly was down in the dumps.

California was a beautiful place. He tried to tell himself that. Everything was green and plastic. Everything was new. Everyone was young. God, he hated it. Everything and everyone too.

Don't be so quick to judge, he chastised himself. You're just an old man in a bad mood.

Penelope had been trying to convince him to move out to the West Coast. He was resisting but she was persisting. She was like her mother that way. You'd be close to us, she said. Your grandchildren will get to know you. You could go fishing with Seth and to Great America Park with Jeannette. You could live in the pool house, it's a full apartment. You'd have your privacy. We wouldn't smother you, Dad, I promise. And I'd worry less if you were here. Please, Dad, please.

It was tempting in a way. They were family, after all, not Martians. But when he looked down at himself—a self in a brand new green Lacoste shirt, plaid slacks and white loafers—he felt like a strange man in a strange land. Penelope forced these clothes on him and he'd been too polite to say "These aren't me, honey. I'm a corduroy kind of guy." And to add insult to injury, he felt like a damn fool wedging himself into that fancy yellow Porsche they let him use. So he simply didn't drive anywhere. He sat and stared out the window. Glutzing. He sat and waited for a respectable period of mourning to be over and he wondered how long it would take. Probably forever, he guessed.

Here it was almost a year since Mary Margaret had died, and instead of getting easier it got worse. He told himself he should snap out of it, especially since he had been more of a caretaker than husband to her during their last years together. But still he felt empty inside. Forty-eight years of marriage is a lifetime, and now he was left with half a life. No one with whom to share his memories or his rye toast or his rare off-color jokes.

Now Mary Margaret was on the wrong side of the grass in Raven's Wing, Connecticut. He sighed. At least he hadn't let Penelope talk him into cremation. Trevor got mad just thinking about it. He was a man of tradition and to him cremation indicated a fast-food mentality about human disposal, oblivion served up by Colonel Cinders. Sometimes he thought that was the way the world was going. Sometimes he felt out of step, out of sync. Sometimes . . .

He tried to push these thoughts away, tried not to think about the other underlying cause for his loneliness. Tried not to think about Mildred Bennett. Because when thoughts turned to Mildred, conflicting emotions were sure to follow. All right, he had been attracted to her. He flushed with embarrassment, even now, just thinking about it. He was a damn fool, that's what. Twenty years his junior she was. Fifteen, he corrected himself. Okay, fifteen.

Big deal. When she's ninety, you'll be a hundred and five. Besides, ninety's a long way off. She's only fifty-eight. And you're only seventy-three.

Only. Out here seventy-three seemed very old indeed. He suspected that Californians stuck old people in file cabinets so as not to detract from the youthful image of this state. He pictured room upon room of Steelcase drawers holding senior citizens in neat little alphabetized compartments.

His thoughts returned to Mildred. If the truth be told, he'd been stung with disappointment when she packed her bags and went back to New York City. True, he had Forrest and Irene for company, but they were so wrapped up in each other that he felt like a third wheel. Also—though he would scarcely admit this even to himself—Forrest and Irene were country people. They were wonderful folks but their interests were quite different from his. Once he'd had the temerity to ask if they might like to go to the ballet. They'd howled with laughter and asked why anyone would want to watch a bunch of fairies dancing around in pointy shoes.

Oh well.

"Hi, Gramps."

Trevor's ten-year-old grandson, Seth, sat down next to him on the sofa. He set his skateboard on the jarring lime-green carpet. Trevor could see Snoopy on that skateboard, wearing sunglasses with a legend emblazoned under him in red letters: "Joe Cool."

"Hi, Mr. Cool." Trevor tried to sound cheerful.

"Aw," said Seth, "that's kid stuff. I'm gonna get another board, decorate it myself. They got a good one over at Hanson's Sports. Top of the line. Three hundred bucks."

Trevor whistled. He wondered whatever happened to kick-the-can and mublety-peg, but he had the good sense not to ask.

"Gramps, you gotta get out of yourself."

"Out of myself?"

"Yeah. You're too introspective. Too quiet. Staring out the window all the time. Going to bed at seven . . ."

"And what are you doing?" said Trevor too sharply. "Practicing psychiatry?"

The boy hung his head, his crewcut spikes pointing in Trevor's direction. Trevor felt a pang of guilt. He had snapped without meaning to. He reached out and ran his big hand gently over Seth's prickly scalp. "It's okay," he said. "Never mind me, Seth."

"We're worried about you is all."

"I'll be fine, Seth. It takes time." It's not like your Saturday morning TV programs, boy. Not like *Pee Wee's Playhouse,* no indeed. You don't turn on the magic screen and flip the channel. But Trevor said none of this.

"Yeah. I guess."

You guess? You didn't even know her. Trevor wanted to shout the words. You don't know what it's like! You're too young. But still he said nothing.

"Oh," said Seth. "I almost forgot. You got a call."

"Really?" In spite of himself, Trevor perked up.

"Yeah. While you were in the shower. Some guy. Said his name was Forrest. Said you should get your ass back to Raven's Wing right away."

"Seth."

"Well that's what he said!"

Trevor decided a lecture on civilized language could wait. He reached for the phone. Little did he know that this was the lifeline that would save him.

"Forrest?" said Trevor. "It's me."

Seth watched his grandfather. He became very intent, saying "Yes, yes" or merely grunting in response. Then he said, "Right away. You can count on it." He hung up, and his eyes were very bright indeed.

"Gramps, you okay?"

Trevor couldn't believe it. Another case. All of them. Together.

"Grampa? Grampa?"

He hardly felt Seth's hand on his elbow. "I've got to go," he said.

"Go? Go where?"

"Home."

"But Mom said—"

"I don't care what your mother said, boy. I've got to go. Now."

Trevor ran into the guest room and stuffed randomly selected garments into a travel bag. He would take a plane, any plane. He would pay full fare with no advance reservation.

"She's gonna be awful upset," said Seth. He followed his grandfather back into the living room.

"Tell her I'm sorry," said Trevor. "Tell her I have no choice. I've got to . . . well, tell her . . . oh, just tell her I left the Porsche at the airport."

Seth watched his grandfather race out the front door. He looked different suddenly. Seth wasn't sure what it was. He looked upset, yes, but he looked younger too. Like one of those old people in that *Twilight Zone* story who played kick-the-can and turned into kids. Yes, he looked younger. Seth heard the roar of the engine and raced outside, hoping he could catch his grandfather.

"Wait!" he cried. He ran to the end of the driveway. "Wait!"

Trevor buzzed down the window. "What is it, boy?"

"Goodbye, Grandpa. I just wanted to say goodbye."

"Be good, Seth."

"Yeah. And good luck. That too."

"Sure," said Trevor. "Don't you worry."

Trevor raced away in a cloud of spinning gravel and exhaust. Now that, thought Seth, is the way that car is supposed to be driven.

7 The blue and white box of Kleenex sat on the desk between them, squat and square, a bunker of sorts on the clean green blotter underneath. It had been weeks since she'd reached for a tissue, weeks since she'd shed any tears in this office. The days of crying were long gone, thank goodness.

"You've come a long way, Mildred," said Dr. Withers.

Patricia Withers folded manicured sausage fingers against the curve of her stomach and leaned back contentedly. Her face was made up like a kewpie doll. Her hair was tightly permed. Sometimes Mildred half expected her to burst into a rendition of "The Good Ship Lollypop." The Shirley Temple of psychiatry. At this thought a laugh bubbled in the back of Mildred's throat and she swallowed it down.

The barest hint of a self-satisfied smile tugged at the corners of Dr. Withers's ruby red lips, and Mildred watched to see if that smile would blossom into a full-fledged grin. If it does, thought Mildred, her face will crack, and I certainly don't want to miss that.

In the past Mildred made an effort to resist such negative thoughts about Dr. Withers lest she be branded "therapy resistant." After all, she reasoned, I'm paying good money for this woman's advice. She comes highly recommended. People beat a path to her door. Dr. Withers had told Mildred this herself on more than one occasion. Told Mildred that her "slots" were highly sought after and, indeed, that Mildred's prime-time slot could be filled by any number of willing patients on a moment's notice. In a minute, Dr. Withers had said. Mildred found this bit of supposed inside information galling but ignored her feelings for the sake of mental health.

However, today these thoughts, along with disparaging thoughts about Dr. Withers's physical attributes, intruded with relentless frequency.

Dr. Withers wasn't morbidly obese, but she was decidedly plump. Mildred wondered if she treated anorexic patients and how her plumpness affected them. Maybe she placed a stack of donuts on the desk instead of Kleenex. In her mind's eye Mildred pictured Dr. Withers with Twinkies lodged in her mouth and ears. It was not a pretty sight.

Mildred herself was now quite trim and had, in fact, struggled mightily to shed twenty pounds since her divorce became final last March. She suspected Dr. Withers did not like the svelte new Mildred, suspected Dr. Withers did not approve of her trendy new frosted hairdo or the soft pastel makeup either, but she kept her suspicions to herself.

The first time Dr. Withers had approached Mildred in the starkly futuristic chrome and glass reception area, Mildred had the distinct sensation of being overpowered by a runaway balloon from the Macy's Thanksgiving Day Parade. Indeed, Dr. Withers bobbed forward as though tethered to the ground by the tippy tips of her toes. Then she had shaken Mildred's hand in a mighty bone-crushing grip that caused Mildred's diamond-encrusted emerald ring to leave an ugly purple bruise for a week.

At this moment Mildred made a conscious effort to remember that bruise and that pain.

"Yes," agreed Mildred affably. "A long way. And I want you to know I'm most grateful for your help."

"Now, now," said Dr. Withers predictably, "let's have none of that. You helped yourself, Mildred. Indeed, without cooperation of the patient, this kind of therapy cannot achieve maximum success."

Maximum success. Mildred wondered exactly what that was and if there might be such a thing as minimum success. Did Dr. Withers consult some sort of wall chart or rotating slide guide in evaluating her patients? She suspected that the Withers Maximum Success Program took years to accomplish, and she didn't intend to stick around to find out.

"Well," said Mildred agreeably, "if you say so. In any case, I wanted to come here today to tell you face to face."

"Tell me what face to face?" said Dr. Withers, arching a penciled eyebrow.

"That I won't be coming anymore."

"What?" said Dr. Withers, her jaw dropping into three chins.

"I'm feeling ever so much better," Mildred went on.

"Oh," said Dr. Withers darkly, "those feelings of well-being are deceptive, take it from me."

"I had a low period after the divorce, I admit. And my life seemed rather empty after all the excitement and publicity of last fall."

"That," said Dr. Withers primly, "was a fantasy world, Mildred. Pie in the sky. It's time to wake up and smell the coffee."

Mildred looked at Dr. Withers with narrowing eyes. She decided not to mention that Dr. Withers never so much as offered her a cup of coffee or tea or even a glass of tepid tap water during these tedious weekly sessions. Dr. Withers wasn't of good breeding, Mildred could tell that right off the bat, always asking about dreams and sex. Under her haughty professional demeanor, she was ill mannered and ill tempered too. She probably could derive benefit from a therapist herself.

"It was real enough at the time," said Mildred back. "I missed Forrest and Irene terribly." She hesitated. "And Trevor." Trevor most of all.

"They are like family to me. I was betwixt and between. But now my feelings of despondency have dispersed." She paused and smiled at this unintentional alliteration.

"But we've only just begun," said Dr. Withers.

Ah, thought Mildred, I was wrong. She's going to sing Karen Carpenter's song instead of Shirley Temple's. And we all know what happened to Karen Carpenter.

"No, really," protested Mildred politely. "I'm feeling wonderful. I've lost some weight, had my hair done."

"Cosmetic changes," sniffed Dr. Withers, "nothing more."

Mildred remembered endless days of dry whole wheat toast for breakfast and Lean Cuisine for dinner. Hours running on the relentless electronic treadmill. Her eyes narrowed to slits. Cosmetic changes indeed.

Dr. Withers looked at Mildred's obstinate expression with increasing agitation. Her eyes darted from Mildred's face to the box of Kleenex to the comforting array of degrees on the wall to the dusty dry philodendron over on the windowsill.

"To me they're more than cosmetic changes," said Mildred, keeping her voice neutral. "And I'm afraid that we haven't only just begun, Dr. Withers. We've only just finished."

"I beg your pardon?" said Dr. Withers, not trusting her ears.

"This kind of talking therapy is simply not for me," Mildred went on. "My daughter wheedled me into it. You know how young people are today. So open. Ready to broadcast their innermost feelings at a moment's notice." She sighed. "It's just not for me, I'm afraid. It's simply not my style. I'm a private sort of person. A stiff upper lip sort of person. I believe in putting one foot in front of the other and getting on with one's life."

"As an emotional cripple?" said Dr. Withers archly.

Mildred's cheeks flamed with color. Automatically she reached down to pat Winston, her aged bulldog, a diversion that usually served to soothe her.

"I wish," snapped Dr. Withers, "you would desist bringing that smelly mongrel to my office."

Mildred stiffened. "His name is Winston. He doesn't smell and he's hardly a mongrel. He took best of show at Madison Square Garden. His stud fees, when he was in his prime, were far higher than your hourly rate, I can assure you." Now the gloves were off.

"Really," said Dr. Withers with uninterest.

"In any event, Dr. Withers, I will comply with your request. I will desist in bringing Winston. And I will desist in bringing myself." She picked her Gucci bag from the floor and placed it squarely in her lap, a pointed clue that this conversation was to be terminated.

"Now, now," soothed Dr. Withers, "you know you don't mean that."

"Oh but I do."

Dr. Withers stared at Mildred in disbelief. "You're

actually serious about terminating therapy?"

"Yes," said Mildred. Finally this woman was getting the picture.

"But you can't do that. You're not ready."

"I think I'm the best judge of that," snapped Mildred, losing her temper.

"Well!" huffed Dr. Withers. She sat there fuming for some moments. She flipped open her calendar book and started rifling through pages. Mildred watched dumbfounded, wondering what was going on. Suddenly it dawned on her. Dr. Withers was calculating the loss of income incurred by the loss of a patient in a prime-time slot. Mildred felt like handing her a jar of white-out and a calculator.

"You simply cannot abandon therapy on such short notice," sputtered Dr. Withers.

"Nowhere," snapped Mildred back, "did I sign any contract with a clause for thirty days' notice. Besides," she added, unable to resist, "there are other patients eager to fill this chair. In a minute. You said so yourself."

With that Dr. Withers became overtly angry. She stood and started to pace. Her face became inordinately flushed under all that war paint. If there was ever any possibility of Mildred reconsidering, it vanished at that very moment.

I am trapped in an office with a crazy therapist, she realized. It felt like she was in one of those dreams Dr. Withers was so insistent on hearing about. Ever so slowly, Mildred rose from the chair and eased toward the door, walking backward step by step.

Dr. Withers whirled in her tracks. "And where do you think you're going? This session isn't over!"

"Oh but it is."

"Ach," croaked Dr. Withers in disgust. She waved a dismissive hand, then groped for a Kleenex.

For one brief moment, Mildred experienced a sympathetic reaction and with it the urge to comfort this unattractive and obviously distressed woman. It was her nature to offer comfort, no matter what, no matter who. But Dr. Withers herself shattered the moment when she cleared her throat with a disgusting rattle and spat indiscreetly into the Kleenex.

"I was wrong," said Dr. Withers, looking briefly into the wadded Kleenex as she removed it from moistened lips. "You haven't come a long way at all. You'll backslide into depression like a shot."

Mildred had had enough. "Come along, Winston. We're leaving." Gently but firmly she closed the door behind her.

"Come on!" she said, tugging the leash with impatience. But Winston was not a dog to be rushed. He sniffed at piles of old magazines on the chrome and glass coffee table, magazines which had always irked Mildred because when you're paying $125 for a paltry fifty-minute hour, the least you can expect is up-to-date periodicals.

Without warning Winston hiked his leg. Mildred stared transfixed as a torrent of urine cascaded onto the magazines, down the chrome leg of the table and into the carpet.

Lord, she should have anticipated this. Winston's bladder control wasn't what it used to be. Well, what was a person to do? She couldn't leave him in the apartment for any length of time, and she couldn't very well diaper him. The vet said once that the needle was the answer. But she couldn't bring herself to do such a drastic thing. He was the only family she had left.

Mildred watched in horror as a dark stain spread on the Oriental carpet. Hastily she looked around the reception area for witnesses. Fortunately, Dr. Withers was too cheap to hire a receptionist and too discreet to allow patients to overlap, so no one had seen Winston's transgression.

She spied a dry copy of *Vogue*, a recent issue at that, addressed to Patricia Withers, M.D. Without a second thought, Mildred tucked it under her arm and walked out.

She read it all the way home. Cosmetic changes indeed.

8 Forrest Haggarty was back to Jonathan Maine early the next day. "You said you had more to tell me," he said a mite too eagerly.

"Yes," replied Jonathan softly. "Follow me."

They walked through a cavernous tiled foyer, up a free floating staircase, down a long hallway lushly carpeted in mint green. The walls were stark white. To Forrest the house had a cloistered, almost institutional, feel about it. He could see no evidence of children anywhere.

"Sure is a tidy house," marveled Forrest. "Lord, when our kids were young 'uns they ran Queenie ragged. Toys strewn all over, friends trooping in and out, the refrigerator door open more than it was closed. Kool-Aid, that's what they drank. They called it *bug juice*. God-awful stuff."

"The children are away most of the time," explained Jonathan. "Claudia's grown and Cameron and Lauren go to boarding schools. Helga takes care of Timmy."

Until, thought Forrest, Timmy's old enough to be shipped off to boarding school too. "I see," he said carefully.

Jonathan stopped in midstep as though reading Forrest's thoughts. "I tried to make things easy for Esther."

"No need to explain."

"The children were more than she could cope with. She loved them, but—"

"It's okay, Jonathan. From what all I can see they're turning out just fine."

Jonathan looked Forrest square in the face, his eyes suddenly full of worry. "What am I going to do, Forrest? What the hell am I going to do?"

"Huh?"

"For years I've left the job of parenting to others. Hired people—nursemaids, teachers, camp counselors. I've never done it myself. But I want to now. I want to rebuild this family, but, God help me, I don't know where to begin."

Forrest's face broke into a smile revealing crooked yellow teeth. "Don't you worry about it, Jon. You'll figure it out. It'll come to you, sure as shootin'."

"I don't know."

"It will," Forrest insisted. "It's natural, being a father."

"I hope so."

Jonathan led him into an office of black leather and Plexiglas. The room was totally devoid of color except for a swirling abstract painting on one wall.

"Interesting," commented Forrest as he eased himself into a yawning, Y-shaped chair.

"Oh, that?" Jonathan glanced at the artwork. "Claudia painted it. When she was in high school. She was very talented."

"She dead or something?"

"No, why?"

"You talk about her like she is. You said *was*."

"I meant *is*. She *is* very talented."

The picture looked pretty ugly to Forrest. Well, he thought, to each his own. He turned his gaze to a set of photographs on a nearby credenza. There were at least a dozen, providing an intimate glimpse of the Maine family . . . Jonathan and Esther's wedding picture, Claudia mugging at the camera as a toddler, Claudia as an adolescent on horseback, Cameron and Lauren in Halloween costumes, Lauren making her first holy communion, Timmy crying on the lap of Santa Claus, the family clustered under an umbrella at the beach. The collection looked like a shrine.

"Your kids are real beauties," said Forrest.

"Pardon?"

"I've always been partial to tow-heads. And Claudia, she's mighty pretty too, with those big brown eyes and brunette hair."

"Esther's coloring," said Jonathan.

"The others favor you then."

Jonathan shrugged. He folded his hands and waited for Forrest to get on with his questions.

"So," said Forrest, unable to hide his eagerness. "You said you had more to tell me."

"Yes," replied Jonathan. "This isn't going to be easy. We've always been a private sort of family. Very self-contained. I find it difficult, I must say, to share certain matters with outsiders. But I thought it through last night, and there are a few things you should know."

"Okay."

"Esther had some problems."

"You mentioned something along that line last night."

Jonathan stood up and walked to the window. He put his hands on the frame and stared outside. "Jesus, I didn't know it was going to be like this."

"Take your time, Jonathan."

He took a deep breath. "She wasn't what you'd call crazy or anything. Nothing like that. Just fragile. Delicate emotionally. She had always been quiet. More than shy, I'd have to say. Of course, her natural shyness was compounded by her speech impediment."

"I never heard about any speech thing."

"Stuttering. She was afflicted badly. It began when she was a small child and was pretty ingrained when I first met her. As I told you last night, she hardly said two words the first time we met. The fact was, she couldn't say two words."

"I met her once or twice. I don't remember hearing her stutter."

"Because we worked on it, she and I, and we succeeded. With the help of a fine speech therapist and
endless practice sessions with me, Esther got the problem under control. You know, breathing exercises and
relaxation techniques can work wonders. It's all a matter
of relaxing the larynx really."

"Uh huh." Forrest couldn't help but remember
Cameron's fight for air.

"In any event, Esther overcame her stuttering but never
her extreme shyness. She held back with people to the
point of being reclusive. It reached its worst point after
Claudia was born."

"What happened?"

"She suffered from postpartum depression. The baby
blues, people used to call it. But Esther's condition was
unusually severe. She refused to leave her room. Wouldn't
go near the baby, and got hysterical when we tried to bring
the baby to her. I hired someone to help with the baby and,
in time, Esther seemed to recover."

"Seemed to?"

"Yes." Jonathan looked pained. "The fact is she never
fully recovered. There was a pattern of reclusiveness,
especially during her pregnancies. When she started to
show, she stopped going out. I thought you knew. I thought
everyone knew."

"No," said Forrest, "I heard no such thing." As former police chief, Forrest prided himself on knowing
most of what went on in Raven's Wing. He knew
about Martha Pringle who lived in a mansion on Main
Street and drank herself into oblivion daily, often calling Town Hall to harangue employees about imagined
sex scandals and aliens from outer space. He knew
about Webster Stiles, who had a collection of child
pornography stashed in a file cabinet in his attic. He
knew about Sonny Joiner who squashed his nuts flat
as nickels while unloading sacks of grain at Young's
Feed Store. Hell, he knew about damn near everybody.
He was the J. Edgar Hoover of Raven's Wing, only

the files were all stored in his mind. It was safer that way.

Except Esther Maine. He didn't know a damned thing about her. What the hell was there to know anyway? A woman like that?

"For a while I was so busy building the practice I wasn't fully aware. Then I found out everything was being delivered. Groceries. Dry cleaning. Diapers. Everything. She was living like a Carmelite."

"A what?"

"A cloistered nun. Never showing her face. Never talking to anyone. Praying all the time. Listening to Gregorian chants on the phonograph. When I confronted her, she broke down and admitted it. She was terrified to leave the house, really terrified. I feared she might be agoraphobic."

"Agora what?"

"Agoraphobic. A person with an irrational fear of being outside. Of going places. That sort of thing."

"I see."

"It can be more or less severe. Different people set up different boundaries for themselves. Some venture outside but won't cross a particular highway, for example. Others, like Esther, won't leave the house at all. They stay inside for years. Decades even. It's a living death. They draw the blinds and wither away without ever having seen the sun shine."

"Jesus. What did you do?"

"I hired household help, for one thing. Of course, I urged her to see a psychiatrist, but she wouldn't hear of it. So I did what I could. We worked on the problem together following each pregnancy. I encouraged her to do little things, one step at a time. It took more than a year after Cameron was born to get her out the front door. The panic attacks she experienced were frightening to witness. They must have been hell to go through. But she forced herself.

"We progressed to walking to the mailbox. We set goals. Small goals, to be sure, but she persevered. It took years, Forrest. Finally, when Claudia entered kindergarten, Esther walked her to school. It was a rite of passage for them both. The children were a great motivating factor. By the time Lauren came along she attended occasional PTA meetings, charity events, and the like. Eventually she seemed to be okay most of the time within the confines of Raven's Wing."

"Raven's Wing is a safe place," agreed Forrest.

"Yes, and I was satisfied to let it rest at that point. Frankly, I thought her progress had peaked, so I stopped pressuring her. You can imagine my astonishment when she expressed the desire to go into the city."

"Ah yes," said Forrest, "the city. When did that start?"

"A year or so ago. She wanted to try it, she said. I was against it at first but finally agreed. She went once a week, always following a strict routine: had her hair done, lunched with her sister, did a little shopping, and that was it."

"The sister," said Forrest. "What's her name?"

"Constance Townsend. Husband's name is Fred. They've got a place in the East Seventies." Jonathan recited the address and phone number.

"Anyway, on her trips to the city Esther would stay one night, always at a suite at the Regency. It's a lovely hotel, very expensive—and very safe. I never had the slightest worry."

"Until this time."

"Yes. I've gone over it again and again in my mind. There simply was no clue that anything was wrong. And yet . . ."

"Yes?" Forrest pressed.

"And yet something must have gone wrong. On July eighteenth Esther went to the city as usual. Only this time she didn't come home the next night, which was most *un*usual. I tried calling, but there was no answer. I became worried, and as yet another night went by I became quite frantic."

"What about the children?" asked Forrest.

"Oh," said Jonathan distractedly, "they were worried too of course. Claudia's away, but the others—well, I tried to shield them. Tried to hide my concern. But children have a way of sensing these things."

"Did you go to the police?"

"Not at first. I didn't know where to start, you see. Then too, I kept hoping for the best. Her car was parked at Darien station, and I tried following her tracks. I went to the Regency, and they said she'd registered and never checked out. All her things were still there.

"So I waited in that room, hoping she'd come back. I waited and I waited and I waited. And I knew something was horribly wrong. I called all the hospitals. I started going to the police."

"I see."

"And I stayed at the Regency—in that room—with her things—still hoping she'd come back. During the day I went from station to station. They told me they'd file a missing persons report. Told me it was in the computer and that I didn't have to go to more than one station. But I couldn't help it. I couldn't just wait and do nothing." Jonathan held his hands up hopelessly.

"Finally an officer took pity on me—or maybe he was sick of my badgering. He did some checking and found out there was an unidentified body at the morgue that fit Esther's general description. He took me down there."

"Yes?" said Forrest.

Jonathan closed his eyes as if to shut out the wrenching memory. "They rolled her out in a stainless steel drawer in the morgue. I looked, waiting to say *No, that's not her*. But it was. Even under the bruises and the broken bones, I could see . . ."

"Esther."

"Yes." He looked at the ceiling and forced himself to continue. "I'm a doctor. I've seen death and should be used to it. But when it's your own, there's no getting used to that. Her face . . . was all pushed in. Purple. Broken, horribly broken. All my training, my carefully cultivated detachment as a physician, went right out the window. I came totally apart, I'm afraid. I remember wanting to reach down and smooth it out. Fix it somehow. I'm supposed to be able to do that, aren't I? Of course that was impossible. Her skull was fractured in the front, her cheekbone and forehead shattered."

The words that came to Forrest's mind were *beyond repair*. Sourness blossomed in his stomach. "What did they tell you?"

"She'd been found in some hotel, a place I'd never heard of, registered under the name of Camille Smith with no identification whatsoever. The manager found her in the tub with the shower still running. At first they thought she slipped and fractured her skull."

"What caused them to change their minds?"

"They didn't change their minds exactly. But there was an autopsy, and it raised some doubts. The fracture, combined with the way she was positioned in the tub . . . well, she could have fallen forward face first, or . . ."

"Or what?"

"She could have been battered and moved there. The physical evidence was inconclusive."

"I see. Can you think of anyone who might have wanted to harm her?"

"No. Esther never hurt a fly. Never said a harsh word or even so much as contradicted anyone."

Forrest tried to ask the next question gently. "The autopsy," he said, "did it show any evidence of . . . well, had anyone assaulted her, you know . . . in an intimate way?"

"No," said Jonathan quickly. "Thank God." He looked at Forrest with agonized eyes. "But that's small consolation, Forrest. I simply could not accept her death. It made no sense. I couldn't for the life of me understand why she was there. And the police were no help at all. They gave me plastic bags of bizarre clothing they claimed was hers and told me they'd be in touch."

"Then what?"

"I came home and . . . well, I almost went crazy. Locked myself in this room for three days. Wouldn't speak to anyone. Finally I sent Lucille and Helga away with the children and I ransacked the house. Yes, I ransacked my own house. Trying to find something, anything, that would be a clue."

"Did you find anything?"

"I don't know. Maybe." Jonathan Maine turned slowly and walked to the desk. He extracted a small key from his pocket and unlocked a drawer. He removed a small burgundy notebook tied with a pink ribbon. He held it out to Forrest.

"What's this?" said Forrest.

"Some sort of journal."

Forrest rifled through the pages eagerly.

"It won't help much, I'm afraid. There are no names. Just a few poems." He hesitated. "By Camille Smith."

Forrest flipped through the pages. "Any of this mean anything to you?"

"No," said Jonathan.

"I'll hang on to these for the time being," Forrest said, slipping the packet in his pocket. "Maybe we can learn something from them."

"I never knew she wrote poetry," said Jonathan softly.

"She had the heart of an artist. Just like you."

"They're love poems, Forrest."

"Ah yes," said Forrest. "They do look like that."

> *A silk stocking, a wisp of hair,*
> *Gone are the days of May,*
> *When a gentleman caller courted me*
> *And told me what to say.*
>
> *He held my hand, he spun me 'round,*
> *He made me feel so grand.*
> *And why he chose to leave me*
> *I'll never understand.*

9 "Not much of a love poem," sniffed Irene. "Some fella up and left her. Big deal."

"Unless," said Forrest, "it was the fella that killed her."

"Yeah," agreed Irene, "that's one way of looking at it."

"There's something about that poem," said Mildred. "It sounds rather Victorian. Like something from another era."

"The first verse," said Trevor thoughtfully, "is like something a schoolgirl would write, not a forty-three-year-old woman. It's sentimental. Virginal."

"And vague," muttered Forrest. "Too damn vague. I don't see how this here book's going to help us, at least not right now."

"So what do you propose we do?" asked Mildred.

"First I'm going to tell you everything I could find out about Esther Maine. It's not much, but it's a start."

"And then?" said Irene.

"Then we're going to pay a visit to the St. James Hotel. Then we're going to talk to that sister of hers. Then we're going to get a look at the autopsy report. And then . . ." He let his voice drift off. Then he didn't know what the hell they were going to do. He hoped they'd have some concrete leads.

"Seems like a lot of runaround," sighed Irene, "and a lot of time."

"Well," said Trevor agreeably, "time is something we have plenty of now, isn't it? Besides, I think Forrest is right. I think we should cover the bases properly, handle it like pros."

"Pros," snorted Irene. "Who you kidding, Trevor?"

They sat in a dark wood-paneled room that had once been Connor Bennett's library. A massive air conditioner droned from one of three windows that overlooked a magnificent garden to the rear of the building. The walls were lined with books, with Mildred's popular mysteries, thrillers and romance novels slowly edging out her ex-husband's dry biographies and business-related nonfiction. In the center of the room a large mahogany table that had once served as headquarters for Connor Bennett's spontaneously called weekend business meetings now lay strewn with Chinese takeout.

"Have another egg roll," offered Mildred. She eyed Trevor sideways. When she first found the three of them waiting in the lobby downstairs, he had unexpectedly thrown his arms around her. Then once he realized what he had done he backed off in embarrassment. But in those unguarded moments when he forgot himself she had seen how much he cared. She hadn't imagined it. "It's so good to see you again, Mildred," he had said. "So *good*."

But ever since they came into the apartment, he seemed preoccupied. Why just look at him now, she thought. Sitting there stiffly, not saying anything. Sipping his wine, studying the grain of the wood table as though it were some rare form of hieroglyphics. She wondered if she'd done anything to offend him and, if so, what on earth it might be.

Irene leaned back in her chair and tried to swallow her impatience. She didn't like taking things stepwise. She was an intuitive person and liked getting to the heart of the matter right off the bat. Still, she told herself, things could be worse. New York City wasn't half so bad as expected. With the extra time allowed, she could do some weeding and pruning in that garden out back. Maybe plant some bulbs for next spring.

"Do you folks want to hear what I have to say or not?" grumbled Forrest.

"Don't mind Forrest, Millie," put in Irene. "He's just out of sorts because of Cameron."

"Oh hush," said Forrest.

"Cameron wanted to come with us," Irene went on. "Of course we had to tell him no. We had no choice, much as I like the boy. There's no telling what we might find out, you see."

"Where the hell was I?" said Forrest.

"Steps," said Mildred. "You were talking next steps."

"Yes," said Trevor. "Tell us what you know about the mysterious Esther Maine."

"Mysterious," said Forrest, "is a good way to describe her."

From what Forrest had been able to piece together, Esther Maine was a nice lady, bland but nice. Quiet, conscientious, a good mother, she was a person most comfortable on the side-lines. As Jonathan indicated, she was a person who dutifully baked cookies for the PTA, stuffed envelopes for the Muscular Dystrophy Fund, delivered for Meals on Wheels. Her halting speech, combined with deeply ingrained shyness, made her avoid any situation in which she might attract the slightest bit of attention. So, while she would serve on a committee, she would not chair it. While she would attend a PTA meeting, she would not speak. While she would sit behind the cash register at the Thrift Shop, she would never speak up if a customer walked out neglecting to pay for merchandise stashed in a tote bag.

Still, she had lived on this earth for forty-three years, Forrest reasoned, a supporting player and not a star, but nonetheless a human being with hopes, feelings, and dreams like any one of us. There simply had to be more. Determined to get a better picture of the woman behind the name, Forrest had spoken with her mother, Lucille Jamison.

"She seemed nice enough," he said. "At first."

"Take a cookie, Mr. Haggarty. I baked them myself.
"I'm touched, I must say, that you've come to talk to

me. I've been consumed with grief ever since Jonathan called me about Esther, and it's a relief to share it with someone—a relief to know someone even cares—especially a man such as· yourself. . . .

"Oh? You want to go back that far? To the beginning? All right. I don't see the point, but I guess you know your business.

"We lived in the Branchvale section of town back when Esther first came to us. Not a fancy section, but clean and crime-free. Neighbors kept their front yards tended and their junk cars out back. There were no colored, of course. Not like today.

"Esther was a foster baby, I suppose you know that. We took her in for a variety of reasons. Evan and I already had Connie and wanted a second child—Evan was quite set on it. But the doctor said it would be dangerous for me to carry another. So fostering seemed like a good alternative. Yes, the state gave us money for Esther's care, and yes, we were people of modest means, but the money certainly wasn't a deciding factor. In any event, we took her in and it worked out nicely for both sides.

". . . Sides? I do declare, Mr. Haggarty, if I didn't know better, I'd think you were twisting my own words against me. I didn't say sides, no indeed. I certainly didn't see little Esther as being on another side. . . .

"We wanted a boy but took Esther. Evan came home one day with her out of the blue. Pleased as punch, he was. He held her up as though she were some sort of prize. Said it was an emergency. Said the social worker needed a place for her real fast. Said she'd been abused.

"I've got to admit, I wasn't thrilled at first. Esther was a wild child. Unruly. She had lice nits in her hair and worms coming out her fanny. There were cigarette burns on her bottom too. It was very difficult at first. I taught her to eat with a knife and fork, got her potty trained, bathed her, fed her, clothed her. Of course, she never could dress herself right, even when she was older. Always wore the most god-awful color combinations.

"Then there was the business of not talking. That was the most unnerving thing. A three-year-old child comes into the house and doesn't say boo for weeks on end, just looks at you with big bug eyes—it turned out she needed glasses—and people started hinting she wasn't normal. Neighbors started looking at her funny and us too. They kept their children away and Connie suffered for it.

"So I had a talk with Evan. I said, 'Look, honey, if she's retarded this isn't the best place for her. We have to send her back. It's the kindest thing all around.' Evan set his mouth in that stubborn line of his and I could see a disagreement looming. Fortunately it didn't come to that. Eventually little Esther made sounds. It just took a little encouragement, you know the kind I mean. When coddling doesn't do the trick, a firm hand can work wonders.

"After that she stuttered, but at least she talked. . . .

"Evan? Oh he was right partial to her. He never looked twice at poor Connie, but Esther was the apple of his eye. When she was little he played with her and dressed her up in frilly clothes and took her on shopping sprees. Just the two of them. With money we didn't have, but that's how Evan was.

"Esther took it hard when we divorced. By then we'd legally adopted Esther, and Evan wanted to take her and leave Connie with me. Did you ever hear such nonsense? I wouldn't hear of it, of course. Between you and me, Evan couldn't be relied on for diddly. He never did earn a steady paycheck, and caring for a child? Well, that was way beyond him, believe you me. . . .

"She never said so out right but, yes, I suppose Esther missed Evan. He would come by, rarely, to see her, though he broke his promises more often than not. That's the way it is with men sometimes. Out of sight, out of mind. But once in a while he'd come over and take Esther to a movie or for a soda at Bissell's Drug Store. Once he took her to the Danbury State Fair up at the old fairgrounds where *the mall is now and she threw up all over herself on the ferris wheel.*

"Evan, quite frankly, was a good-for-nothing dreamer, always talking of money-making schemes. He filled Esther's head with nonsense, and she believed it. She thought the sun rose and set on Evan P. Jamison.

"Yes, it's true Esther was alone much of the time. Connie was a little older and had many friends. Connie has always been outgoing and popular, unlike Esther. Esther was always off in a corner by herself. Reading. Daydreaming. Whatever. It was her way.

"Evan didn't pay child support or alimony, and someone had to put food on the table. Plenty of children today have working mothers and don't suffer for it. Of course, back then it was frowned on, especially in a prosperous town like Raven's Wing. People thought less of me, I suppose. But I had to ignore their uppity ways, I had no choice. And the people who looked down their noses were the quickest to hire me, I can tell you that. People in this town love having someone at their elbow in a white uniform. Dr. Bradford's dead wife, she was the worst. Acted like she never went to the toilet. Now don't frown like that, Mr. Haggarty. What's true is true.

"Esther was always well behaved, always toed the mark in school too. Never made any trouble. Quiet as a mouse, she was. Once I went to one of those parent-teacher conferences they have at the grade school and her teacher is talking to me and all of a sudden in the middle of the conversation I realize the teacher is talking about some other child. Not about Esther. Then I realize the teacher didn't even know who Esther Jamison was, even though she was in her class.

"After that I never went back. What was the point?

"Oh, I take that back. Once I did go back. If you nose around enough, I suppose you'll find mention of it in her records, so I may as well tell you. A guidance counselor at the high school called, and said she wanted to chat. That's the very word she used. Chat. Like we were going to have

high tea or something. So I took a morning off work and went in to meet Little Miss Chatterbox. I must say, she had some nerve. She said Esther was withdrawn. She said she didn't have any friends. Worst of all, she said Esther told her affection was a foreign language in our house. Can you imagine a child saying such a thing? I knew it was a lie, and when I confronted Esther, she denied everything Miss Chatterbox said. . . .

"After Evan moved out, I supported the three of us by working my hands to the bone. I've earned every penny Jonathan and Freddy send me today and more, not that I'm not grateful.

"First I cleaned houses like I told you and then later I started cooking for a caterer over in Stamford. Francesco's Catering, perhaps you've heard of it. They're famous around here. I made decorative hors d'oeuvres and pastries for exclusive affairs.

"Anyway, when Esther graduated high school Francesco offered her a job serving. She didn't want to take it, but I put my foot down. She couldn't just sit around the house.

"Of course, it was hard for her because of her stutter. Francesco painted me a picture one day, and it wasn't pretty. He said she would weave around the guests all mute and stiff and push platters of food at them. The staff laughed at her. They called her the gray ghost, said she should be working the haunted house down at Disney. But Francesco felt sorry for her. Once she dropped a whole tray of chocolate mousse on an expensive Oriental rug and he didn't even dock her wages.

"I remember she used to throw up from nerves before every party. Finally I said why don't you just pretend to be someone else. Anyone would have been an improvement. Ha! She got real quiet and thought about it a moment. Then she said she'd tried that before and it scared her. She might get lost, she said. Talked about a stranger in the mirror. Did you ever hear such nonsense?

"Maybe she was crazy even then."

10 "Lord," said Mildred, "that woman gives me chills."

"Lucille Jamison was always a hard woman," said Trevor. "She had a tough row to hoe raising two girls with no help from a good-for-nothing husband."

"It's plain she was partial to Connie," said Irene. "I bet she treated little Esther awful. I bet she abused her."

"Now Irene," cautioned Trevor, "we don't know that."

Forrest studied his hands. "We didn't look close at youngsters back then. Didn't listen to them close either. Kids turned up with bruises sometimes, and we didn't ask questions. Or if we did, we accepted their explanations right quick."

"I remember a boy in my third grade class," said Mildred. "His name was Jamie. He came to school one day with a black eye. And my mother told me Jamie's mother did it. She was horrified, but she didn't do anything. And no one else did either. That's just the way it was."

"That's physical abuse," said Trevor. "Mental abuse can be just as damaging, perhaps even more so. But even if it existed with Esther and even if anyone had reported it, nothing would have been done. Then or now. Even today the welfare people leave mental abuse cases alone. They're too hard to prove."

Irene folded her napkin into a tight little square and sighed. "I wish . . ."

Forrest looked at her. "Wish what, Reenie?"

"Wish we'd gotten Esther instead of her going to Lucille

and Evan. Earl and me wanted a baby something awful. We applied for a foster child once."

"Why Irene," said Mildred, "I didn't know that."

"Yeah, we did. Only they said no. 'Cause Earl couldn't read. Can you believe it? They said an illiterate person didn't qualify." She looked down at her hands. "I'd forgotten all about it, till now."

"Horses' asses," snapped Forrest. "They hang their degrees on the wall and wear clunky college rings and think they're hot shit."

"At least Esther's life took a turn for the better," Trevor reminded them, "when she met Jonathan."

Forrest brightened slightly. "That it did. She met Jonathan at one of those fancy parties. He had a fine education and came from a solid middle class family. He was ambitious too, a go-getter. But ambition or no, Jonathan was hardly what you'd call a ladies' man. He was paunchy and unathletic. A panty-waist, inexperienced with women. Took a real shine to Esther though. Took her under his wing, you might say. He provided her a means of escape, sure, but the marriage turned out to be more than that. They loved each other dearly, everyone could see it. It was a match made in heaven."

He paused, considering. "Of course, Lucille talks about the marriage from her own point of view. . . ."

" . . . *Esther was on the verge of being fired when Jonathan Maine came along, so I suppose it looked to most people like he rescued her. But I knew differently. I knew about the money. How could I not? Evan made sure everyone knew, everyone from here to East Jabib.*

"*The Lotto money, Mr. Haggarty, and I'm pleased as punch that subject has come up. It's been troubling me for more than twenty years, and I've kept my mouth shut. It wasn't my way to ask for financial remuneration, even when it was due. But now that Esther's gone, I've decided to make my feelings clear. Right is right, after all, and I think, by rights, Jonathan should give that money to me. With interest. Don't you agree? It's nothing to him. A paltry sum by his standards today. And I'm her mother, after all. I mean, fair is fair, don't you agree?*

"That's just what I am doing, Mr. Haggarty. Trying to tell you. On Esther's wedding day Evan told about some money Esther had. Secret money. He got drunk at the reception, per usual, and started to blubber, also per usual. And when he blubbered, he blabbered. There he was, whining and crying into his champagne, telling everyone who would listen that it was he who bought a lucky Lotto ticket, he who gave it to Esther and he who was entitled to the winnings. One hundred thousand dollars. He announced it for all the world to hear. I could scarcely believe my ears.

"That's when I saw the light. Oh, I know it wasn't a vast sum as lottery winnings go. But on our side of the tracks it was a veritable fortune. And, believe me, it was nothing to sneeze at on Jonathan's side either. People in Raven's Wing who live well are always overextended. More to the point, a tidy sum like that represented the stake Jonathan needed. The stake to get his practice up and running. The stake to pay for his equipment. The stake to help him cultivate proper contacts.

"Course, Jonathan said he loved her, and I think he did. They fit together like fiddle and faddle. Two odd ducks, they were, and in such a hurry to get married. Of course, when Claudia was born seven months to the day after the wedding weighing a healthy eight pounds, I saw the light again.

"So there you have it: the story of the money and of Claudia all rolled into one.

"Speaking of Claudia, I guess you heard from Jonathan about that postpartum business. Let's not gild the lily, Mr. Haggarty. There's a better word for what was going on than postpartum and it's malingering. Lots of women tire easily after giving birth, but they get up and make the best of things. Not Esther though. She took to her bed and wouldn't so much as touch that newborn baby. Then Jonathan catered to her, which didn't help. Why, I had *to do everything. Between you and me, once she said she was afraid she might hurt the child. Said she had thoughts about killing it. Can you imagine such a thing? I told her to hush. I told her never to say such a thing again. . . .*

"Evan? He died. It happened shortly after Esther married. He was living in a dilapidated hotel over in Norwalk and somebody robbed him, then slit his throat neat as you please for good measure. Stole his few dollars. Stole his lottery tickets. Stole his miserable sorry life, which was all he really had.

"It was ironic, now that I think of it. Him being robbed. The man never had two nickels.

"Now tell me what you think, honestly. You being a man of the law. Do you think I have a chance at that Lotto money after all these years? Legally speaking, that is?"

11 "What a witch," pronounced Irene. "I'm sure if she'd just ask Jonathan nice, he'd give her the money."

"Sure," agreed Forrest, "but Lucille's been so desperate and so suspicious for so long she can't believe anyone would do something generous. And I bet she's worked herself into a real lather, afraid now that Esther's dead Jonathan'll stop sending her monthly allowance."

"Well it certainly was a blessing that Esther met Jonathan," said Trevor. "She really did escape."

"Yes," said Forrest. "The marriage seemed to work out well for both of them. At least as well as it could, considering Esther's reclusive temperament."

"The postpartum depression," said Mildred, "do you

remember anything about it, Trevor?"

"Vaguely. I wasn't Esther's physician, but I'd hear things around town. Apparently her pregnancies—all of them— affected her badly. Each time she withdrew from the world. Wouldn't leave the house. Fortunately Jonathan was very understanding with her. After he saw how Claudia's birth affected her, he brought in help. I suppose that was the start of him having people 'do' for her. Lucille certainly wasn't any help, despite her recollection to the contrary."

"Esther managed to recover after each birth," put in Forrest, "and there was no more talk about killing babies. That's all it was, thank God. Crazy talk."

Irene chewed on that thought for a moment. "Seems lately I've been hearing about women killing their babies, Forrest. You got to take such talk serious. Why just the other day they had a woman on *Oprah*—"

Forrest snorted in disgust.

"Sometimes you can learn things on those shows," defended Irene.

Ever the peacemaker, Trevor tried to get Forrest back on track. "Why don't you go on with the story, Forrest?"

"Okay." He rolled his eyes in exasperation. "Jonathan set about to help Esther as best he could. He not only hired help for the house, he hired a speech therapist too. And he worked with Esther himself to help her overcome the fear of going outside. Each time, bit by bit she seemed to get control of her life.

"Seems it took a long time for Esther to get pregnant again, or maybe they planned it that way, since she had her troubles with Claudia. In any case, it wasn't until Claudia was five that Cameron came along. Claudia had flashing dark eyes and was outgoing. Cameron was washed-out-looking and cranky—a contrary, unattractive, sickly baby. The kind people hold briefly then pass along gratefully to the next pair of available hands. By this time, though, the days of watching pennies were over. Jonathan was successful. His clients included an occasional Broadway star or Colony Club socialite."

"You'd think," said Irene, "that if the pregnancies affected Esther so badly, they'd quit having babies. I mean, why not settle for one? Or two? But no, they went on, and along came Lauren and then Timmy."

"I must admit," said Trevor, "I was particularly surprised when Timmy came along. It was only a couple of years ago, mind you, and by then Jonathan and Esther were in their forties. It's not so easy keeping up with a toddler. On top of that, they'd been to hell and back that year with Claudia."

"What about Claudia?" snapped Forrest. This was irritating. Sometimes Trevor here seemed to know more about the Maines than he did. He was a doctor, but still and all. "What'd she do? Get herself pregnant or something?"

"No, nothing like that. I wish it had been that."

"I thought she was away at school," said Irene. "Some fancy college. Barrington."

"Bennington," corrected Mildred. "An avant-garde school. Of the same ilk as Bard and Oberlin and Antioch." She knew them all. If there was a school for rebellious youth, her daughter Molly had sought it out and applied for admission. They'd taken a grand tour, she and Molly. It was a grim memory. She'd seen more than enough of the *Less Than Zero* crowd. Cynical affluent young people who thought they knew it all.

"She went there for a year," said Trevor, "then transferred to an art school in Brooklyn. Pratt Institute, I think it was. She stayed a month or two, then dropped out. The family kept it quiet at the time. Children from Raven's Wing families aren't supposed to become drug addicts."

"A drug addict?" exclaimed Irene. "Claudia Maine? Get out."

"What sort of drugs?" asked Mildred. "I mean, all young people smoked marijuana for a while there. Not that I'm saying it was right, mind you. But my own daughter—"

"Nothing so tame as marijuana," said Trevor. "I'm talking hard stuff." He shook his head. "The ones that come to mind—well, let's see—there was heroin, cocaine, amphetamines, Seconal, Dilaudid, Darvon, methadone, Quaaludes—"

"All right," said Forrest. "We get the picture."

"She used every known common addictive chemical by every route of entry."

"Jeesum." Irene's mind filled with visions of disgusting routes of entry.

"Christ," said Forrest.

"No one told me what happened exactly. Claudia had always been rebellious. A handful. Apparently she fell in with a rough crowd. Street dealers, not students. It was a terrible thing. She was so gifted."

"Yeah," agreed Irene. "I remember reading about her in the paper once. Some kind of artistic genius, they called her. Had a bunch of paintings on exhibit over at the savings bank. I went to take a look. Figured why not, it was free. They were kind of weird, though. Wasn't nothing I could recognize."

"Not weird to everyone," said Trevor. "Not to art critics. And with her father's connections at some of the galleries, there's no telling how far she might have gone." He shook his head sadly. "But she threw it all away."

"What happened to her?" asked Mildred.

Trevor closed his eyes for a moment, remembering. "One night out of the blue Jonathan brought her to the house. Literally carried her in. Mary Margaret about threw a fit. It was bedlam, Claudia crying and threatening and carrying on. And the language. Well, I never heard such filth. Jonathan had tracked her down and literally kidnapped her from the city, from an abandoned building or penthouse suite, who knows?

"He'd gotten her just in time, believe me. She was at rock bottom. She was psychotic from the effect of the drugs. Hallucinating . . ."

The word that came to mind was *wasted*. Trevor had never seen anyone like that before, and he hoped he never would again . . . chalk-white skin, waxy glazed eyes, limbs studded with festering scabs and needle tracks.

"The veins in her arms had collapsed. She'd taken to injecting herself everywhere, her groin, her anus."

Mildred folded her hands and thanked her lucky stars that Molly had gone to a nice quiet avant-garde school like Hampshire College.

"She looked like a concentration camp victim."

"So what'd you do?" asked Forrest.

"Jonathan knew I had privileges over at Norwalk Hospital. He wanted her there, not at Doctor's Hospital in the city where he's affiliated. So I got her a bed and told him to get her over there fast. She was on the verge of cardiac arrest. Plus she had hepatitis and venereal disease. Not AIDS, thank God for that at least. In any case, we got her admitted. Then later, when the physical crisis had passed, Jonathan got her into a drug treatment program at Silver Glen."

"And she was cured?" asked Irene hopefully.

"I don't think so. I asked Jonathan about her a couple of times, and for a while he seemed hopeful. Then one day he told me she was gone. Just like that. Took off, he said. He couldn't even talk about it. He was devastated."

"It must have been terrible for them," said Mildred.

"For Esther especially. As hard as it was for Jonathan, I think he managed to come to terms with it. But Esther never did. For some reason she blamed herself. Seemed to believe she'd contributed in some way. Of course, she hadn't. She was a good mother, but she seemed to take it as divine retribution for some sort of sin."

"Sometimes," said Forrest, "I wonder about the church. Does more harm than good, seems to me."

Irene looked at Forrest sharply. "Don't go blaming the church. Folks like you just get things twisted in their minds, that's all. Why, look at that John List fellow. When he killed his entire family so's they could go to heaven, folks didn't blame the Lutheran church, did they? Course not. They blamed him. But when it's the Catholic church, it's a whole 'nother kettle of fish. People like to place blame."

"Maybe," conceded Forrest. "But the church played a part. You got to admit that."

"Oh hush!" said Irene. She turned to Trevor. "So where's Claudia now?"

"I don't know. Nobody does. She might be dead. Odds are, she is."

Forrest wondered why Jonathan hadn't told him about Claudia. Wondered why Jonathan glossed over the troubles of his first born, saying she was "away at school." Maybe it was too painful to discuss. Maybe he was embarrassed. Maybe he figured Trevor would fill him in.

But Trevor wasn't finished. "I remember wondering if they had Timmy as some sort of replacement. I mean, Esther was so upset about Claudia and then all of a sudden Timmy turns up."

He remembered the day clear as glass, the day Jonathan and Esther came to his house with Timmy in Esther's arms. Trevor was semiretired and not taking on new patients, especially infants. But he'd given the other children their checkups, and Jonathan was insistent.

"I examined the baby," Trevor recalled, "then referred them to Tom Bradley, the young fellow who took over my practice. Jonathan sure seemed the proud papa. He was beaming. 'Here's another one,' he said. 'Imagine. Being a father all over again at my age.' "

"What about Esther?" asked Mildred.

"Esther?" Trevor thought for a moment. "I don't know. She seemed tuckered out from the birth. Quiet. But happy. At least I thought she was."

12 Jonathan and Esther Maine prospered during the course of their marriage. They moved through a sequence of houses in Raven's Wing, each grander than the last, before settling in the stone and glass contemporary on High Ridge.

"A monstrosity," pronounced Forrest, who deemed such houses contemptible rather than contemporary.

"Very out of character, that house, with the rest of the neighborhood," said Mildred, sighing.

At the time of Esther's sudden death, Jonathan and his wife owned the residence in Raven's Wing, a vacation house on Little Chebeague Island off the coast of Maine, various stocks and bonds amounting to about $3 million, and the practice which had turned into a veritable gold mine. Indeed, the practice was now an expansive corporation with field offices in Boca Raton, Scottsdale, Santa Fe, and Beverly Hills. Banker friends of Forrest's confided that Jonathan Maine's worth, on paper at least, was in excess of $20 million.

"Jeesum," said Irene, "they don't seem that rich."

"They don't live high," explained Forrest. "Just a family vacation at the house on Chebeague every summer, private schools for Cameron and Lauren, and a few luxuries at home—the pool and the housekeeper, but nothing lavish considering their means."

"There's something here," said Mildred. "Something we should consider right off the bat."

"What's that?" replied Forrest.

"We all know that nine times out of ten when a woman is murdered it's the husband who did it. Perhaps Jonathan killed Esther. Perhaps he found the poems not after she died, but before. Perhaps he was suspicious. Perhaps he followed her to that hotel room—"

"Perhaps, perhaps, perhaps," mimicked Forrest. "Christ on a crutch, Millie, don't you think I thought of all that?"

"Well he is a friend," Trevor reminded him. "Your judgment may be clouded."

"Being a friend doesn't mean diddly," Forrest shot back. "I checked out his alibi, and it's rock solid. He was home in bed the night Esther died. He came home early from work. Had allergies something awful. Took an antihistamine and it knocked him out. They swear Jonathan was home. Lauren was sleeping over at a friend's that night, but I talked to Cameron and Helga, see?"

Helga Marie Dominski stepped onto the front porch and approached the front door, hand raised tentatively. There was a creaking sound. "Oh!" She whirled around and faced Forrest with accusing eyes. "You startled me."

He rocked again, repeating the sound. "Sorry, Miss Dominski. I guess everyone's a little on edge right now."

"I should say."

"Have a seat with an old man. Reenie put out some lemonade. Homemade." He traced a drippy smiley face on the pitcher.

The housekeeper sat down stiffly. "Dr. Maine said you wanted to talk to me." (So let's not pretend, Mr. Haggarty. Let's not pretend this is a social call. This is not a happy time, Mr. Haggarty. Not a happy time at all.)

She was a big beautiful woman, five-ten, maybe taller. Her looks were more Scandinavian than Slavic, featuring porcelain skin, ash-blond hair now twisted into a thick braid that trailed down her back, and clear blue eyes flecked with green. Worried eyes.

Forrest studied her for a moment and watched her gaze fall to her lap.

"You already talked to Cameron," she said, not looking up.

"Yeah."

"I hope you didn't upset him. He's a sensitive child. He's been through enough."

"You really care about those kids, don't you?"

She looked up at him, fire in her eyes, and in the barest instant she looked like she would kill for those children if she had to. Then the brittle protective shell dissolved and her face softened. *"Yes,"* she said quietly. *"I care."*

"Don't worry, Miss Dominski. I may not look like it, but I can be a gentle man."

"Good." She folded her hands tightly. And I hope you'll be gentle with me, she seemed to say silently. *"I don't know what more I can add."*

"Well, Cameron's a little vague on what happened that night. He doesn't remember anything much after his father came home."

She jutted her chin toward him. *"What's to remember? It was an ordinary night, Mr. Haggarty. A night like any other. There was nothing special about it."*

"Still, he's a bright boy, with a mind that remembers almost too much most times. A boy like that—like you said, a sensitive boy—you'd think that night would be etched in his mind forever. You'd think he'd never forget. After all, he remembers the day he heard what happened right down to the very last detail."

"Of course. Because that was when her death became real to him. We all remember where we were, what we were doing, at shattering moments like that."

"I guess. But one way or the other I need to know about that night. Anything you can tell me might help. Even details that seem trivial. I hope you'll cooperate."

"Why?" She turned her face away. *"It's over."*

"For Cameron's sake. This matters very much to him. He can't make his peace with it until he has some answers. He's the one who asked us to investigate."

"And if only he hadn't!" She snapped her mouth shut, then shrugged her shoulders hopelessly. "No good can come of this, Mr. Haggarty. There's been pain enough in this family—pain enough to last five lifetimes. What good will knowing do? Mrs. Maine died a terrible violent death. Knowing how and why won't help anyone."

"Still," he said evenly, "I aim to find out. How. And why."

"Do what you want then, but it won't help Cameron. I know him very well. He blames himself for his mother's death. Ah, that surprises you? It shouldn't. He has always been protective of her. Now he feels he should have protected her from this. That is why he seeks this investigation of yours. He looks for absolution, Mr. Haggarty. For himself. From himself. Of course, he will never receive it."

"But that's crazy."

"Perhaps. Nevertheless, he will never forgive. You see, that afternoon was very ordinary. Dr. Maine came home early from the clinic. At three o'clock. He has allergies. It runs in the family. Cameron has them too, you must have noticed."

"Yes," he said impatiently. "And then what happened?"

"Nothing 'happened,' Mr. Haggarty. Dr. Maine came home and went straight to bed. We had instructions not to disturb him. I remember I had trouble keeping little Timmy quiet. But it didn't matter because Dr. Maine took strong medication and was sound asleep."

"You're sure of this?"

"Quite sure. I could hear him snoring through the door. I heard him when I put Timmy to bed and again later—at ten o'clock—when I went to check on Cameron."

"Cameron was home all evening?"

"Of course. Where would he go? He attends boarding school and doesn't have friends here. I sent him to Great Pond for a swim that day, hoping he would meet some of the local youngsters, but"—she shrugged her shoulders *again*—"*he came home alone. As always. He ate his dinner, he watched a little television, he went to sleep. And while he was sleeping peacefully, his mother died. It is that simple. And that terrible.*"

"*You've been with the family a long time?*" he asked suddenly.

"*Yes. Well, actually not so long. It just seems so. My life began when I came to the Maines. I have no family. This family, these children, they are my family. I came after Timmy was born. To help Mrs. Maine.*"

"*And how was she?*"

"*What a question. Do you mean was she nice? A nice lady? A caring person? A good employer? Yes! She was all of those things. She was a saint, Mrs. Maine was.*"

"*Was she a good mother?*"

Helga paused. "*Yes. Distant on occasion. The children found that hard to understand. She had mental problems. But she was always gentle. Always caring. Life was just too much for her sometimes.*"

"*Not anymore it isn't.*"

Helga paled and looked away.

"*What about her relationship with Dr. Maine? Did they get along?*"

"*Always. I would have known if they didn't. They never squabbled. Never had those bickerings some couples have. They were always polite with one another.*"

"*But did they love each other?*" he pressed.

"*Oh yes!*" *Helga looked down at her ringless hands.* "*They loved each other very much!*"

The four sat silently for some moments, pondering.

"What about Esther Maine's things?" asked Mildred. "Any clue there?"

"I looked through the carton the police gave Jonathan," answered Forrest. "It supposedly contains her personal possessions from that West Side hotel—toiletries, makeup, clothing. The curious thing was the strange assortment of clothes. Stuff that didn't go together at all."

"Like what?" asked Irene.

"Like fancy evening dresses, frilly blouses with pearl buttons, and designer suits."

"None of that seems out of place," said Mildred.

"Yeah? Well what about a black leather skirt? What about red satin shorts? *Real* short they were. Left nothing to the imagination. And a cheap red wig too. Believe me, there was trashy stuff there. Undergarments with holes in strategic places. Lotions and notions. Stuff you don't want to hear about."

"I want to hear," said Irene.

"Irene," said Trevor gruffly, "that's her private business."

"Not anymore," corrected Forrest. "She's dead. There's no private business when you're dead."

"So tell," persisted Irene.

"Adult toys," said Forrest darkly, "and that's all I'm going to say on the matter. Jonathan insists they weren't hers. Insists she never would have owned such contraptions."

"My," sighed Mildred, "this is getting downright sordid."

"Oh," said Forrest with relish, "you ain't seen nothing yet, Millie."

Trevor winced. Forrest seemed to enjoy these investigations so, seemed to enjoy uncovering other people's secrets. He once told Trevor that no one had the right to end a human life before its time, and Trevor supposed that these investigations gave his old friend a sense of purpose. He respected Forrest's sense of commitment but sometimes suspected it bordered on obsession.

If pressed, Trevor would admit that he himself felt drawn to Forrest's quest for rightness, perhaps even his quest for retribution. Nevertheless, he maintained enough detachment to be repelled by the crime at the same time.

He and Forrest had their differences, that was for sure. Seventy years on this earth and Trevor still wasn't sure how he felt about capital punishment, for example. Forrest had no qualms, no reservations, not the slightest quibble. Forrest believed in capital punishment for the same reason he opposed abortion: You protect the innocent from harm. No matter what. It was one of Forrest T. Haggarty's Basic Rules of Life. No exceptions, period. Capital punishment, Forrest maintained, served both to punish and to rid society of its abominations. Mankind had a duty, a moral obligation even, to rid itself of evil.

One time Trevor reminded Forrest that it had been proven that capital punishment was not a deterrent to murder. "Oh yes it is," Forrest snapped back, " 'cause there's no way a dead man can murder again." Trevor didn't have a quick comeback for that one. " 'Sides," Forrest went on, "I don't give a rat's ass if it's not a deterrent in the broader sense. It's punishment, and that's good enough."

When Trevor countered that it was a punishment meted out unfairly with the black and poor suffering in percentages far disproportionate to the numbers of their crimes while the white and rich got off, Forrest's answer was that there should be more capital punishment, not less. Pile it on, he said. Everyone who earned the punishment should partake, white and rich included. "And none of this lethal injection shit, neither," Forrest said. "It's too easy. Too kind. After all, the monsters who poured Drano down the throats of those victims in Utah didn't give them a humane choice. Did they say, 'What'll it be—Drano or cyanide?' Well did they?"

Sometimes Trevor envied Forrest the strength of his convictions and sometimes he was appalled by them.

"So," said Forrest, interrupting Trevor's thoughts, "tomorrow we start at the Hotel St. James."

"Hotel St. James?" repeated Mildred.

"That's where they found her," whispered Irene. "Esther Maine. Her face stove in. Blood running down the drain. Cold as stone."

Mildred gasped. Irene had a way of describing things in such grisly detail.

"You'd best prepare yourself, Millie," said Forrest. "The St. James is not exactly a place with three stars in the Mobil Guide."

"You know what I picture?" said Irene. "A dump. A pit. A den of sin."

"I don't suppose," said Mildred hopefully, "that I might be put to better use performing some other worthwhile task while you all visit this St. James establishment— doing research at the library or what have you. I mean, I won't be offended if you leave me out."

"Oh no," said Forrest. "You're not getting off the hook that easy, Millie. We all go. We must get a feel for the place, the scene, the victim—"

"If she was a victim," reminded Trevor.

Forrest went on, ignoring this interruption. "Much as I hate to admit it, Millie, you might pick up on something I miss. Trevor has a good eye too. And Irene . . ." He stopped, at a loss to think of what Irene's contribution might possibly be.

"Irene is good with people," put in Mildred quickly. "The desk clerk, the housekeeper, that sort of thing. You never know who might have seen what."

"Exactly," said Forrest gratefully, knowing Mildred had saved him from a cold shoulder that evening.

"Thank you," said Irene. She leaned back in her bowback Windsor, forgetting about the St. James for the moment, and gazed contentedly at the ornate relief on the plaster ceiling. "This place here really is something, Millie. Like living in a museum almost."

"A mausoleum is more like it," said Mildred without enthusiasm. "I'd really like to sell it and move into something more manageable."

"Well, I for one never thought New York would be like this."

"New York," said Trevor, "isn't like this, Irene. At least not for most people." In spite of the fact that Trevor Bradford was well traveled and a retired physician of comfortable means, he couldn't help but be somewhat intimidated by Mildred's apartment. He had, of course, known that some people live like this. People like Trump and that Helmsley woman. But he'd never connected the Mildred Bennett he knew with this sort of wealth. Two floors, twelve rooms, three fireplaces—he had counted— a living room the size of a hockey rink. Genuine Picassos and Renoirs on the walls and a magnificent Steinway grand that nobody even played. He could tell because when he'd allowed himself to gingerly touch one of the keys, dust had come up on the tip of his finger.

"Go ahead," Mildred had encouraged, "play away." But he couldn't. It was all too overwhelming. He knew old-fashioned songs like "Fly Me to the Moon" and "Don't Sit Under the Apple Tree (With Anyone Else But Me)." Simple plain songs. Nothing classical or fancy. "Oh I couldn't," he said and turned away.

"My son Sam used to play it," she said wistfully and turned away too.

All of this served to make him more tongue-tied than ever. A gold digger, that's what she'll think I am. He concentrated on eating a spare rib as delicately as he could and tried not to think about the strings of pork caught in his bridgework.

13 Mildred's nose wrinkled with distaste. The vestibule of the St. James Hotel smelled vaguely but unmisstakably of urine. No amount of Lysol could scrub it away. The floor might be Italian marble and the dainty chandelier overhead leaded Irish crystal, but clearly the hotel had fallen into disrepair. It was painfully obvious that street people in this dreary neighborhood now utilized the once-imposing entryway as a lavatory.

Yet there was evidence that someone was trying valiantly, hopelessly, to stem the tide of decay. Mildred could tell that in its time the St. James must have been a gem of a hotel. The lobby was graced with a worn but well-vacuumed Oriental rug, the real thing, it looked like to Mildred. Potted plants in the corners were lush and well cared for. And the front desk was of antique mahogany polished to a high gloss.

But the clientele seemed oblivious to the faded grandeur. Mildred watched out of the corner of her eye and shuddered. Young women—and a few not so young—sauntered through the lobby wearing miniskirts or satin hot pants that exposed garters and fanny cheeklets. Makeup was thickly applied, with a trowel it seemed. Yes, the St. James was, she suspected, one of *those* places.

Mildred spied a gaunt woman wrapped in a raggedy sweater. Her face resembled fish skin in its unhealthy pallor. She slumped to one side on a sofa, mouth agape, yesterday's *Post* clutched grimly in inky hands.

"You okay?" asked Irene. She grabbed the woman's shoulder and gave it a squeeze.

"Irene," whispered Mildred, "for pity's sake."

"Maybe she had a heart attack," said Irene. "A body could die in this city, die and *decay,* and wouldn't nobody know it. Or care."

"The woman," whispered Mildred, "may be decayed but she's not dead." She rolled her eyes to the ornately carved plaster ceiling and was greeted by leering cherubs in gold relief.

"Best leave her alone," advised Trevor. "I don't think she's had any heart attack." He nudged the woman's shopping bag discreetly with his toe. There, wedged between tangled skeins of yellow yarn, was a half-empty pint of Richardson's Wild Irish Rose, eighty proof.

The emaciated woman jolted awake with a start. "Huh?"

Irene jumped back. "Never mind!" she cried.

The woman looked at her menacingly. She let sheets of newspaper fall and clutched the shopping bag to her chest, stabbing herself with a knitting needle in the process. "Shit!" she said.

"Oh, for Christ's sake," muttered Forrest. Some investigative team this was, stopping to examine every bit of human flotsam spit up by the streets of Manhattan.

"Sorry I woke you," apologized Irene. She pictured the knitting needle impaled between her breasts. "I thought maybe you was sick, that's all. But I can see you're not. Sick, I mean. I can see you're fine."

"Fine!" exhaled the woman. She staggered to her feet and leaned forward precariously. Irene felt a blast of alcohol. Her eyes almost watered.

"Don't anyone light a match," said Forrest. "We'll have an explosion."

Mildred turned to Irene, repulsed by this vagrant who swayed like an apparition before them. "She's got one tooth."

"Flossing must be a breeze," whispered Irene.

"What!" barked the woman.

"May I help you?" A small prissily dressed man fluttered forward from the front desk. He wore a pathetically hopeful expression, but his face switched channels quickly as he glanced angrily at the fish-white lady in the moth-eaten sweater.

"I must apologize for Cora here," he said, shooting one final glare at the lady in question. "You see, she was a resident at the St. James when the hotel was in its prime." He arched an eyebrow and spoke as though Cora weren't even there. "A schoolteacher, can you believe it? Then she retired and ran out of money. She sleeps in a shelter at night, but keeps coming back to our lobby during the day."

"I'm on automatic pilot," said Cora matter-of-factly, "a homing pigeon without a nest."

"I haven't had the heart to turn her away," added the desk clerk.

"Heart schmart," mimicked Cora. "I give him good money to let me sit here, and he cops a feel every time I doze off."

The desk clerk spread his hands. "She's out of her mind, as you can see. I inherited the St. James from my uncle last year and never thought it would be like this, I must say. Sometimes I think this place is turning into a mental institution." He turned on the interloper and shook his finger. "You sorely test my patience, Cora. You push me beyond all reasonable bounds."

"Mr. Generosity," muttered Cora sullenly. "He gave me an inch, so I could take a flying leap."

Forrest cringed. "Oh boy."

"Forrest," said Mildred, "be kind."

"If you'll come this way," said the desk clerk, "I'll get you checked in and show you to your rooms." He touched two fingers to slick Brylcreemed hair in a sort of jaunty salute.

Mildred hastened to set things straight. "Oh, we're not here to check in."

Clearly disappointed, the man seemed to deflate before their eyes.

"We're here to see a room," said Forrest.

"You're planning," said the desk clerk carefully, "to all stay in the same room?"

"No," explained Trevor. "We just want to *see* a room."

"*Look* at it," said Forrest.

"As in 'examine,' " said Mildred.

"I see," said the clerk stiffly. "And which room did you have in mind?"

"Lemme see here . . ." Forrest flipped open his black spiral notebook. "Room three-twelve."

Color drained from the clerk's face. "Oh my. I don't think that's such a good idea. No one's stayed in that room since . . ."

"Since Camille," supplied gaunt Cora.

"Since who?" asked Mildred.

"Camille," said Cora, who suddenly seemed in possession of her sobriety. "Three-twelve was Camille's room."

"Yes," affirmed the clerk. "Ms. Smith always stayed in three-twelve."

"Always?" said Trevor.

"Every Tuesday, right as rain. She booked it right straight though, every day of the week, a whole year in advance even though she only came on Tuesdays. She didn't want anyone else staying in that room. She was a very particular woman, Ms. Smith."

"A *peculiar* woman," corrected Cora. "Quiet. But nice. Real nice."

"A terrible accident, it was," said the clerk. "We have nonskid bath mats. Apparently she chose not to use hers." A worried look crossed his face. "I do hope there won't be any sort of litigation. We're hanging on by our fingernails as it is."

"No indeed," Mildred reassured him. "Nothing like that."

"Good," said the clerk in relief. His face turned somber again. "Ms. Smith, rest her soul, will be sorely missed here, I can tell you that."

"You bet she will," snapped Cora. "The St. James doesn't get many guests anymore. People aren't exactly beating down the door. Bookings have fallen off."

"People don't come here like they used to," admitted the desk clerk. "They prefer the big chains—the Hilton, the Sheraton—"

"The HoJo's," put in Cora. "They got good fried fish at HoJo's." She smacked her lips.

"Yes," said Mildred, trying not to imagine Cora's single tooth sinking into a greasy fillet of fish.

"Okay," said Forrest impatiently. "Now if we could just have a look-see at that room, Mister . . . ?"

"Higgins," said the clerk in a voice that tried to be assertive. "I am the owner of the St. James. And I'm afraid a 'look-see' as you call it is out of the question."

"Oh yeah?" said Forrest belligerently. "And why is that?" He drew himself up full height and moved toward a now cowering Mr. Higgins.

"Oh," said Higgins, wringing his hands, "I don't know. Somehow it just doesn't seem right. Ms. Smith paid for the room through December, and dead or alive it's still hers now, isn't it? Showing it to you people, strangers at that, would seem an invasion of privacy."

"Oh for Christ's sake," muttered Forrest.

"Doesn't seem an invasion of privacy to me," said Cora reasonably. "Not after the way the police tramped through there, the way they carted off her body in a black zippered sack, the way they shoved her things in plastic Hefty bags—"

"Cora please!" said Higgins. "Where's your sense of decency?"

"Decency, shmecency," replied Cora.

"We got permission from her husband," Irene put in. "Dr. Jonathan Maine. He has authorized us to investigate what happened."

"What happened," said Higgins tightly, "is that Ms. Smith slipped in the tub and fractured her skull."

"That," said Forrest hotly, "is debatable, and if you stand in the way of our investigation—"

"Forrest," whispered Trevor, "couldn't this be better handled without a display of temper on your part. I mean, maybe a little financial encouragement—"

"Huh?" said Forrest.

"The money, Forrest. Didn't Jonathan give you some—"

"Money?" said Cora hopefully.

"Oh. *That* money." He reached into his pants pocket and pulled out several loose bills. Cora's eyes bugged out and Higgins made an obvious effort to study the tips of his shiny shoes.

"Here." Forrest held out a twenty. "This should cover the price of admission."

Higgins seemed to reconsider. "Well . . . I suppose it

could be applied to our restoration fund. And since you say Ms. Smith's husband is aware of your venture . . ." The bill vanished into the folds of his blazer. "All right then . . ." He pivoted primly on one foot. "If you'll just follow me . . ." He paused to look at Cora. "And you," he said, "stay here."

"Screw that," Cora shot back. She gathered up stray sheets of newspaper and stuffed them into her shopping bag. "There's plenty I could tell these nice people and it wouldn't cost twenty neither. Hell, I'd be happy with ten."

Tired gray walls and peeling paint?
Look once, look twice, you'll see that it ain't
A bad sort of place to contemplate
Or wait for a man you appreciate.

14 Common and tacky, thought Mildred. Her eyes took in a dark musty room, a screaming turquoise seascape print on the wall, hung crooked at that, a threadbare tufted bedspread, and cheap plastic-veneer furniture scarred with over-lapping cigarette burns.

"Nice place," remarked Irene. "A black-and-white TV, touchtone phone, all the comforts."

"We redecorated a couple of years ago," said Higgins. "I must say, I don't like to come in here though. Not after . . . well, you know." He swept across the room and flung open the drapes.

"Not much of a view," commented Forrest as he surveyed the brick wall outside.

"Ms. Smith preferred this room," defended Higgins. "I showed her several of our best, and this was the one she selected. She liked the privacy, the lack of street noise." As if on cue, someone in the room next door moaned in what could have been agony or ecstasy.

"Uh huh," said Forrest. Some privacy. "The room next door—we'll want to talk to the occupant."

"Oh," said Higgins hastily, "the current occupant isn't the same one as when Ms. Smith was with us. We're not a residential hotel, you see."

"Well then, we'll talk with whoever was there at the time," said Forrest absently. His eyes traveled up sooty bricks. Here and there he detected rectangles of newer, pinker brick where old windows had been walled shut. One window, however, remained intact. As he angled his head just so and looked up into it he spied some kind of office. A well-dressed man in a tie and white shirt looked down at him furtively, then turned away.

"I can look it up for you," said Higgins, "but it won't do a bit of good."

"Folks here don't tend to use their real names," explained Cora. "They come, they stay an hour or two, they go. Or maybe I got that in the wrong order." She grinned lewdly.

"I'm sure you understand," said Higgins, wanting to drop the subject.

"Indeed," said Mildred.

While Higgins and Cora hovered, Forrest, Irene, Mildred, and Trevor wandered about in silence, each engrossed in thoughts of what it must have been like to be Esther Maine or Camille Smith, for indeed they were one and the same, in this dreary room, in this wasted neighborhood, for the last hours of her life.

Mildred smoothed the bedspread without thinking. She straightened the cheap plastic ashtray. The room bore no signs of a struggle, not even a stray thread as evidence of its former occupant . . . the closet was empty, hangers shoved to one side in a tangle of black wire, the ratty shag carpet looked freshly raked, the bathroom appeared in absolute and bleak order, with shrink-wrapped plastic glasses on the sink and a paper strip in place across the toilet.

"We had to replace the fixtures in the tub," Higgins called in to Mildred. "At considerable expense, I might add. She had fallen into them."

"How thoughtless," muttered Irene.

"Odd," said Mildred almost to herself. She bent down on the tiled floor and ran her hand gingerly across the bottom of the rust-stained tub.

"What's odd?" asked Forrest.

"The surface of this tub is like sandpaper."

"It's an old tub," apologized Higgins. "We're planning on replacing them. Someday."

"The point," said Mildred, "is that one couldn't slip in this tub, Mr. Higgins, even if one tried."

"Well—" stammered Higgins.

"You got a point, Millie," said Irene, kneeling down and feeling the porcelain for herself. "You could file your nails on this here tub. Yep. You sure got a point."

"You bet she does," said Forrest, glaring at Higgins now.

"Well," said Higgins again, "the police said—"

"What about the shower curtain?" snapped Forrest.

"What shower curtain?"

"That shower curtain." Forrest pointed. "Was it in or was it out when you found her?"

"Why," stammered Higgins, "I don't know."

"Well think about it!"

"There's no need to raise your voice." Higgins crumbled to the bed and put his head into his hands. "I—oh dear—let me think. Please."

"Hurry up, for Christ's sake!"

Higgins looked up, his face ashen. "Someone called—I don't know who—and said something was wrong in Room three-twelve. I thought it rather odd."

"Someone called?" said Mildred.

"Who?" demanded Forrest.

"I don't know!"

"Man or woman?" pressed Forrest.

"I said I don't know! It sounded as though the person was speaking through a handkerchief or something. It was all very indistinct. When I realized what they were saying, I rushed upstairs to check it out. And when I got there I heard water running, The shower—"

"What about the door?" asked Mildred.

"Huh?" Higgins looked at her as though dazed.

"The door, Mr. Higgins. Was it unlocked?"

"Well yes, now that you mention it, I suppose it was."

"You *suppose?*" cried Forrest. "You *suppose!*"

"All right!" shrieked Higgins. "The door was unlocked! Are you happy now? I didn't think anything of it at the time. I was intent on—"

"Mr. Higgins," interrupted Mildred, "a woman alone in a hotel wouldn't leave her door unlocked." Especially in a hotel like this.

"Maybe this one would," commented Irene darkly.

"Let the man continue," said Forrest.

Higgins made an effort to compose himself and proceeded to reenact his horrible discovery. "As I was saying, the water was running, I could hear it. I called out—*Ms. Smith? Ms. Smith?*"

Forrest, Irene, Mildred, and Trevor hung on every word.

"When there was no reply, I entered the room, with some trepidation, I must say. I continued on toward the noise, toward the bathroom."

The four leaned forward expectantly.

"And there"—Higgins paused dramatically—"she was."

"Dead?" said Irene.

"Of course she was dead!" snapped Forrest. "Christ, Reenie, why the hell do you think we're here?"

"Dead in the tub," said Higgins triumphantly. "Demure until the end. On her knees as though in supplication. Her face pressed to the drain."

Somehow Irene had been hoping the story might turn out different in the retelling.

"The shower curtain," Forrest reminded Higgins.

Higgins looked at Forrest quizzically for a moment. "The curtain? Oh yes, the curtain. Let me see . . . There was water on the floor. It was a terrible mess. I think I put the shower curtain back in. Yes. I distinctly remember now. It was most certainly out. And," he added almost proudly, "I reached over and turned off the water."

"Christ!" screamed Forrest.

"I did it quite automatically," explained Higgins. "Besides, the police didn't seem to care. They said of course the water would be on when someone slips. They're hardly going to turn it off as they fall, are they?"

For a moment Mildred thought Higgins might actually be waiting for an answer. Then he let out a laugh that bordered on hysteria.

"Besides," he went on, "they didn't look for fingerprints or anything like that. They just carted her away. They said—"

"I don't care what the police said," snorted Forrest. "Can't you see?" He turned to his friends. "Can't anyone see? Lady goes to take a shower, she sure as hell isn't going to leave the door unlocked. And when she takes a shower, she sure as hell doesn't leave the curtain outside the tub. Something's mighty rotten here."

"Easy, Forrest," said Trevor. "We can see, all right. Easy." He turned to the cringing man. "Mr. Higgins, you said something about supplication. That she was on her knees. The position of the body, sometimes it gives a clue. Could you elaborate?"

"Yes," replied Higgins. "It was, as I said, rather like she was kneeling. Like she was kneeling forward with her head thrust forward. Crouched over the drain. There was a bloody smear down the tile. And the bent faucets. But her face was hidden. Almost modestly, I might add. Ms. Smith was a lady to the bitter end."

Forrest stalked over to Higgins, bent down and put his

crooked nose right up to Higgins's shiny pointy one. He was so close he could smell the man's Right Guard, which was failing at the moment.

Higgins shrank back. He removed a perfectly pressed handkerchief from his breast pocket and blotted his forehead nervously.

"Okay, Mr. Higgins," said Forrest in a deceptively conciliatory tone, "so you saw her kneeling. What else did you see?"

"Nothing," cried Higgins. "I swear it."

"Well, let me tell you a thing or two. I'm seeing something, Mr. Higgins. I'm seeing that you blundered in here and destroyed evidence."

Higgins looked as though he might throw up.

"Destroying evidence is a crime, Mr. Higgins. A serious crime."

"But—"

Forrest reverted to his police persona and spoke very quietly, very reasonably. "Now, I want your cooperation, Mr. Higgins. I want to know about Esther Maine or Camille Smith or whatever the hell you choose to call her. More to the point, I want to know specifically what she was doing here in your establishment."

"Doing here?" gasped Higgins.

"Yes, goddamnit! Something fishy is going on, Mr. Higgins. The lady sure as hell didn't slip in that bathtub of yours. Somebody stove her face in, and you helped them get away with it."

"I did nothing of the kind! I never intended—"

"Nobody gives a shit what you intended, Mr. Higgins. Ignorance is no excuse. You, Mr. Higgins, are in deep caca!"

Forrest paused a moment and let that sink in. "But . . ." He let the word dangle tantalizingly.

"But what?" said Higgins in a pathetically hopeful voice.

"But if you'll fill us in about the lady, we're in a position to make things easier for you. For starters, we won't report you to the police."

"Oh my," said Higgins wretchedly. The handkerchief fluttered in his hands like a white butterfly.

"Forrest," admonished Mildred, "there's no need for such blatant intimidation." Bullying, really. That's what he was doing.

"Leave him be, Millie," said Irene. "Sometimes it's the only way to loosen a stiff tongue."

"I don't want any trouble," said Higgins quickly. "She was a nice lady. It's terrible what happened. But I don't want any trouble."

"You'll be in trouble up to your eyeballs," threatened Forrest, "if you don't tell us what you know."

"There's nothing to tell," insisted Higgins. "I swear. She was quiet. Minded her own business."

"But Mr. Higgins," said Trevor, "we can see, well . . . what kind of place this is."

"Yeah," said Forrest. "A place that charges hourly rates. A place where you got to squeegee the sheets."

Mildred blanched. Irene guffawed. Trevor shut his eyes.

"We've fallen on hard times," admitted Higgins. "We can't afford to discriminate as far as our clientele is concerned. Nonetheless Ms. Smith was different. She was a lady. She kept to herself."

"She never had any visitors?" asked Mildred.

"Never," insisted Higgins.

"Occasionally," corrected Cora.

"Cora!" pleaded Higgins.

"Once in a blue moon she had men friends. Not often like the other ladies here. But she had callers once or twice as I recall."

"Oh dear," said Mildred. "You mean boyfriends?"

"Johns," said Irene. "That's what she means, Millie. They call them johns. There was a segment on *Donohue*."

Mildred objected instantly. "For heaven's sake, Irene, let's not get carried away."

"We run a nice hotel here," interrupted Higgins nervously. "With honest, hardworking people. Ms. Smith minded her own business. She didn't make any trouble. So she had a few visitors now and again. Rarely, I might add. It wasn't any big deal." He tried to laugh again and it came out a shriek. "After all, we're all adults here."

"Really," said Mildred. This was preposterous. Esther Maine was a lovely woman. A woman of refinement. The mother of four children. They all made it sound as though she were a wanton hussy. "Forrest," she whispered, "this is patently ridiculous."

"Tell us about her visitors," Forrest demanded.

"I don't concern myself with the private lives of our guests," said Higgins. "Or with their guests' comings and goings."

"There were a couple of them," offered Cora helpfully. "Nice fellows, they were. Neat. Clean. With pressed suits, attaché cases and the like. They gave the place an air of class, I'll tell you that."

Mildred shuddered.

"So they came regular," said Forrest.

"Nope. Camille was here for months all by her lonesome. Then traffic picked up a mite toward the end there. Takes a while for word to get out sometimes. But toward the end she had a couple of gentleman callers, as I recollect."

"Look Mr. Higgins," said Trevor reasonably, "we're not trying to get you into any trouble—"

"Right," said Forrest sarcastically. "So a lady was murdered in your hotel. So you destroyed evidence. So you want to forget all about it. So who gives a shit?"

Higgins looked so stricken, Mildred was afraid he might have a heart attack.

"With your financial troubles here," Trevor interjected, "who can blame you for wanting to avoid an investigation? But don't you worry, there's probably no need for it to come to that."

"The police never asked me about any visitors," said Higgins quickly. "If they had, I would have told them. But they said it looked like an accident, and they were the experts. I thought fine, let sleeping dogs lie."

"Of course," said Trevor. "We understand."

"But the point," said Mildred gently, "is that it probably wasn't an accident, Mr. Higgins."

"I suppose," agreed Higgins reluctantly.

"So look," said Forrest, "we'll make it easy on you. Just tell us who those gents were who came here. Camille Smith's visitors—"

"I really can't," said Higgins honestly. "As you yourself have surmised, our clientele is transient to say the least. I'm afraid Ms. Smith's infrequent visitors blended in with all the others. And I certainly didn't ask them for identification. We pride ourselves on discretion here."

"Well," said Mildred helpfully, "perhaps you can at least describe any visitor who might have come the night she died."

"I wish I could." Higgins twisted his handkerchief into a tight little knot. "But I've been working two shifts just to keep this place afloat. I have a tendency to doze off at the desk in the evening, and I'm afraid that night was one of those times."

"And what about you?" Forrest turned on Cora. "What did you see." He patted his pants pocket. "I'll make it worth your while."

"If you're thinking about slipping the salami to me, you can think again, mister."

"Jesus," said Forrest. "I don't believe this." He withdrew the crumpled bills once again and shoved them in Cora's face. "I'm talking cash, lady. Cold hard cash. Now what's it going to be? Are you going to be helpful or are you going to be poor?"

Cora looked at the money with unabashed longing. She squinched her eyes shut and tried to picture Camille Smith's visitors. But her mind was dulled by too much alcohol and too little nourishment. Dulled by fear too. Fear of not finding a safe place to sleep. Fear of dying on the street and having people step over her. Fear of losing her mind, or what little was left of it. Once upon a time she had feared losing her pride, but that was gone a long time ago.

She sought out Irene's sympathetic eyes. When she finally spoke up, her voice was bitter and discouraged. "I'm sorry. I'm not as sharp as I used to be. I wish I could remember for you folks, but I can't. And not just for the money either. For Camille. She was my friend. She was kind to me." She turned to Forrest. "A heck of a lot kinder, mister, than you're being now."

"It's okay, honey," said Irene. "Don't you worry."

"Of course it's all right," agreed Mildred. Appalled at Forrest's lack of sensitivity, she reached out, snatched the cash, extracted five twenties, and pushed them into Cora's open hand.

15 "Couldn't sleep?"

Trevor Bradford looked up at Mildred standing at the kitchen door. She wore a pink terry cloth robe with a belt cinched around her newly slender waist. Without her makeup she looked vulnerable and approachable.

"Kept tossing and turning," explained Trevor. Ever the gentleman, he moved to get up.

"Sit," she said, waving him down. "I guess that makes two of us then. Thoughts kept whirling in my head. Horrible, intrusive, unpleasant thoughts. Finally I gave up. I must say, having your company during an attack of insomnia is a pleasant surprise."

"Oh," he said, feeling unexpectedly flattered. "Well."

She went to the stove and lit a flame under the copper tea kettle.

"I got myself a drink," he said. "Hope that's all right."

"Of course. I'd be upset if you didn't. I want you to feel comfortable here, Trevor." She looked at him with concern. Since he'd arrived, he hadn't seemed very comfortable at all. He seemed so preoccupied.

"Just a little scotch," he went on, "with hot water from the tap. Sounds awful to most folks, but it's soothing to me. Easy on the stomach too."

"Unlike this afternoon," said Mildred, "which wasn't so easy on the stomach."

"Ah yes," he sighed. "That." He thought for a moment. "Don't be too hard on him, Mildred."

"Hard on who?"

"Forrest."

"Oh him. Well, he can be an aggravation. I didn't like the way he treated that Cora one bit, bullying her."

"He wasn't bullying her, Mildred." Trevor smiled. "All this time and you still don't understand Forrest."

"Oh I don't?"

"No. To him it wasn't bullying. Sure, he got too caught up in things and he was relentless with her. But he offered her a deal, plain and simple. He treated her as an equal."

And I didn't. That's what you're saying, isn't it? I handed her cash out of pity. "I see," she said.

"He can be hard to take sometimes," Trevor offered. "Overbearing."

"He's so narrow-minded. So intense. So bossy. And since he's come to the city, I've become aware of another disagreeable trait."

"What's that?"

"He's prejudiced. You should hear some of his remarks."

Trevor waved his hand dismissively. "He's prejudiced in general, yes. But when it comes to specifics, when he meets an individual, he's not at all. For example, I bet you didn't know he's become buddies with the fellow on the third floor."

"Collin Farraday? The opera singer?"

"Yes. They play checkers every afternoon."

"Checkers?" Mildred was amazed. Collin Farraday had just returned from a run of *Don Giovanni* in London. He was very dignified. Very proper. And very black. She couldn't picture him hitting it off with Forrest at all. Then again, maybe she was the one with the preconceived notions.

"I've been worried about Forrest."

"Trevor, you're always worried about him. Forrest's going to be all right. He'll outlive us all."

"Possibly. But I'd call him once a week when I was in California, and the way he was back in Raven's Wing wasn't good. Talk about intense . . . He had nothing to do all day but worry about that big house of yours. He became obsessed with order. Knives had to be in the dishwasher blade down, so he wouldn't stab himself on the points. The ketchup bottle had to be thoroughly cleaned before the top went back on. He put reflector poles along the driveway so delivery men wouldn't drive off the edge of the gravel onto the grass."

"Reflector poles? In my driveway?" Mildred was not pleased.

"And then he had this thing about dogs."

"What about dogs?" She glanced at Winston sleeping at her feet.

"He'd start cussing and screaming every time a dog wandered onto the grounds. He'd pick up dog poop and put it in neighbors mailboxes. He even put up a sign down by the road: '*Curb your dog. Or else.*' "

"Oh no!"

"Oh yes. So I thought maybe this case would help. I know I told him after the heart attack that he had to take it easy, but I figured anything would be better than his obsessing on little things. Of course, I should have known what would happen. Now he's obsessing on something big. He's obsessing on Esther Maine's murder."

"That's just the way he is."

"It's got him churning, I can see that. He's fond of the

boy—Cameron. And Jonathan is pretty high on his list too. They're good people. Quiet. Never hurt anyone."

"Just the sort of people Forrest likes to protect."

"And avenge, when they've been hurt."

"I don't think vengeance is going to make them feel any better."

"It's not. And Forrest knows it. He just can't help himself."

"He plays God, always running the show. Why do we put up with him?"

"Because we love him."

"Sometimes I'm not so sure about that."

They were silent for some moments waiting for the water to boil. As Mildred occupied herself with fetching a bag of Lemon Lift tea and placing it in a porcelain cup, Trevor became acutely aware of his silk robe, which was starting to fray at the cuffs, of the white T-shirt that showed underneath, and of the old leather slippers on his veiny feet. He swirled the warm scotch in the snifter and wished he presented a better appearance.

"So," she said as she sat across from him, tea in hand, "what do you make of all this, Trevor?"

"This business with Esther Maine? I don't know what to think. It's so bizarre. I mean, the woman I knew—the Esther Maine who lived in Raven's Wing and devoted herself to community and family—well, it hardly seems possible that she could be the same woman they found at the St. James."

"But she was," said Mildred. "That much is clear. And apparently she went there willingly." She took a sip of her tea.

"You wouldn't believe it if you'd known her, Mildred. Esther Maine was a sweet lady. Almost childlike sometimes. And remember what I said about her reaction to Claudia's illness? She took it very much to heart. Told me she wished it were her instead of Claudia. Said it should have been her."

"It sounds as though she felt guilty for some reason.

Because she rejected Claudia as a baby perhaps. Or maybe Esther always lived some sort of double life."

"Maybe," he said absently. "You know, something's been gnawing at me since we were in her hotel room."

"Oh?"

"We know they found the body in the bathtub. We know the door was unlocked with no sign of forced entry. And we also know that Esther Maine was a timid sort of woman."

"Yes."

"She certainly wouldn't leave her door unlocked, and the door wasn't forced. The only way someone got in there was if she let them in. So I don't think this was a random sort of thing—a burglary gone bad or some deranged psychopath who followed her off the street."

"She knew her killer."

"Exactly. Not only did she know him, she trusted him. She unlocked that door and let him in. She may even have been expecting him."

"Champagne," said Mildred suddenly.

"Huh?"

"Champagne. Just before we left Mr. Higgins mentioned champagne. He said it was chilling in a plastic ice bucket next to the bed when he discovered Esther Maine's body."

"There!" said Trevor. "You see!"

"It makes sense," agreed Mildred. "So we have to find out who she was waiting for. And about her double life. There's something underneath all this. Some secret."

"Yes."

"I must say, I can't understand this double life business. I mean, for years I lived in a marriage that wasn't exactly made in heaven, but I never dreamed of doing anything so unseemly as staying in a hotel like the St. James. Or any hotel, for that matter."

"It's hard to figure," agreed Trevor. "Especially knowing the family."

"That's what I mean," said Mildred in frustration. "What

could be so terrible that would drive a person to do the things she did? To stay in a place like that?"

"Her childhood was rather bleak."

"Yes, but she grew up and married a man who loved her. Besides, if she was unhappy, why not just walk away?"

"Maybe it was something inside her," said Trevor, "and you can't walk away from that."

"I suppose," she agreed. From the living room came the sound of the grandfather clock striking two.

"Mildred, why did you leave Raven's Wing?"

He'd switched tracks so suddenly, it knocked her off balance. "Why, I—"

"I thought we were a good team, the four of us."

The four of us. There it was.

"Well," she said pointedly, "no one asked me to stay."

The remark flew right over him.

"I mean," she went on, "Forrest and Irene have each other now, don't they? And you have your patients." She saw him start to protest and waved him off. "Oh, I know you're supposed to be retired. But you still are involved with many of your long-term patients. They refuse to see anyone else, and you accommodate them. Don't try to tell me different."

"Maybe now and then," he conceded.

"And that's fine. That's well and good. You've got something to keep you going, you see." And I, on the other hand, had nothing. But she didn't say that.

"I see," he said carefully.

No, she thought sadly. I don't think you do.

"Mildred," he said suddenly.

"Yes?"

"I was thinking . . ."

"Yes?"

"Well, being we're here in the city and all. It might be nice to take in some cultural events."

"Irene did mention something about wanting to see the Bronx Zoo," said Mildred without enthusiasm. She tried not to make a face. "I've never really been partial to penguins and hippos."

"Oh I didn't mean that. Actually I didn't mean us. All of us I mean. It just occurred to me that, well . . ."

"Yes?" She leaned forward expectantly.

"I mean if you're not booked up . . ."

Booked up? Mildred blinked. Why for heaven's sakes, he was going to ask her out. On a date.

" . . . I thought maybe we—you know, you and I— could go to the ballet. Or the opera. Or something." The last words sounded lame to his ears.

"I'd be delighted," she said without hesitation.

"I mean, it wouldn't have to be a date exactly."

Her face fell.

"Unless you wanted it to be, of course. It could be for companionship or for a date, whichever you prefer." Now he felt like a babbling idiot.

"A date," she said, "was what I had in mind."

16 "Well now, if this don't beat all." Irene sat at the dining room table hunched over the largest telephone book she'd ever seen in her life, her bifocals pressed close to the tiny print.

"If what don't beat all?" said Forrest absently. "Pass me the toast, if you will Millie. And don't hang a face, Irene. I'm not planning to butter it."

"Claudia Maine," said Irene. "The name stuck in my head. All night long I kept hearing Claudia, Claudia, Claudia. On and on. Like the good Lord was trying to tell me something."

"Yes?" said Mildred, trying to be polite. Sometimes Irene seemed to have splinters in the windmills of her mind.

"And now, sure enough, here it is! C. Maine right here in the New York City phone book. I wonder if it's the same one?"

"Probably not," said Trevor.

Irene continued to study the page. "I suppose it's a common name, Maine. But wouldn't it be something? Claudia Maine herself right here in your neighborhood, Millie."

Mildred looked up in interest. "My neighborhood? Where exactly?"

"Four-oh-five East Tenth Street."

"Not exactly the same neighborhood," said Mildred primly. "In the Village, East is rather different from West, I'm afraid."

"East is rather dangerous, is what she means, Irene," said Trevor. "Abandoned tenements, drug dealing on the street, riots in Tompkins Square . . ."

"The area, as I understand it," said Mildred, "has the highest rate of violent crime in Manhattan. Not of burglary, of course, because there's little to steal. But of violent crime. I recall the police commissioner saying that to me once at some sort of fund-raiser."

"In any case," said Forrest, "Irene can take care of herself, and today Irene will pay a visit to this C. Maine." It was as good a way as any, thought Forrest, to keep Irene out of trouble.

"I get all the prize jobs!" complained Irene. But underneath she was pleased to be delegated such an important assignment.

"I think she should at least call first," said Mildred. "It's only polite."

"Millie," replied Forrest, "this isn't a time for niceties. Miss Manners wouldn't last ten minutes out there on these streets."

"But—"

"But nothing. This is a time for surprise. The element of surprise can be helpful. Throws people off balance."

"If this person is, in fact, Claudia Maine," said Trevor, "I doubt she needs to be thrown any more off balance than she already is."

Forrest frowned briefly at this remark, then glanced at his notebook and turned back to Mildred. "And as for you, Millie, I've got a plum assignment indeed."

"I can hardly wait," she said. She concentrated on buttering a sesame bagel.

"You're going to pay a visit to Esther Maine's sister."

"Very well," said Mildred.

"Constance Townsend."

Mildred froze. "Excuse me?"

"Constance Townsend."

"I certainly hope you're not talking about Constance Townsend of East Seventy-second Street."

"That's the address I got here. Seventy-four East Seventy-second."

"Mrs. Frederick Townsend?"

"Right. Frederick P. Townsend. I mentioned the name last night."

"Yes, but it didn't register. I certainly didn't think it was the same Townsend."

"The same Townsend as who?"

"The same as the Townsends I know, that's who. Townsend is a common name, for heaven's sake." She dropped the bagel, wiped her fingers on her napkin, and smoothed her frosted hair. "You're not going to do that to me."

"Do what to you? I'm not doing anything to you. It couldn't be more perfect. She's high society. And you're not exactly low-life. You'll be like two peas in a pod. The fact that you know this pair makes it so much the better."

"It most certainly does not," said Mildred, "and my speaking with them would be totally inappropriate."

"Inappropriate?" repeated Forrest in disbelief.

"Constance Townsend is on the board at the Metropolitan Museum of Art. So am I. Constance Townsend is a member of the Colony Club. So am I. Constance Townsend is chairing a committee for funding the new SPCA shelter. I am a member of that same committee. We're not close friends, but we do know each other socially." She stopped and shook her head at the awkwardness of it all. "No. I simply cannot approach her under these horrific circumstances. It would be most insensitive."

"Listen to that, will you?" He threw up his hands. *"Inappropriate,* she says. *Insensitive,* she says. You know what I think, Mildred? I'll tell you what I think. I think you're afraid to approach Constance Townsend and her husband because it will jeopardize your hoity-toity social position, that's what I think."

"That's ridiculous!" Mildred shot back. "I've never cared a whit about social position."

"Sure," said Forrest. "That's why you belong to all those snooty little clubs. Clubs that exclude folks. That's why you won't meet with Constance Townsend. Because you don't care squat about social position."

"A whit," she snapped.

"Whatever," said Forrest.

Irene looked at Mildred and wondered what she would decide. She wondered too if maybe Millie did care more about the trappings of money and position than for her friends and their investigation. And if, indeed, Mildred did care so much, she wondered how they could continue to be friends. Maybe to her it was all just a game. Maybe I'm just a novelty for her, thought Irene. Someone good for a laugh. Someone she'd never take to one of her fancy parties.

Mildred might have been a snob on occasion, but she wasn't insensitive. In a breath Mildred took in Irene's concerned, almost hurt expression. Damn Forrest anyway. He did this on purpose. He knew exactly what he was doing. Once again, he had cleverly managed to strike a nerve all around. Manipulator! she wanted to shout.

"Okay," said Mildred.

"Okay what?"

"Okay I'll talk to her. Now are you happy?" She felt reasonably secure making this offer because it was summer in the city and no one who could afford otherwise spent the dog days of August in Manhattan. Unless, she thought, they're crazy. Like me.

"Good," said Forrest. "But if she's out at the Hamptons or up at Newport or one of those places where the swells go when it's hot, you track her down. We've got money for train fare. Or an airplane ticket."

Oh he was a weasel. Totally impossible. He managed to appear deceptively ignorant when in reality he had a mind like a steel trap. And it always trapped her. Always.

"All right!"

"Well," said Trevor mildly, "I guess that leaves me. If I know you, Forrest, you've got something special in mind for me too."

17 Two hours later Trevor was making his way toward the offices of the New York City medical examiner, buried deep in the bowels of LaGuardia Hospital. It wasn't easy. LaGuardia was a city unto itself, a towering soot-stained monolith of gray granite covering four square city blocks and arching thirty stories into the sky. It had taken Trevor a tedious hour of navigation through an intricate maze of color-coded corridors to get this far and now he wondered if he'd ever find his way out again.

"Excuse me," he blurted in desperation as a wisp of a man rushed by. The man wore a spattered green scrub suit and bore an uncanny resemblance to the late Malcolm X. His nameplate said DR. MATTHEW LEVEAUX.

"Are you speaking to me?"

The voice was clipped and intimidating. Trevor detected a Bahamian accent. The man thrust his small bearded chin forward and looked at Trevor through round rimless glasses with dark unblinking eyes.

"I'm looking for the chief medical examiner."

"You and everyone else," said Leveaux. "He's on vacation. So, I might add, is everyone else with any seniority in his employ. And with any sanity. Apparently I have neither, and I'm a very busy man right now, Mister. . . ."

"Bradford," said Trevor. "Doctor."

"Dr. Bradford. So if you'll excuse me."

"I'm sorry," said Trevor, not giving up. He grabbed the man's arm, and Leveaux recoiled. He was tense, Trevor realized. Spring-loaded and ready for mayhem.

"I'm sorry," said Trevor again. He removed his hand. "Look, I'm trying to locate the doctor who performed an autopsy on an Esther Maine. Or Camille Smith."

Leveaux backed away a step. This fellow might be crazy. Lately a lot of crazies had been wandering the corridors of LaGuardia. The most flagrant and tragic had been a mental defective by the name of Oscar Bloodgood. Bloodgood had walked through the wards of LaGuardia with impunity, masking his insanity behind a white coat and a stethoscope. It wasn't until Bloodgood raped and killed a young pathologist—a young *pregnant* pathologist—who was working alone one weekend that his monstrous charade had been exposed. Still, this Bradford fellow appeared rational enough, though clearly out of his element in this public hospital.

"Dr. Bradford," said Leveaux wearily, "do you have any idea how many autopsies the medical examiner's office performs here at LaGuardia?"

"No," admitted Trevor. He pictured a gruesome assembly line of cadavers.

Leveaux ran a hand over closely cropped hair. All he wanted to do was take a shower, eat a slice of cold pizza if he had the energy, and collapse into bed. But he looked at this neatly dressed out-of-towner with his carefully combed silver hair and handkerchief folded just so in his breast pocket and decided his shower could wait an extra thirty seconds.

"Can you be more specific?" he asked, not unkindly. "Smith or Maine, you say? Which was it?"

"She used both names, but I think the name would have been Camille Smith when they brought her in."

"They?"

"The police. She was registered at the St. James Hotel over on West Thirty-eighth Street and apparently fractured her skull in the bathtub." (*Actually she fell down and battered herself to death, Dr. Leveaux. How's that for far fetched?*)

"And when was that?"

"She was found on the night of July eighteenth."

Shit, thought Leveaux. Forget the pizza, forget the sleep. "Wait here," he said. "I'll be right back." He disappeared behind a milky glass door embedded with wire mesh.

Ten minutes later he returned. "I called it up on the computer. Both names. We have her listed under Maine. You know, now I do remember. July eighteenth. It was a crazy day. That evening we had four new arrivals, not counting your friend Esther Camille. A floater from the East River. A vagrant run over by a Checker down in Tribeca. A heroin overdose from God knows where. And a suicide from the Upper East Side. Man slit his own throat. I admired his steady hand. Didn't pause or flinch. Very decisive. Very clean. Very effective. I could tell it was the work of an experienced hand. Turned out he was a surgeon."

"Yes," said Trevor, trying to hide his impatience, "but what about—"

"I remember your woman because they brought her in just as I was going off duty. About two A.M. I looked at her briefly. Fractured skull. Broken cheekbone. Eyes crushed into the sockets."

"Eyes," repeated Trevor woodenly. No one said anything about eyes.

"Yes indeed. Quite a mess she was. Murphy was on duty."

"Murphy," Trevor repeated. He jotted the name down. "Do you know where I can find—"

"You're in luck. Murphy's here now, getting caught up on paperwork. Shoveling sand is more like it, but we all have our illusions."

"Where—"

"You see the end of this corridor? Way down there where the bomb shelter sign is?"

Trevor squinted at the dimness but could see nothing.

"Yes," he said.

"Go all the way down. Turn right. Follow the blue linoleum stripe on the floor to where they're doing construction. Cover your ears, because those jackhammers can do permanent damage. A handkerchief over your nose wouldn't hurt either, what with the dust, some of which is probably asbestos . . ."

Lord, thought Trevor. He wondered how he could cover his ears while holding a handkerchief over his mouth.

" . . . down a ramp," continued Leveaux. "Murphy's office, if you can call it that, is on the right. Number three-ten."

"Thank you," said Trevor, moving away.

"If you start to feel a chill, you've gone too far."

Right, thought Trevor, wondering if Leveaux was referring to the refrigerated storage area.

By the time he finally reached another rippled glass door embedded with chicken wire that bore the number 310 in chipped black paint Trevor was exasperated indeed. His eardrums felt as though they had been ripped asunder and his dark suit was covered with chalky white powder.

He slapped away the dust in an effort to restore his dignity. He examined a frayed index card Scotch-taped to the door frame. P. MURPHY, M.D. it said in neatly typed letters. He knocked once and walked in.

An obviously hassled secretary with frizzy strawberry blond hair paused from her typing at an old Underwood and looked at him in annoyance. Overlooking her expression for the moment, he noticed that she had finely chiseled, delicate features and a sprinkling of cinnamon freckles across her nose.

"Yes?" she said, shoving her glasses up the bridge of that nose.

"I'm looking for Dr. Murphy," said Trevor. He craned his neck in an effort to look beyond the secretary. The room was more a lair than an office. It appeared to have been a closet at one time. He spied a sink in the back and another desk wedged behind the redhead. Murphy was nowhere in sight.

"Murphy's busy right now," she said shortly.

"Well if you would just tell him I'm here." Trevor tried to filter exasperation from his voice.

"And who," said the girl haughtily, "may I ask are you?"

She was a petty tyrant, he could see that right off. One of those infuriating mean-spirited people who are stepped on all the time and seize a moment of glorious power when the opportunity for revenge presents itself, creating misery for those unlucky enough to be in a position of supplication.

"Dr. Trevor Bradford."

"As if," muttered the girl, "that explains everything." She returned to her typing. "I'll see that Murphy gets the message. Leave your name and number, and Murphy may call. Or Murphy may not, depending on Murphy's mood."

"Listen, Miss," said Trevor, "perhaps you're in the habit of being surrounded by cadavers who are in a position to overlook your rudeness. But I happen to be very much alive and would appreciate some simple consideration."

"Is that a fact?" she said. She eyed him with amusement.

"Yes, it's a fact. So if you'll kindly direct me to Dr. Murphy, wherever he is, I won't take up any more of your time."

She removed her glasses, smoothed back the defiant tangle of hair and clamped it down with an orange clasp shaped like a ladybug. Then she stood up and offered her hand.

"Dr. Patricia Murphy," she said. "At your service."

"Oh." His face flushed with embarrassment. He closed his eyes momentarily before taking her small hand in his. "I apologize, Dr. Murphy."

"Chauvinist," she said, smiling.

Before his very eyes she had transformed into a very nice, very approachable young woman. New York City had strange effects on people, Trevor decided. It made them rush. It made them insensitive. But if you scratched the surface, sometimes they could be downright human.

"Caught in the act," he said, smiling too. "Mea culpa."

She removed a stack of files from a battered plastic chair and he sank into it gratefully.

"Well," she said, "from the looks of your suit you walked the gauntlet to see me. I guess the least I can do is give you five minutes. Coffee?"

It was a nice way of telling him she was very busy and that five minutes plus coffee was all he was going to get. But that was okay.

"No thanks," he said. "I'll get right to the point. I'm here to inquire about one of your . . ." He groped for a word. "Patients" didn't seem quite right.

"Cases?" she supplied.

"Yes. A forty-three-year-old Caucasian female brought in by the police on July nineteenth. Apparent cause of death massive head injuries. You may not remember, but—"

"Oh boy," she sighed. "This is one that won't go away." She opened a drawer and extracted a file.

He looked at her, perplexed. "What do you mean?"

"Well, just that for death of unknown cause, this case seems to be generating a lot of interest. First the police, then her husband, then that other guy." She flipped open the folder and scanned the contents.

"Which other guy?"

"I don't know. Things get crazy around here. I can hardly remember one day to the next. He was average looking, stocky maybe. With dark curly hair. He showed up asking questions."

"What kind of questions?"

She thought for a moment. "How did she die? What did the police think? Were there any leads? Like I was supposed to know, huh? Anyway, it was a little irregular, but sometimes talking to these bozos is easier than arguing. So I gave him five, like I'm giving you, no offense."

"What did he say?"

"Nothing. He just listened." Murphy seemed to reconsider. "Well, actually he did seem concerned about one thing—whether the death would be ruled accidental or a murder. He kept asking me about it. I was rushed and distracted. It was one of those days, you know? So I told him we thought it was an accident. He seemed satisfied, and off he went."

"Did he show any identification or leave a card?"

"No."

"I see." This was developing into more than Trevor had expected. He made a mental note about Patricia Murphy's mysterious visitor and pressed gamely on. "Maybe you'd be kind enough to tell me what you remember about this case."

"Sure. She was a lady without any ID. Husband came in several days later to identify the body. We were storing it until he arrived. We do that for two weeks before sending them off to Potter's Field. It's standard procedure."

"I see. I'm interested specifically in your impression of her injuries. I understand you did the autopsy?"

"Yes." Her eyes narrowed suspiciously. "Oh, I get it. There's more to this than the police thought, right? They're reopening this case. Or maybe," her eyes widened, "the family's going to sue. Of course. I should have seen it coming."

"No, nothing like—"

"Well let me tell you, I am sick and tired of the litigious nature of our society, Dr. Bradford. Sick and tired. Do you have any idea how much time these lawsuits take? How much of the city's money is wasted?" Patricia Murphy's face was flushed and she felt herself starting to rant, but she didn't care. "No one's responsible anymore for their own actions. Someone trips on the sidewalk, and they sue the city. Never mind they weren't looking where they were going. Someone slips on a grape, they sue Foodtown. Sue sue sue, that's all people know anymore, and I for one am—"

"So am I!" cried Trevor, trying to derail this runaway train of thought.

"—sick and tired." She stopped. "You are?"

"Yes! I'm with you a hundred percent. I hate lawsuits, and I'm certainly not here to start one. Or to contribute to one in any way."

"Oh," she said. "Well. Good." She reconsidered, wondering now about the purpose of his visit. Her mind started to churn forth other possibilities, none of them good. "I want you to know my work was thorough. I stand by it. If you're going to drag me into court to testify about some sort of crime that may have been committed or— God forbid—corruption in the ME's office . . ."

"No, nothing like that. Her husband simply asked me to get some additional details, that's all. It was a tragedy for him, and now that the shock's wearing off there are some questions in his mind. So he asked me to look into this. As a friend." It wasn't a lie exactly.

"The husband . . ." She leaned back in her chair. "Now there was a candidate for grief therapy if I ever saw one."

"He was understandably upset, I'm sure," said Trevor.

"Dr. Bradford, I've seen a lot of distraught relatives in my time—"

Trevor almost smiled at her words. She was barely thirty if she was a day.

"—but this fellow took the cake. He was much more than distraught, I can assure you. The man was almost incoherent. Kept hugging her. Kissing her. We had to pry him loose. Bear in mind, she was a mess. It had been—what?—four or five days?" She shook her head. "Refrigeration can accomplish just so much. I'm sure this woman didn't look anything like his wife. I understand she was nice enough looking at one time."

"Yes," said Trevor, "at one time."

"Most people will look once," Murphy went on. "Sometimes they'll force themselves to look again. It's a necessary process, of course. Agonizing as it is, confronting the death of a loved one forces them to say goodbye. You can see it happen. They look. It registers. And then they back away. As much as they love that person they back away."

This was true. Trevor had witnessed this phenomenon many times and had even experienced it himself. The moment someone became dead they became something other as well. Something alien. Something dangerous almost. He had experienced that inner chill when he looked down at Mary Margaret. There was the awful realization that this shape, this form before him, was no longer Mary Margaret but some sort of monstrous impostor. And with that knowledge came the uneasy feeling that perhaps we are all impostors, fleeting spirits hiding underneath the deception of a body. That thought frightened him. He backed away from the body in the casket and from the awful thoughts too. Most people do.

"Well," said Trevor, "he's a doctor. A plastic surgeon at that. He's used to accidents, used to seeing tragic physical abnormalities. Maybe he could look past them more easily than most."

"That was the other thing," Patricia Murphy said suddenly. "The plastic surgery. I had already done the autopsy and he insisted on examining the body. So I showed it to him. He was her husband, I know, but he also was a doctor, so I thought he could handle it. I thought wrong. He went off the deep end, like I told you. And then he said something rather strange."

"Oh?"

"He said he appreciated how careful I had been."

"Careful?"

"Yes. You know how it is when we do the cranium."

"Yes," said Trevor, quickly. "No need to elaborate." Despite his best efforts not to, Trevor envisioned pretty petite Dr. Murphy peeling Esther Maine's forehead down over the nose like a rubber mask to reveal her naked skull. Jesus, he thought, how on earth could she choose this line of work?

"Well, when he composed himself, he said I'd done excellent work. I'm always careful, of course. So many funeral directors are stubbornly determined to prepare these bodies for viewing. I try to leave them something to work with. I try to be delicate. This one, though, was too far gone. Or so I thought. I was sure it would be a closed casket."

"As a matter of fact, it was," said Trevor. "For the sake of the children. But you said he said something strange. What was it?"

"He said he was going to reconstruct her face. Himself. I don't flinch easily, Dr. Bradford, but the thought of a man working on his own wife, performing plastic surgery after death, well, I found that a little unnerving."

Trevor found himself making excuses. "As I understand it, Jonathan Maine loved his wife very much. And he was a man whose work revolved around creating beauty—or an ideal of beauty. I think I can see how he couldn't bear to see the person he loved most destroyed."

"I guess," said Murphy.

"So," said Trevor, "what did you find?"

"It wasn't an easy case, Dr. Bradford. First off, they brought her in through all that dust you just walked through. The bag was unzipped, don't ask me why. Some of our orderlies are ghouls, maybe they wanted to have a look. Anyway, plaster dust got on the body. So any evidence that might have been detected was tainted by the time I did my examination, what with all that chalk. Anyway, I did my best. I cleansed the wounds and examined them closely."

"And?"

"The wounds could have been caused by a fall."

"You sound doubtful."

"Well . . ." She hesitated. "We're under some pressure here to reduce the active caseload for the police." She saw Trevor's shocked expression. "Listen, Dr. Bradford, let's face facts. Manhattan detectives are up to their eyeballs in homicides. It's better, isn't it, if they can concentrate on cases that are not so iffy?" She didn't wait for a reply. "So, all right, we're under some pressure ourselves to cut the wheat from the chaff. The injuries could have been caused by a fall, and that's the conclusion in the report."

" 'Could have been' doesn't sound very convincing."

Murphy seemed to waver. "Okay. So maybe I wasn't totally convinced. I'll admit it's unusual that someone dies by falling *forward*. Backward, yes. There's less protection to the brain. But forward, the brain is well protected. There's a lot of bone there, as you know." She knocked her forehead with her knuckles. "Plus," she said, holding both hands out now, "a person shields herself instinctively during a forward fall with an arm or a hand."

"Of course!" said Trevor eagerly.

"Plus," continued Murphy, "for a forward fall there was a lot of damage. It must have been a very hard fall. The woman was large and heavy. Not obese, mind you, but big. Still, even at that, there was a lot of facial trauma."

"And what about the eyes? I heard something to the effect that they were damaged."

"Yes. According to the police she fell forward onto the fixtures in the bathtub. It was remarkable in a way. She'd managed to impale herself on two spokes from the faucets and then slipped down, face flat on the drain. Never saw anything quite like it before." She saw Trevor's expression. "It's grisly, I know, but frankly I've become immune to it."

"Is it possible," began Trevor carefully, "—conceivable—that someone could have killed her first, then held her head and smashed it forward on the faucets?"

"Anything's possible, Dr. Bradford," replied Murphy. "But it's hardly probable. There was blood in the grout, so I heard. And as I understand it, the police found no evidence of forced entry into her room. And a lady doesn't simply allow someone to bash her face in, even a lady as inebriated as this one."

"She was drunk?"

"The level of alcohol in her blood supports the conclusion that she fell in the bathtub. You might say she was literally falling-down drunk."

"I see."

"I suppose you want to see the autopsy report too."

"Actually I would."

"That's against the rules."

"Oh," said Trevor with resignation. "Of course."

"I'm not supposed to show it around, you know," she said defensively. "It's confidential."

"I understand."

They were silent for some moments.

"She was only forty-three," said Murphy almost to herself. "Did she have any children?"

"Four," said Trevor quietly.

"You think maybe someone did this to her?"

"Yes," said Trevor. "I think maybe."

"So what's it to you?"

The question caught him off guard. "She was . . ." Oh hell, he thought, go ahead and say it. "She was my patient when she was a child. My responsibility."

"I see," said Murphy carefully.

Patricia Murphy turned a thought over in her mind. "I have to go to the ladies' room, Dr. Bradford. It's a hike from here, and I'm liable to be gone a good ten minutes. I'm sure I can trust you not to touch anything on my desk. And most certainly not to touch the autopsy report right here . . ." She pointed to it with her pencil.

18 New York City detectives say the second-best witness is the victim. Trevor Bradford had never heard of such an axiom but knew intuitively that Esther Maine in her own way would try to tell him something.

He picked up a brutally explicit Polaroid photo and forced himself to look. The woman's face was like a mass of rotten plums. Split lips revealed jagged broken teeth. Her nose was a flat purple mushroom.

In Victorian times, police and medical examiners gazed into the eyes of the dead, hoping to detect the lingering image of the killer. But Esther Maine's eyes had been bludgeoned, and sodden craters were all that gazed up at him now. He felt a cry lodge in his throat.

Tell me, Esther. Tell me.

Something caught his eye . . . a faded scar, the size of a dime, on the woman's left cheek near the ear. Not new but old . . .

"Okay, honey, off with those clothes and onto the scale. Let's see how much you weigh."

The child was dressed in a gray hand-me-down dress that had once been white. The cotton fabric was limp from repeated washings and decorative pink threads were broken, creating gaps in the intricate hand-stitched smocking that spanned the chest. Around the hem he could see distinct lines, like rings on a tree, evidence of old hems that couldn't be pressed out. He had the feeling it was her best dress, washed and pressed for this visit to the doctor's office. The thought made him sad.

She appeared not to hear him, and at first Trevor took this for modesty. Sometimes seven-year-old girls could be that way. Unexpectedly demure, reluctant to undress, crossing their arms over breastless chests.

"Esther, honey, would you like me to wait outside while you put on this gown?" He held out a voluminous paper robe, the kind he offered to his skittish old maid patients. It would look ridiculous on a child, but if it made her feel better, so be it.

She turned, as though his words registered for the first time. Her hair fell back from her face. It was then that he noticed an angry red laceration surrounded by the halo of a purple bruise high on her left cheek.

"Well," he said with false heartiness, "what's this?"

He reached toward the wound and she flinched.

"Let's take a look, shall we?"

He lifted her small stiff body onto the examining table. A scared rabbit, that's what she was. He turned her chin gently but firmly in his hand, the better to examine the cut.

"How'd this happen?" he asked casually. When she didn't answer, he pressed. "Tell me, Esther. Tell me."

She stiffened and tried to turn away.

"Never mind," he said. "We'll just call it a beauty mark, okay? You're mighty pretty in any case. Of course I'll bet plenty of folks have told you that already."

"No."

There it was. A word. Only a word, but her tone, her expression, said so much more. She looked at him with a pinched, almost fearful expression. Her face closed up. She didn't believe this offhand compliment, wouldn't accept it.

I'm not pretty, her expression seemed to say. Don't make fun of me.

"Well you are."

He continued the examination, not bothering to have her disrobe. Somehow he'd manage, despite the dress.

"You know," he said, "by rights this cut should have had stitches. Too late for them now, though. It's healed over. But you'll have a scar, I'm afraid."

She seemed not to care. She studied her pink socks.

"Now I'm going to take a look in your ears." *Trevor had learned to warn skittish patients what he was going to do before he did it. Of course, as gentle as he was with children, it was nothing compared to the almost obsessive caution he exercised with adults, especially older females. As a result of his courtly demeanor and classic good looks, Trevor Bradford had experienced more than his share of embarrassing situations when he first started his practice.*

Like the time an old maid teacher—a teacher who had taught him back in grade school, for gosh sakes—screamed and accused him of "fooling with her privates." Jesus. It had taken a lot of explaining and a lot of soothing to settle the neurotic woman down. Then, after he'd barely managed to regain his equilibrium, another patient—this time a proper suburban matron with four children and a golden retriever—reached out during an exam, put her hand over his penis and gave it an encouraging squeeze. She found him attractive, she said.

After that Trevor made a habit of having Nurse Granger in the room whenever he examined a female over twelve years of age.

But now there was no Nurse Granger. Only Trevor Bradford and a seven-year-old girl who seemed inordinately shy. He looked in her left ear, above the scar, because it was the closest to him. He didn't like what he saw.

Trying to maintain his casual demeanor, Trevor examined the ear more closely. He then proceeded through Esther Maine's checkup as though nothing were amiss. He listened to her heart, her lungs. Looked into her mouth. Pricked her finger for blood. (She didn't so much as flinch, which he found unusual.) Tested her reflexes. Normal, normal, normal. Everything was normal.

Except that ear.

Finally Esther's ordeal was over. Her dress was half on and half off. He helped her rebutton it. He helped put on the scuffed saddle shoes and tied the broken knotted laces. Then he reached into a drawer. "Here," he said, holding two barrettes. "A reward for being such a good patient. Take your choice. Red or green."

She looked at first one, then the other, confusion etched on her face. She seemed to be concentrating very hard.

Maybe she can't tell the difference, Trevor realized. Maybe she's color-blind. The trait is rare in females, but possible. He pressed them into her hands. "Take both, honey. You deserve it."

"Adornment is sinful."

It sounded like another voice. An adult voice. Jesus.

"Wait in the reception area, honey. I want to have a word with your father."

Moments later Nurse Granger came back into Trevor's small office and said Evan Jamison was nowhere to be found.

"Try the Cannonball Pub," said Trevor tartly. "Odds are he slipped away to have a few. Don't call. Just go over and get him."

Nurse Granger stared at Dr. Bradford and started to sputter. Her voluminous tits inflated and deflated under her starched white uniform. "Dr. Bradford, there are patients . . . in the reception area . . . overflowing . . . in case you haven't noticed . . . I haven't got time to—"

"This is more important. I don't want that poor child to have to sit in a crowded room filled with flu and strep for hours while Evan Jamison quenches his insatiable thirst.

The pub's right next door, Madeline. Just get his goddamn ass over here."

In fifteen years Nurse Granger had never heard Dr. Bradford use such coarse language. Words of her own came to mind. Her mouth dropped open. Then, reconsidering, she snapped it shut. She pivoted on one orthopedic white shoe and stalked out.

Ten minutes later a slightly flushed, slightly sheepish Evan Jamison appeared at Trevor's office door. He shook Trevor's hand firmly, trying not to exhale in the doctor's face.

"I stepped out to make a phone call," he said.

Bullshit, Trevor wanted to say. Trevor, who never used vulgar language. But he said nothing, just let Evan shake his hand.

Evan Patrick Jamison was the very picture of a drunken charmer. He bounced from job to job as a salesman, and never lasted very long at any one of them. Unlike Willy Loman, he had never been able to get by on a shoeshine and a smile without supplemental support from a bottle of Mother Fletcher's Whiskey stashed in the glove compartment of his big Buick. Trevor had told Evan more than once to cut back on his drinking, especially with all the driving he did, but his words fell on deaf ears.

Trevor looked at Evan now. The man's pleated brown slacks hung like a skirt on bony hips. His screaming yellow tie bore an old stain, bourbon or Worcestershire or salad dressing from one of those envelopes they give you in cheap diners. His rugged face, once strikingly handsome, was now blotchy and puffy. Gray bags framed his bloodshot eyes. Yet somehow, amazingly, the old twinkle was still there.

Trevor felt sad and angry all at the same time. The man was a buffoon, a gracious buffoon but a buffoon nonetheless. Everyone in Raven's Wing knew how henpecked he was. Everyone knew he was out of a job more often than not. Everyone knew that when Evan Jamison's watch was gone from his wrist sure as shootin' you could find it in the window of the pawnshop over in Danbury. Yet he put on such airs, dressed so flamboyantly, acted as though he were better than anyone else. The King of Sheba. If he stepped in dog shit, he'd tell you it was pâté. In a way you almost had to admire him.

No, thought Trevor angrily. *I don't admire him. He's a grown man. A grown man should have control. A grown man should care for his family. A grown man should be just that, grown up. Experts said alcoholism was a disease, and maybe it was. But it wasn't a disease like cancer or diabetes. It was a disease that could be stopped. It was a disease that allowed you the luxury of a second chance. If you were willing to take it. If you had the guts.*

But Evan didn't have the guts. He continued to drown in booze and excuses. The pity was that others were drowning along with him. Others like Esther.

"I appreciate your taking Esther on such short notice," Evan went on. "She's tickled as can be to be going to day camp—"

Sue Lancaster, president of the Community Center, had pulled some strings and gotten Esther a place in the town day camp free of charge. She then called Trevor and asked if he would give Esther the required physical. Of course, he said.

"—of course, at first Lucille wasn't real keen on her going. Didn't want to accept charity, she said. 'Charity?' I says. 'It's not charity. I'll pay the Community Center back soon as I'm on my feet,' I told her. 'With interest.' And you too, Doc. I'll pay you too."

"Whenever," Trevor said, knowing full well Evan would never pay him. He didn't care, of course. But he resented having to join in Evan's game of pretend. "Sit down, Evan."

"Sure." Evan sat. He leaned back and crossed a foot over his knee, revealing a dime-sized hole in the sole of his shoe.

Trevor put his pen back in the pocket protector of his white jacket, buying some time. When he spoke he chose his words carefully.

"There's a problem with Esther, Evan."

"Huh?" Evan uncrossed his foot and leaned forward. "Is she sick?"

"No. Nothing like that. It's that cut on her cheek—"

"Oh, that." *Evan leaned back in relief. "Esther's always got something. That's just the latest of a string of bumps. You know how kids are."*

"No, Evan. I don't know."

"Kids have accidents, Doc."

"Not like this they don't."

"Look," said Evan agreeably, "what's the big deal? A cut on her cheek . . ."

"The big deal is that her eardrum's broken."

"What?" The color drained from Evan's rosy pickled complexion.

"You heard me."

"Her eardrum? I had no idea. I didn't know. I—"

"Someone . . ." Trevor's voice rose and he stopped himself. It would do no good to have his words reach the packed waiting room. "Someone cracked her on the side of the head, Evan. About a week ago, near as I can tell. Cracked her on the side of the head, broadside, with the back of their hand, it looks like. Wearing a ring or some such"—he spat out the word—"adornment!"

"I don't wear any rings," bluffed Evan. He held up his hands. "Not even a wedding ring."

"Someone cracked her so hard they broke her goddamn eardrum!" This time Trevor's voice rose to a shout that carried far and wide.

In the waiting room Nurse Granger jacked up the Muzak.

Evan's voice dropped to a meek whisper. "I was away last week, Doc. All week. On business."

"I don't want to hear your lame excuses."

"Lucille gets awful exasperated when Esther won't talk, see? And if I try to interfere it just makes things worse."

Trevor didn't particularly like Evan's wife, Lucille. She was stiff-necked and humorless. But she was conscientious about those girls, while Evan was erratic and unpredictable.

"I don't care who did it," he snapped. "It just better not happen again."

"It won't," said Evan. "I'll make sure."

"No," corrected Trevor. "I'll make sure. I'll make sure because every month from now on Esther's coming back for another checkup." He whipped open his appointment book and started filling in dates with his Cross pen.

"But I can't afford—"

"Every month. The first Wednesday. That way no holidays will interfere and no long, lost weekends. At six P.M. An evening appointment. So neither of you will have to miss work."

"But I won't be able to pay—"

"And if I find anything amiss, a bruise or a fracture or so much as a hangnail that shouldn't be there . . . anything at all, I'm calling the welfare people. Understand?"

"I said—"

"I don't want your money!" shouted Trevor. "I want you and Lucille to take care of this child. I want you to pay her some attention. Some affection."

"But I do," protested Evan. To Trevor's astonishment Evan Jamison turned weepy. "I love Esther. More than anything. She's nearest and dearest to my heart. I love her with my soul, Trevor, my very soul."

Lies, thought Trevor bitterly. Lies. The man disgusted him.

"Get out of here, Evan."

Evan Jamison scrambled to leave. This time he didn't tarry to shake Trevor's hand. He hurried to the door and called over his shoulder, "We'll have her here, Doc. Wednesdays. Six sharp."

"Evan," said Trevor, unable to stop himself.

"Yes?"

"Don't you even care?"

"About what?"

"About whether she's deaf. In that ear."

Evan seemed to totter slightly, then regained his equilibrium. "Of course I care," he replied. "I just assumed—"

"Never assume, Evan."

"Well is she? Deaf?"

"There's some scarring, but the eardrum appears to have healed. I don't know how, but it did. I did some tests and she can hear. When she wants to."

"Thank God," said Evan.

Evan brought Esther back every month for a year thereafter. There was never any further evidence of abuse, but there was never any change in the child's withdrawn nature either.

The memory rose like bitter bile within Trevor as he looked down at the picture of Esther Maine. Damn me, he thought. Damn me for believing him. Damn me for believing something as feeble as monthly checkups could make a difference in a little girl's life.

Angrily he stuffed the horrifying photo into his jacket pocket. She had told him something. Not much, but something. Maybe she would tell him more.

19

Irene didn't like this neighborhood at all. Not one bit.

Originally the plan had been for her to take one of those taxicabs. Forrest had given her the cash to do so. Mildred had coached her on how much to tip. But it all seemed exorbitant and outrageous and totally unnecessary. Besides, 405 East Tenth Street wasn't that far away. Besides, the people who laid out New York City were considerate enough to number the streets in logical order. So finding your way wasn't a problem.

Being a thrifty person, Irene stashed the cash in her shoulder bag, slung the bag crosswise over her chest, and decided to walk.

It had been a mistake.

She'd navigated east to Fourth Avenue. Taken in by the sights, sounds and smells of the city, Irene whirled about several times as she walked. And she became disoriented. Then, rather than continuing east, Irene proceeded south. Soon the numbers she relied on to navigate vanished. She noticed family-type names . . . Cooper, Jones, and Bleeker. An anxiety attack took hold. She was on a street of the damned called the Bowery.

She wandered about in agitation. Her panic at being lost quickly turned to revulsion as she observed bodies strewn hither and yon. Men—and women too—stretched out on grates, on stoops, in the gutter even. Why you'd need a backhoe just to scoop them all up.

They were drunk, she realized. Dead drunk. And she was lost. Dead lost.

She felt like a lost child and wanted to cry. She wondered if she could retrace her steps.

"Spare change?"

"What!" screamed Irene.

A mountain of a man wearing what looked like animal skins stuck a massive grease-encrusted hand in her face. He was black, which was no comfort as far as Irene was concerned. His hair hung down in dreadlocks. The whites of his eyes were yellow. Behind him trailed a two-wheeled shopping cart piled high with bales of clothing and knick-knacks.

"Or maybe you want your windows washed." He reached into the cart and pulled out a rag and a blackened bottle of Fantastic.

Irene stared at him in fear and amazement.

"Or maybe," he said pointedly, "you want your pipes cleaned."

Irene didn't like the leer on his face. She didn't like the way he stepped forward so brazenly, invading her space. And she didn't like his smile, a smile that revealed three distantly spaced teeth in a gaping black hole of infinite depth.

"You just shut your dirty mouth!" she snapped. She thought of slapping him but did not know where she could wash her hand after.

As soon as the words tumbled out, a sense of doom washed over her. Now he will kill me, she thought. I'll be dead on an unnumbered street called the Bowery, one body among many, and no one will even know.

"Man's gotta make a living," the man in skins muttered. He turned away and shoved the Fantastic back into his cart.

She eyed him warily, but felt the barest bit of sympathy creep in. He looked like he could use a good meal.

"Man's gotta do what he's gotta do. Shit. Birds gotta swim. Fish gotta fly."

"It's not like that," she said without thinking.

"Not like what?" He eyed her warily.

"You got it all wrong. Birds swimming and fish flying, for gosh sakes." With that, Irene forgot her fear and revulsion and sang a few bars.

"Fish gotta swim, birds gotta fly. I gotta love one man till I die." Her voice swelled at this point. "Can't help lovin' that man o' mine!"

Thirty feet away two winos propped against one another on a stoop clapped feebly. Someone across the street whistled. It was as much appreciation as the Bowery could muster.

"Hey," said the black man in surprise, "that ain't half bad."

"Thank you," said Irene modestly.

The man turned to leave.

"Wait," she said.

He swung around.

"I'm lost," said Irene, throwing her cards on the table.

"You and everyone else, lady."

"No, I mean I'm really lost. I'm trying to find four-oh-five East Tenth Street and I'm stuck on this here Bowery Street. I thought maybe you could direct me."

The man looked at her like she was crazy.

"I'm willing to pay," she offered desperately.

"How much?"

"A dollar."

"A dollar!" He hooted and turned away again.

"Five!" she cried.

He whirled around. "Do I hear ten?"

"Robber!" she yelled.

"Okay," he said finally. "I'll tell you what. I'll take you to that address. For a five and another song."

"Another song?"

"Yeah. Go ahead. Sing. And it better be good."

Which was how Irene came to sing "Stormy Weather" on a hazy hot summer morning on a street called the Bowery.

"You know, Quinten," she said some minutes later as

they walked north, "I do believe you could get a chorus together over on that Bowery. All those folks hanging around with nothing to do."

Quinten looked at Irene with pity. "Maybe," he said grimly.

His strides were long. She had to take three steps to match his every one.

"So," she said breathlessly, "where'd you get those skins?"

"Skins?"

"Yeah. Those clothes."

"Oh these." He looked down at himself. "I made them myself."

"Is that a fact?" She looked at the enormous stitches of twine and knew they'd been done by hand, not on a Singer.

They were passing a row of brownstones now, some of them restored to Victorian splendor, some of them gutted hulks, and some crammed with poor families barely hanging on. Gentrification had broken out like chicken pox, a building here, a building there. Yuppies lived cheek-to-jowl with welfare recipients and crack dealers and felt like pioneers. They told themselves they would make a killing in real estate. They reassured parents that it was safe, but kept automobiles for weekend getaways stashed in other boroughs.

"Yeah. When I got out of Nam I had trouble adjusting. I was in the VA Hospital for a while, but I couldn't take it. They took away my clothes, pulled my teeth, and pumped me full of Thorazine. Finally I said fuck it. I took a hike. Had to get myself straight. Headed for the woods."

"The woods?" This Irene could understand and appreciate. She herself had lived in the woods in Raven's Wing—in a log cabin she built herself—until she took up residence with Forrest in Mildred's grand accommodations.

"Yeah. The woods of Pennsylvania. The Poconos. I lived there until the developers displaced me." He grinned unexpectedly. "They turned my lean-to into a time-share."

Quinten was an intelligent man, Irene could see that.

"Hey," she cried suddenly. "There's the Good Humor man! Want an ice cream bar?" She reached into her purse and started to hurry toward the white enamel truck.

"Don't," said Quinten softly. He clutched her arm with an intensity that scared her.

"Huh?"

"He's not selling ice cream."

"He's not?"

"Take a good look . . . Do you see any kids running up to that truck? Well do you?"

"No," she said carefully.

"Watch."

What she saw was an occasional man or woman scurry up to the ice cream vendor. Money was handed over and the man or woman would come away. Without any ice cream.

"There's no ice cream to be seen."

"Right. He's selling something else."

"Something else like what?"

"Like drugs."

"Lordy."

"Good Humor guy's been using this cover for months now. It's perfect. Every time he pulls up folks can hear that loony tune music for blocks."

"Golly."

"I called the police. Gave them an anonymous tip. I'm not sticking my neck out, you understand. Don't want to end up dead. Course, the police did nothing. They're probably in on the take."

"Jeesum."

He turned his attention away from the ice cream man. "There," he said, pointing way down the street. "That's the place you're looking for. Four-oh-five."

She squinted through steam rising from the manholes in the street. It occurred to her that hell must be close to the surface in New York City.

"How can you see?" she demanded. Maybe he was trying

to trick her. Maybe he just wanted to leave her here.

"I can see," he said slyly. "I got eyes can see behind the trees. I got ears can hear choppers before they take off."

Oh boy, she thought, a nut case. Jesus help me. But Jesus was nowhere to be seen and Quinten was still her best bet.

"I know that place," he went on. "It's a halfway house."

"Halfway to what?"

"Lady, where you been? It's a place where crazies live."

Now there, thought Irene, is the pot calling the kettle black.

"Oh."

"Sort of a shelter, but nicer."

"I see." She wondered why he didn't live there if it was so nice.

He seemed to read her mind. "I applied to live there once, but they rejected me. Said I didn't have adequate social skills."

"Social skills? *That*," said Irene, "sounds crazy."

"Just as well," Quinten went on. "They have a lot of rules there. Especially about times. You got to be on time for meals. You got to be on time for curfew. You got to be on time for urinalysis. You got to toe the mark. Their mark."

"Oh."

"They got rules upon rules. Like no cohabitation."

"Co-what?"

"No fraternization."

"Pardon?"

"No screwing."

"Oh."

"That all you can say? Oh?"

"Well," stammered Irene, "I'm a little out of my element here. Over my head, you might say."

"Listen," he said, seeing the apprehension on her face, "you give me the five you owe me. Then I'll follow you down there. I'll wait. And I'll walk you back . . ."

"Oh," said Irene, "I'd be ever so grateful."

" . . . for another five," he continued.

"I should have known."

"And for a—"

"Not another song!"

"Kinda had my heart set on 'Summertime.' "

It may be summertime, thought Irene, but the living sure isn't easy. She could have taken one of those taxis for less than this was costing her.

But Irene knew when she was licked. "Okay."

She left Quinten sitting on the stoop.

As it turned out, a nice blue-haired lady wearing blinding white dentures answered Irene's timid knock. Sixty-five or thereabouts, she filled a faded housedress to capacity with a well-padded body. In one hand she held a rag, in the other a canister of Endust.

"Yes?" said the woman politely.

"Sorry to disturb you, ma'am. I'm Irene Purdy and I'm looking for a person by the name of Claudia Maine. Probably she doesn't live here. Probably it's someone else. Probably it's just a big mistake. But, see, there was this 'C. Maine' in the phone book, and I figured I should check it out."

The woman seemed to process this information slowly.

"Ah," she said at last. "Claudia. Of course. She's most likely at work. Most of them are this time of day. But let me check the board." She turned to leave, then remembered her manners. "I'm Doris," she said. "The housemother. Do come in."

Irene followed Doris through a living room, dining room, and into a large kitchen. Though furnished with tired hand-me-downs and Goodwill pieces, the place was clean and homey. There were braided rugs on the floor, colorful prints of country scenes on the walls, and an ample stack of magazines on a coffee table in the living room. Irene spied *Psychology Today, Spy,* and *Guns and Ammo*. The television, she noted, was a Panasonic color model.

"Nice place you got here," said Irene.

"We're proud of it," said Doris agreeably. "I try to make it as homelike as possible. Some of our residents have been in institutions for years. And living in this city isn't easy."

"I should say," agreed Irene. "It could drive anybody bats."

Doris laughed. "Yes. It requires an incredible amount of perspicacity simply to cope with daily living. Taking subways, handling money, dressing for survival, never mind success. Everything is demanding. So this place is a refuge of sorts. We give them a little help, just a little, mind you, a safe place to recoup and regroup."

Irene was amazed when Doris led her to the board in the kitchen. It spanned an entire wall and consisted of a list of names to the left, followed by an array of boxes containing grease-penciled notations.

"Here now," said Doris proudly. "As you can see, we can peruse pertinent information about each resident at a glance. Medications. Family ties. Daytime phone numbers. Some of our residents hold full-time jobs, others spend the day in sheltered workshops, and still others participate at outpatient therapeutic environments. And over here"—she ran her finger clear across the board—"is where residents check in and check out. Now let's see about Miss Claudia."

Her eyes scanned the scribbled data. Apparently each resident checked in and out on a daily basis. After curfew the boxes were wiped clean and made ready for the next day.

"Oh dear," sighed Doris.

"What's the matter? Where is she?"

"Nowhere. That's just the point. Miss Claudia has signed in sick. Again."

"So she's here?"

"Yes. Unfortunately." She saw Irene's expression and her tone turned confidential. "Miss Claudia isn't sick, at least not physically. She's malingering. Doesn't like her job at the Insurance Institute. Of course, compiling actuarial statistics isn't everybody's cup of tea, but she's got a good mind and she was lucky to get that job, let me tell you. It pays decently and it's a nice environment and the benefits are good and . . ."

"And what?"

"And, well, it's so much more than our other residents can ever hope to achieve. So very much more. But Miss Claudia takes it for granted. And now she's going to blow it. Going to blow this opportunity because of excessive sick days."

For a moment Irene feared Doris might cry, she was becoming so wound up.

"She called in sick four times in the past month alone."

"Maybe she really is sick," ventured Irene.

"No," said Doris. "If she's sick, it's from stinking up the place with turpentine and paint. She paints bizarre pictures at all hours with no regard to the other residents here." As if that wasn't enough, Doris piled on more criticism. "She's spoiled rotten, you know, what with that fancy family of hers providing a safety net. The way her mother keeps giving her money—" She stopped abruptly. "Of course, that's all over now."

Maybe, thought Irene, that's why she's sick. Heartsick.

Doris directed Irene upstairs to "Miss Claudia's" room, which was, she said, at the end of the hall to the right.

"I'd go with you," said Doris apologetically, "but unless I'm mistaken, I hear the Good Humor man, and I don't want to miss him."

For once Irene was at a loss for words.

Doris hurried off. "Pleasure having met you," she called airily over her shoulder.

"Likewise I'm sure," muttered Irene.

She made her way to Claudia Maine's room following her nose. The scent of turpentine was unmistakable. When she got there the door was ajar, and at Irene's gentle knock it swung wide open.

"Hello?" she called. "Anybody home?"

"Go away," groaned an exasperated voice. "I'm not going to work today. I'm sick."

Irene was not put off by the less-than-cordial welcome. She ventured inside, finding herself in a small room cluttered with rags, squashed tubes of paint, and partially completed canvases. One caught her eye in particular. To her untrained eye it looked like some kind of test canvas—something on which an artist might have applied unorthodox color mixtures. Then she stepped back and looked again. Upon further examination, Irene could detect an intricate pattern in a swirl of multitudinous dots so painstakingly applied. There was a woman. She had long brown hair. She was sleeping in a field of flowers. Her hair intertwined with daisies, black-eyed Susans and Queen Anne's lace. It was an arresting portrait. Irene stood there transfixed.

"What are you looking at?"

"That there. It's your mother, isn't it?"

"Never mind who it is. Who the hell are you?"

Claudia Maine lay prone on a bed by an open window, fanning herself with a copy of *Vogue*.

"I do believe that's the prettiest picture I've ever seen."

Claudia eyed Irene irritably. "What are you anyway? Some kind of art critic? Or some kind of mutant?"

Irene didn't know what a mutant was, but from Claudia's tone she knew it was no compliment. Still, even with her sharp tongue and obnoxious manner, Claudia Maine was quite possibly the most beautiful young woman Irene had ever seen. Even with that fresh mouth and tangled brown hair. Even wearing a baggy stained T-shirt and spattered dungaree cutoffs. Even without makeup and covered with a sheen of perspiration. Prettier even than the model on that magazine she was waving back and forth. Claudia Maine was everything Irene was not. Tall. Thin. Young. Attractive. And articulate, that too.

"I'm Irene Purdy, and I'm trying to pay you a compliment."

"Well don't bother."

Irene decided to try another approach. "I'm a friend of your father's, honey." It wasn't a lie exactly.

Claudia shot up from the pillow in alarm. "Does he know I'm here?"

"Well, I don't know. I mean, I don't *think* so. He never said—"

Claudia slumped back. "Forget it. He knows. I should have known she'd tell."

"Who'd tell?"

"Never mind. I'm not feeling well, so if you don't mind, I'd appreciate it if you'd get the fuck out of here."

Irene cringed. This wasn't going to be easy.

"Dr. Bradford sends his regards."

"Huh?" Claudia Maine's head shot up again and for the thinnest slice of an instant the veneer of toughness cracked. "How do you know him?"

"He's a friend of mine too. In fact, we're sort of working together on—"

"Oh shit." Abruptly Claudia covered her mouth, leapt from the bed, and bolted down the hall. In the distance Irene could hear her retching into a toilet, at least she hoped it was into a toilet. Without thinking, Irene hurried after her. She came upon Claudia bent over the bowl and gently placed her hands on the girl's shoulders.

"There," she said. "There, there."

When Claudia finished, she wiped her mouth with the back of her hand and struggled to her feet. Irene put the lid down and flushed the toilet.

"Sit," she commanded.

"I'm okay now," said Claudia sullenly.

"Sit!"

Obediently Claudia sank to the seat. She watched warily as Irene briskly ran a washcloth under the tap and wrung it out.

"That's not my washcloth," she muttered. "They give you shit around here if you use someone else's washcloth."

"Anyone gives you trouble, just refer them to me." She blotted Claudia's face gently. Then she took both the girl and the washcloth back to Claudia's bedroom.

"Lie down."

"Uh," said Claudia, giving in to her queasiness, "maybe I will. Just for a moment."

Irene blotted Claudia's face again, then folded the cool washcloth and put it across the girl's forehead.

"Why are you doing this?"

"Because," said Irene, "I can't help myself. I'm a nurse. Or I was once. Awhile back."

She removed Claudia's tattered sneakers and opened the window wider. When she asked the next question she was looking out that window into the bleak East Village neighborhood.

"When's the baby due?"

Claudia grimaced and closed her eyes. "It's that obvious?"

"No, although it soon will be. I've done enough midwifing in my time to recognize the signs."

"April." The word fell out of her mouth, squashed and flat. "It's due in April."

"Well," said Irene, not knowing what else to say. "Well, well."

"Have you ever done an abortion?"

"No," replied Irene quickly. She was silent for some moments. "Well, once," she finally admitted. "A girl who said she was raped. I don't know if it was true, and I didn't press. She was all of twelve. Her family didn't know, and she didn't feel she could tell them. They wouldn't believe her, she said. I always suspected maybe her daddy—never mind. Anyway I helped her out. I did it. But to this day I don't feel entirely right about it."

Claudia looked at Irene carefully.

"I mean, I know a lot of people feel different and they're entitled. But for myself, well, I just couldn't do such a thing again. Ever. To me it's alive, no matter how it got put there. I hope you're not asking—"

"Oh no," said Claudia. "I don't want that." She sank deeper into the pillows and sighed. "My mother wanted me to have one, that's all."

"I see," said Irene, thinking most mothers want what's easiest for their child, never mind for some grandchild that isn't born yet.

"No," said Claudia. "You don't see. It's fucking complicated, that's what it is."

"Do you think," said Irene carefully, "you could make an effort to talk a little nicer?"

"Nicer?" Claudia looked at her like she was crazy.

"Those words—*that* one word in particular—it bothers me."

"You mean fuck?"

"Yes! And you know darn right what I mean!"

Claudia smiled in spite of her misery. "Okay."

"Good. So where were we? Oh yeah. Why's it so complicated?"

"If I'm pregnant, I get thrown out of here for starters. That means I have no place to live."

"Oh."

"And since I've been pregnant I've stopped taking my meds. That means I could go crazy again."

Irene scoffed. "What do you mean crazy? You seem right as rain to me. Why just look how we're sitting chatting. Like normal folks. Don't talk about crazy."

"Well my doctor wouldn't like it, I can tell you that. When I came off smack the second time—" She saw Irene's expression. "I came off smack all by myself. I guess you didn't know about that. No one knew about my getting better, my coming here, except her."

"Her who?"

"My mother." Before Irene could get a word in edgewise, Claudia rattled on. "Anyway I went through detox and got myself straight. Then I needed a place, see? So they—the social worker, the rehab counselor, the probation officer— recommended me here. Which was okay, except they had these conditions here and one of them was that I see someone for regular medical treatment. A shrink. The city pays, it's part of the program. And he's okay, but like all shrinks he likes to prescribe meds. They can control you that way, you know."

"Seems like an awful lot of 'theys,' " muttered Irene.

"Well 'they' run the show, take it from me. Only now that I'm pregnant I stopped taking the meds. On the sly, of course. Think I should tell him?"

"No," said Irene quickly. "Don't tell him anything. I mean, if *they* run the show maybe *they* could force you to get rid of the baby. Say you were incompetent or something. Not that you are, of course."

"Of course," replied Claudia. Without warning she grabbed a pallet knife crusted with crimson paint and pointed it at her belly.

"Stop that!" Irene snatched the pallet knife from her hands and tossed it aside.

"See? Even you think I'm crazy."

"I do not. It's just this place. It gives me the creeps, if you want to know the truth. As for you, I think you're doing good. Real good."

"Sure. I'm not taking my meds because they might hurt the baby. But because I don't take them, the voices might come back. I heard voices because of the drugs, and believe me they weren't friendly. I figure with my luck the voices will come back. And I might kill myself. Or the baby. How's that for good?"

"I see," said Irene glumly. "So why do you want this baby anyhow?"

"Lady, my life's so fucked, sorry, mucked up, how could I not want it? It's a chance to do something right for a change. Look at me. Would you believe I was once considered gifted?"

"Sure I would," said Irene. "And I do. I believe it still, looking at that there picture."

"That? It's garbage. Amateurish. Overly sentimental."

"I love it."

"Lady," said Claudia, not unkindly, "you're a trip and

a half. Okay, so forget the painting. Look at this place. I've fallen about as far as a person can go."

"Some have it worse."

"The assholes around here maybe. Like Doris Day down there."

"Her last name's Day? Ain't that something! Do you think she's related?"

"I hate to burst your bubble, but that's not her real name. She told you she was the housemother, right? Well, she's not." Claudia read Irene's shocked expression and continued. "And Doris Day is who she thinks she is today. Yesterday it was Betty Crocker. Day before that it was My Little Margie. Tomorrow it will probably be December Bride or June Cleaver. She's stuck in the fifties. Crazy as a loon."

"Oh stop," said Irene, laughing in spite of herself.

"Has its good points, though. When she was Betty Crocker she made some marijuana brownies that were out of this world."

Claudia turned suddenly wary. "So you say your name is Irene. Why're you here anyway? Did my father send you to check up on me or what?"

"No," said Irene. "Nothing like that. Me and some of my friends—Dr. Bradford, you remember him?"

"Yeah. He was a nice guy. Not bad looking either for an old coot."

Irene chose to ignore the last remark. "Dr. Bradford and Millie Bennett and Forrest Haggarty—"

"That old fart?" Claudia arched an eyebrow. "I remember him. He was chief of police. Folks said he was nuts."

Another pot calling names, thought Irene sourly. She masked her irritation. "Well," she sniffed, "that was a long time ago. Anyway, your father hired us to find out what happened to your mother."

Claudia turned her face to the wall. "My mother slipped in the bathtub."

"Maybe not," said Irene. "There are what they call *inconsistencies*. Even the police report can't make up its mind. It says 'cause of death unknown, pending investigation.' "

Claudia bit her lip. "I didn't know that."

"And then there's that place she was staying. Under an assumed name. And—"

"Listen," interrupted Claudia. "I'll admit the surrounding circumstances seem bizarre, but it had to be an accident. I can't see my mother as the type to get herself murdered."

"I see," said Irene, "and what type might that be?"

"Someone with enemies. Someone with secrets. Someone blackmailing someone or being blackmailed themselves. That kind of someone. See, I read up on it once. There's this thing called victimology."

"Oh yeah?"

"The FBI invented it. They study the murder scene and the wounds and all that, but they also study the victim. They do what's called a 'psychological autopsy.' They try to figure out what was going on in the victim's life that caused him or her to be in that particular spot at that particular time when they died."

"Right! They've got a fancy word for it, but that's exactly what we're trying to do."

"I see." Claudia considered this for a moment. "So you're talking to a lot of people. People like who?"

"The desk clerk at the hotel where she died. Higgins. And another lady who was there. A lady who knew your mother."

"Yeah?" Claudia looked up. "Who?"

"Lady by the name of Cora Parks. She hangs out there. Ever heard of her?"

"No."

"Well it would help us a lot if you'd cooperate too, cause it would give us a leg up on this thing. So tell me: Did you see your mother that day? The day she died?"

"Yes."

"Lordy," breathed Irene. Pay dirt.

"I remember that day very clearly. It was the last time I saw my mother alive."

Irene sat down on the edge of a chair next to Claudia's bed and leaned forward expectantly.

"Like I said, she knew I was here. I told her when I first entered the program." Without waiting for a reply, Claudia plunged on. "I never in a million years thought she'd come to see me, but she did. Every week. She'd meet me at the office at five, and we'd go have a drink. Just us girls." Claudia's mouth twisted. "Like—how did you put it—normal people? Mother and daughter at the Top of the Sixes, the city at our feet, slugging down kir royales. That's what she'd order for me. A kir royale. You're not really supposed to drink on meds, but one kir royale was okay."

"It must have been fun."

"Actually it was pathetic, but what the hell, she seemed to get a kick out of it."

"So you saw her after work that day?"

"No. I called in sick that day. She came to see me that afternoon. Here."

"And what happened?"

"I told her about the baby."

"No!"

"Yes. She didn't take it well either. I didn't expect joy and rapture, but I didn't expect her to get so freaked. It was a sight to behold. She didn't want me to go off the meds. Wanted to know who the father was too." Claudia rolled her eyes. "As if I knew. Hey, I'd say if I knew, right?

"She started crying about how I was ruining my life— as if there was anything left to ruin. She said she wouldn't always be around to take care of me. It got rather ugly."

"Why would she say a thing like that?" interrupted Irene. "That she wouldn't always be around."

Claudia thought for a moment. "I don't know. It was a heated argument. Words were hurled back and forth. I didn't think about any hidden meaning at the time."

"So what happened then?"

"Suddenly she got very calm. She said it was a tragedy but that we would get through it. We. Like it was her baby, you know? She whipped out her little black book and said she'd make an appointment for an abortion. Just like that."

"And you refused."

"Damn right. Then she pulled the rug out from under me. Said she wouldn't help me get my own apartment. That was my plan, see? That she would help me get situated. I needed some place to go, any place. But she cut me off without a dime. Left me high and dry. Up shit creek without a paddle."

The words were defiant but there was no mistaking the pain and anger beneath them.

"It surprised me that she would be so insistent about abortion, her being so religious and all. But she made up her mind, and that was that. She reasoned, she pleaded, she cried. Finally she gave up. She left, and I never saw her again."

Another scenario leapt to Irene's mind. "You didn't," she asked carefully, "try to talk to her? You know, go to her hotel later. To make up?" Or to ask for money, to demand money. But Irene didn't say that.

Claudia looked at Irene with respect. The lady was smarter than she looked. "As a matter of fact I did. But I went to the Regency"—she spread her hands—"and of course she wasn't there."

"I see." Irene tried not to sound skeptical. "So that's what you were doing that night. Going to the Regency. You knew nothing about the St. James."

"No. I walked to the Regency, and when she wasn't there I walked back here. I do that quite often, walking. It's a long way from there to here, and I walked in the door just before curfew at ten."

"It must have been hard, her rejecting you like that."

Claudia didn't say anything.

"I mean, looking at that painting—"

"Will you forget that damn painting! Jesus." She ran a hand through her tangled hair. "Okay, so maybe it was hard. She used to call me her brown-eyed beauty, even at the worst times. Back when I got sick, she stuck by me. She was the only one who did."

"Your daddy did too."

"Him? Yes, I suppose he did. In his way. But we don't talk very often. We're not estranged or anything like that, but he has trouble dealing with what happened. With him things are black or white. You're a success or you're a failure, and I'm the latter. He's sure I'll end up a bag lady. Sure I'll end up in some SRO hotel wearing a moth-eaten sweater huddled in front of a black-and-white TV with no vertical hold eating cat food cold from the can."

"Lord."

" 'Course I wouldn't eat it cold. The cat food, I mean. I'd heat it up first."

"Aw go on."

"Look, you've got to understand my father. He has this picture in his mind of the perfect family. And we were it. Only I spoiled the picture. It was hard for him to cope with. For a while I tried. After the drugs screwed up my mind, I tried very hard to act lucid. He'd come visit me when I was in the hospital and he'd hold my hand and I could tell it was killing him. So I tried to act okay, like normal people. But it was such an effort. I got so exhausted, pretending."

"What was it like?" asked Irene suddenly.

"You mean being crazy? What a question."

"Sorry. Forget I asked."

"No, it's okay. No one ever asked me flat out before. People pussyfoot around it. At least you're honest."

She stared at the ceiling as she spoke. At first her voice was flat and devoid of emotion, almost as though she were speaking of someone else. "I never really thought it was the drugs, I thought it was me. Something *in* me. My mind didn't work anymore. I didn't care what I wore, what I ate, if I ate, if I slept or who I slept with.

"Combine that with hallucinations. I saw people wearing strange clothes and heard them saying things they supposedly weren't saying. Voices told me I was a stupid bitch. Told me I was a slut. Told me I was ugly. Told me to do things. Violent things. To others. To myself. That led to paranoia." Claudia was talking very fast now. "I mean you see strange people and hear strange things, and everything is all wrong. You start to think this is being done *to* you. I was afraid to eat because I was sure there was glass in my food. I lost thirty pounds in a month."

"But they let you out of the hospital. You must have been cured."

"Are you kidding? I escaped. That sounds melodramatic. Actually I just walked out one day with the clothes on my back. It was like prison in there. I couldn't take it anymore. And most of all I couldn't take what it was doing to my parents. They always looked so pathetically hopeful, always tried to say just the right thing. So I figured I'd make it on my own, come back some day and prove I'd done it, you know?"

"And you did make it."

Claudia looked around at the dismal room . . . at clothes hung on nails . . . at an empty can of Diet Pepsi that served as an ashtray . . . at a heap of soiled jeans and T-shirts over in the corner . . . at a lone roach crawling lazily up the bureau.

"In a manner of speaking," she said grimly.

They were silent for some moments.

"I wish to hell I knew what I was going to do."

"I'm sure if you talked to your father—"

"Forget it. He's got enough on his mind."

"Maybe you'll inherit something," said Irene. She stopped short, realizing the implications of her words.

Claudia's face closed up. "Maybe," she said noncommittally.

Irene looked at Claudia wondering if the girl had it in her to kill her own mother. Wondering if maybe those voices in her head had told her to do so.

"Listen, I didn't want her dead, if that's what you're thinking."

"I wasn't thinking that. I wasn't thinking anything."

"Well I didn't."

"I know."

"I could talk to her because she understood. She'd had problems of her own, see? And I always had the feeling she almost expected me to crack up. I'd catch her looking at me when I was growing up, looking at me funny. Like she was worried. I suppose that sounds crazy. Anyway, when I entered this halfway house, she came to see me. My mother, coming into the city. You have no idea what it took for her to do that."

"She must have loved you very much."

Claudia said nothing. Irene thought she saw a tear streak down her cheek, but the girl flicked it away as though it were a gnat.

"You think I'd kill her? Well do you?"

"No," said Irene with more conviction than she felt. Inside she wasn't sure about Claudia, not sure at all.

20 When Mildred called Constance Townsend, she was relieved when the maid answered the phone and told her "Miz Townsend is indisposed."

Of course, thought Mildred. She's lost her sister. She's in mourning.

Then someone picked up on another extension.

"It's all right, Monique. I'll take the call."

At first Mildred didn't think it was Constance. The words were thick and throaty. Then she realized that the woman had been crying.

Mildred offered her condolences. Constance accepted them. Stiffly. Mildred said she would like to come by to call. This afternoon, if Constance was up to it. Constance said yes, she was receiving visitors. And perhaps they might discuss redelegating some of the more pressing responsibilities of the SPCA benefit.

She's going to dump all the work on me, thought Mildred in annoyance. Then she chastised herself for being selfish and unsympathetic.

Constance suggested that Mildred come by that afternoon for tea. A time was agreed upon.

And now Mildred stood at the shiny red enamel front door of the Townsend home, a four-story limestone building on East Seventy-second Street. It was, Mildred knew, a highly desirable address. Of course, Mildred was used to desirable addresses and knew how to dress for them. She wore an off-white linen suit, bone patent leather sling-back pumps, and a single rope of very good pearls. In one hand she clutched a box of Godiva thin mints and in the other a bone patent leather handbag.

She steeled herself for the conversation that was to come and the questions she would have to ask. True, she would ask them ever so tactfully, ever so delicately, but Constance Townsend was nobody's fool and there was a distinct risk of unpleasantness. Mildred hated confrontations and breathed a silent prayer that the conversation would not turn awkward.

Pink and white geraniums bloomed around her. She stared into a polished brass knocker. Her bowed reflection peered back. Very well, she decided. She dropped the knocker with a dull thud.

An elderly butler of the stiff-upper-lip school opened the door and ushered Mildred in. Very few people—even those of ample means—employed butlers anymore, but James had been with the Townsends since Constance's husband Freddy was a baby. Sometimes, thought Mildred, Freddy still acts like a baby. Maybe he should have a nursemaid.

Mildred followed James through thick mauve carpet and tried not to think that Constance Jamison from the wrong side of Raven's Wing had married into big bucks indeed. Such thoughts were crass and really not characteristic of her. James led her upstairs to the living room on the second floor.

"Mildred," said Constance.

"Constance," said Mildred.

Constance Townsend rose gracefully from a loveseat covered in apple-green silk damask. She wore a pink chiffon concoction that was, Mildred supposed, intended for lounging at home. It swirled around Constance like cotton candy on a stick and did not meet Mildred's criteria for appropriate mourning attire. Her body was thin to the point of emaciation, her face lifted into a permanent expression of surprise, and her fingernails professionally buffed, shaped, and polished in pearly pink. Constance Townsend was beautiful, Mildred supposed, in a dry, desperate, calculated sort of way.

They clutched each other briefly and brushed dry kisses on one another's cheeks.

This, thought Mildred grimly, is the way we say hello. A hollow, numbing ritual devoid of real affection. She shoved these thoughts aside and sat down next to Constance.

"I'm so sorry," she said genuinely, "about your sister's tragic death." In spite of herself, and in spite of Constance's off-putting formality, she gave the other woman's hand a squeeze.

"Oh," said Constance absently. She extricated her hand. "Yes. Well." She appeared slightly unfocused for a moment. "It came as a shock. We'd had lunch together that very day. At least I'll always remember Esther that way. Eating lemon sole at the Palm Court. Sipping a good Chablis."

Mildred nodded sympathetically.

"Speaking of which, may I offer you something to drink?"

Constance, Mildred realized, had artfully shifted gears, managing to veer away from the emotional topic.

"Well," said Mildred, "a cup of tea would be very—"

"Nonsense," scoffed Constance. "I had something stronger in mind. A glass of sherry perhaps? Or a shot of bourbon?" She leaned forward unexpectedly. "What do you say?" She gestured vaguely toward the hallway. "James will pour whatever you'd like."

"Well, I don't know . . ."

"I've already got a head start on you." It was a challenge.

Oh dear, thought Mildred. So that was it. Although she hadn't picked up on the fact straightaway, Constance did seem slightly less steady than usual.

"Maybe a glass of white wine," said Mildred, trying to be agreeable, "with seltzer, plenty of seltz—"

"Screw the seltzer," said Constance.

Minutes later James tottered in bearing a silver tray with a glass of white wine for Mildred and a small prismed glass of iceless bourbon for Constance.

"He's old as Methuselah," confided Constance after the man crept out, "but he's got his good points. Going blind and deaf, so he's very discreet." That said, she winked.

Mildred was unsettled by both the remark and the wink. What, she wondered, does she mean by *that?* She suspected Constance might be more than tipsy; she might be drunk. But then Constance seemed to get hold of herself.

They chatted for a while about family, friends, and social gossip. As expected, Constance deftly managed to unload a host of disagreeable chores connected with the SPCA benefit onto Mildred's shoulders. The most vexing was coordination of telephone solicitation of prominent people, friends and acquaintances all, urging them to buy tickets at a thousand dollars a plate for food on a par with Kal Kan. Mildred hated, absolutely hated, such telephone work. The very idea of going hat in hand and asking for money, no matter how worthy the cause, was most disagreeable. She consoled herself with the fact that at least she would be able to delegate most of the calls.

Then she pictured Forrest calling Saul Steinberg . . . and Irene on the wire with his wife Gayfryd . . .

"No!" she blurted.

"I beg your pardon?" said Constance.

"What I mean is, Constance, I can't." She saw Constance's stormy look and blundered on. "I'm afraid I haven't the time. I'm, well, I'm rather involved."

"Why you sly devil," warbled Constance. "Dating already!"

"No. Not that. Not dating."

"Well, for heaven's sake, what is it then, Mildred? What could possibly be more important than the SPCA benefit?"

"It's a long story," she replied.

Mildred waited as James refilled their glasses, then sought to explain.

"Constance . . ."

"Yes?"

Briefly she explained the situation as it had developed . . . her country house in Raven's Wing, her friendship with Forrest, Irene, and Trevor . . .

"How very charming," said Constance automatically. Clearly she had no inkling of what was coming.

Mildred plunged on and told about Forrest's encounter with Cameron Maine and Forrest's subsequent conversation with Cameron's father Jonathan . . .

Constance's flawless face froze.

Oh dear, thought Mildred. This is not going well.

"How very intriguing," said Constance, not sounding the least bit intrigued.

Despite the distinct chill in the air, Mildred pressed on and revealed that they had agreed to investigate Esther Maine's death. She then related the visit to the St. James Hotel but managed to skirt some of the less savory details.

"So you've already begun your little diversion," said Constance icily.

"I wouldn't call it a diversion, Constance. We take this very seriously. It's not some sort of game."

"I suppose Jonathan has given you money for this."

"No," protested Mildred automatically. Then she remembered the ten thousand dollars. "Well, yes. He gave Mr. Haggarty a stipend—a modest stipend—to cover expenses."

"I'll give you more. To stop this nonsense."

Mildred looked at her dumbfounded. "Constance, it's certainly not a question of money. Cameron Maine asked for help. We're giving it."

"Out of the goodness of your hearts, I suppose," said Constance archly.

Mildred realized that the bourbon had loosened Constance's tongue, and it was an angry tongue indeed. She tried to think of a way to placate the woman.

"You don't see, do you?" Constance went on. "You'll drag my dead sister through the mud. My family too. There will be scandal." It seemed to be the worst thing she could think of. Suddenly she turned weepy.

"Oh dear," said Mildred. Hastily she fished a handkerchief from her purse. She handed it to Constance. "I don't think it will come to that, Constance."

"What will it come to?" Constance sniffed noisily into the handkerchief. When she withdrew it her nose was very red. Her mascara, however, was intact. "How do you think I feel?" she asked. "I have lunch with my sister and four days later she turns up dead at the morgue. In a public hospital for goodness sakes."

Mildred wondered which was worse to Constance, the death or the public hospital. "I know," she said sympathetically.

"Her face was so battered, we couldn't even have proper calling hours at Campbell's. And Jonathan was no help at all. Babbling nonsense about how he was going to make her pretty again, for pity's sake. I opened the casket and looked. The result was a travesty. A crazy quilt! And he calls himself a plastic surgeon! Dr. Frankenstein is more like it."

Constance shuddered and drew herself up in her seat. "The man's demented, if you ask me. Just like Claudia.

It runs in the family. Maine genes, not Jamison. There is inbreeding there, you mark my words."

"Esther was your adopted sister," Mildred reminded.

"That's right," said Constance hastily. "I tend to forget. I loved her like a blood sister, after all."

"Of course," said Mildred. She decided to continue gently. "Constance dear, aren't you the least bit curious about what happened to Esther?"

"Curiosity killed the cat," snapped Constance. She took one large swallow, finishing off her bourbon.

"Maybe curiosity is the wrong word. I mean, wouldn't you like to know what happened? Wouldn't you like to see justice prevail?"

"Justice?" Constance looked at her as though she were mad. "Honestly, Mildred, sometimes you are naive. Can't you see this could do more harm that good?"

"Why?"

"There's no telling where this might lead. Esther had everything—social position, money, a devoted husband, loving children . . ."

The undercurrent of jealousy in Constance's voice was all too obvious.

" . . . but even with all that, she was never a particularly stable woman. She was an emotional recluse. I must admit, I was surprised as anyone when she started coming into the city. And then during the past year there seemed to be a change of sorts. It was astonishing really. She was more talkative, chatty even. She seemed inordinately— how shall I put it—happy?" Constance made a disagreeable face.

"I wonder why."

"I have no idea. Maybe she finally came to her senses and appreciated all the good things she had."

Before Constance could go on, they were interrupted by the slam of a door and the sound of Freddy Townsend, who had come home early from work. Early as usual. As head of the family business, Freddy could keep any hours he pleased, and those hours were minimal indeed.

His great grandfather had been a man with the remarkable foresight to invent the first tampon (though Mildred always suspected it had really been great grandma and grandpa got the credit). Now Freddy spent his abbreviated days plotting market penetration of plastic applicators into the Third World. He talked about it at cocktail parties even. Mildred tried to avoid him whenever possible.

"Constance, pet!" he called from the hallway. "I'm home!"

"Ugh," muttered Constance.

Mildred detected a domestic storm on the horizon and hoped it would hold off until she was gone.

"Ah Mildred!" said Freddy as he strode into the room. Freddy never walked, he was a strider from way back. "What a pleasant surprise."

"Freddy," said Mildred, offering her cheek.

He set his Manhattan on the coffee table and plopped himself into an overstuffed chair. In his younger days, Freddy Townsend had been a fullback at Dartmouth. Now he seemed nearly as overstuffed as the chair itself. He had discarded his suit jacket somewhere along the way and now sprawled before them in navy blue trousers, a rumpled white shirt monogrammed on the pocket, and a yellow silk tie which hung loosened under his collection of chins.

"So," boomed Freddy, "how's the family? Damn shame about you and Connor."

"The family," said Mildred, "is fine. Such as it is." She wondered how a grown man could allow himself to be called something so ridiculous as Freddy.

"Mildred and some acquaintances are investigating Esther's death," blurted Constance without preamble. "Jonathan hired them."

For the barest instant Freddy Townsend looked stunned. "I beg your pardon?" he said.

"They've already talked to some miserable little man at the St. James Hotel. Some desk clerk."

"The owner," Mildred corrected. "And I wouldn't say we were 'hired' exactly. Jonathan just asked us to look into the circumstances. I'm sure you'll agree they were a bit curious."

"I always thought so," concurred Freddy. "But what the hell, the police said it was an accident, and they're the experts." He casually lit a Dunhill cigarette and exhaled a stream of slate smoke.

"Not exactly," said Mildred. "As of now the cause of death is officially listed as 'unknown, pending investigation.' "

"Well I'll be damned," said Freddy. "But I thought they were dropping it. The police, I mean. We heard there wasn't anything to go on."

"There isn't," said Mildred. "At least not much. I was hoping you might add something to the picture. Do either of you have any idea why Esther was at the St. James Hotel?"

"I should say not," sniffed Constance.

Freddy looked at Mildred guilelessly and shrugged his flesh-padded shoulders.

"Well," said Mildred tentatively, "the owner of the hotel seemed to be aware of—how shall I say it—I mean, apparently she had secured the room for the long term. On an annual basis, paid in advance."

"I'm sure he's mistaken," said Constance primly. "Esther never mentioned anything of the sort to me. What on earth would she have wanted with a dreary little room like that? She would have mentioned something so bizarre to me, I'm sure. We were sisters after all."

"For God's sake, Connie," said Freddy, "there are people who prefer to keep some things to themselves." He turned to Mildred. "I don't see what you're driving at here, Mildred."

"Well," began Mildred once again. For the life of her, she wished she could think of a way to approach this tactfully. But she couldn't.

"Well what?" said Constance.

"The man seemed to think—seemed to imply—oh dear. There simply is no delicate way to put this, I'm afraid. He indicated that Esther had a number of recent visitors at the St. James."

"Visitors?" said Freddy.

"Men visitors," said Mildred.

Constance blanched and took a hasty sip from her empty glass.

Freddy hooted. "What the hell, Mildred. We're all adults here. If Esther had something going on the side—not that I'm saying she did, mind you—it was no crime."

"If she was murdered," said Mildred, "that was a crime."

"If," repeated Freddy.

"I must point out," said Mildred reluctantly, "that the clientele at the St. James seems to be oriented toward, well, a certain kind of occupation."

He tossed down his drink. "Oh for heaven's sake, Mildred, spell it out."

"Toward prostitution." There.

Freddy Townsend coughed as a spray of booze shot up his nasal passages. "Good Christ."

"I'm not implying that Esther was involved in such sordid transactions, of course."

"You'd better not be!" cried Constance. "Tell her she can't say such things, Freddy. We'll sue. There are laws—"

"Please," interrupted Mildred. "We're not the police. And while there are questions here, let me assure you that we have no intention of doing anything official or of making this public in any way. That's part of why Jonathan hired us. To be discreet."

"I should hope so," said Freddy angrily. "For God's sake, Mildred, the woman's dead. What's to be gained by these trashy innuendoes?"

Mildred stood her ground. "Listen Freddy, we have evidence indicating that somebody killed Esther."

That caught Freddy Townsend's attention all right.

"So far numerous factors point to that fact. What we don't know is why and who. Is there anything either of you can tell me that might help us find Esther's killer?"

"Maybe it would be better all around," said Freddy, "just to leave it alone. She's dead, after all. Nothing can bring her back."

"Nevertheless," demurred Constance, "if someone did this thing, perhaps they should be punished."

Freddy looked at his wife in disbelief.

"Go ahead," challenged Constance. "Ask your questions, Mildred. But I can't imagine anything we say will be of help."

"Who might have wanted to kill her?"

"No one," said Constance instantly.

"Certainly not us," snapped Freddy.

"Oh Freddy, Mildred was hardly implying—"

"Certainly not, Freddy. I'm only trying to determine . . ."

They talked for a long while. Mildred proceeded to go round and round with Freddy and Constance, eliciting endless pointless details about Esther Maine, her habits, and her friends. According to Constance nothing seemed amiss during lunch that day.

"I don't know what you expect us to tell you," said Constance finally in exasperation. "Why don't you just talk to that psychiatrist of hers?"

"Oh for heaven's sakes, Connie," said Freddy. "He's not going to be any help."

Mildred blinked. "She was seeing a psychiatrist?"

"Yes," said Constance. "It was ridiculous really. Totally uncalled for. But the court insisted, and she had no choice."

"I'm afraid you've lost me," said Mildred. "The court?"

"Oh," said Constance. She waved her hand, dismissing the matter. "There was some trumped-up incident about shoplifting of all things. The very idea. It was totally absurd, of course, and totally blown out of proportion."

"What incident?"

Here Freddy took over. "There was a misunderstanding over at Van Cleef and Arpels," he said. "A dumbass clerk—pardon my French—accused Esther of trying to leave the store with some trinket."

"A trinket?"

"A diamond bracelet," said Constance airily. "It was totally preposterous, of course. Esther had no taste for jewelry, and if she'd wanted a diamond bracelet, Jonathan would have bought her one. In a minute. A much finer piece than the bracelet in question, I might add."

"But it got sticky," continued Freddy. "The clerk wouldn't back down. Esther got quite hysterical. She called me, and I brought my lawyer into the picture. He said it would be dangerous to try to pay off the little weasel. So it went to court."

"Perfectly ghastly," shuddered Constance.

"Fortunately it was a first offense."

"A first offense," echoed Constance.

"And the judge dismissed the case."

"On the stipulation," added Constance, "that she see a psychiatrist. So she did." Constance smiled.

"I see," said Mildred. "And what was the name of this psychiatrist?"

"Dr. Alexander Blaustein," said Constance proudly.

"Shrinks always seem to be Jews, don't they?" commented Freddy, apropos of nothing.

"Everyone who's anyone sees Alexander Blaustein," said Constance. "All the best people."

"I don't," said Freddy.

I didn't, thought Mildred. I saw the Goodyear Blimp. "I don't think I've ever heard of him," she said.

"I'm not surprised, Mildred," said Freddy. "He's well known among people who count, but Blaustein keeps a low profile. He doesn't usually see women either. His patients are men. The movers and shakers, don't you know."

"But he made an exception for Esther?" asked Mildred.

"Yup," said Freddy proudly. "I got her to him through a connection—fellow at my club. Some mucky muck who's got plenty of contacts. We wanted someone discreet, of course, and this chap said Blaustein is as discreet as they come."

"I see. Well, I suppose we could talk with him." She took off her glasses, put them in her purse, and snapped it shut. "One last question," she said at last. "I hate to ask. It's just a formality really."

"Yes?" said Freddy warily.

"Where were each of you on the night of July eighteenth?" She held her breath and waited for thunder to rumble.

"Oh for Christ's sake!" snapped Freddy. "This really is going too far, Mildred." He crushed out his cigarette angrily.

"Go ahead, Freddy," said Constance. "Tell her."

Once again Mildred detected the hint of a challenge in Constance's voice.

"Very well," said Freddy shortly. "I was here. We were together. Constance and I. Weren't we, pet?"

Mildred looked to Constance for confirmation.

"Yes." Constance smiled grimly. "I suppose we're each other's alibis, aren't we? Isn't that what one would call it?"

"Yes," said Mildred.

No further details about Esther Maine emerged from Constance or Freddy Townsend after that. They sat united in stiff replies and clipped tones. They promised to call if they thought of anything else, but Mildred doubted they would.

"Very well," she said finally and stood up. "I'd best be going." Once again she squeezed Constance's hand, this time not allowing it to be wrested away. "Constance, I really am sorry about your loss. And I will try not to make it any more painful than it already is."

"Will you?" said Constance hollowly. Mildred's interrogation, such as it was, seemed to have rattled her badly.

She slumped back in the couch and didn't bother to get up. Even her chiffon seemed to have wilted.

"I'll hail you a cab," said Freddy, bolting to his feet.

"James will help me," said Mildred.

"It's rush hour," said Freddy smoothly. "Two hailers are better than one, and James is worse than none."

He walked her down to the marble foyer and stopped at the front door. He stood there for some moments fiddling with the change in his pocket.

"I guess you'll be looking at Esther's life pretty closely," he said at last.

"It will require that, yes," said Mildred.

"Probably won't find out a damn thing."

"Maybe not," she replied. "Last time might have been beginner's luck."

Freddy remembered the last time now. The time they'd tracked down that serial killer. It had been in all the papers. Christ.

"Listen . . ." Freddy studied his reflection in one of his gold cuff links. "If you find out anything, let me know, okay? Before you tell Constance, I mean. She's vulnerable right now, and I'd like to help her through this, to whatever extent I can."

"How very decent of you, Freddy," remarked Mildred dryly.

"Well," he beamed, "that's just the way I am. The way I was brought up, you know. Breeding will tell, after all."

"Indeed," said Mildred.

Hoping the fresh air would do her good, she walked up to Fifth Avenue and hailed her own cab.

"So," she said bitterly, "did you put the make on her too?"

"Shut up," snapped Freddy. "You don't know what the hell you're talking about, Connie."

"My, aren't we testy."

"Why the hell did you have to tell her about Blaustein?"

"I got her off our backs, didn't I?" Constance smiled mirthlessly. "Maybe I did you a favor."

"Or maybe," said Freddy, "you did yourself one."

"Go to hell."

Before the others got home, Forrest received a phone call. "How's everything going?" asked a voice without preamble.

"Jon? Is that you?"

"Yes."

"It's only been a couple of days, Jon. Not much can happen in—"

"I know, but I'm going crazy sitting here, Forrest. The days are endurable because I have my work, but the nights . . . I lie awake, wondering. And here I sit in the clinic, about to go home, about to face another night . . . Can't you tell me anything?"

"Well . . ." Forrest tried to think of something positive. "We went to the St. James and talked to the desk clerk. Turns out the guy owns the place. And he remembers Esther."

"He does?" Jonathan's voice escalated hopefully.

"Yeah. His name is Higgins, Gordon Higgins. He dozed off at the desk the night she died, but we'll talk to him again. Could be he'll remember something."

"I hope so."

"Someone else was there too, not that she'll be much help. Lady named Cora Parks. She's homeless, hangs around the lobby. She knew Camille, I mean Esther."

"What did she tell you?"

"Nothing worth diddly. Cora's alcoholic. In a constant fog." He could sense Jonathan's disappointment. "But what the hell, maybe the fog will lift."

"Maybe."

"Now don't go getting discouraged. This is only the beginning. Mildred's out talking to Constance. Trevor's talking to the ME. And Irene's—" He stopped himself, not wanting to tell Jonathan about Claudia. Hell, maybe the name in the book wasn't even Claudia anyway.

"What about Irene?"

"Nothing," lied Forrest. "She's just tagging along with Millie. Just try to relax, Jon. Try to forget about this for the time being. I know it's hard."

"Impossible is more like it."

"Don't you worry, we've got other cards up our sleeve. Tomorrow I'm going to talk with folks in the building across the alley from the St. James. I noticed an office with a good view of room three-twelve. There was a guy looking down at me. Who knows? Maybe he saw something. Maybe he was working late."

"Maybe." Jonathan didn't sound hopeful.

"Buck up, Jon. Something will turn up."

"I hope so, Forrest. Now that this has started, I want to play it to the end. I want to get the sonofabitch who did this. Sometimes I think I could kill him with my bare hands. I have dreams about . . . about killing him."

"Jesus, Jon. Don't talk like that. Go home. Be with your children. They need you, Jon. Remember that."

21 "There's something going on," said Mildred that evening.

"What?" asked Irene. "What's going on?"

"Something between Freddy and Esther. He was so edgy when he saw me to the door, fidgeting, playing with his change and his cuff links. I think he's hiding something. And whatever it is, he's afraid we'll find out."

"It sounds to me," said Trevor, "as though both of

them were hiding something. Freddy and Constance, I mean." And me too, he thought. He fingered the photo in his pocket, which, for some reason he couldn't quite understand, he was reluctant to share just yet. Maybe it was privacy. Maybe Esther deserved some shred of it, even now.

"They do a disturbing little dance," Mildred went on, "the way they parry with one another. There was a distinct undercurrent of hostility, yet they seemed inextricably bound together in some way."

"Maybe one of them did it," said Irene, "and the other is protecting them."

"Perhaps," said Mildred, "but I really can't imagine Freddy or Constance killing anyone. Neither is the type."

"Oh yeah?" said Forrest. "No one's the type, take it from me. That's what makes finding the killer so damn difficult."

"What we have to find out," said Trevor, "is what provoked the crime. It might not have been justifiable, but nonetheless something provoked Esther's murder. Some catalyst."

"Folks kill for a lot of reasons," put in Forrest. He eased back in his chair and took a quick sip of ginger ale. "Greed. Anger. Fear. Jealousy."

"Craziness," added Irene.

"Yeah," agreed Forrest. "Hell, maybe it was Claudia. She had motive. And opportunity."

"Claudia doesn't act crazy," said Irene. "She acts angry."

"Oh," said Trevor, "I don't think Claudia could be prone to such violence."

"Trevor," reminded Forrest, "you haven't seen Claudia Maine in—what?—a year or more?"

"Something like that," Trevor admitted. "And it pains me greatly to hear about her current situation, I must say."

"It's not so bad," Irene reminded him. "I just hope they don't throw her out on the street."

"What about Jonathan?" asked Mildred. "What about that awful business of reconstructing her face?" She looked to Trevor, whose own chat with Dr. Murphy had corroborated this ghastly piece of information.

"I told you," said Forrest, "I checked out his alibi."

"Still seems mighty strange," said Irene.

"I for one am worried," said Trevor, "about the fact that someone else is asking questions about Esther Maine's death."

"Whatever do you mean?" asked Mildred.

Trevor told them about Dr. Patricia Murphy's visitor.

"That's unnerving," said Mildred. "Whoever it was could be the murderer. He's bound to hear about us if he talks to the same people involved in the case. I'd say our paths are likely to cross."

"I don't like it," said Irene darkly.

But Forrest was not about to be deterred by some phantom out there asking questions. "If he is, we'll find him before he finds us. And the best way to do that is to concentrate on the murder. During the act the perpetrator will almost always reveal his pathology."

"Say what?" said Irene.

"Under stress during the act the murderer gives away information about himself. Take the scene, for example."

"The scene was no help," said Trevor. "It had already been cleaned thoroughly. The police didn't even follow proper procedure. They just assumed it was an accident, zipped the body into a bag and packed up her belongings."

"That in itself seems strange, the lack of clues I mean. And the position of the body, that too. And I keep thinking about her eyes. You know, the way they were crushed. The killer must have done it after she was dead. I keep thinking there's a clue there too."

Forrest had tried to say exactly that to Chief Ballinger at the Midtown Precinct earlier that afternoon. But Patrick Gerrard Ballinger would have none of it. . . .

• • •

"Forget it," Ballinger told him bluntly. *"Like I told the husband, the lady took a dive in the bathtub. I don't care what the medical examiner says. It was a freakish accident, nothing more."*

"But—"

"But nothing. There was blood in the grout and no splatters. Her face was flattened against tile. I saw the impressions myself. Then she slid onto the faucets."

"But this case—"

"This case—not that there ever was any case—is closed. Don't waste your time."

"It's my time to waste," said Forrest doggedly, *"and I for one don't think you're giving this woman's death its due."*

A cynical smile blossomed on Ballinger's florid face. *"Death its due? You got a way with words."* Then the smile evaporated. *"Look, pops—what'd you say your name was?"*

Pops. The barb stung. *"Forrest,"* he snarled. *"Forrest T. Haggarty. Former chief of police of Raven's Wing, Connecticut."*

"Right," said Ballinger in a bored tone. *"Look Haggarty, things are different in Connecticut. A wealthy area like that. You have one homicide—what?—every ten years or so? Every ten years tops, and you think it's a big fucking event. Here it's different."*

"I don't think so," said Forrest, thinking murder is murder no matter where it happens.

"I got homicides coming out the wazoo. More than we can keep up with. Good people, bad people, all kinds of people, see? The only way we make any headway is to concentrate on stiffs that matter."

"What's that supposed to mean?"

"It means," said Ballinger evenly, *"I don't have time to waste on dead hookers. Even rich ones. That's what it means."*

Forrest held himself very still, afraid for what he might do or say. Afraid for his heart too, because right now he *was so angry he thought it might jump out of his chest.*

"She was a wife," he said quietly. "A wife and a mother of four children. That counts for something."

"Yeah?" said Ballinger. "From where I sit she was also turning tricks at the St. James Hotel. You came in here to tell me that like it was some big surprise or something. Hell, you think I don't know what goes on in my precinct?"

"You don't know for a fact she was engaging in prostitution," Forrest shot back.

"She was staying at the St. James." Ballinger grinned. "That's enough for me."

"You know, Ballinger, for a dead hooker this case sure seems to get you riled. Why, it almost seems like you've got some kind of hard-on for this lady."

Ballinger reacted instantly. Color poured into his face and he gripped the edge of the desk with meaty hands.

"Look, Haggarty, I don't have to take this shit! I knew who the lady was, I knew what was going on, and I looked the other way. Big deal. In the great scheme of things a bored housewife hooking on the side wasn't the biggest crime in the world."

Yeah, thought Forrest. And maybe she did you a favor or two to look the other way.

"If you want to know the truth, I didn't like the broad very much. She disgusted me, in fact."

"Why?"

"You want me to paint you a picture? Here was a lady who had everything—family, money, social position. The works. And what does she do? She fucks around where she's got no business fucking. No business at all. Tricks for kicks, that's what it amounted to. Not like some junkie trying to earn her next fix. Hell, that's understandable. It's got more dignity by comparison. This was sick."

"You seem to know a lot about her," commented Forrest.

"Get out of here," said Ballinger quietly.

But Forrest was determined. "What'd you know about

her, Ballinger? Come on, you two were friendly, right?"

"If you don't get out of here right now, I'll have an officer escort you to the street, Haggarty. Or to a holding cell."

"You didn't even try to find out who did this," Forrest accused.

"Reilly!" barked Ballinger.

"Well you didn't!" repeated Forrest.

A thin, nervous officer materialized. He had very white skin and red-rimmed eyes.

"Show Mr. Haggarty out."

"Yes, sir." Officer Reilly grabbed Forrest's elbow and hoisted him to his feet, "This way."

"I know the way," snarled Forrest. Already Reilly had him halfway out the door.

"You said there were no splatters," Forrest cried, "but—"

"Jesus Christ," roared Ballinger. "Get him the fuck out of here! Someone give me a break!"

"—I bet you didn't check everywhere! I bet you didn't!"

"Jeesum!" exclaimed Irene. "Why didn't we think of that?"

" 'Cause everyone can't be as brilliant as me, that's why."

Mildred's response was less enthusiastic. "I suppose that means we're going back to the St. James tomorrow. To check for splatters."

"Nope," replied Forrest smiling, "cause I already did."

"And what did you find?" said Trevor.

"Huh? Oh. Yeah. I found 'em. The splatters. They were around the doorframe. Tiny brown flecks. I didn't need a lab to tell me what they were."

"So she was murdered," said Trevor.

"No doubt about it."

"And that police chief's covering it up. You see? It's just like I said."

"Not necessarily," replied Forrest. "Ballinger's just

afraid of looking like the asshole he is. We're not stepping back now, Trevor. Not after all this."

"We really should keep going," said Mildred. "For Esther's sake. Why, I almost feel she's here with us."

"I thought you might be less inclined now, Millie, considering her reputation."

"Esther Maine didn't have a reputation," said Trevor thoughtfully. "Camille Smith did."

"A hooker," said Irene. "Who would believe it?"

"Now Irene," chided Mildred, "like Forrest said, we don't know that for a fact."

"Well Cora over at the St. James said she had men friends."

"Still," said Mildred, "the woman isn't here to defend herself. So let's try not to be judgmental."

"It would be helpful," added Trevor, "if we could determine who her, ah, friends were."

Irene turned to Forrest. "What's the next step?"

"For one thing, Trevor's going to have a little talk with Alexander Blaustein. Doctor to doctor."

"It's August," reminded Mildred. "Psychiatrists always vacation in August."

"Well, Trevor will just have to track him down then." Forrest grimaced. "I sure as hell hope he isn't in Europe."

"I'd kinda like to visit Claudia Maine again," said Irene. "I think I could get close to her. Underneath all that nastiness she needs a friend."

"I was hoping you'd see it that way, Reenie." Forrest looked at his notes. "And you, Millie, I want you to cozy up to Constance and Freddy."

"I doubt they'll be very receptive."

"You never can tell. Give Constance time to sleep on it. She might need a friend too."

"Not if she's the killer," said Mildred. "But then I can't imagine that she is."

"Just be careful," said Trevor.

"Right," said Forrest. "It's like walking through a mine field. Watch your step."

"And what about you, Forrest?" asked Mildred. "Who are you going to see?"

"Never you mind," said Forrest cryptically. "I got someone in mind, but it'll probably turn out to be a dead end."

"I say we forget all this for the time being," interrupted Irene. "I'm hungry. What about dinner?"

"Mildred and I planned to go out," said Trevor.

"Great," said Irene enthusiastically. "Where we goin'?"

"Irene," said Mildred gently, "Trevor and I thought we might make it a twosome this one time. I hope you don't mind."

"Mind?" Irene's look of puzzlement dissolved into embarrassment. "Oh! Sure, Millie. Great. That's just great. Forrest and I always said you two should get together, haven't we Forrest?"

"Oh for heaven's sake," sputtered Mildred, "it's only dinner."

Forrest sighed. "I suppose Irene and I can get a hot dog somewhere. One of those Sabrettes on the street or the like."

"There are chicken cutlets in the fridge," said Mildred, "and fresh vegetables. And frozen yogurt."

"Christ," groaned Forrest.

"Don't knock it until you've tried it," said Mildred. "And anyway you have. The ice cream you had last night was frozen yogurt, and you couldn't tell the difference."

"I could too," replied Forrest. "I was just being polite."

"That," said Mildred, "is a contradiction in terms."

22 The first thing Gordon Higgins noticed when he entered his tiny apartment on the eleventh floor of the St. James Hotel was that the room was stifling hot. Damn, he thought, the air conditioner isn't running. He hoped it wasn't broken. The unit was a top-of-the-line Emerson Quiet Kool that he'd purchased just that past spring. Six thousand blessed BTUs hooked up to an automatic timer set to kick in precisely at 8:30 P.M. so his small apartment would be cool and comfortable upon his arrival at nine.

Please don't let it be broken. Not tonight. The return of Mr. Haggarty was more than I could take. I'm sweaty and tired and about ready to collapse. If the air conditioner is broken I'll have to sleep in one of the regular guest rooms. God forbid.

Gordon flipped on a lamp, brushed past a glowing tank of tropical fish, and bent over to check the timer. It was in perfect order. Then he noticed that the master switch on the Emerson itself had been turned off.

Strange. Maybe I brushed against it or something.

The mournful sound of a distant siren made him look toward the only other window in the room. He smelled the cloying scent of garbage mingled with street exhaust and realized that the double-hung window was wide open.

Gordon Higgins froze in place. Despite the sweltering heat, he felt a chill. He never opened that window. It had been painted shut, intentionally so. The air outside was filled with carcinogens, noxious pollutants and airborne filth. Gordon, who tended toward hypochondria, drank bottled water and breathed filtered air whenever possible. He tried to keep his body pure. In fact, if he could have done so without looking like a screwball, he would have worn a gas mask on the street.

His mind churned with possibilities. Clearly someone had entered his apartment. Someone had opened his window. Someone who was, perhaps, still here.

Gordon licked his dry lips and slowly surveyed the tidy living room . . . his precious stamp collection neatly arranged on the leather-topped desk . . . the *Smithsonians* stacked in precise chronological order on the coffee table . . . the carefully dusted Mayan figures he'd purchased in the Yucatán with his late wife on their honeymoon.

These objects had once been a source of comfort. Now they looked alien and threatening. This was no longer home, it was a place of danger.

I must leave. At once.

It was then that he heard a familiar snarl. Walter. The cat had been with Gordon ever since his wife died and now was the only family he had. Gordon had selected Walter at the shelter on East Ninety-second Street when no one else would have him. Walter was an arrogant seal point Siamese with arresting blue eyes and enormous balls. He was a beautiful specimen, everyone said so. But unfortunately Walter had a taste for human flesh. If you held your hand up and clicked your fingers, Walter would leap to extraordinary heights in the hope of drawing blood. When the SPCA attendant put on a leather glove and demonstrated this, Gordon was amazed.

Gordon, who appreciated things of beauty, took possession of the cat no one wanted and promptly had him altered. He hoped the surgical procedure would deter Walter from staking out his territory by spraying in inappropriate places, and it did. He also hoped it would ameliorate the animal's aggressive tendencies. It did not.

He scooped up the cat and tried to keep his voice calm. "It's all right, old buddy. Everything's all—" He whirled around.

The face was grotesque, mashed flat under a nylon stocking. Whoever it was was wearing a trench coat—Gordon's trench coat—and holding a handgun.

My gun. Oh my God.

"Take whatever you want," said Gordon. "There's money in the register downstairs. Not much, but you can have it. And I've got some things here, valuable things." It was a lie, of course. Gordon had nothing of value. Gordon was in hock up to his eyeballs. But he was desperate. "I've got a diamond engagement ring. It was my wife's." God, he hoped the silent figure didn't carry a jeweler's loupe. "She's dead. Leukemia." Gordon seized on his wife's death like a lifeline. "We were married for five years, five of the happiest years of my life. We didn't have children, couldn't have children. And when we went for tests, it turned out she had—"

A hand lashed out and whipped the gun brutally across Gordon's forehead. He dropped the cat and lurched back, clutching his bloody face in both hands, blinking back pain and tears. He struggled mightily to rein in his pain and terror. He could not believe this was happening.

"My stamp collection," he managed to say. "You can have that. It's worth thousands."

The shape in the trench coat advanced and Gordon staggered back against the sill of the window.

"Anything!" he cried. "I'll give you anything!"

Pressed under the nylon, the flat lips seemed to smile. The gun dropped to Gordon's feet.

He felt weak with relief.

"Thank you," he heard himself saying. "Thank you."

Suddenly a pair of hands reached out and shoved him. To his horror, he felt himself fall backward into the open window.

"No!" he cried. "Noooooooooooo!"

For one exquisite moment his knees locked around the

lip of the window. But only for a moment. He felt disembodied hands flip his legs up and out, felt his heels scrape against the concrete ledge, and felt himself fall free.

The fall seemed to last forever. City lights swirled around him.

Relief washed over Gordon one last time. He was dreaming. Of course. Soon he would wake up. Soon everything would be fine.

Gordon Higgins clung to his delusion all the way down. He marveled at the beauty, the clarity, of the street below as pavement rushed to greet him.

23 "Do you think we have sex enough?"

"Jeesum, Forrest, what a question."

Forrest hiked himself up on one elbow, leaned over Irene, and kissed her enthusiastically. "Well, do you?"

"You don't hear me complaining, do you?"

"No, Reenie. But maybe you're just being kind. Maybe you don't want to hurt my feelings. Maybe—"

"Hush," she scolded. "How can you ask such a question, now, after . . ."

"Well," he said as he snuggled against her, "it's just that we had a dry spell there after that business with my heart."

"A dry spell. You sure have a way with words, Forrest, I'll give you that."

"Okay, so I'm not a romantic man by nature."

"You do all right," she said. She wrapped her arms around him and held him tight. "More than all right."

"Ahhh, Irene," he sighed contentedly, "what would I do without you?"

"That's something you don't have to worry about. Not now. Not never."

They dozed for a while.

Forrest's mind swirled with fragments of the case. He saw vivid images in exaggerated color, some of them horrifying . . . A long dark corridor flanked by countless doors . . . a scurrying rat with tiny lantern eyes . . . a splintery window frame that held a pale and bloodless face . . . a broken porcelain doll, naked and exposed, without any eyes.

"No!" he cried.

"Hurry up, Dad, it's late."

Late, he thought, it's late. Hurry. His fingers moved slowly, fumbling at folds of fabric.

"How's it going to look if the guest of honor doesn't show?"

Guest of honor? He got up, looked out the window and suddenly felt better. It was a beautiful spring day in Raven's Wing, a day like no other, unfolding like a flower after the deep freeze of winter. Pussy willows and forsythia all around. He could see the town clear as day from his room high in the sky just as though he were in a tree house.

Why, just look . . . there was the old high school . . . and Town Hall . . . and the library before they put the addition on. Jesus, he could see every Main Street shop clear as day. Squash hurried about in the news store, while Florie cheerfully served cherry Cokes to kids sporting greasy ducktail haircuts and black leather jackets. Only Squash wasn't cheerful, oh no. He had a business to run, and smartass punks who nursed nickel Cokes for an hour would drive him to bankruptcy. Plus they shoved pink wads of gum under his Formica counter.

One day Squash would rip out the entire soda fountain in a frenzy of modernization, and the kids with the ducktails and white T-shirts who propped themselves against the brick front of the news store would disappear. Gone to do other things like bowling or balling or whatever the hell kids did.

Forrest raised his fist in salute and did a jig. "You showed 'em, Squash!"

Then his face clouded over. It was an old view. The town wasn't like this anymore. "What's going on, Scott?"

"Here, Dad, let me fix your tie."

"Where we going?"

"To a party, that's all."

"Oh, I get it. My retirement party, right?"

"Sort of."

"They never did give me a retirement party, you know. Forty years on the force and I never got one."

"There. You look good." Scott appraised him one last time. "But can't you do something about that hair?"

"What's wrong with my hair?"

"Well, it's all stuck out. Like Brillo. You look like a wild man."

"I am a wild man. Takes a wild man to keep a lid on this town. Why I remember—"

"Don't start, Dad, we don't have time."

"Oh I'm not starting nothing. But, Jesus, I just thought of that kid they called Charlie Horse, remember him?"

"Yeah. He died in Vietnam."

"I know. But I mean before that. Remember back when he worked after school at DeLoria's Drugs."

"Oh yeah, right." Charlie Horse Hauptman had supplied Scott and his friends with rubbers. Rubbers with pinholes in them.

"DeLoria was crazy to hire Charlie Horse. I tried to tell him. 'DeLoria,' I says, 'letting Charlie Horse Hauptman work in your drugstore is like letting Adolf Hitler manage a Glade factory. There's no telling what'll end up in the canisters.'"

"That's not funny."

"DeLoria didn't think so either. 'Specially after what happened with the Preparation H."

"Dad, we've got to get going."

"Don't you want to know what happened!"

"All right, what happened?"

"It was back before they had tamper-proof packaging, see? Hell, they probably invented tamper-proof packaging 'cause of Charlie Horse Hauptman. 'Cause Charlie Horse squeezed out the Preparation H and squeezed in Infrarub."

"Christ."

"Burned like hell. Franny Watson—"

"Old widow Watson?"

"The very same. She's the one that bought that tube, an' by golly she was smartin'. She raised one helluva hullabaloo. She always was a tightass, and this only made it worse. Two fellas from American Home Products hightailed it down here from Hartford and settled out of court with old Franny. She got sixteen thousand dollars."

"A pretty penny back then."

"You betcha. Franny with the golden fanny, that's what I always called her after that.

" 'Course, DeLoria knew who did it. I'd tried to warn him, but he wouldn't listen. Then when the shit hit the fan, so to speak, he didn't dare tell on Charlie Horse, cause he'da been liable, being it was his store an' all, see?"

"Yeah, Dad, I see."

"Oh he was a pisser all right, that Charlie Horse. I remember the time he put a nest of condoms—unused, but still—under a heap of cole slaw in the deli case over at the Stop N Shop. And Artie O'Leary, he's behind the counter, spoonin' up some slaw for Tillie Potter. Tiller had a real fondness for cole slaw, at least until she saw—"

"Dad, we've got to go!"

"All right!"

Forrest put on his one and only sports jacket. Suddenly his face clouded.

"What is it, Dad?"

"I made him join the army."

"What?"

"Charlie Horse. I made him go sign up."

"Don't start with that, Dad."

"It was the thing with the Brylcreem that did it. What the hell'd he put in there? Nair or some such thing, and that was the last straw. Ripley Crane bought that tube, and he was awful pissed. I had to tell Charlie Horse to get out of town. Told him to join the army. Told him 'that'll learn you not to put condoms in the slaw and Nair in Brylcreem.' Told him—"

"Dad, stop this! Don't go blaming yourself about things long past! You can't take responsibility for every blessed—"

"And he died. Charlie Horse went to Vietnam and he died."

"Yeah." Scott Haggarty looked at his watch, exasperated. "Look, we're all going to die. Some sooner, some later. Nothing stays the same. This town's going to change, and the people in it too. Sometimes I think you'd like to put Raven's Wing and everyone in it under a plastic dome paperweight with swirly snowflakes inside. Some things won't keep . . ." He looked at his watch again. "And this party's one of them. So come *on*."

They went to the Community Center. Everyone Forrest knew was there. People shook his hand, slapped him on the back. It was like old times. All his children were there, and their children too. He drank champagne and no one told him he couldn't. His heart, apparently, was working just fine so he decided to make the most of it. The champagne went to his head.

"What is this," he laughed, "my funeral?"

Everyone stopped talking and looked at him funny.

"Party!" he cried. "Go ahead, have a ball!"

"Dad," whispered Scott.

"Huh?"

"Over there . . ."

"What?" Forrest looked. That was when he saw her.

Queenie. His wife of more than forty years. She was sipping champagne and talking with some of her friends. Giggling. She looked beautiful, like a young girl.

"Oh my," he whispered. He had almost forgotten. Almost.

"You've got to tell her."

Forrest watched his wife, savoring her enjoyment.

"Dad, you've got to tell her."

"Tell her what?"

"That she's dead."

"Oh, Scotty, I can't do that." He shrank back. "Please. Look how happy she is. 'Sides, Queenie's not the only one. There are others here, plenty of others who are . . ."

"Where?" The word was a challenge.

Forrest looked around and saw that he was wrong. He looked from his son Scott to Mildred Bennett to Sonny Joiner from the feed store to the new first selectman, a lovely woman named Sue Mannington . . . to Trevor Bradford . . . to Irene.

Irene. Oh dear. This was a dilemma.

"Mercy," he said.

"You've got to tell her, Dad. No one else can."

"But . . ."

Yet he realized it was true. It was his responsibility and no one else's. So he turned away from his son. He went to his wife of more than forty years and took her hand. She looked at him happily and followed him over to a sofa in the corner. And he told her. Just like that.

She wasn't angry or sad or even surprised.

Somehow he'd known she wouldn't be.

"I'm dead," she said and vanished. Just like that.

She was kind enough not to say, *"And so are you."*

He woke up in a sweat.

"Forrest, honey, you okay?"

He lay there, eyes wide open. "I think so."

"What happened? Bad dream?"

"Not exactly. Strange, not bad."

"You and your dreams," she scoffed, curling herself into the hollow of his stomach.

"I miss her, Irene."

"Who, honey? Who you miss?"

"Queenie." The admission pained him. He wouldn't hurt Irene for the world. "Even with you at my side, sometimes I miss her."

"It's okay, Forrest. Sometimes I miss Earl. Sometimes he just sneaks up on me, you know? And all of a sudden I get teary."

"Oh," he said. "Well." To his surprise he was relieved.

"It's natural, honey, and it's okay."

Suddenly his arms tensed around her. "What's that?"

"What's what?"

"Damned if I didn't hear something . . . There it is again."

"Oh that." Irene jumped out of bed. "That there's the intercom. We got ourselves a visitor."

"A visitor?" said Forrest. "At this hour?"

24 "So what have you been up to all these months?" asked Trevor.

"Oh," she said lightly, "nothing much. Busy with charity work and the like."

"The Manhattan Women's Club?"

"Well," she began, feeling slightly defensive, "yes. It's not all a bunch of snobs, you know."

"I know," he said quickly.

"They do good work."

"And anyone can join."

"Trevor." The implication stung. Of course anyone couldn't join. The Manhattan Women's Club maintained a degree of exclusivity, it was true. That was the way the Club had been since its inception, that was the way it would continue to be, and that was no fault of hers.

"I'm sorry."

"Well I hope so." She looked at him carefully and decided to be forthright. "You've been walking on eggshells ever since you arrived."

"Well, this restaurant . . ."

"I don't mean the restaurant." Although, indeed, the restaurant had been a poor choice. It had started to pour and they ran into a place, any place, as a refuge from the storm. Once inside they discovered the building had been a church in another incarnation, a Catholic church no less, with all the trappings still intact. Stained glass, stone statues and, goodness, even stations of the cross or whatever they were called. Above Mildred's right elbow Christ lurched in frozen relief, stumbling under the weight of his cross for the second or third time, plaster blood and tears streaming down his face. He looked ghastly.

"It's more than this restaurant, Trevor. You haven't been yourself since you came to my apartment."

"Perhaps I feel a bit intimidated," he conceded.

"Whatever for?"

"I knew you were of comfortable means, Mildred, but I never imagined it was like this."

"Like what?" She had no idea what he was talking about.

"Renoirs and Picassos, the antique Steinway, three fireplaces, twelve rooms—"

"Fourteen," she corrected before she could stop herself.

"All right, fourteen. You never told us, Mildred, never gave any indication."

"Indication of what?"

"Of your wealth."

"Of course not," she protested. "It's not something one talks about. What was I supposed to do, Trevor? Say 'Hello, I'm Mildred Bennett. I have fourteen rooms and twenty thousand shares of AT and T. I am a woman of considerable means.' Should I have said that?"

The sing-song imitation of herself was endearing. "No." He smiled. "Of course not."

"These things you point to were Connor's choices, not mine. Good investments, he called them. But anyway they're nothing to be ashamed of."

"Oh I didn't mean you should be ashamed." It's just that I am. In a way. But he didn't say that.

"I don't see what it's all got to do with us."

"I'm a country doctor, Mildred. A country doctor of limited means. An old country doctor at that."

Ah ha, she thought.

"For heaven's sake, Trevor, you're not old."

"I'm fifteen years your senior."

"Who's counting?"

"I guess I am."

"Well, don't. Sometimes you sell yourself short, you really do. Why I remember when I was in high school and you first set up practice in Raven's Wing."

"I was only twenty-eight."

"And so handsome. We all had crushes on you, you know."

"You did?"

"Of course. My old friends would be green with envy if they knew I was sitting here with you right now."

Trevor sat there feeling pleasantly embarrassed and more than a little flattered.

"And as far as the money question is concerned, can't we just put it aside for now? Can't we just enjoy ourselves?"

"People will think I'm a gold digger," he mumbled.

"They will not," she shot back. "And so what if they do? Besides people are hardly watching our every move. We're in New York City after all, not Raven's Wing."

"I suppose."

"Don't you worry about digging any gold. Who do you suppose is going to pay for this fancy dinner?"

"Well, I intended—" He saw the laughter in her eyes and smiled in spite of himself. "Oh, all right. Forget it. Enough said."

"Good. Now what do you think we should order? I'm starved."

"Me too."

They opened heavy menus shaped like biblical tablets and studied them in silence.

"Oh dear," said Mildred finally.

"Oh dear is right. There doesn't seem to be any regular food on this menu, does there?"

"I don't know. The candied crab cakes with mango chutney looks intriguing."

"What about the jalapeño pasta with lobster and cucumber? Now there's a tempting dish."

"Or the polenta studded with braised mushrooms. A steal at nineteen-ninety-five."

"Ah. Polenta."

"I know it's not something anatomical," said Mildred, "but it certainly sounds like it is."

"I know. I'm going to the doctor to get my polenta checked."

Mildred laughed.

"Well I don't want it. It reminds me of California." He sighed. "I suppose we could just order salads and forget the placenta. I mean polenta."

"Let's forget this restaurant entirely. I have my teeth set for a juicy hamburger. Medium rare."

Trevor brightened. "So do I. With french fries and ketchup. Maybe a side order of onion rings. And some kind of pie for dessert. Pecan. Chocolate cream. Key lime." He lowered his voice conspiratorially. "All the stuff Forrest can't eat."

"Now you're talking. That sounds ever so much better than"—she looked at the menu once again and winced—

"curried bratwurst flambé." She cocked her head and thought a moment. "Listen, there's a little place down the block. Kind of a hole in the wall, but they make decent martinis and great burgers."

"Wonderful. Let's get out of here."

They ran through the rain to Chumley's, a tiny dark restaurant at the end of a path behind a leafy courtyard. A Mets game played on a silent flickering TV stuck against one wall. The two of them ordered Beefeater martinis and ate large salty pretzels hard as granite.

"Was the divorce painful?" he found himself asking.

"Yes. But it was rather like having a tooth extracted. Painful at the time, but a relief afterwards. The divorce itself was not so painful as the years that preceded it . . . the silences that stretched between us, the affairs he had, the bitterness between us. It affected me, I'm afraid. I did some things I'm not so proud of."

Not that she'd tell Trevor in detail, of course. Some of the things she'd done had been childish. And some had been downright disgusting. Like the time she scoured the toilet bowl with Connor's toothbrush and later watched, delighted, as he brushed his teeth with his usual vigor and precision.

"But nothing was as painful as when we lost Sam. You go through something like that, and everything else pales by comparison."

"Of course," he said, taking her hand under the table.

"Well, you know what I'm talking about, losing Mary Margaret so recently."

"It stopped me in my tracks for a while, I admit it. And even now I have my moments. But I've often thought divorce is worse on a person. At least with a death there's a finality to it. And there's no anger—except the anger at being abandoned. With a death there's sadness, but at least there are the good memories."

"Oh I'm not angry at Connor anymore. I almost feel sorry for him in a way. He's blundering around, making a fool of himself. He married his last girlfriend, you know."

"Really?"

"Couldn't stand to be alone. Why is it like that with men anyway?"

"I don't know," he said automatically. He almost told her he couldn't stand being alone either. Couldn't stand coming home to an empty house. Couldn't stand eating stale crackers and Cheez Whiz alone in the kitchen. Couldn't stand waking up in the morning with no one beside him. And most of all he couldn't stand going to bed at the end of a day no one cared to hear about. But he told her none of these things.

"Anyway he married her. The bride wore white, can you imagine? And Molly was maid of honor."

"Molly?"

"My daughter."

"For heaven's sake," sputtered Trevor.

"I know, I know. It didn't seem right to me at the time either. But I got used to it. It's a new world we're living in, Trevor. Emily Post just doesn't cut it anymore."

"People should still have consideration for other people's feelings. And a child might show more sensitivity for a parent, if you don't mind my saying so."

"It's all right. Really. Molly and I are closer now than we've ever been. We talk on the phone. See each other once a week or so for dinner. We even go shopping together sometimes." She paused. "Of course, she lets me do the buying."

"My children are the same," he commiserated. "Sometimes they seem so grasping. So selfish." He dropped his voice. "My son tried to swindle me out of my house."

"No!"

"I tried not to believe it at first. I tried to tell myself his heart was in the right place and that he was only being kind. But I was living in a fool's paradise."

"What happened?"

"After Mary Margaret died, he came over for a little chat—all the way from Chicago. He never visits, so I knew something was up. Anyway, he said he thought the house was too much for me to manage. I almost agreed—what with mowing the lawn, cleaning the gutters, getting the driveway plowed in winter, and the like. Plus the place needs a new roof. It's always something."

"Did he suggest a condominium?"

"Not exactly. He offered to buy the house from me, and let me live in it for the time being."

"For the time being?"

"Yes. Actually that part was never clearly defined. But the price was. He offered me half of the market value."

"Well for goodness sake, why only half?"

"That was what he could afford. When I pressed him on this point he as much as said he wanted his inheritance now. That was how he looked at it."

"Why that little weasel!"

"He made no apology for it either. Seemed to think it was a most reasonable expectation. That it was his *due*. Sometimes I blame myself. I raised him, after all."

"Don't, Trevor. It's the way all young people are today, especially those raised in comfortable circumstances. They have no idea how to work for anything."

"Sometimes I think I should just do what old Lucas Petry did."

"What was that?"

"His kids were after him to sell his farm to developers. They said the market was right, that they were thinking of his best interests. His golden years. But what they really wanted was to get their hands on that money."

"Oh dear."

"Lucas was in failing health and knew he couldn't keep up the place. But he fixed their wagons."

Mildred leaned forward. "How?"

"He went and sold the farm. For a pretty penny too. But then he took all the money—in cash, stacks of it—put it in his silo, and burned the whole place down."

"No!"

"Yes."

Trevor didn't have the heart to tell Mildred the rest of the story. Didn't have the heart to tell her that Lucas Petry knew he had Alzheimer's. That Lucas lay down in the corn crib while the farm burned around him. That Lucas never tried to run, just let himself burn along with his place.

"You look so sad all of a sudden."

"Me? Oh no, just thinking. You know, about folks."

Mildred held Trevor's hand and decided to veer to a happier subject. "Molly and I took a vacation together last March. You wouldn't have believed it. We went to Cozumel. Club Med."

"Club what? Oh God, I remember. One of those swinging singles resorts."

"It was her idea," laughed Mildred. "Not mine. She got it into her head that it would be a good way for me to meet somebody. Lord, it was awful. Hairy-chested dentists from Long Island wearing so many gold chains it's a wonder they didn't sink in the swimming pool."

"So did you?" asked Trevor with studied nonchalance.

"Did I what?"

"Meet anybody?"

"No one I cared for. No one like you."

25 By the time Mildred and Trevor got home it was late indeed. They were startled to find Forrest sitting in the living room reading a copy of *Modern Maturity*.

"You didn't have to wait up, Forrest," said Trevor. "I have her home safe and sound. See?" Trevor gestured to Mildred with exaggerated flourish.

Mildred giggled and curtsied.

"You two are three sheets to the wind."

"We are not!" cried Mildred. She tried to regain her equilibrium.

"Now, Forrest," said Trevor.

"Okay," sighed Forrest. "Never mind. We got ourselves a problem."

"What sort of problem?" asked Mildred, her celebratory mood dissolving into concern.

"Higgins."

Trevor blinked. "Gordon Higgins? The owner of the St. James?"

"The very same. Seems he killed himself."

They recoiled as though simultaneously slapped.

"Took a dive out his apartment window."

"When?" asked Mildred shakily.

"Just a few hours ago. Fell eleven stories. Went right through the roof of a Volvo sedan. They had to hose it down after."

Suddenly hamburger and french fries and chocolate mousse pie congealed into a ball and tumbled around in Mildred's stomach.

Trevor hovered at her elbow. "Mildred, are you all right?"

"Yes," she said after a moment. She walked unsteadily to the sofa and sat down next to Forrest. She didn't feel all right at all. She feared she might throw up.

Forrest snorted. "Apparently he was despondent because of his wife. She died of leukemia a few years back."

"How did you hear about all this, Forrest?" asked Trevor.

"Cora told us, me and Irene."

Mildred looked at him curiously. "Cora?"

"Cora Parks. You remember. The rummy from the lobby. The one with the knitting. She was standing on the sidewalk when it happened, taking in some air. Heard a high-pitched shriek, looked up, and saw a body careening down. Really shook her up."

"Lord," said Trevor, "the poor woman. Where is she now?"

"In one of the back bedrooms." Forrest jerked his thumb.

Mildred snapped out of sympathy and into sobriety. "She's where?"

"I think it's a maid's room. Got a bitty bathroom with a bathtub on claw feet."

Mildred felt her hackles rise. "She can't stay here."

"Well I didn't know where the hell else to put her. She's all we've got now, our only witness. It's a lucky thing she found our address in her pocket and made her way here, I'll tell you that, what with the condition she was in."

Mildred shuddered, imagining very well the kind of condition Cora must have been in.

"That snooty doorman of yours wanted to call the cops and have her carted off to Bellevue."

"That's exactly where I'd like to put her," she said sourly.

"We got to protect her. Her and the cat too." He made a face. "Damn cat."

Mildred's eyes narrowed. "What cat?"

"Higgins's cat. Weird blue eyes. Mean son of a bitch. After Higgins took his leap, Cora ran up to his apartment. Between you and me, I think maybe she was going to see what all she could grab. But all she grabbed was the damned cat."

"And she brought it here?" Mildred's voice edged up hysterically. "A cat!"

"Don't worry, I fixed up a litter box. Found a porcelain roaster with flowers—"

"My Rosenthal!"

"—and Irene found some cat food."

Mildred felt like crying. "There's no cat food in this apartment. Winston can't abide cats." She could not believe she was having this conversation.

"That's true," said Forrest mildly. "Winnie piddled all

over the carpet when he saw that cat—don't worry, we cleaned it up. We got Winston settled down all right, then Reenie scouted around for some cat food. Found a can of pâté—looked like baby shit—and another bitty can of sardines."

Mildred threw her head back against the sofa and closed her eyes.

Trevor tried to veer away from the subject of the cat. "Forrest is right about protecting Cora. We can't have her walking the streets now, can we?"

Why not? thought Mildred. Half of Manhattan is homeless. They walk the streets and are none the worse for wear. But in her heart she knew this attitude was cruel and uncharitable. Her mind searched for a more acceptable solution to this most disagreeable situation . . . Cora . . . the cat . . . protection . . . sanctuary . . .

"I know!" she cried.

"Huh?" said Forrest.

"Martha Abbington."

"Who the hell's Martha Abbington?"

"We do charity work together sometimes. Martha is very into the homeless cause. She's on the board of Harmony House."

"What's that?" asked Trevor.

"Harmony House is a residence for senior citizens. Very fine. Very expensive. But they take indigent cases on occasion." Especially if the indigent person in question has connections, but she didn't say that. "They even take pets. I'm sure I can get Cora in. Tonight if need be." She moved to get up. Tonight it would be.

Trevor knelt beside her. "Mildred honey, it's a wonderful idea you have. A wonderful generous idea. But you can't call this Abbington woman now. It's nearly midnight."

Mildred slumped back in the cushions. "I suppose not," she said. "But first thing in the morning that's what I'm going to do." That woman, she thought. That cat. They both go. First thing in the morning.

"Right," said Forrest. "First thing in the morning. We'll each do our thing. Trevor'll see that shrink. Irene'll see Claudia again. And me? I intend to chat with the fellow who works in the office across the alley from Esther's room. Who knows? Maybe he saw something."

"Harmony House!"

The words cracked like a whip. There, swaying in the doorway, wearing one of Mildred's finest silk nightgowns, was a very inebriated Cora Parks, her freshly laundered hair wrapped in one of Mildred's monogrammed towels, an empty glass in her hand.

"It sounds like a loony bin. Or a funeral home. I don't want to go!"

Forrest yawned and got up. "We'll discuss it in the morning."

"There's nothing to discuss," said Mildred firmly. "She goes or I go."

"Do you have any more of that sherry?" Cora asked no one in particular. "My glass has run dry."

26 "Sir, as I've already explained, Mr. Winkler simply cannot see you without an appointment."

"You could at least call him."

"There's simply no point."

Simply, thought Forrest. And this is simply bullshit. He surveyed the massive receptionist planted squarely in his path and wondered if he'd met his match. She wore lace-up orthopedic shoes, a voluminous flowered dress, and was as shapely as a cement pillar. She reminded him of the old maid teachers he had back in grade school, bright, stifled women all of them, with sagging tits that stretched down to their belts.

He sat himself in a cordovan leather sofa. "Well then, I'll just have to wait until he comes out, won't I? The man can't stay in there forever."

Rita Lynn Peters looked at the stubborn old man and felt her blood pressure rise. Damn, why was this happening? Why today of all days, her last day on the job? I've had enough bad luck lately, thought Rita Lynn bitterly. Give me a break.

"You'll have a long wait," she remarked darkly. "He works very long hours, Mr. Winkler does."

"Oh yeah? What kind of work?" The musty reception area with its ponderous furniture and sterile matted prints on the walls gave no indication of the underlying purpose of Parker McKenzie and Swaine.

"Management consulting. Look, Mr. . . ."

"Haggarty. Forrest T."

" . . . Mr. Haggarty, today's my last day here and I don't want any trouble."

"I'm not making trouble."

"Yes you are. You're an unauthorized visitor. If you insist on sitting there, I'll have to call security. It's my job."

"How come you're leaving?" asked Forrest, trying to change the subject.

Rita Lynn considered the question and felt her stomach start to churn. Damn his snoopiness anyway. Of course she wouldn't tell him why she was leaving. She wouldn't tell anyone. She wouldn't tell him it was because of a stupid baby shower.

"Because of a stupid baby shower," she blurted.

"Huh?"

God, she could remember it clear as day, the horrific circumstances of her demise at Parker McKenzie and Swaine. The horrific *humiliating* circumstances . . .

• • •

After the first glass of champagne at Madeline Kroll's baby shower, Rita Lynn had known she should exercise temperance, but somehow she didn't care. She batted mascaraed eyelashes at Niles Johnson and told him he was cute. Niles Johnson was head of the accounting department, but Rita Lynn didn't care about that. He was also half her age, and she didn't care about that either.

Underneath it all what Rita Lynn did care about was the fact that now, at forty-eight, she still lived at home with her parents. In Queens. She had no social life to speak of, no contact with friends, except at the office. And at the office her coworkers thought she was an ogre. Most of the time Rita Lynn supposed they were right.

As the receptionist of long standing at Parker McKenzie and Swaine, Rita Lynn was the unofficial office manager and rather like the assistant principal in a high school. She was the disciplinarian. She kept the attendance records. She docked the clericals if they were late or if sick days taken exceeded those allowed. She monitored the lunch hour with a vengeance, always watching and jotting down on a jotter block the names of those who sashayed back tardy. Rita Lynn never went out to lunch herself. She ate a single clump of tuna at her desk, ready to bolt on elephantine legs to the sound of any unanswered telephone. She was a martyr.

In reality Rita Lynn Peters was shy, so much so that if someone else walked into the ladies' room while she was going to the bathroom, she'd sing "The Battle Hymn of the Republic" to drown out the sound of the tinkle. But every once in a blue moon Rita Lynn let loose, and the baby shower was one of those times. There were three bottles of Great Western Champagne for the shower— or so everyone believed. Rita Lynn, keeper of the office kitty and organizer extraordinaire of the shower, had surreptitiously secreted a fourth bottle in a Glad bag packed with ice stashed in her waste basket. Every now and again she'd slip away from the party to the privacy of her reception area cubicle (or "cubby," as she called it) for a refill.

Rita Lynn eyed everyone carefully. She wanted to be sure they were having A Good Time. That, after all, was the purpose of this gathering. They stood in a cluster around the mound of pink and blue packages piled on Madeline's desk. It looked like a shrine. The old clunker of a typewriter was virtually buried in presents, though you could still detect a pair of yellow booties dangling from the carriage of the machine. Rita Lynn thought those booties lent a particularly festive touch, and she was glad she'd knitted them. People chatted politely, sipped flat lukewarm champagne, and nibbled on tea cakes (baked by Rita Lynn herself).

God, thought Rita Lynn, this party is a blast.

She took another sip of her bubbly and moved closer to the crowd. She supposed she should mingle. But suddenly she was assailed by a series of unexpected and unpleasant thoughts: I have made this party for Madeline Kroll. Madeline is married. Madeline is going to have a baby. Madeline has everything. I have nothing. *Bam. Bam. Bam.*

Rita Lynn's free hand flew to her mouth to stifle a cry that lodged in her throat. The other hand—the hand holding the plastic cup of champagne—trembled so violently she thought it might spill.

"Rita Lynn?" The voice came from Ethel Murton, a secretary from the executive suite. Ethel was remarkable in that workers at Parker McKenzie and Swaine liked her even less than Rita Lynn. Ethel was a snob who usually declined to associate with lowlife such as Rita Lynn or Madeline, but this time she had sniffed out the champagne. Now her face was a mask of concern. "Rita Lynn, honey? Are you all right?"

Honey? Rita Lynn wanted to hurl the word back like a grenade. Honey! But she had steadied herself. She set down her glass on a credenza and leaned against a lateral file cabinet. When she refocused her eyes, she saw Ethel's

*face peering at her. It looked like the bowed fish-face
reflection you see in a spoon.*

"You have a face like a fish," said Rita Lynn.

*In a split second there was dead silence. People looked
at their feet in embarrassment. Then one person stifled a
snicker and it was as though the floodgates burst open.
Everyone broke out laughing. Hysterically. It was a new
feeling for Rita Lynn—people laughing with her instead
of at her.*

"I beg your pardon," said Ethel Murton, blanching.

*"A tuna, I think," Rita Lynn went on. "Or a carp
perhaps."*

*Someone guffawed. Someone else—Rita Lynn thought
maybe it was Henry Pruitt from data processing—hooted,
"A bottom feeder!"*

*"No," said Rita Lynn thoughtfully. "That's not it." She
savored a long moment of contemplation. "A largemouth
bass, I think. A very largemouth—"*

*Pandemonium broke loose. No one dared talk to Ethel
Murton that way. She was secretary to Norman Winkler,
executive vice president of the firm, and as such she
wielded extensive, albeit unofficial, power.*

*"Well!" Ethel drew herself up to full height. "I never!"
She staggered back several steps, turned on her heel,
and stalked off, her sizeable fanny jerking right-to-left,
right-to-left in double-time tempo.*

*Suddenly Rita Lynn was surrounded by coworkers. They
were smiling, slapping her on the back. She couldn't
believe it. Flushed with glory, she hoisted her plastic
glass yet again. . . .*

"So why so blue?" asked Forrest. "Sounds like you
done good. Why leave?"

"Good?" repeated Rita Lynn in unabashed misery.
"Good? I got fired. You call that good? Twenty years
at Parker McKenzie and *Swine*, and I get fired. Canned.
For one unguarded moment of frivolity."

"That stinks," said Forrest sympathetically.

"So now I'm out of here."

"You're better off," said Forrest. "Screw them."

Rita Lynn liked this man's logic. "Yes," she said. "Screw them."

"What the hell do they do here anyway?"

"You mean what kind of service? Well, the firm employs experts on business. Financial systems, management structure, production, things like that."

"Oh. Right."

"Other companies hire experts from PMS"—she tittered at this abbreviation—"to tell them how to solve problems. How to make their own companies perform better. How to improve the price-earnings ratio, as it were."

As it were. Jesus. "I see," said Forrest, whose intention had merely been to get her talking, not to get a crash course about management consulting. "And that Winkler fellow, he's that kinda expert?"

"Him?" Mr. Winkler had been the one who fired her. She made a prune face, rearranged it back to normal, then made the face again. What the hell, it was her last day. "No one knows for sure what Mr. Winkler does. Like I said, he's our executive vice president."

"Sounds impressive."

"He thinks so." She lowered her voice. "Actually he married into the firm. His wife is Barbara McKenzie . . ." She paused dramatically, as though waiting for Forrest to drop to his knees in homage. " . . . daughter of one of the founders."

"I see."

"They live in Greenwich. In a mansion. They had the company Christmas party there last year. Wrote it off, I'm sure."

Forrest paused as though deep in thought. "You said he works long hours yet no one knows what he does?"

"Oh," she replied, slightly flustered now. She looked over her shoulder at the doorway behind her. "It does seem a little peculiar. He never goes home at five—is here till God knows when. Sometimes I think he sleeps here. But his responsibilities are purely administrative, and he has a host of assistants to handle those chores, so we can't figure out why—" She narrowed her eyes. "Why do you want to know about him anyway?"

"It's no big deal," answered Forrest slyly. "He may have witnessed a murder, that's all."

"A murder," breathed Rita Lynn. "Mercy."

"Woman right across the alley. At the St. James Hotel."

"You don't say." Rita Lynn digested these facts. "We heard it was an accident."

"Maybe not," said Forrest knowingly. "It's being investigated."

"Oh, that poor woman." Rita Lynn was a person who lived her life vicariously. She was an avid reader of the *National Inquirer* and the *Star*. She passed her evenings watching *America's Most Wanted* and *Hard Copy*. In a flash she pictured the victim as she pictured herself: ungainly, unattractive, unwelcome. Her eyes filled up and Forrest was afraid she might cry, but she recouped quickly, dabbing the corners of her eyes with a lace handkerchief extracted from her ample bosom.

"We heard the commotion next door, what with the sirens and all. When we came in to work the body was already gone." She tried to filter the disappointment from her voice. "But the police were milling around. Investigating. I suppose it was ghoulish, us watching like that."

"Not at all," reassured Forrest. "Folks always look. They're scared and they want to understand." Before it's their turn in the zippered bag, but he didn't say that.

"I'm getting out of this city," Rita Lynn proclaimed.

Forrest nodded sympathetically.

"I'm going to Alaska. Oprah Winfrey had a show about all the men in Alaska. The ratio's very good. So that's where I'm going."

Forrest eyed Rita Lynn and winced inside. Good ratio or no, he doubted that the pickings would be abundant for Rita Lynn, but he said nothing to discourage her. Who knows? he thought. Maybe a girl like her could find happiness in the frozen north. Maybe she'd look better under a parka. Stranger things had happened.

"So you think Mr. Winkler may have seen . . ." She let the sentence hang.

"His office is right across from the victim's room. And you yourself said Mr. Winkler makes a habit of working into the night."

"My goodness," said Rita Lynn, "I never thought of that." She paused, considering. "You know, now that you mention it, Mr. Winkler did seem particularly upset the day after it happened."

"How so?"

"Well, we were all distressed, of course. I mean, having someone die practically on our doorstep as it were. But Mr. Winkler was absolutely ashen. He staggered around here like a zombie. It was spooky. He wouldn't go into his office either. See, we were all in there looking down at the police, but he holed up in the conference room, which is most unusual. In fact, I believe he went home early that day. Said he was sick."

"Interesting," said Forrest.

"He's creepy," said Rita Lynn. She wrapped her arms around herself as though feeling a chill.

"How so?"

Rita Lynn looked over her shoulder again. Satisfied that no one could hear her, she went on. "I don't know," she said, "just creepy. The girls don't like to be near him, I can tell you that. You get the feeling that he's—I don't know—watching or something. That he'd like to . . . well, it's ridiculous, I'm sure, but there was a rumor awhile back that he was watching women in the ladies' room. Behind the wall. One girl sued the company. It was all very hush-hush. She's not here anymore. I heard PMS paid her off."

"Hmmm," said Forrest noncommittally.

"I've never been involved in a police case before," said Rita Lynn, her eyes glazing with anticipation. "Look, Mr. Haggarty . . ."

"Yes?"

"I'm sure if Mr. Winkler knew *why* you were here he'd want to help. I mean, if he actually *saw* something, well, surely he'd want to cooperate."

"Surely," said Forrest, not believing it for a minute. He didn't think Rita Lynn believed it either, but now realized she wasn't as dumb as she looked. Besides, it was her last day. Forrest watched as Rita Lynn's manicured finger tapped out Norman Winkler's number. Then she winked at him. Well, what the hell, thought Forrest. Nothing's sweeter than the taste of revenge.

27 Norman Winkler appeared to be a small man lost behind a mahogany desk the size of Rhode Island. The green desk blotter before him was clean and without doodles or frivolity. Pencils stood poised at attention in a walnut cup, points sharpened, erasers fresh and unblemished.

Winkler himself was as perfect, as precise, as obsessively neat as his surroundings. He wore a white shirt starched so hard it could have cracked. His silk tie was a somber maroon, plain and without the intrusive polka dots or stripes. His suit was simple and expensive, a navy blue single-breasted variety from Sulka's, custom made at a cost of $1,200. The shoes on his feet were dainty wingtips of Italian goat skin polished to a high gloss.

Forrest may have missed the finer subtleties of Winkler's attire, but not the compulsive neatness of his surroundings. A place for everything and everything in its place. Winkler was obviously that kind of man, besides being a priss and a wimp.

Forrest stepped inside and closed the door behind him. "How do you do, Mr. . . . ?"

"Haggarty," said Forrest. He took the man's delicate birdlike hand in his own and gave it a shake. They sat down, facing one another across the expanse of desk. Winkler looked at his watch. It was a reflexive habit, continually checking the time through days that progressed with interminable slowness, and it was something Winkler would do frequently during the conversation to come.

"Miss Peters at the front desk mentioned something about some sort of crime?" Winkler pursed his lips with distaste after saying the word, then smiled incongruously.

"Yeah. Lady at the St. James Hotel right across the way. Registered under the name of Camille Smith."

Winkler's face remained blank. He drummed his fingers on the desk impatiently. "I remember something about an accident. Several weeks back, I recall—"

"We think it was murder."

The drumming stopped abruptly. "We?" repeated Winkler. "And just who, may I ask, is we?"

"Me and my team. I'm a private investigator. Hired by the family."

"I see," said Winkler shortly. "And I suppose you have appropriate credentials."

"Of course." Forrest produced a letter signed by Jonathan Maine, as well as a card identifying him as chief of the Raven's Wing police department, expired to be sure, but with the date carefully smeared into illegibility.

"Very well," sniffed Winkler. "Nevertheless I don't see why you're here. I really can't help you, Mr. Haggarty, and I'm a busy man, so if you'll excuse me . . ."

"No," said Forrest quietly.

"No?" Winkler cocked his head as though he'd heard incorrectly.

"You see, Mr. Winkler, your office here has a bird's-eye view of room three-twelve. Camille Smith's room."

"That's all well and good, Mr. Haggarty, but I assure you I didn't see a thing."

"Well now, Mr. Winkler, I think maybe you did."

Winkler tried to smile condescendingly and managed to look constipated. "That's a matter of conjecture and a monumental leap of logic, Mr. Haggarty. As I said, I'm a busy man. I work late hours for that very reason. I have neither the time nor the inclination to observe—"

"Some people like to observe," said Forrest, not missing a beat. It was a stab in the dark, but what the hell.

"I beg your pardon?" Winkler folded his clammy hands on the blotter.

Forrest stood up and ambled over to the window. "Why, just look here—you've got a bird's-eye view of several rooms over there at the St. James."

Norman Winkler's little bird eyes darted nervously from Forrest to the window to the door and back to Forrest.

"People in a hotel like that, well, there's no telling what goes on, is there? All sorts of hanky-panky, I'd wager. Quite a temptation, I'd say. For a man like you."

"I'm sure I don't know what you're talking about, Mr. Haggarty." Winkler reached for a pitcher of water and fumbled with a glass. He managed to spill equal amounts of water into the glass and onto the blotter, leaving a spreading stain.

Forrest wheeled around and his voice escalated. "I think you do, Norman. I think you know very well."

"And I think you'd better leave," said Winkler with as much bluster as he could manage. "I don't have to take this abuse."

"You see, Norman, I saw you looking when I visited Camille Smith's room a couple of days ago. Perched at this very spot, you were." Forrest indicated the windowsill. "Perched real comfortable like. And you know what? I think you look a *lot*, Norman. I think you get your rocks off by looking, that's what I think."

"That's preposterous!" cried Winkler. "You may leave this instant."

"Look," said Forrest reasonably, "I have connections. We folks in law enforcement stick together. One call to Chief Reynolds over in Greenwich, and he'll be only too happy to tell me if there have been any complaints about a peeper in that fancy town of yours. Or in your neighborhood. And I'm sure he'd appreciate a tip from me, Norman."

"You wouldn't."

"Oh but I would, Norman. Don't underestimate me."

"I'll sue," said Winkler evenly. "You can't barge in here and threaten me with ruination. With innuendo. You can't—"

"That's just the point," said Forrest. "I can, and I will. Make no mistake. I'm seventy-five years old, Norman. What do I have to lose, after all? Money? Reputation? Hardly. But you? You stand to lose a lot. You got a wife? Kids?"

Winkler looked at his hands. "You really are a bastard," he said quietly. He sat there for some moments, weighing his alternatives. His mind as unclear. He was rattled. Like the horoscopes say, it was not the right time to make decisions.

Winkler was on the verge of talking, Forrest could see it. He reached inside his rumpled seersucker jacket and pulled out Esther Maine's book of poems.

"What's that?" asked Winkler in a ragged voice.

"Just listen . . .

> *I feel his eyes upon me,*
> *The sweetest caress of all.*
> *The kindest touch doesn't ask for much,*
> *Yet will perchance enthrall."*

"Don't," said Winkler.
But Forrest ignored him.

> *"No more than a smile across the way,*
> *No more than a silent plea,*
> *Gives a notion of his devotion*
> *And that's more than enough for me."*

"That's enough!"

"It's about you."

Winkler sat there stonily for some moments. "Look," he said finally, "I didn't do anything wrong, Camille and I had a very special relationship. I certainly never hurt her."

"But you knew her." Forrest leaned forward eagerly at this revelation.

"In a way," Winkler hedged.

"In *what* way," demanded Forrest, his impatience getting the best of him.

"We had something precious, Camille and I."

"Spell it out for me, Norman."

"Can't you tell by that poem? *The kindest touch doesn't ask for much."*

"So?"

"So, if you must know, it was a platonic relationship. A pure relationship. I at my window and she in her room. We never met and I assure you we never touched."

"I see." Forrest was disappointed. The man really was just a peeper. He'd been hoping for more. Still, maybe he saw something.

"Somehow she seemed to know me," Winkler went on. His voice vibrated with barely concealed emotion. "She seemed to know what I wanted. We never spoke, but she seemed to know. Haven't you ever had that feeling about someone? Someone you've never even met?"

"Yes," Forrest lied. "Tell me about it, Norman."

"It will go no further?" said Winkler.

Forrest lied again. "No further."

"And I want you to stop calling me Norman," he said sullenly. "It's overly familiar, if you don't mind my saying so."

"Yeah, yeah. Look, *Norman,* the faster you start talking, the sooner I'll be out of here."

"All right." Winkler inhaled deeply, as though trying to steady himself. "There was nothing much to it, actually. You might say that's the story of my life. Nothing much to it."

And to your physique as well, thought Forrest, but he held his tongue.

"Last February or so I happened to notice a woman over at the St. James Hotel on Tuesday nights. An attractive woman. A woman of class and breeding. Rather unexpected, considering the ambience."

"Go on."

"Well, I noticed that this lovely creature stayed at the St. James each and every Tuesday. In the very same room. The rest of the week the room was dark and vacant. But on Tuesday nights, the lights came on, and she was there." Winkler's expression turned wistful.

"And what did you see?"

"I could see," he breathed, "when she got ready. When she dressed. Did her hair. Applied makeup. Little things like that."

"She left the drapes open?"

"Oh yes. I was sure she believed the office was empty. I was always careful, you see. I'd put the lights out and sit here in the dark. You must understand, I'd never intentionally frighten anyone. I am, as the experts say, harmless. God knows, I've paid enough of them to analyze this embarrassing propensity of mine. In any event, I thought she was unaware. And I thought wrong."

"She *knew* you were watching her?"

"Apparently so. Sometime around April her preparations . . . how shall I say it . . . became more imaginative. More uninhibited. More provocative. She would prolong the ritual of undressing into a kind of exquisite torture. She would parade before the window. Naked." He lowered his voice. "She would play with herself."

Jesus, thought Forrest.

"I considered stopping at that point, considered forgetting the whole thing. I now realized that she knew, you see, and it had become dangerous for me. I thought about stopping. But I wouldn't. Or maybe I couldn't. You see, I had come to look forward to our Tuesday nights. More than that, I had come to live for them. It was like having a date or something. There was a closeness between us, an intimacy. It was almost palpable, and it was growing."

Forrest sighed. A real nuthatch.

"I don't expect you to understand," said Winkler shortly.

"Norman, did you notice anything unusual about Camille's performances?"

"Unusual?" Winkler looked puzzled. "You're asking *me?*"

Forrest smiled. Winkler was not entirely without a sense of irony.

"Now that you mention it, there was something that caught my fancy early on. I suppose *you* might consider it unusual. As I mentioned, Camille was a lovely woman, obviously a woman of refinement and culture. She was well groomed and impeccably dressed in stylish, tasteful clothes. I notice those things."

I'll bet you do, thought Forrest.

"I got the feeling that she was lonely too," said Winkler, almost to himself. "So very lonely . . . Where was I?"

"Something unusual," Forrest prodded.

"Oh yes. When she changed her clothes—and when she made herself up—a transformation of sorts occurred. She wasn't classy anymore. She was cheap. Trashy. Almost grotesquely so. Florid makeup, a tawdry red wig, black underwear with holes in strategic places. You get the picture."

"Ah, but Norman, you said she knew what you wanted."

"Exactly," said Winkler without apology. "So of course you can see why our relationship was so special. She *knew what I wanted.*" He paused. "And I suppose she became an obsession."

"So that's it?"

"Not entirely. In June I got a letter."

"A letter?" Forrest leaned forward so fast he almost spilled from the chair.

"A love letter. Marked personal. How she got my name I'll never know, but somehow she did. I almost died when I got that letter. Thank God no one else opened it. Secretaries these days are such blithering idiots, and nosy too."

"What did the letter say, Norman?"

"It said that she loved me." His voice escalated in disbelief. "And that she knew I loved her."

"How did you feel about that?"

Winkler gulped. "I was terrified."

"So you killed her."

"No!" cried Winkler. "I could never do that. I loved her, don't you see? Once my panic abated, I came to appreciate what she had done. The risk she had taken. I came to see that our relationship had evolved to a higher plane."

"Admit it, Norman. You were hooked. You weren't only terrified. You were excited."

"Yes," replied Norman. "Our intimacy had assumed deeper proportions. Dangerously so, but I didn't care. She knew my name, where I worked. Our relationship was now more binding than ever. That appealed to me. And, of course, there was one other benefit as well."

"What was that?"

"As long as I had Camille, I seemed to be able to hold myself in check at other times. I behaved myself. So you can see I wouldn't want to lose her—and I'd certainly never harm her."

"Did you save this letter?"

Winkler looked horrified. "Of course not. It was too risky. I destroyed it. And I never responded either. There was no need. She knew how I felt, I could tell."

"And when you watched, did you see anything else? Besides Camille Smith, I mean. Did you see any visitors? Any men friends?"

Winkler seemed stung. "Never. We shared our private moments, Camille and I, and then she drew the curtain. I was never aware of any visitors."

"But there was a visitor on Tuesday, July eighteenth," pressed Forrest.

"There was—" Winkler stopped himself. "I saw nothing. The drapes were drawn."

"Liar! The drapes were open when the desk clerk found her!"

Winkler twisted a paper clip. His eyes darted about nervously. "Then someone must have opened them later."

Forrest tried to rein in his impatience and anger. "Listen, I don't want to scare you, but if you saw anything, anything at all . . ."

Winkler turned his face away.

" . . . you could be in danger."

"Please," whispered Winkler, "I don't want to get involved."

Forrest's voice was gentle. "You already are involved, Norman. Can't you see that?"

Winkler sat there, drumming his fingers nervously on the desk. "I need to think," he said at last. "What if what I saw—if I did see anything, and I'm not saying I did—wasn't distinct? I mean, what if they were just shapes?"

"Shapes?"

"Shadows," he blurted. "It all happened so quickly. I was so startled when they came."

"They?" repeated Forrest. "You mean there was more than one?"

"Three came that night," admitted Winkler. "First one. Someone heavyset. I could see them sitting, talking perhaps. He didn't stay long."

"Ah," said Forrest. "Could you identify him?"

"You mean in a police lineup or something? I doubt it. I don't know. Maybe."

"Then, after him, she had another visitor?"

Winkler shuddered. "Yes."

"What happened?"

"She was going through her usual ablutions. Preparing for her bath and whatnot. And there must have been a knock at the door because she crossed the room. I can't see what's happening at the door, it's out of range. Take a look for yourself, if you like. In any event, she went toward the door." Winkler's voice cracked. "And . . ."

"And what?"

"And moments later someone dragged a body—her body—across the room. Toward the bathroom. Then he turned off the light."

"He?"

"I don't know!" cried Winkler. "I can't be sure. The person was in a hurry and moved quickly. It seemed like a blur."

"Did you call anyone?" Forrest remembered Higgins saying that someone called the front desk.

Winkler squirmed. "No. I was too scared. I waited, kept watching, hoping that the light would come on, that she would get up. That everything would be okay. That it would be, you know, some kind of grotesque game. Sex play or something."

"It was no game, Norman."

"I know," he said miserably. "A while later—an hour or so later—someone else came. The lights came back on and a man stepped into the room—I could tell this time. I'm not sure but I think he was different from the first one. Of smaller stature."

"What'd he look like?"

"Average height. Black hair. Curly."

"So you could identify this man?"

"Possibly."

Forrest rubbed his hands together. "Good. Now listen to me. Don't tell anyone else about all this, understand? Let it be our little secret for now."

"Oh don't you worry," said Winkler miserably. "I won't tell a soul. I'm already sorry I told you."

"Oh no. You've done the right thing. Everything's going to be okay. You want whoever did this to Camille to pay, don't you?"

"Yes," admitted Winkler.

"So just sit tight for a few days. Go about your business as usual. I'll be back to you as soon as I can get some pictures."

"Pictures?"

"Yeah. To help you identify those visitors."

"Oh I don't know—"

"But in the meantime call me if you think of anything else. Or if you get scared. Or if you just want to talk." Forrest reached over and stuffed a scrap of paper in Winkler's breast pocket. The man's shirt was damp with sweat. "Okay?"

"All right," said Winkler weakly.

Forrest turned to leave, then stopped. "One more thing, just out of curiosity . . ."

"Yes?"

"What are you going to do now that Camille is gone?"

"I don't know," said Winkler hollowly. "I miss her, you know. It sounds crazy, but I really do."

28 The house stood out stark and white against a brilliant azure sky. It shimmered like a sugar cube, set as it was on a bluff edged with dune grass. There were no windows, at least none Trevor could detect. It looked as square, as impenetrable, as a Rubik's cube.

With new found resolve Trevor navigated the black

Lincoln along the sandy driveway. He felt suddenly invigorated by the beauty of the day and glad that this leg of his journey was almost over. The drive out to the Island had been unexpectedly harrowing. He'd had no idea that the Long Island Expressway would pose such a gauntlet. First he traveled past neighborhoods of gutted buildings glorified with Day-Glo graffiti, rust-crusted metallic cinders that had once been automobiles, and clusters of idle young men. Except for the climate, it could have been Beirut. He'd thought of Nancy Reagan and wondered how she'd do telling those fellows to "Just say no." Face to face. How would she do?

He'd been afraid to pull over on the shoulder to look at his map, afraid someone might strip the car as he watched helplessly. He said a silent prayer that he not take a wrong turn. After all, wasn't that what happened to that Sherman fellow in *Bonfire of the Vanities?* In a neighborhood just like that too? Oh God.

So he gripped the wheel with slippery hands and pressed on along the Long Island Expressway. On and on and on. Then he progressed through a series of connections he'd written on a Post-it note and affixed to the dashboard.

Finally, miraculously, he came to a place, a place that seemed like Valhalla, a place called "The Hamptons."

Relief washed over him. He felt almost at home. Main Street of Westhampton was quite similar to Raven's Wing, Connecticut, with its small shops and quaint signs. I have run the gauntlet, Trevor congratulated himself, and emerged alive.

From Main Street it was but a short drive to Sandpiper Road and the home of Dr. Alexander Blaustein.

He opened the car door and smiled to himself. Mildred had told him Long Island sinks an inch every August under the weight of all the shrinks on vacation. He touched the sand gingerly with his foot and wondered, indeed, if it might be true.

Trevor knocked on the front door several times, but there was no response from within. Funny, he thought.

He'd spoken directly with Alexander Blaustein before coming out. The good doctor had returned his call almost instantaneously after Trevor left a rather convoluted message with his service. He spoke with a hint of a cultured European accent, which may or may not have been genuine. Blaustein had been gracious and accommodating. They'd made an appointment. Trevor glanced at his watch. Two o'clock. He was on time to the minute.

Suddenly he heard squeals of laughter coming from the rear of the house. He followed the sound.

"Daddy, oh Daddy—" The child's voice broke into ecstatic shrieks, followed by a splash, silence, then more laughter.

"My turn! My turn!"

"No more," gasped an older voice. "Daddy is going to swim his laps."

Trevor heard wails of disappointment.

"One more throw, Daddy! One more!"

"Me! Me! Me, Daddy, me!"

"It's *my* turn, Jamie!"

"Is not!"

"Is!"

"Is not!"

"All right, my darlings," laughed the older voice.

Trevor rounded the corner.

"One more throw for each of you." A small muscular man with bristly salt-and-pepper hair and a beard to match glanced over at Trevor and waved a hello. "Just one more, and that is it. Daddy has a visitor."

The children, a boy and a girl, looked at Trevor from the shallow end of a shimmering turquoise swimming pool. They both had bright red hair and freckles and might have been twins. Dr. Alexander Blaustein intertwined his fingers and deftly lifted the girl and then the boy overhead into beautiful well-executed arcs that landed them into the deep end. From there they dog-paddled back to him.

"Okay," he said with mock severity. "Now you must stay on this side of the rope. That is the rule."

"Awwwww—"

"I mean it, Julie. The deep end is off limits until I am finished. And I will be watching. I will be right over there . . ."

Alexander Blaustein hoisted himself out of the pool in one smooth motion, threw a towel around tanned shoulders, and offered Trevor his hand. His body was lean and well toned. Trevor wondered if Blaustein might be one of those men of small physical stature driven by relentless macho instincts to work out daily on Nautilus machines, run ten miles, then swim forty laps.

"Dr. Bradford," Blaustein said.

"Dr. Blaustein. It's good of you to see me on such short notice."

"I am always pleased to make time for a colleague," said Blaustein cordially.

"I really am sorry to intrude."

"Ach, but there is no intrusion." Blaustein led Trevor to an enormous, multitiered redwood deck and they settled into cushioned patio chairs. Trevor could see that from where Blaustein positioned himself he had an unobstructed view of his children as they splashed happily in the pool.

"Nice kids you've got," said Trevor.

"Thank you. Yes, they are good children. I only wish I could see more of them. I live for August, at which time they spend the month here with me."

"Ah," said Trevor sympathetically. "You're divorced?"

"Yes. Six years it is now. We suffered from a difference in cultures . . . she was a California girl and I a European man." He arched his eyebrows. "You are divorced also?" The question was tossed out unexpectedly.

"No," said Trevor quickly. "Widowed. Or widowered. I never did get the terminology straight."

"May I offer you something?" asked Blaustein solicitously. "I think we have some lunch meats. Rye bread. Soft drinks. A beer perhaps?"

"Oh no," protested Trevor, "I wouldn't want you to

go to any trouble." As if on cue, his stomach rumbled loudly, an embarrassing reminder that he hadn't eaten since breakfast.

"Ach," said Blaustein, "again with the trouble. As I said, Dr. Bradford, there is no trouble. I myself haven't eaten lunch as yet, so you would do me a favor, you see. Then I would not be eating alone." That said, Blaustein stood up and went inside. "Chicken salad all right?" he called back.

"Wonderful," said Trevor.

"And raspberry seltzer!" said Blaustein enthusiastically as he sat himself back down. "I am rather a health enthusiast. We don't have any beer, after all. My apologies."

"Seltzer will be just fine," said Trevor.

"Daddy, can Jamie and I go dig on the beach?" The little girl materialized before them. She hugged a damp towel around herself. Her body vibrated with barely contained energy. Rivers of water ran from her compact body onto the raw redwood planks.

"Julie, what did I tell you about splinters?"

"I know, Daddy, I know, but can—"

"Look at those feet. Feet without sneakers."

She started to jump up and down. "I know, Daddy, but can we—"

"I don't want to see any tears tonight when I remove those splinters."

"Can we, Daddy? Can we?"

"Very well."

She flew away.

"But only to the top of the ridge there!" he called after her. "Where I can see you! You are not to go down by the water, understand?"

"Yes!" she cried. "Yes!"

He turned back to Trevor. "I worry about them. I suppose I am an overprotective parent. But the things I hear in my work, well . . . And the media doesn't help now, does it? What with the relentless horror stories about children being snatched away. Perhaps I worry too much, but—"

An astoundingly well-endowed young lady clad in an abbreviated string bikini set a tray of chicken salad sandwiches and Sundance raspberry seltzers between them. Trevor tried not to gape. She nodded hello to Trevor and turned to leave.

"Thank you, Jennifer," said Blaustein.

"Nice . . ."—Trevor groped for a word—" . . . sandwiches."

Blaustein grinned knowingly. "Indeed," he said. "Help yourself." He grabbed one for himself and shoved the platter in Trevor's direction. "So," he said between mouthfuls, "you said you are hired by the family to look into the death of Esther Maine?" He shook his head sadly. "Such a tragedy. Terrible. How, may I ask, is the family doing?"

"As well as can be expected," said Trevor. He felt as though he were reciting lines. "Her husband is . . . coping."

"The older boy," pressed Blaustein, "and the younger sister, Lauren? How are they?"

"I really don't—"

"It will be particularly bad for them," said Blaustein darkly. "Teenagers. Everyone thinks they are grown up. Everyone thinks they are fine. Mark my words, they are neither. They are still children. This will have negative repercussions for a long time to come."

"I hope not," said Trevor.

"Oh it will," said Blaustein darkly. "I see such people in my work. Scarred people. People who never grow up because of such a tragedy. Arrested development. Arrested by pain, Dr. Bradford. Pain."

"Yes," said Trevor, wanting to get back to the subject at hand. Wanting to get back to Esther Maine. "Dr. Blaustein," he said, "I understand your practice is mostly limited to males."

"Not mostly," said Blaustein shortly. "Entirely. I had enough with bored American women when I was on the West Coast. Wealthy neurotics, hysterics, and borderlines. They entered therapy as though it were some sort of diversion. A hobby, for goodness sake. After a time I found it difficult to be sympathetic."

"And yet," continued Trevor, "you made an exception for Mrs. Maine."

"Yes. As a favor to a friend I broke my rule. She was a referral."

"Oh? And who referred her?"

"Another patient of mine. I'm not at liberty to divulge his name. Suffice it to say he was a member of her brother-in-law's club. I treat men in powerful positions, Dr. Bradford—corporate presidents, government officials, men from here and abroad. They prefer that their stockholders or their constituents or their governments remain unaware that they are consulting a psychiatrist. Surely you understand."

Heady stuff, thought Trevor. "Of course," he said. "But I would like to ask you about Esther Maine herself."

"I will do what I can to help," said Blaustein agreeably, "though of course you realize that the doctor-patient relationship is confidential."

"Of course," said Trevor. He'd anticipated that Blaustein might react this way and had formulated a response just in case during the drive out. "Still, it is true that the woman is dead. I hope, considering the circumstances, that we might be able to speak candidly about her. Confidentially, of course."

"I don't know," said Blaustein. For the first time his voice betrayed a slight undercurrent of uncertainty. Unconsciously he stroked his beard.

"There's another way to look at it," ventured Trevor earnestly. "I'm a doctor. In fact, I was their family doctor for quite some time. Why not suppose we were simply consulting about her case? Suppose you were seeking my advice?"

"Instead of vice versa," said Blaustein abruptly. "Seeking advice about a dead patient?"

"Well," fumbled Trevor, "it's just a way to look at it, that's all. I thought it might help."

"I will make up my own mind," said Blaustein. "And I haven't said I won't help. I will. It's simply a matter as to what degree. Please tell me what you already know."

It was a demand, not a request. Trevor looked at the good doctor and felt himself being drawn into some sort of bargain that was not necessarily to his liking.

Blaustein shot a glance at his children on the bluff. Assured that they were safely preoccupied with shovels and buckets of swimming pool water, he turned his attention back to Trevor.

"Well," Trevor began, "we've got a puzzling personality here. Pieces that don't seem to fit together at all."

"And how is that?" replied Blaustein noncommittally.

You know damn well how, Trevor wanted to say in exasperation. But he didn't. If this was the way Blaustein wanted to play the game, he would play it. He just hoped he'd get some insights in return.

"We have a woman who was a pillar of the community in Raven's Wing, Connecticut. Respected in a town that doles out respect grudgingly at best. She did a lot of good in her own quiet way. Delivered for Meals on Wheels. Sang in the choir of the Catholic church. Never said no when they needed someone to work the bake sale for the Cancer Crusade. She was quiet. Shy. A good mother. And maybe folks didn't notice her much, but plenty of people relied on her, I'll tell you that. Plenty."

"Obviously," said Blaustein primly, "too good to be true." He bit off the word, making it "gut." He took a sip of his seltzer.

"We also have a woman—the same woman—who was arrested for shoplifting in New York City. As I understand it, that was what brought her to you in the first place."

"This is true," concurred Blaustein.

"And finally we have a woman who appears to have been leading some sort of double life. A woman who, while supposedly staying at the Regency Hotel every week was, in reality, checked in at a very different sort of hotel called the St. James. A woman who called herself Camille Smith. A woman who, we have come to understand, had several visitors at that hotel, men visitors. A woman who may conceivably have accepted financial remuneration in return for sexual favors."

Alexander Blaustein once again looked in the direction of his children. He sipped his seltzer. If Trevor's little speech had disturbed him in any way, he didn't show it.

"Well?" said Trevor.

"Well, what?" said Blaustein shortly. "Just what do you want me to say, Dr. Bradford?"

Trevor threw up his hands. "Can you provide any insight here? What the hell was going on with this inexplicable behavior?"

Blaustein sat there watching the horizon, and Trevor continued in frustration. "Look, anything you can tell us might give us a lead on what happened. The lady didn't take a fall in the bathtub, Dr. Blaustein. She was bludgeoned. I'll quote the autopsy report if you'd like. I'll show you a picture." He thrust the gruesome Polaroid at Blaustein's averted face. "Someone did this to her, Dr. Blaustein. The police don't seem to give a damn. And I must say you don't seem to either."

Blaustein winced. "Put that away. For God's sake."

"So who was she?" Trevor pressed. "Who was this Esther Maine?"

"Haven't you guessed?" said Blaustein quietly. He turned his gaze back to the horizon. "Mrs. Maine was a painfully shy woman. A desperately lonely one too. She would do anything—indeed, *be* anything that anyone wanted her to be. And that, Dr. Bradford, was the pity of it." His voice trailed off. "Such a terrible pity."

"What do you mean?"

"In some ways," said Blaustein, "you appear to know more about Mrs. Maine than I. Although what you say is consistent with my client as I knew her, I did not know the specifics. The name of the hotel, for example—or even that there was one specific hotel. I knew something of her behavior pattern, I knew that something very dangerous was going on, and we were exploring the roots—"

"Trying to figure out the cause of the fire without putting it out?" The words spilled from Trevor's mouth before he could stop himself.

"I beg your pardon, Dr. Bradford?"

"You knew she was engaging in dangerous behavior and you didn't try to stop her?"

"A curious choice of words, Dr. Bradford." Blaustein spread his hands. "It is not up to me to stop such behavior. It is up to the patient."

Trevor took a deep breath and reigned in his irritation. "I have a couple of theories about what may have been going on," he said finally. "They'll probably sound like pop psychology drivel to you."

"Go on," said Blaustein.

"The different names. The bizarre variations in clothing found in her hotel room. The totally contradictory modes of behavior and character. It could add up to a case of multiple personalities."

"Wrong," said Blaustein flatly. "Come, come, Dr. Bradford, you know that true multiples are rare indeed. Documented cases are greatly exaggerated. They sell books and movies, that's all. And when they do occur, there are many, many personalities involved. Such an abnormal disorder would have been detected long before now."

"Well," said Trevor, "still—"

"You are on the wrong track. That much I will tell you."

"What is this," demanded Trevor, "twenty questions?"

Blaustein ignored the outburst. "You mentioned a couple of theories?"

"All right," said Trevor. "Articles have been cropping up in professional journals lately about another condition. We used to call it nymphomania."

"It is not called that anymore," said Blaustein quickly. "There is more compassion, more understanding."

"Okay, so it's not, but from what little I know the symptoms haven't changed. An apparently insatiable sexual appetite. There have been cases where women, respectable women even, sneak out of the house at night and engage in multiple, compulsive encounters. Encounters without any real satisfaction or fulfillment."

"Ah, but there is fulfillment," Blaustein corrected. "Therein lies a part of the problem. It is an addiction, as strong in its hold as alcohol or drugs. Perhaps even stronger."

"So that's it," said Trevor.

"Bingo," said Blaustein.

29 They sat across from one another in the Chef's Touch, a tiny coffee shop on a side street in the financial district. It was three o'clock and the lunch crowd had long since dispersed. A sullen waitress slammed watery cups of coffee on the stained Formica table, then withdrew a pad and tapped her pencil against it.

"Anything else?" she asked.

"No."

The waitress shoved the pad back into a pocket in her apron. "Figures."

They waited for her to leave.

"I know I wasn't very nice last night."

"Never mind that. You were just distraught. You'd been through a lot."

"I'm used to being on my own. Not used to people doing for me." She fingered her dress distractedly. She looked down at stylish new shoes, at hose without runs, at the genuine leather handbag clutched in her lap. A handbag with spending money inside. It all seemed to belong to someone else. The body too.

"I can't believe this is me."

"You look nice."

Lord knows, thought Mildred, they never would have let her in Harmony House looking like she did before, a vagrant.

Mildred had thrown the ensemble together hastily, then marched Cora over to Martha Abbington's. From there they went to Harmony House and filled out innumerable forms. From there they went to the dentist.

"I'll look better when I get teeth."

"You look fine." Just try not to smile. *Please*.

Cora took a noisy sip of coffee.

Mildred looked around. Where is he anyway? she wondered.

"Who knows? Maybe I'll even go to AA. I've been thinking about it. I've tried to cut back in the past but it never worked out somehow. Maybe it would be easier in a club like that. They have a meeting in the basement of St. Michael's right down the street from Harmony House, so it'd be convenient."

"Sounds like a workable plan," said Mildred carefully. She glanced at her watch and then to the door. Maybe he wasn't going to show up. Damn.

"Still, drinking's the only real pleasure I get out of life." Cora craned her neck. "When's this fellow coming anyway? Shouldn't he be here by now?"

"He's late. I just hope he comes at all. I was rather cryptic on the phone and hoped that piqued his curiosity, but you never know."

"Well, I don't think that waitress is going to refill our cups forever. As it is I'm about to float away." Cora grimaced slightly. "Think they'd mind if I used the ladies' room?"

"Of course not. You're a patron."

Mildred realized that in all likelihood Cora was escaping for a shot from a bottle stashed in her handbag. But what could she do? Then another thought crossed her mind. Maybe Cora was escaping period. As Cora got up to leave, Mildred grabbed her arm. "Don't desert me, Cora. Please."

"Don't you worry. You've piqued my curiosity too. I wouldn't miss this."

Mildred kept her eyes glued to the door. Scant seconds after Cora's departure a very wilted Freddy Townsend stepped into the frigid air conditioning of the Chef's Touch, damp curly hair matted to his scalp, a navy blue jacket slung limply over one shoulder. Heat, humidity and air pollution had put a damper on Freddy's customary swagger, or maybe he was just nervous.

He looked around for a moment, then spied her. "Mildred," he called out heartily.

She winced. His good cheer seemed forced. It grated, and the volume did too. She gritted her teeth and waited while Freddy wedged himself into the booth.

"God," he sighed, "this is a hole in the wall. Really Mildred, we could have met some place more comfortable. My club, for instance." He spied Cora's coffee cup and looked at her in surprise. "Someone's joining us?"

"Yes," she said airily, "just a friend. She'll be along shortly."

"Hmmm. I must say you're being very mysterious, Mildred. Mind telling me what all this is about? I assume you've discovered additional information about poor Esther."

"Perhaps," she said carefully. "We'll see."

His tone turned agitated. "What the devil is that supposed to mean?"

"Just bear with me, Freddy. Just wait until . . . ah, here she is now. Frederick Townsend, I'd like you to meet Cora Parks."

Reflexively Freddy shot to his feet and offered his hand. "Pleased to meet—" His nostrils were assailed by an aroma of Ivory soap and cheap whiskey. Abruptly he withdrew his hand.

Cora ignored this ill-concealed insult. She stood at the edge of the booth and studied Freddy Townsend's flushed face.

"Yes," she said at last, "I've seen this man before. I'm sure of it."

"My good woman," said Freddy in the most conciliatory tone he could muster, "I'm afraid you're mistaken. We've never met, and I certainly don't even recall hearing your name before." Freddy looked to Mildred. "Who the devil did you say she was?"

Cora threw the name out like a bone. "Cora Parks. But you wouldn't have known my name until right now. Wouldn't have known I was even there. I looked different then. Raggedy. Not so presentable as now."

Presentable? thought Freddy. The woman's mad. She's no more presentable than Ma Kettle. Take those clothes, for instance . . . why they're hopelessly out of style and swim on her at that. And the hair . . . a rat's nest. And upon closer inspection it appears . . . yes, it certainly appears as though she hasn't any teeth. Freddy's upper lip curled slightly.

"Wouldn't have known you were where?" He turned to Mildred, a mixture of revulsion and confusion written on his face. "Mildred, I'm afraid I'm at a loss here."

"Cora knew Esther, Freddy. You see, she was an occupant of sorts at the St. James Hotel."

"Yes," confirmed Cora. "Of sorts. I spent my days in the lobby. Long days, they were. I dozed a bit, it's true. Took a little nip now and then, I don't deny it. But I saw plenty, and I saw you. There. At least once. I'm sure of it."

"Oh, for Christ's sake," sputtered Freddy. "Really, Mildred, this is outrageous. Totally preposterous. I assure you I've never set foot in that hotel. The St. James, you say? Rubbish! The woman is confused. Demented. Surely you don't take her seriously. I know a boozer when I see one."

Cora glared at him.

"Or worse yet, she's deliberately lying." Freddy narrowed his eyes and turned them appraisingly on Cora. "Of course. That's it. You know a mark when you see one, don't you? You're trying to secure some kind of financial remuneration here. With Jonathan Maine's money."

"I am not!" Cora drew herself up indignantly. She fought the urge to slam Freddy with her hefty new handbag. "I saw you at the hotel. I know it. I wouldn't forget a man such as you."

Under other circumstances Freddy might have accepted the remark as a compliment, but then Cora proceeded to elaborate.

"What with that pompous demeanor of yours. And all those trappings too: the fancy suit, the gold cuff links, that paisley tie. I wouldn't forget paisley as ugly as that. Not to mention that cheap face-lift."

"Cheap face-lift!" cried Freddy.

"You ought to ask for your money back," said Cora. "It's sagging. Sagging bad."

Mildred tried to get this back on track. "You always wear paisley," she reminded him.

"Well," he huffed, "no one's going to convict a man for wearing paisley for Christ's sake!" Self-consciously he straightened his tie.

"Thank you, Cora," said Mildred.

"That's it?"

"For now."

Mildred waited until Cora was gone. "What's going on, Freddy?"

"I might ask you the same thing," he snapped, "but I don't intend to dignify these accusations by further discussion."

"Freddy, face it. We have now confirmed that you were at the St. James. Cora's not mistaken, and you know it. If need be, we will pin down the specific dates and times. We will secure collaboration from other witnesses."

"Witnesses?" he repeated in disbelief. He steadied his hands on the table.

"Yes. Others will turn up besides Cora. Why, even as

we speak Forrest's talking to a man who works across the alley." She arched an eyebrow. "Directly across from Esther's room. Who knows what he saw, Freddy?"

"Jesus." He looked around the shabby luncheonette. "Can't a man get a drink around here?" When no response was forthcoming, he bunched his shoulders into an angry hunch. "Shit," he muttered to no one in particular, "what a fine mess this is."

"Look Freddy," said Mildred gently, "no one's accusing you of the murder."

"No? You're the one talking about witnesses and collaboration. If that isn't accusing, I don't know what is. So you look, Mildred. Look and listen good. Nothing happened between Esther and me. You've got it all wrong."

"Oh? Then how do you explain—"

"I explain nothing, you understand? Nothing!"

"Freddy, there's no need to shout."

He lowered his voice and spoke through clenched teeth. "You listen to me, Mildred. Esther Maine was my sister-in-law, got it? My sister-in-law, period. I saw her at weddings, funerals, and Christmas. Once or twice a year, if that. I gave her a peck on the cheek. And that, my dear, was that." Abruptly he stood up. "Jesus Christ, this has gone far enough."

"But—"

"But nothing! You're trying to drive me crazy! I was never in that hotel, Mildred, and you can't prove it with some drunken old crone."

Mildred strove to keep her voice reasonable and calm. "I'm just trying to find out what happened to Esther. I thought you wanted to find out too."

"You're trying to pin this on me," replied Freddy. "I can see that plain as day. Well it won't work, Mildred."

"I—"

"Just back off. Back off now, you understand? Or you'll hear from my attorney."

That said, Freddy Townsend turned his back on Mildred and stalked out of the Chef's Touch.

30 Trevor eyed Alexander Blaustein skeptically. "No," he said finally. "I don't buy it. Esther Maine was a shy person, afraid of people. Certainly not the type to engage in sexual escapades."

"Come, come, Dr. Bradford," scoffed Blaustein. "Surely you are not so naive. Perhaps she was those things you say, and perhaps she was not. Whether she was or wasn't is immaterial. Because whatever the case, she could not help herself. It was a compulsion, something she could not resist."

"Oh? And why did she feel this compulsion?"

Blaustein wiped his lips carefully with a starched linen napkin. "We had not yet progressed in the therapeutic process to the point where she trusted me enough to reveal her innermost thoughts. I can, however, speak in general terms of such cases. If you like."

"Please."

"You see my little girl playing on that sandbar?"

"Yes."

"She is six years old, Dr. Bradford. Six years old. To her I am God. A potentially dangerous situation for a six-year-old—*if* the one who is supposed to be God takes unfair advantage."

"You're telling me Esther Maine was molested as a child."

"I am telling you nothing of the sort. I don't know if she was or wasn't. But I *am* saying that in the large majority of cases women who engage in compulsive and promiscuous sexual behavior were indeed abused at an early age. You might like to consult my book, *Sexual Promiscuity Among Females.*"

No thank you, thought Trevor, I think I'll pass. But not wanting to bruise the good doctor's ego, he scribbled a note on a scrap of paper.

"In such cases," Blaustein went on, "molestation was often the first real attention the victim received."

Trevor thought of the child in his office and didn't want to hear.

"There follows a drive, an absolute craving, from an empty gut. That is how the victims themselves describe it. A craving for attention, for power, for punishment. It is all intertwined, you see."

"What about the shoplifting?"

"A preliminary warning. A flare, you might say. A cry for attention. And for help."

"Ah," said Trevor. "And what about her marriage?"

"What about it?"

Trevor felt like screaming. All shrinks were the same, answering questions with questions. "Was she neglected? Slapped around maybe?"

"Her marriage was totally unrelated to her compulsion. She never mentioned ill treatment. She seemed devoted to her husband."

"And yet she sought companionship elsewhere. Did she tell you the names of the men she was involved with?"

"She did not."

"Did she describe them to you?"

"Only in vague, dreamlike terms. Mrs. Maine was a highly romantic woman and, despite her compulsion, rather Victorian in her attitudes about sex. Her notions about men and about physical love in particular were childlike and unrealistic. Of course, there are men who are drawn to such naïveté."

"And she talked about these men?"

"Yes. She called them suitors. As I said, her descriptions of them were vague and dreamlike."

"But one of these vague dreamlike men may have killed her, Dr. Blaustein."

"Perhaps."

"Let me understand this," said Trevor. "She came to you for treatment regarding the shoplifting. It was a cry for help. She came to you, and she got worse."

"People often do," said Blaustein simply, "before they get better. But she was making progress. Given time, she would have made a breakthrough." He shook his head and sighed. "What happened was a tragic waste. It's a shame you don't have any concrete leads."

"Oh but we do," said Trevor. "Or, I should say, we might."

"Oh?"

"There's a man who works across the way."

"Indeed."

"Yes. We're talking to him today. And there's a woman who frequents the lobby. Alcoholic, unfortunately. But she knew the victim."

"Ah yes," responded Blaustein thoughtfully. "I believe Mrs. Maine mentioned this woman in one of our sessions. Her name escapes me at the moment."

"Cora," said Trevor. "Cora Parks."

"Of course," said Blaustein. "Cora Parks."

"Did you love Esther Maine, Dr. Blaustein?"

Blaustein stiffened visibly. "I beg your pardon?"

"Did you love her?"

"I love all my patients," said Blaustein. He looked at Trevor with unblinking eyes. "It comes with the territory and is part of the process. If you are asking did I act on that love in a physical way, the answer is unequivocally no."

"Did she love you?"

"That too is a phase of the process. Perhaps she did. A little bit." Blaustein looked away and reached for his seltzer.

"What about the abuse? Do you have any idea who might have done it?"

"If indeed it occurred, there are many possibilities. An uncle. A cousin. An older brother. Her father. The parents lived apart, as I understand it. Her father was but an infrequent visitor to the home. She adored him. This she told me more than once."

"I see," said Trevor.

"One other thing," said Blaustein. "Perhaps I shouldn't tell you this, but it may help."

"Yes?" said Trevor.

"The oldest child. Her name is Claudia?"

"Yes."

"She is not, as I understand it, the husband's child."

Trevor set down his glass. "You're mistaken, Dr. Blaustein. I was there after the baby was born. Jonathan was very proud of his daughter."

Blaustein shrugged. "I am only telling you what she told me, and she told me the first baby was not his."

"I don't understand then. I don't understand at all."

"Neither did I. I tried to elicit more information from her, but she resisted."

Trevor sat there, stunned.

"It occurs to me that her relationship with this person— with Claudia's father—may have continued over time. That possibly he . . ." He stopped. "But who knows? Perhaps it is nothing."

"Perhaps," said Trevor. "Unfortunately we may never find out. If what you say is true, Esther Maine may have taken the name of the father to the grave with her."

"Possibly," said Blaustein smoothly, "but not necessarily. Ask her husband. If indeed he is committed to find the murderer, perhaps he will tell you."

"Even at the risk of exposing this secret to Claudia."

Blaustein shrugged again. "Who knows? If Esther Maine's mother is still alive, you might ask her. Sometimes there are family secrets. Conspiracies of silence."

"Yes," said Trevor grimly, "sometimes there are." He got up to leave, then sat back down. "One last question, Dr. Blaustein . . ."

"Of course."

"Did you think you could save her?"

"Save?" Blaustein stopped and considered the question. "What an odd way to phrase it. I thought I could help her, yes."

"But you didn't."

"I would have."

"But you didn't."

"You sound angry, Dr. Bradford."

"I'm trying not to be, Dr. Blaustein, but I can't help thinking that you knew what was going on. At the very least, you suspected what was going on. Something very dangerous, didn't you say? And yet you did nothing to intervene."

"Intervene?" Blaustein repeated in amazement. "Again you bring this up. Therapy in itself is an intervention of sorts. I help the patient help herself. It is not my place to intervene further."

But Trevor couldn't stop. "You did nothing to intervene. Oh no. You were busy digging for roots. And while you were digging, the patient didn't get better. The patient died."

Blaustein flushed. "And you? What about you? You were her doctor all those years. When did this all begin, Dr. Bradford?"

Shocked, Trevor rose and reeled back from the table. His only thought was to get away from this man and from the accusations turned back against him.

"As long as you are dishing up blame, Dr. Bradford, save a portion for yourself."

31 Irene found Claudia Maine surrounded by boxes and packing paper.

"I called your office, and they said you quit." The words tumbled out as a breathless accusation.

"Yes," said Claudia shortly. She continued placing stereo cassette tapes into a corrugated container and barely glanced at Irene.

"And all these boxes . . . it looks like you're moving or something."

"It does look that way," replied Claudia.

"So are you? Moving?"

"Yes."

"Oh," said Irene. For some moments Claudia kept packing, and Irene kept watching. Finally she could contain her curiosity no longer. "So where you moving to?"

"None of your business."

"I'm only asking 'cause I'm concerned, is all."

"Well don't be."

"You being pregnant and all."

"I'll manage."

"Only yesterday you said you'd have no place to live."

"That was yesterday," said Claudia. "This is today." She glanced at the squat woman planted in her doorway. "What's that?"

Irene looked down at the shopping bag in her hand as though discovering it for the first time. "This here? Why, it's for you."

"Me?" Claudia strove for indifference. "What on earth

would you possibly want to bring me?"

"It's a blanket. A baby blanket. I mean, I know the baby's not due till April, but April can be chilly sometimes. And you'll want to take her for walks and such, 'course if you do I sure hope it's not in this neighborhood. Or he, maybe it'll be a he instead of a she and you'll take him for walks. Wherever that may be."

Claudia stared at Irene in disbelief.

Irene pulled the blanket from the bag. White tissue paper floated to the floor. "I got it in yellow. That way, boy or girl, it'll be okay."

Claudia blinked but said nothing.

"I would have knit it myself," Irene went on, "but my fingers aren't as limber as they used to be, and besides I wanted you to have it right away."

"Well," said Claudia. "I don't know what to say."

"You could try 'thank you.' " Irene smiled and handed her the blanket.

Claudia took it in both hands and brushed the satin edge against her cheek. "Thanks," she said gruffly.

"You're welcome, I'm sure." Her tone turned wistful. "I'm awful fond of babies. Never had one myself. We didn't know if it was my plumbing or Earl's. Didn't want to know neither. But the fact was we couldn't. Sometimes I wonder . . ." She stopped herself and looked around. "Well, never mind that. We are as God made us."

"I suppose."

"Well, I guess I'll be going."

Claudia looked at her but said nothing.

"I mean, I might as well, right? Now that I know you're okay and all." Irene moved away a step. "Don't go moving those cartons yourself, though, you hear?"

"I hear."

"You need anything, just give a holler." Irene reached into a pocket. "I wrote my number down on this here scrap of paper. I'll just set it on the table. You call me, any time. Day or night."

"Okay."

Irene turned to leave.

"Wait."

Irene whirled around.

"Maybe you could help me pack. I mean, I'm supposed to move tomorrow. It's all happening so fast. I'll never get everything done." She looked at Irene and let down her guard the barest bit. "I really could use the help."

"Why sure," said Irene, her face brightening. "I'm good at packing. Just tell me what to do. But if you don't mind my asking, I'd sure like to know where you're moving. I'll rest easier knowing you and the baby are in a safer neighborhood, don't you know."

Claudia chose to ignore Irene's prying. She busied herself with surveying several partially finished canvases. "I don't know what I'm going to do about these," she said. "They're still wet."

"I said," persisted Irene, "I'd rest easier knowing—"

"Oh all right," replied Claudia in exasperation. "If you must know, I'm moving back to Raven's Wing."

"Go on! You aren't either!"

"I am too. In fact, my father has invited me to come home."

"You don't say!"

"See? I knew you'd think it was just too bizarre."

"Oh no," said Irene. "I think it's fine. Real fine indeed. People who need each other should stick together. You need him, he needs you. And it sure won't hurt Cameron and Lauren and Timmy none to have their big sister around. What could be better? It's just that the last time I was here, it sounded like . . . well, you talked like . . ."

"Like I hated him?"

"Sort of."

Claudia sat down on the bed. Unconsciously she put her hands on her as yet flat stomach. "I don't know," she said. "I suppose I do. Or did. It's all so confusing. He came over last night from the clinic. And he looked so—I don't know—he looked so down."

"He's taking it hard, Claudia."

"I know. And she must have told him where I was, because all of a sudden he shows up out of the blue just to see how I'm doing."

"That was nice."

"Yeah, I thought so too. Only I played it cool. There's a lot of fences between us. Anyway he got to talking. Asked me what I was going to do. I fumbled around with that one for a while. Then he asked me if I needed any money. I was about to answer when all of a sudden his face sort of lit up and he said why didn't I come back home? Said I could live in the pool house. I mean, it's big enough, that's for sure. Two bedrooms and a decent size living room—with northern light, which is great for my painting."

"And you accepted."

"Like a shot." Claudia seemed to switch channels to her hard side. "Any port in a storm. You know how it is. After all, I don't have a whole lot of choices."

"Oh come on, Claudia," scoffed Irene. "Don't give me that. You're tickled about the idea, I can see it all over your face."

Claudia smiled then, allowing a fleeting, unguarded instant of happiness to wash over her face. "Yeah," she admitted. "I guess I am."

Irene proceeded to stow stacks of paperbacks in an empty carton. "Gosh," she said happily, "we'll be neighbors. Maybe you'll let me babysit."

"That would be a help." She was silent for some moments. Finally she stopped what she was doing and looked at Irene. "Any more ideas about what happened to my mother?"

"Not really. We're nosing around, talking to this one and that. Trying to get some kind of picture."

"You know," said Claudia thoughtfully, "there was something I didn't tell you. I thought of it later. I don't know if it will help."

"Try me," said Irene. She grabbed a handful of Claudia's T-shirts and started folding each with practiced hands.

"Well, toward the end there—during the last month or so—my mother seemed different."

"Your aunt said the same thing. That she seemed happier."

"Yes. She'd always been quiet and sort of mousy. But now that I think about it, she brightened up around then. Smiled more. Talked more. Seemed to enjoy herself more. I even remarked on it once."

"And what did she say?"

"She got very mysterious. Then she laughed." Claudia stopped, remembering. "She had a beautiful laugh. But she said the strangest thing. I mean it was so ridiculous that I laughed too and put it entirely out of my mind."

"So what was it?"

"She said, 'Maybe I'm in love. What do you think of that?' "

"And what *did* you think?"

"I thought she was joking. But now I don't know. I keep thinking about it. What if she was having an affair or something?" Claudia considered this for a moment and squinched up her face. "No. Not in a million years. No way."

"Claudia, how can you be so sure?"

"I knew her, that's why." Claudia was silent for a moment. "Or at least I thought I did. Jesus. What if she was seeing someone?"

"Yeah," said Irene. "What if?"

"And what if the guy killed her? I guess that sounds crazy, doesn't it?"

"No," said Irene softly. "I don't think it sounds crazy at all."

32 Beatrice Watson paused with her mop and little wheeled bucket outside one of many offices along executive row. Ten o'clock and sure enough, he was still here. Damn. She had thought a night job, even a menial one like this, was a good way to put herself through college. The work wasn't terribly taxing, and though the hours were long, there was ample time to study. Sometimes she even wrote papers on one of their PCs. But this man was a decided disadvantage. He gave her the creeps.

She leaned down low and looked under the door. The light was on this time. Sometimes he sat there in the dark and sometimes the light was on. Either way it was downright creepy. Now he was doing something even creepier. He was talking to himself. Again.

She squatted on her haunches there in the hallway, listening to muttered whispers from within. She braced herself on the linoleum and pressed her ear to the door. As in the past, she took care to hold a wet sponge in her hand, lest the door swing open suddenly.

Creepy, creepy, creepy, talking to himself like that. The man might be a big-shot executive with a fancy office, but to Beatrice those things were no more than a clever disguise. He was crazy, a textbook example of psychosis. Everyone knows people who talk to themselves are crazy, thought Beatrice. This is fact. Just look at street people. Sometimes they not only talked, they ranted. Sometimes they spit. It was disgusting. Why just the other day an old man dressed in urine-soaked rags hawked a disgusting oyster right onto her best Sunday coat. It made her want to upchuck just remembering.

She looked at a brass plate to the right of the door. *Norman L. Winkler.* *L* for lunatic. She pictured the word written in red crayon right there on the wall and smiled in spite of herself. Then the mutterings behind the door became markedly louder and Beatrice became fearful. It almost sounded like someone else was in there with him. Maybe he wasn't talking to himself.

In spite of her fear, Beatrice squatted closer.

"I have children," she heard him say. "A family."

Whoopie shit, thought Beatrice sourly. We've all got family, mister. Some nights this Winkler fellow babbled this and that about a wife that didn't understand him. Or about his children doing drugs. Sometimes he babbled about wanting to chuck it all and run away with some lady named Camille.

"I saw nothing," she heard then. "A shape, nothing more . . . I don't know, I tell you! I don't know!"

Beatrice perked up at this. He was flying off on a new tangent now, talking of shapes.

"I couldn't see! She fell backwards. Whoever it was dragged her out of view."

Beatrice froze at these words. The man was talking about someone dying. Someone being killed. Maybe something to do with that woman across the street. The way he stared out that window for hours on end, maybe he saw something.

I'd best get out of here, thought Beatrice. I don't want to hear any more.

She didn't move.

The voice behind the door edged up hysterically. "Leave me alone!"

More mumblings.

"I didn't tell him anything, I swear it! Please, you're hurting me!"

Nut or no nut, this Winkler fellow was definitely talking like someone was in there with him. Beatrice stood stock still for a moment, frozen in a dilemma. To help or not to help.

"Oh God, please!"

Unable to stop herself, she reached for the knob. The door was locked. "Mr. Winkler, are you okay?"

The answer was a long time coming. When the voice answered it was hoarse and raggedy. "Yes, Bea. I dozed off. Had a bad dream. Just go on home."

She forced herself to say the next: "You don't want me to clean your office?"

"No."

"You sure?"

"Yes. Please. Just go."

Guiltily she heaved a sigh of relief, got up, and left. But all the way home on the subway she thought about Mr. Winkler. The man had always been twitchy and creepy, but this night he sounded really scared. She hoped he was all right.

33 Forrest Haggarty slept fitfully on the couch in Mildred's living room, his snores mingling stereophonically with those of Winston, who lay on the floor next to him. As frequently happened in his dreams, Forrest felt a pull away from New York City and back to Raven's Wing. I'm a country boy, he would have told anyone who cared to listen. I don't belong here. He wondered how things were going in town . . . wondered if the Family Y had closed for lack of funds, like everyone said it would . . . wondered if they'd erected that fancy barricade around the fountain so

folks wouldn't drive into it anymore . . . wondered if folks
were still walking their canines on Mildred's property,
leaving dog poop hidden in the grass like land mines . . .
but most of all he wondered how the Maine children were
getting along. . . .

Cameron Maine looked at him with eyes flat as nickels.

*"Look, boy, I'm doing the best I can." He reached
out to put an arm around the youngster's shoulders, but
Cameron pulled away.*

*The boy's too old for a hug, Forrest reminded himself.
'Sides, you got to be careful with kids today. One spontaneous gesture of affection and folks think you're a pervert
or something.*

"How you doing, anyway?"

The word fell out automatically. "Fine."

*That's what he tells everybody, probably. That he's fine,
when you can see plain as day he isn't. When you can see
he's holding himself in tight, like something might explode
inside if he lets go.*

"I heard how you handled the funeral and everything."

The boy's reply was matter-of-fact. "Someone had to."
*Cameron directed his gaze over Forrest's shoulder as he
went on. "I can't seem to cry. I don't know why. I go to
bed at night and put my face into the pillow and wait for
tears, but I'm bone dry. It's like part of me died along
with her."*

"You're in shock, that's what it is."

*"Doesn't matter. I'm too old to cry anyway. I have
responsibilities now. I have to make sure my father's all
right, make sure Lauren's all right, make sure Timmy's
all right."*

"Just make sure Cameron's all right, you hear?"

"I'm fine."

"Yeah, sure."

"I can stand it."

*Forrest doubted he could. Maybe for now he could
hold himself together, but sure as there's lightning in*

August he'd crumble someday, and when he did it would be bad. Forrest felt a sudden and inexplicable urgency to contain a tragedy as yet unfolding. It was the same way he'd felt back in the big war when a live grenade exploded during a training exercise. He'd watched in helpless horror as bodies of his buddies burst open like overripe watermelons. Faces blown away. Hands gone. Feet and fingers flying in the air. A spray of pink. All in amazing slow motion.

"Timmy doesn't even remember her anymore, you know that? Only a month and already he's forgotten."

"Little ones forget fast, the good with the bad. It's a blessing and curse. But you remember, and you miss her."

"I miss little things. I miss her meat loaf. Stupid, isn't it."

"No," said Forrest. "Not stupid."

"The other night I realized I'd never taste that meat loaf again. No two people make meat loaf exactly the same, you know. And I miss asking what's for dinner and hearing her say 'mockingbird's eyelashes.' I miss seeing her in the garden surrounded by her gladiolas. I miss hearing her stories. She used to tell great stories—" He stopped himself and looked away. "It's okay. It wasn't any big deal."

"Someday you'll make up some yourself. You'll tell them to your own children."

"If I live that long."

"Hush up, boy! If you live that long? What a thing to say!"

"Forrest, honey, wake up."

"You listen to me! You've got years left. *Years.*"

"Forrest!"

"Huh?"

"You were talking in your sleep something awful."

He looked up and into the faces of Irene, Trevor, and Mildred peering down at him. "I must have dozed off."

He looked at the clock. "Jesus, it's after eight."

"He looks peaked," decided Irene. "Don't he look peaked?"

Forrest swung his feet to the floor. "I feel fine, Reenie. Never better." He'd never admit how that dream gave him a chill. Never. "Can't a man take a nap without folks deciding he's got one foot in the grave?"

"Of course," said Mildred. "We hate to wake you, but we held dinner as long as we could. We want to review the case while we eat."

"I must say," said Trevor, "I'm rather curious about the man across the alleyway."

Forrest smiled. "I wasn't sure it would amount to anything. But now we've got ourselves a second potential witness."

"Do tell!" exclaimed Irene.

"His name is Norman Winkler, and I think he'll cooperate."

Forrest told his friends about the peeper while they ate a dinner of veal marsala, green beans almandine, and wild rice. It wasn't half bad, even if Mildred did get it out of *Weight Watchers Cookbook*.

"Well," said Trevor when he was finished, "this case gets more outlandish every step of the way."

Mildred set down her napkin. "This Winkler fellow might be more than a witness, Forrest. Think about it. The letter she sent could be construed as blackmail. Or consider this: Even though it may have been no more than a diversion to her—a dangerous diversion, to be sure—Esther may have provoked the man to murder. You yourself said he was thrilled at her attentions, but he was terrified too."

"And more than a little jealous," added Trevor.

Irene nodded in agreement. "They got a point, Forrest."

"I know," he conceded. "But he did love her, in his way. I know loving someone can be a motive to murder, but in this case I don't think so. Winkler's a passive person. An observer. Not someone who acts out."

Mildred turned to Trevor. "And what about you? What happened with Alexander Blaustein?"

"I thought you'd never ask."

Trevor related the details of his visit that afternoon to Esther Maine's psychiatrist, including the bombshell he dropped about Claudia's questionable paternity.

"Of all the wicked things!" said Irene. "Jeesum, I sure hope you're not going to tell Claudia."

"Of course not," said Trevor. "That's the last thing the poor girl needs to know."

Forrest remained quiet. He wondered whether Jonathan knew about Claudia and, if indeed he did, how much it bothered him. It certainly must have way back when he was a newlywed. But maybe he made his peace with it.

Trevor set down his fork. "There's another thing," he said quietly. "It's just a hunch, but I think there may have been something going on between the two of them—Esther and her doctor."

Forrest looked at Trevor keenly. "That's unlike you, going on hunches."

"You're right," Trevor agreed, "but other factors got me thinking."

"Other factors like what?" asked Irene.

"I made a few calls this afternoon to the American Psychiatric Association and the American Psychoanalytic Association to see if either of them had any grievances filed against Alexander Blaustein. The answer was yes in both cases. Dr. Blaustein, it seems, is a man with a past."

"What kind of past?" pressed Forrest.

"Five years ago he left Los Angeles in disgrace after several of his patients accused him of seducing them."

Mildred set down her coffee cup. "My word."

"It's not all that unusual, unfortunately. Some psychiatrists have been known to take advantage of patients' vulnerability. But in Blaustein's case it was pretty extreme. It turned out to be any physician's nightmare. Four patients got together and filed criminal charges. When those didn't stick, they filed a civil suit. From what I understand their case was compelling. Dr. Blaustein settled out of court for a tremendous amount of money. He was ruined professionally, financially, and personally. His marriage fell apart."

"So that's why he only takes on men patients now!" exclaimed Irene.

"Possibly. He may want to avoid temptation—and the possibility that some disgruntled woman will make a false accusation."

"He seems to have recouped well enough," said Forrest.

"That he has," agreed Trevor. "Dr. Blaustein has built a remarkable practice, no doubt about it. He's president of something called The Confidential Trust. It's a consortium of psychotherapists offering personal therapy, management consulting, and a modern hybrid of the two—executive coaching. For three hundred and fifty dollars an hour, they treat titans of industry and government in the privacy of the client's home or office."

"So why take Esther Maine as a client?" asked Forrest. "He couldn't have been earning that much off her."

"Unless," said Mildred, "she was giving him money. Lots of money."

Forrest seemed to consider this. "It's a possibility. One we'll have to check out."

"Wait'll you hear about Millie's day," said Irene.

"Now," said Mildred modestly, "it wasn't really any big deal."

"Go on! It was too." She turned to Forrest and Trevor. "Millie here may have cornered the killer."

Forrest's head swiveled. "What?"

"Oh I wouldn't go that far," said Mildred. "I mean, Freddy Townsend isn't necessarily—"

"Freddy Townsend? What about Freddy Townsend?"

"Well I saw him today and—"

"What makes you think he's the killer?"

"Let her speak, Forrest!" Trevor felt like dousing Forrest with his wine. The man could be so overbearing sometimes.

"Thank you, Trevor." Mildred took a sip of her coffee. "Now where was I? Oh yes, I saw Freddy Townsend today and introduced him to Cora."

"You didn't!" cried Forrest.

"I most certainly did."

Forrest buried his face in his hands. "Christ, I don't believe it."

Mildred looked at him in confusion. This had been a brilliant stroke on her part. How could he be angry? "Forrest," she said in a quivery voice, "did I do something wrong?"

"Wrong?" said Forrest sarcastically. "Wrong? Oh no, what you did was fine, Millie. Mighty fine."

Trevor looked at Forrest. "Forrest, for heaven's sake what's the matter?"

"Never mind. If you're all too dumb to see it, just never mind." Forrest looked at his cleaned plate. "Shit," he muttered.

"Well," said Mildred, standing up, "I don't have to take this abuse!"

Trevor touched her elbow. "Don't go, Mildred. Please."

"Yeah, Millie." Irene looked at her with concern. "We want to hear what happened. Forrest's sorry he snapped." She looked pointedly at him. "Aren't you, Forrest."

"Jesus," said Forrest irritably. "Why doesn't anyone tell me what's going on around here? We're supposed to work in concert, not in all directions. We're supposed to work like professionals. We're supposed to have a plan."

"Yes," said Mildred icily. "With you in charge."

"Christ, you're like a bull in a china shop, handing over a witness on a silver platter."

"I did not!"

"Oh yeah? What the hell do you call it then? You've placed her in danger."

Mildred's lower lip started to quiver. "I've known Freddy and Constance for years. They wouldn't—"

"Oh yeah? Maybe they would. If anything happens to Cora Parks, it'll be your fault."

Mildred's eyes filled with tears. She bit her lip and looked away. "Nothing will happen," she managed to say.

Irene put her arm around Mildred's shoulder. "Millie, don't." She glared at Forrest. "Now see what you've gone and done? You're the bull in the china shop. Say you're sorry."

Forrest hunched his shoulders and looked at his plate.

"Say it!"

"Oh, all right. I'm sorry. Let's forget the whole thing. No use crying over spilt milk."

"Actually . . ." began Trevor. He meant to confess that he too told someone about Cora Parks. He'd told Dr. Blaustein out at the beach house. Trying to impress the man. But Irene interrupted, and the moment was lost.

"Tell 'em what happened, Millie."

Mildred dabbed her eyes and straightened up in her chair. "Very well." She proceeded to relate her meeting with Cora and Freddy. "And you know what? Freddy lied to me! He denied ever having set foot in the St. James Hotel."

"There," said Forrest. "You see?"

"That doesn't make him a killer," she insisted. "He's a pompous ass, yes, but not a murderer."

"I don't like this, Mildred," said Trevor. "It could be getting dangerous."

"They wouldn't dare hurt me."

"They might if they feel trapped," warned Forrest. "No matter. You just leave Freddy Townsend to me from now on."

"Not on your life!" shot back Mildred. Why the nerve of the man! "You gave me Freddy and Constance, Forrest. You *assigned* them to me when I didn't even want them. Remember?"

He grunted.

"I was a good soldier and I accepted the assignment, distasteful as it was. Now that things are getting dicey I'm not bowing out. Freddy Townsend is nervous as a cat. He's getting ready to talk, I can feel it. If you start meddling he'll clam up. And Constance?" Mildred hooted. "She'd never talk to you, never in a million years."

"Oh yeah?" snapped Forrest. "And why not?"

"Because," replied Mildred, "*you* are the bull in the china shop. Especially when it comes to dealing with people's feelings."

Forrest turned to Trevor. "Maybe you can reason with her. She's your girlfriend."

Trevor's impulse was to protest the remark, but he decided instead to ignore it. While it wasn't quite accurate yet, if he had his way it soon would be.

"Don't look at me, Forrest. I don't feel any better about this than you do, but when Mildred sets her mind on something there's no changing it. Plus she's got a point about her relationship—and access—to Freddy and Constance."

"I'm glad you realize that," said Mildred, closing the matter to further discussion.

Finally Irene told the group about her day of packing with Claudia, told them how Claudia was moving back to Raven's Wing with the encouragement and support of her father.

"Well," beamed Mildred, "that is wonderful news."

"Jonathan really seems to be making an effort," said Forrest. "When he said he was going to try to get closer to his children I didn't believe it. I thought it was beyond him."

"They need each other more than ever now," remarked Trevor. "Maybe some good will come out of this tragedy after all."

34 Jonathan Maine and his son Cameron jogged up the long driveway of crushed white stone. They wore sweat-soaked T-shirts, gray gym shorts, and matching Nikes. When they reached the crest of the property they sat by the side of the pool, their white legs dangling in the cool chlorinated water.

This daily run had been born of Jonathan's despair. One night he simply could stand it no longer. Helga fluttered at his shoulder, the inevitable white ghost forever lamenting about his lack of appetite, urging him to taste this or try that, pouring him yet another glass of wine. Jonathan gulped the wine but scarcely touched his food. He stared stonily at his plate of barbecued chicken, potato salad, and steamed broccoli. The hollandaise sauce had congealed, forming a sticky skin.

He steeled himself and looked at the bleak faces around the table. Cameron. Lauren. Lucille. Timothy. Faces full of expectation and need.

"What do you want?" he said. "What!"

Lucille, who disapproved of displays of emotion, set her mouth in its inevitable grim line. Lauren looked away, her eyes filling with tears. Cameron, predictably, said, "It's okay, Dad. Okay."

Like a mantra, the word seemed to reverberate in his head. *Okay. Okay. Okay.* Jonathan threw his napkin down on the table.

"No it's not," he snapped cruelly. "Nothing's okay anymore. It never will be okay again. Got that? Everything stinks and I can't make it okay anymore. I can't!"

The words rang in his ears and he reeled from the table. He staggered outside to the patio, where he was confronted by his sculptures. The statues stared at him mutely, a study of accusation in alabaster. He hadn't sculpted for weeks, hadn't so much as touched a mallet or a chisel, not since—

Jonathan reached for a hammer left on the patio tiles by a forgetful workman. He hefted it in his hand. He lifted the hammer overhead and smashed it down on one of his finest pieces, a pair of swans with delicate intertwined necks. There was a sharp crack followed by a clatter as delicate necks cracked and severed heads tumbled to the patio tiles. He struck the bodies, the wings, with ever more force. Marble fragments flew like shrapnel. Finally, mercifully, the hammer snapped in two.

"Your hands!" cried Lucille. Her stark black form waved at him from the window, framed in a yellow square of light. "Your hands!"

Yes, he thought. My hands.

"Daddy, please," sobbed Lauren. "Oh please."

"It's okay, Dad. Okay."

Okay, okay, okay.

He turned and fled, a ludicrous figure running down the driveway in a starched white shirt, gray suitpants, and cordovan wingtips. He ran into the blessed blackness of the night, away from his needy family. He ran and kept on running. Down Peaceable Street . . . through Westmoreland development . . . up High Ridge . . . past the Schroeder house. It wasn't until he was almost home, drenched with perspiration, his face streaked with tears, that he became aware that someone was running behind him.

"Cameron?"

"Yeah."

"What," wheezed Jonathan, "are you doing here?"

"Just keep going. You're doing fine. Just . . . keep . . . running."

Afterward when he caught his breath, he tried to make light of the incident. "What did you think?" he scoffed. "That I'd run away?"

"I was afraid," said Cameron carefully.

Jonathan turned away, not wanting to hear.

"Afraid that you were going to hurt yourself."

Jonathan paused, his hand on the front door knob. He didn't look at his son.

"I was afraid," Cameron repeated, forcing himself to say what nobody else would, "that you might . . . kill yourself."

Jonathan's hand dropped from the knob and he turned to face the dark shape that was his son. He put an awkward hand on the boy's shoulder. "I won't, Cameron. You have my word. I won't do such a thing."

Cameron had felt a clutch in his stomach every time he thought about it. Every time he saw the commercial that touted the message *Here's to the man who shaves with a blade*. Every time he saw a length of rope. Or a knife. Every time he heard a firecracker. Now that the words had started, he couldn't stop them.

"I mean, if anything happened to you I'd be left with these children. I don't know that I could manage. I don't know—"

"Never," repeated Jonathan. "I will never do that. You have my word."

"I'm sorry about all this, Dad. Honest to God. I'm so sorry."

Jonathan looked at his son sadly. "So am I."

After that they ran every day. Cameron was a natural. As for Jonathan himself, he ran with the ungainly gait of a man falling over from the waist up and trying to catch up from the waist down. In time, however, his stride improved. He discovered he ran better in Nikes than in Florsheim wingtips. And the exercise cleared his head. He started eating right and drinking less. His paunch was melting away. He was developing something that remotely resembled a physique.

And now, here they sat—Jonathan and Cameron—by the edge of the pool, glasses of iced tea in hand.

"What do you think of Claudia coming back?" asked Jonathan.

"It's okay," said Cameron, keeping his tone neutral. "As long as she's all right."

Cameron had been old enough to witness Claudia at her worst, old enough too to witness the heartache she'd caused her parents. He'd seen how she could disappoint people, how she could hurt people too. He was hedging his bets.

"I'm trying to rebuild this family, Cameron."

"I know."

"Claudia needs a place. And frankly we could use some help around here, what with Timmy and all."

"Timmy has Helga."

"That's true." Thank goodness for that, thought Jonathan. He thought about Helga and forced himself to say the next thing. "But Helga isn't family."

"Grandma doesn't like Claudia."

"Grandma doesn't like most people. Claudia is part of this family. If Grandma doesn't like her, that's just tough shit."

Cameron's face broke into a grin at his father's unexpected and irreverent choice of words.

"Maybe we should have a party," said Jonathan suddenly.

"A party?"

"You know, kind of a welcome home party. For Claudia."

"Who would we invite?"

"Oh I don't know . . . some of her old high school friends. You know, those girls she used to hang out with. Phoebe and Polly and Karen and Barbie."

"They're all gone, Dad. They grew up. They moved away."

"Oh. Well, we could make it a small party then. Just family. Maybe some of your friends."

A very small list, thought Cameron, very small.

"We could invite Aunt Constance and Uncle Freddy. And Forrest Haggarty and his girlfriend. That lady, what's her name?"

"Irene Purdy."

"And the Bennett woman and Dr. Bradford. I've been wanting to see if they've found out anything anyway."

"Yeah," said Cameron, warming to the idea. Maybe a small party would be okay. At least it would be a start. Never in his life could he remember a party here at home. His mother hadn't been one for parties.

At lunchtime when Jonathan told Lucille about the party, she was outraged. "It's too soon," she snapped.

"No," Jonathan shot back, "it's almost too late."

"My Esther's barely in the ground a month, and you're throwing a celebration."

"A party," corrected Jonathan. "For Claudia. A small party."

"People will talk."

"I hope to hell they do. It'd be a lousy party with a bunch of mutes standing around."

"That's not what I meant and you know it."

"We're having the damn party," he said flatly. "This weekend. This family's been in seclusion for too long."

35 "Will you kindly stop pacing!"

"Fine!" He hurled himself into an overstuffed leather chair and blinked at her with red-rimmed eyes. "Maybe you'd prefer I simply got blitzed at nine in the morning." He glared at her glass of orange juice.

"I—" She started to tell him it was only that. Juice. But then she gave up. "It steadies my nerves."

"Christ," he muttered, "what a fine pair we are."

"I can't believe this is happening," she said, turning weepy.

"Please, Constance, don't start again. Not after last night. I can't take it now."

"Oh," she shot back, *"you* can't take it. That's rich, Freddy, really rich. First my sister dies—"

"You never liked her," he reminded her. "Never had a good word to say about the woman."

But Constance would hear none of this. In her mind she had lost a beloved sister and she would wear a mantle of grief for all the world to see.

"—and now people will say you were having an affair with her. How can this be happening? Even in death Esther reaches out and grabs what's rightfully mine."

"People will say, people will say," mimicked Freddy. "That's all you've ever cared about. What people will say."

"You don't know what it's like," she cried. "You never grew up poor. You never had a mother who cleaned toilets for your friends."

"Spare me, Constance. I'm not in the mood."

But Constance was on a roll. "You never had a father who came and went like some kind of gypsy bearing gifts for a foster child but not for you! You never had to worry about getting into the right clubs! You were born into them."

"Playing poor little match girl doesn't become you, Constance, it never did." He hugged himself and rocked in the chair.

She waved him off with a spastic hand. "I pulled myself up from all that, Freddy. I fought tooth and nail. I got that scholarship to Pine Manor."

"Pine Mattress."

"Go ahead, call it whatever you like. It got me out of

Raven's Wing. And it got me into Finch. On another scholarship, goddamnit!"

"Your crowning achievement."

"No," she said bitterly. "My crowning achievement was marrying you." She took a slug of the most powerful juice east of the Hudson.

Freddy stood up and stalked over to his wife. His movements were rigid and jerky. "Look at you! Just look at you! You've done this to yourself, no one else. Lord knows, *I* didn't do it." He stood over her, quivering with exhaustion and unspent anger, his fists clenched at his sides. Then, to his astonishment, his voice cracked and he emitted a stifled cry.

"Freddy?"

He turned away.

Constance fluttered to his side. "Freddy, my God, what's wrong?"

The words, when they came, were choked. "I'm crying, that's what's wrong."

Constance watched him helplessly. She set down her glass. She touched his shoulder tentatively. "Freddy, what is it?"

"I haven't slept in days. I can't concentrate. I—"

She gave his arm a squeeze. "It's all right, Freddy."

"They're going to blame this murder on me."

"Oh no," she said hastily. "No, they won't."

"Yes they will. I have no alibi, don't you understand? I think I better get Harvey over here right now."

Constance sobered up instantly. "Forget Harvey. I know he's been your lawyer for years, but the man's a doddering idiot. Besides, Mildred Bennett isn't the police."

"That's true."

She took out a handkerchief and dabbed his face. "She won't hurt you, Freddy. None of them will hurt you."

"How can you be so sure?" he said thickly.

"I won't let them. I'll take care of you, Freddy. Haven't I always taken care of you?"

"Yes."

"This is all just nonsense, Freddy. It won't amount to anything."

He desperately hoped she was right. He felt her move away. "Where are you going?"

"Out. Just for a while. To pick up some flowers, run some errands."

"You'll be back soon?"

"Very soon." She put on Dior sunglasses and a broad-brimmed straw hat. She walked to the stairway. "And Freddy?"

"Yes?"

"Don't do anything foolish while I'm gone."

"No," he said hollowly. He blew his nose. "Nothing foolish."

After an hour he could stand it no longer. He picked up the phone.

36 "Where the hell am I?"

Her eyes darted around the strange room, taking in the blond plastic veneer furniture, a Westclox alarm clock, and an unfamiliar dress draped over a chair by the window. Her dress. Worn yesterday.

"Oh," she said glumly. "Harmony House."

She looked at the creature. That's what she called him sometimes, though not to his face. He didn't respond to "creature." He responded to "Walter." A strange name for a cat, if you asked her. But he was too old to change. Too old, just like she was.

She glanced down by the side of the bed, into a paper-lined wastebasket where an empty pint of Mother Fletcher's lay tipped on its side. Her medicine, that's what she told the creature last night. I need my medicine. Need it to survive. Tomorrow will be better. *I'll* be better. I won't need it anymore. Or at least not quite so much.

He had looked at her with unforgiving eyes. Blue eyes. Eyes that had seen death.

She remembered drinking herself to sleep last night and thinking of those blue eyes.

"You saw what happened. Higgins didn't jump, did he?"

The creature didn't reply.

"You and me, what a pair. We both know something. But I can't remember and you can't talk."

Unexpectedly the cat jumped on the bed and into her lap.

"Well, well! Aren't you friendly. Could be you're getting used to old Cora." She stroked him gingerly, and he started to purr. "Now let Cora get up and get dressed."

Gently she repositioned the cat into folds of the blanket. She put her bare feet on the cool linoleum and padded over to the litter pan. She cleaned it thoroughly, changed Walter's water, and put out fresh food. Sheba. That lady Mildred had given her a week's supply. Then she washed her hands and face, brushed her teeth, and put on another new dress. It was too big and swam on her like a tent but it still looked better than anything she'd worn in years. Her fingers fumbled at the buttons.

"I'm trying not to want it, you know. I'm trying to put it right out of my mind. Cold turkey's the best way. It's like giving up smoking, that's all."

Only it wasn't. Her fingers trembled viciously. Her stomach did a spastic flip-flop. She could feel herself breaking into a sweat.

You can't do this alone. Dr. Bradford had told her that. You need hospitalization, Cora. She refused. Flatly. She knew what he meant. He meant going to detox, and she wasn't going to do it. Now that she had a chance at a seminormal life, she was going to take it. Whole hog. No detox. No medication. Just me.

And the shakes.

And the dreams.

And the visions.

No. She could stand anything except the visions. If they came, the DT's, she'd get thrown out of this place. There was no telling what she'd do once the DT's started. You see a man with snakes coming out of his mouth, you scream bloody murder. It's normal. You see rats eating away your toes, you fight them off with a baseball bat, no matter you break a few bones, your own, in the process. You do anything you can. You fight for your life.

Please. I have to do this. I have to try.

But she couldn't get the button to go through the hole. Her hands shook worse and her stomach did the two-step and her eyes filled with tears of frustration. She ran to the bathroom, the front of her dress exposing flat, shrunken breasts, and vomited.

She flushed and felt like flushing herself down with it.

"Oh God, Walter, I'm sick. I'm sick bad."

You need hospitalization, Walter seemed to say.

No.

Medication, at the very least.

Medication? You might have a point there. A little medication to tide me over. Just a sip to take away the shakes.

But the bottle was empty and there wasn't another. She would have to go outside. Walk to the liquor store. Buy a pint. Come back.

All of that would take time.

And you'll have to get dressed! To go outside.

I'm trying!

She managed to work one button through, then another. So what if they were in the wrong holes? So what!

Static crackled in the intercom. "Miss Parks, you have a delivery."

She hated that intercom. It was like a spy. "A delivery?"

she muttered to herself. "A delivery from where? Hell?"

"Miss Parks, are you there?"

Not really. "Yes."

"It's a man from Gristede's."

Oh. I need him like I need a hole in the head. The thought of food made her want to vomit again.

"He says Mrs. Bennett sent him over."

"Yeah," she said. "Right. Does he have snakes in his bag?"

"I beg your pardon?"

"Never mind. Send him up."

The man was wearing a pressed shirt that swam on him and a cap like old-time taxi drivers wore. The plastic brim was pulled down way over his eyes. He handed her a lumpy bundle and she tried to give him a dollar. "That's okay," he said gruffly. "Mrs. Bennett already took care of it."

"Would you consider," she blurted, "getting me a bottle. I'll pay."

He looked taken aback.

"I'm . . . I'm sick. I can't go out." Don't make me beg, mister. Please.

He avoided looking at her crooked buttons. His voice was a whisper. "There's already a bottle in the bag."

"You're kidding!" She felt like hugging him.

"No. Enjoy."

She closed the door behind him, hoping he hadn't been lying. Eagerly she rifled through the groceries—through lettuce, tomatoes, Rice Chex, milk, cheese, potatoes, ground sirloin, and more. Your meat, your dairy, your grains, and . . . yes, your fun. There it was, on the bottom of the bag. A pint of Johnnie Walker. Black, no less.

She never stopped to think that the lady Mildred would never send over a bottle, never stopped to notice that the seal was broken either. She unscrewed the cap with trembling fingers and lifted the bottle to her lips. She drank deeply. A look of astonishment blossomed on her face.

Walter watched her collapse to the floor.

37 "Who?" said Trevor into the intercom.

"Blaustein," repeated Doorman John in a bored tone.

In the background Trevor could hear an agitated voice correct the doorman shrilly. *"Doctor* Blaustein."

"Yeah right," snorted John. *"Doctor* Blaustein."

"Send him up!" Trevor released the button and raced to Forrest in the kitchen. "Guess what!"

"What?" Forrest held a slice of butter-drenched toast in his gnarled hand and looked up from two runny fried eggs.

Trevor stopped himself, momentarily distracted by the forbidden breakfast. The stubborn old mule must have galloped to the corner deli for his cholesterol fix while Irene was still asleep. Damn Forrest anyway.

"What're you looking at?"

"Nothing," snapped Trevor, "not a damn thing." He suppressed his irritation. "Blaustein's here. In the lobby. He's coming up."

Forrest paused in mid-chew. Trevor caught a flash of yellow yolk and what looked like crusty fried egg white in the abyss. Then Forrest grinned and spoke through a mouthful. "Holy shit."

Trevor started to back away. "Just stay here."

"Now wait a damned minute—"

"I don't want to scare him off, okay? If you come out it's liable to put the kibosh on everything. Just sit here . . ." He yanked a ladderback chair over by the door.

" . . . and listen. But for God's sake don't come out."

Forrest grudgingly nodded his head. Christ on a crutch, he hoped Trevor wouldn't botch this opportunity.

"Dr. Bradford."

Alexander Blaustein stood tentatively in the foyer. "I'm sorry to intrude so early in the morning. But you gave me your address, and I thought I'd stop by before we left."

"You're leaving? Where to?"

Blaustein looked distinctly uncomfortable. "Just on vacation. For a while."

"Running away? Did I scare you that badly, Dr. Blaustein?"

"No. I've been planning this for a while. Ever since . . ." He seemed to totter.

"Look," said Trevor, "why don't we sit down?"

"All right," said Blaustein gratefully. "I really . . ." He reached out and steadied himself against the wall.

"Dr. Blaustein?"

"It's nothing. It's . . ."

"Do sit down," insisted Trevor in alarm.

"Perhaps for a minute or two." Wearily he sank into a wing chair in Mildred's living room.

"I can't stay long. Jennifer is waiting for me at the airport. With the children. We have a flight to Budapest."

"I don't understand."

"We are leaving the country, Dr. Bradford. Permanently." He gestured to a small suitcase. "I am taking all the cash I can get my hands on and leaving instructions to liquidate as many of my assets as possible. The money, I think, will go very far in my native land. The children and I—and Jennifer—should be able to live quite well for the rest of our lives."

"You're kidnapping them?"

"They are my children, Dr. Bradford. I have a right. I . . . I can't afford to be ruined again. I could never afford—"

"We have no intention of ruining you."

But Blaustein seemed not to hear. "It will come out sooner or later. I had a practice in California before I came here. A very good practice. A highly successful practice. I was a dedicated psychotherapist, Dr. Bradford. Good at my work. Respected in my field." He gulped. "At least until . . . until, one day, a woman came to my office for help. For treatment."

"Yes?"

Blaustein took a deep breath and plunged on. "There was nothing extraordinary about her. She was a housewife from the area, or so she said. Having marital problems, wanted to make some changes in her life and afraid to do so. A typical patient in all respects, if there is such a thing as typical."

"I see," said Trevor, who didn't but very much wanted to.

"She was, as it turned out, the first of four such women . . . but I'm getting ahead of myself.

"Suffice it to say that it was an initial consultation like any other. We discussed why she sought help, what she expected, a timetable for treatment—I do not see people forever, I was very honest that way—and my terms. There was nothing unusual about our meeting. You must understand, my clientele consisted primarily of women from the Los Angeles area. I had no reason to be suspicious. No reason to check her identity or the veracity of her background. No reason to be suspicious."

"Suspicious of what?"

"Of ruination."

"She accused you . . ." Trevor let the words dangle.

"You've already done your homework. She and three others—three other women clients—accused me of things. Terrible things. They conspired. They collaborated. For money. It was a good plan too. Their stories matched. It was all very well orchestrated, too well orchestrated. I should have seen it at the time." Blaustein's voice escalated. "They *accused* me. Accused me of abusing the doctor-patient relationship. Of seducing them."

"And you didn't?"

"Never! It was a pack of lies. Of course, I couldn't prove a thing. I don't videotape my sessions, Dr. Bradford. It was their word against mine, and there were four of them."

"What happened then?"

"I was publicly humiliated. Financially wiped out. Professionally ruined. I had a wife, Dr. Bradford. A wife I love to this day, but who didn't believe me then and certainly doesn't now. I had children—the twins. They were just babies, my beautiful babies. And it all fell apart. Everything. I lost my patients. I lost my family. I lost my money. I lost everything I had worked so hard to achieve since coming to the United States."

"I'm sorry, Dr. Blaustein."

"No matter. When I was barred from practicing in the state of California, I came to the East Coast. I started another practice. A different sort of practice. Specializing in corporations and treating men only. Except for one patient, a woman I took on as a favor."

"Esther Maine."

"Yes." He leaned back in the sofa. "I don't know why I agreed. I thought we'd have an initial consultation, and I'd refer her elsewhere. But when she came to me she seemed so . . . I don't know . . . vulnerable. So very fragile. So I broke my rule and began to treat her. I even agreed to have our sessions in that horrible St. James Hotel."

Trevor nodded.

"I didn't seduce her, if that's what you're thinking. I never touched her."

"But something happened?"

"Yes."

Trevor looked at the psychiatrist steadily. "Did you kill her, Dr. Blaustein?"

"No. I swear it." Blaustein babbled on, whipping himself into a nervous frenzy. "The last night I went to see her, to talk to her. To try to talk some sense—"

"You went to the St. James the night she died?"

"Yes. But I never got to speak with her. When I arrived she was dead."

"Ah," said Trevor. If Blaustein was telling the truth, and Trevor thought he just might be, he could have been the third visitor. "Were you the one who called the front desk?"

"Yes. I panicked. I ran. But I couldn't just leave her like that. In that sordid little room. God knows how many days it would have been. I couldn't just leave her there to . . . to . . . putrefy!"

Again Blaustein's voice cracked. Trevor tried to speak soothingly. "Okay, Dr. Blaustein. You went to see Esther Maine. Why?"

"Because she was threatening me." He saw Trevor's expression and corrected himself. "Not overtly. She was quite unaware of the threat. But to me the nightmare was happening all over again. What happened in California. Esther Maine had a history of promiscuity. She referred frequently to multiple lovers—'suitors,' she called them in her childish way, but it was the same difference. And then abruptly during the course of therapy she seemed to fixate on me. She started calling at all hours of the day or night. Started sending me letters. Poems.

"Then she telephoned one more time. The last time. She said she loved me. We had to meet, she said. She told me to come to the St. James. If I didn't, she said she would confess everything to her husband. She would *tell* him. There was nothing to tell, but what did it matter? I became frantic. I saw the nightmare in California about to happen all over again."

"But surely," countered Trevor, "this happens in your profession. You should have been prepared to deal with it."

"No!" cried Blaustein, highly agitated now. "I could not, as you say, 'deal with it.' Remember, I had been ruined by such women before. That is why I avoid them. And here it was about to happen again, and I couldn't face it.

"In any event, Esther Maine wanted to leave her family. To run away. With me! All because of figments! Figments of her imagination."

"She imagined the whole thing?"

"Yes! I was ever so careful. I never so much as touched her. But she believed I had! Truly believed it. I became highly alarmed. Neither could I comply with her deluded expectations, nor could I risk exposure. And . . ." He paused, weighing his words. " . . . I also feared Esther Maine's husband."

Trevor brushed aside Blaustein's concerns as paranoia. "Come on now, Dr. Blaustein. Jonathan Maine is a reasonable man. An understanding man. You could have talked to him. Under the circumstances, I think you should have."

Blaustein dropped his voice to a hoarse whisper. "You really think so?"

"Of course."

"Then I suggest you find out what happened to Esther's father."

Trevor's eyes narrowed. "What are you talking about?"

Blaustein looked at him knowingly. "I don't know for sure. Let's just say I have my suspicions, Dr. Bradford. So go ahead. Find out what happened to Evan Jamison, what really happened. Then decide how much I should have shared with Jonathan Maine."

38 While Freddy Townsend waited, he tried to pull himself together. He went upstairs and washed his face. He splashed water on his hair and combed it precisely in place. He put on a fresh shirt, one of the few he owned without a monogram. A vacation, that's what he needed. When this blew over, he and Constance would go on a nice long vacation. Maybe a cruise on the Sea Goddess.

James spoke through the bedroom door. "Mrs. Bennett is here."

"Tell her I'll be right down. Offer her coffee or something."

Mildred was shocked by Freddy's appearance. He was a man transformed. He looked like he'd spent the night in the park. His eyes were red-rimmed, his pants a mass of rumples. He hadn't shaved either. And when he took her hand, his was cold and clammy.

"Thank you for coming," he said.

"I'm sorry it took me so long to get here. The traffic was terrible. I ended up walking the last ten blocks."

They sat in two upholstered chairs, their knees almost touching. He reached out and clutched her hands in his. She tried not to recoil at his clutching.

"You want anything? Coffee? Tea? Juice? Connie's got some juice that'll knock you on your keister." He smiled crookedly.

"No. Nothing, thank you. Let's just talk, Freddy. I was surprised, I must admit, to get your call."

"Yes." His head bobbed up and down to some private

tempo. "Talk." His eyes narrowed conspiratorially. "But we have to talk quickly, Mildred. Very quickly."

She eyed him nervously. He seemed on the verge of some kind of breakdown. She wished he would let go of her hands. "Why?"

He lowered his voice to a whisper. "Because she'll be back. Soon."

Mildred found herself whispering in reply. "You mean Constance?"

"Yes. You see, I'm not supposed to tell."

Oh dear, thought Mildred. Freddy Townsend seemed to be unraveling before her very eyes. She'd seen patients like this when she volunteered at Paine Whitney. She wished she'd brought Trevor along or even Forrest. "What is it," she said carefully, "you're not supposed to tell?"

"That I was with Esther the night she died."

Mildred sighed, feigning relief. "I'm so glad you're finally telling me the truth, Freddy."

"Oh, I wanted to all along. But I was afraid because of how it would look. I was afraid you wouldn't believe me." He clutched tighter now. His eyes were pleading. "But you do, don't you?"

"Yes!" she cried. At that he loosened his grip and she pulled her hands away. "Why don't you start at the beginning, Freddy?"

"I wish this didn't have me so rattled. It's not like me to be so rattled." He ran a trembling hand through curly black hair. "I didn't kill her, Mildred. My God, when I found out she was dead, I couldn't believe it. Then the pathologist said it was an accident, and I thought, very well. An accident. Tragic, but at least there wouldn't be any sordid repercussions. Then you showed up, talking about all kinds of witnesses. I didn't kill her, Mildred."

She nodded encouragingly.

His voice escalated. "Well I didn't!"

"I know," she said quickly. "Of course you didn't."

"However bad the extraneous details may appear, the fact remains that nothing happened between Esther and me. I swear it."

"All right," said Mildred agreeably, "so nothing happened."

"I mean," he babbled on, "something happened but nothing happened. Something happened to *her*, in her. Before she died, I mean, if you get my drift."

"I—"

"The woman was severely unbalanced, Mildred, and therein is the tragic heart of the matter. I tried to spare her family the sordid details, but"—he paused—"Esther was a woman with unfortunate delusions."

"What sort of delusions?"

"For one thing, she had a delusion that . . ." He let the words drift off. "Well, it's so preposterous I can't believe we're even discussing it. But indeed, here we are. Discussing it. This is real, right?"

"Right," said Mildred. Good Lord, she wished James would come back. The man was falling apart.

"For some inexplicable reason Esther seemed to believe we were having an affair. And there you are!"

Mildred was not sure she'd heard correctly. "She thought you were? And you weren't?"

"Yes!" he shrieked. "Isn't that absurd? Look, I admit I don't always walk the straight and narrow." He shot an apologetic glance toward Constance's empty chair. "But I'd never stoop so low as to seduce my own wife's sister, a crazy woman at that."

"Crazy," repeated Mildred.

"Exactly! Crazy as a nuthatch! Between you and me, I think it all relates to toxic shock syndrome. She probably used an inferior product—not mine, you understand. Maybe she used generics! There's danger out there, lurking on supermarket shelves, wrapped in plastic. They try to tell you different, but don't you believe them."

"Freddy, please try to think. How did she come to believe you were lovers? If you weren't, I mean."

Freddy looked genuinely perplexed. "Lovers? Oh yes, lovers. Damned if I know. Like I said, the woman was unbalanced. I never even paid any attention to her. I'd see her at family gatherings, and she blended into the woodwork. She'd come here occasionally to see Constance on her weekly visits to the city. We'd kiss on the cheek." He held up his hand. "Nothing more. They were air kisses, Mildred, *air* kisses."

"So when did this delusion manifest itself?"

"It all started after I helped get her out of that mess with the shoplifting. She was pathetically grateful. Okay, I thought, perhaps a little gratitude is in order. But shortly thereafter she began acting bizarre."

And how would you know? Mildred felt like asking. "How do you mean, Freddy?"

"I started getting letters at the office. Letters marked 'personal' and reeking of perfume. Love letters! From Esther. Gushy and sickeningly sweet. Totally juvenile! The return address was that St. James place."

"What did you do?"

Freddy smiled incongruously. "At first I tried to brush it off. I mean, after all—*Esther?*" He laughed but it caught in this throat. "But it was a little unnerving, I must say. An alarm went off in my head. I started to worry that maybe she was some kind of nut. I couldn't help remembering that movie, *Fatal Attraction.* You remember that movie—Glenn Close with a bad perm? Rabbit stew?"

She held up her hand, wanting him to stop. "Yes."

"So I talked to her. I tried to be gentle, Mildred. You know I'm gentle."

I know nothing of the kind. She remembered the strength of his hands. Those big beefy hands. Football player's hands.

"I went to that hotel and told her there had been an unfortunate misunderstanding. I told her I was a happily married man. You know the story."

Mildred couldn't stop herself. "Yes. My husband told it to me many times."

"Oh, I didn't mean—"

"I know, Freddy, I know. So how did she react to your demurs?"

"She said she understood completely. And that, I thought, was that."

"But it wasn't?"

"No. The letters kept coming. And they became more explicit. More graphic. She started acting coy when she saw me. And she started signing another name."

"Camille?"

"Yes." He shuddered. "Then things really got out of hand. I spotted her following me more than once. She showed up at the office unexpectedly. People started to talk. I realized the woman was deranged. There was no telling what she might do."

"Did you tell any of this to Constance?" asked Mildred.

"No! I was afraid . . . well, I've done my share of marital transgressing. I was afraid Constance wouldn't believe me. Constance has always resented Esther." Again he shot an apologetic glance at Constance's chair. "I knew she'd believe the worst, and I knew she'd never forgive me."

"I see."

"And now you can understand my predicament."

"Yes, I'm afraid I can. Whether or not the affair was real could be viewed as immaterial. The result could be the same either way. You went to the St. James again—to end it or to reason with her. Whatever." She waved her gloves. "And when Esther wouldn't listen to reason, you killed her."

"That's right!" he said frantically. "That's exactly how it will look!"

She almost touched his hand, then thought better of it. "Don't get upset, Freddy. Tell me the rest."

"Yes. The rest. I went to the St. James twice. To make matters worse, I went the night she died. I had it out with her and gave her letters back."

"Ah," said Mildred, "so she had them in her possession."

"Yes."

Odd, she thought to herself. They were never found among her things.

"So, yes, I admit it. I went to the St. James. I saw her. I talked to her. But she was very much alive when I left, Mildred. I swear it."

Mildred didn't respond, but sat there thinking. Winkler told Forrest about three visitors. If indeed Esther was alive when Freddy came and went, perhaps he had been the first.

He read her silence as skepticism. "That's what happened!"

"All right. Let's say I believe you. How did she react when, as you put it, you 'tried to reason' with her?"

He scratched his head. "It was curious. And rather pathetic. There she was sitting in this miserable little flat all dressed up in a ridiculous Japanese silk robe as though she fully expected we were going to have some sort of tawdry romantic tryst. She had candles burning and champagne in a plastic bucket. It was like a bad joke."

"I proceeded to talk to her, calmly, reasonably."

"And?"

"And she put on an infuriating cryptic smile. I wanted to smack it right off, that smile." He saw Mildred's expression. "But I didn't, Mildred. I didn't. I forced the letters into her hands . . ."

Mildred nodded.

"And you know what? She said she understood! She said it was all right. She said she had another suitor, that's what she said."

Mildred slumped back in bewilderment.

"Can you believe it? Well I wasn't about to argue. I thought fine. I wished her well and got out of there as fast as I could."

"And she died."

"*Later*. She died *later*. Someone else murdered her, Mildred, not me."

"Did you lie to protect yourself, Freddy? Or did you lie to protect someone else?"

"No. There is no one else."

"Yes there is, Freddy."

"No!"

"You yourself said Constance resented her sister. You said she'd believe the worst."

"She didn't know!" cried Freddy.

"Perhaps she did. Perhaps she followed you that night. Perhaps she waited. And after you left, perhaps she—"

Suddenly a figure appeared in the doorway.

"Liar!" screamed Constance.

Flowers fell from her hand.

39 "Leave Jonathan out of this!"

Irene stood braced like a sumo wrestler in the doorway.

Alexander Blaustein turned toward the intruder. "Who in the name of God is this woman?"

"Irene Purdy," she answered. "Hasn't the poor man suffered enough? And why should we believe what you say anyway?"

"Whether or not you believe me is your choice. I really don't care. I thought it would help, telling the truth. And now I'm leaving."

"That's what you think." Irene stepped in his path.

"Reenie!"

Forrest stepped through the swinging kitchen door. "Sorry Trevor, I couldn't stand it no more." He turned to Irene. "Let him pass."

"What?"

"We've got no legal right to hold him. He came here of his own free will. He gave us this information when he didn't have to."

But Trevor was hardly aware of Forrest and Irene. His mind fixed on Blaustein's words about Jonathan Maine. Old details came flooding back . . . Evan Jamison had been robbed. His throat had been slit. And Trevor remembered the words of Dr. Leveaux. Something about a man who committed suicide. A man who slit his own throat. *The work of an experienced hand. Turned out he was a surgeon.*

No, thought Trevor, it can't be.

"Who are these people!" demanded Blaustein.

He forced himself back to the present. "Don't worry, Dr. Blaustein. They're friends of mine. We're working on this together. Trying to find out who killed Esther Maine."

"I see."

"I'm not sure I do, Dr. Blaustein. Why are you telling us this now?"

"Because," said Blaustein, drawing himself up, "I want to do the right thing. Before I leave. Before I start a new life."

"With Jonathan Maine's money?"

Blaustein stiffened. "Esther Maine gave me some money, yes. But only because she wanted to. And it wasn't a great sum, I assure you."

Trevor scratched his head. "This still doesn't add up, Dr. Blaustein. Your concern, I mean. No offense, but there has to be more."

"You're very perceptive." Blaustein seemed to turn a thought over in his mind. "All right. Remember at the beach house—when you asked if I loved her?"

"Yes."

"I denied it. And I lied. I don't know if it was love exactly, but I was very fond of Esther Maine. Oh, I never told her how I felt, and I certainly never acted on my feelings in a physical way. But I cared very much. And she needed me! Had things in my life been different, well, perhaps I would have run away with her."

"I see."

"She was a person who needed protecting, a person who deserved protecting. And I hope to God you catch the man who killed her."

They were interrupted by yet another buzz from the intercom.

"What is this," groaned Forrest, "Grand Central Station?"

Irene answered the call. Doorman John was to the point. "A police officer is on the way up. I couldn't stop him."

Without so much as a glance back, Dr. Blaustein swept out of the apartment. He brushed past Patrick Ballinger at the elevator.

"Chief Ballinger," said Forrest with false heartiness, "this is a surprise."

Trevor stepped forward and offered his hand, which Ballinger chose to ignore.

Forrest curled his lip. "This," he said tightly, "is Chief Patrick Ballinger."

"Apparently his mama never taught him any manners," said Irene.

"It's okay, Irene." Trevor viewed Ballinger in the same manner he might view a rabid dog. "Best not to rile him," he whispered.

"I'm not here on a goddamn social call," snapped Ballinger. "I'm here to ask the old man here a few questions."

"What old man?" snapped Irene.

"What sort of questions?" said Forrest.

"Questions about this." Ballinger extracted a crumpled scrap of lined notebook paper from his wallet and held it out.

Forrest squinted at the familiar penmanship, not yet realizing its implications.

"That your writing?"

"Yeah," he admitted. "My name. My address. My phone number. So what?"

"So one of my men found it in Norman Winkler's pocket."

Forrest looked momentarily puzzled. Then his face paled. He moistened his lips. "Oh no," he murmured.

"Oh yes. Mr. Winkler was discovered this morning. By a secretary at Parker McKenzie and Swaine. He was in his office, hanging by his necktie from a pipe."

"Oh God," said Irene.

"He was dead, of course. Another 'suicide.' " Ballinger looked at Forrest keenly. "Or might it be something else?"

40 "Mildred, you've got to pull yourself together." Trevor took her hand in his.

Mildred turned away, her expression bleak as she watched the highway streak by. "They're dead," she said almost to herself. "Higgins. Norman Winkler. Cora." Tears spilled down her cheeks. "And Cora's death is my fault."

"That's not true. We don't have the results of the autopsy. The doctor at Harmony House said taking that drink so suddenly could have caused her stomach to hemorrhage. She had bleeding ulcers, Mildred."

Or, thought Forrest, maybe she was poisoned. That could have caused the blood around her lips. But he didn't say anything. He continued to drive, his eyes fixed on the road ahead.

Mildred looked at Trevor hopelessly. "I'm the one

who told about her, Trevor. I just never dreamed that Freddy—"

"Listen Mildred, even if she was murdered—and we don't know that she was—Freddy may have had nothing to do with it. I told Alexander Blaustein about Cora too."

"You?" barked Forrest. "Why didn't you tell us?"

But Trevor ignored him. "Blaustein could have done it—before he came to us. He could have been the one." He turned from Mildred to Forrest. "I didn't even realize what I was doing when I told him. The way he drew her name out of me was insidious. The way he talked, it sounded as though he'd already heard about Cora from Esther. 'Of course,' he said. 'Cora Parks,' he said. And now he's gone."

"Stop it!" said Irene. She glared at them from the passenger seat. "The both of you. What is this? Some kind of competition for taking blame? I told Claudia too, okay? Everyone knew about Cora. So let's wait for the autopsy report, then have a taffy pull. It's going to take days. In the meantime, a break in Raven's Wing won't do any harm."

"I don't feel like going to a party," said Mildred. "Especially if Constance is there."

Forrest took his eyes off the road for a moment and glanced back. "She has some explaining to do, Mildred. Freddy told you where he was the night Esther died. Constance didn't."

"She was too upset to tell me anything. She had James escort me out." She shuddered at the memory. "I've never been thrown out of anyone's house before."

"There's a first time for everything," said Forrest.

Trevor fumbled in his pocket for a peppermint and withdrew the grotesque Polaroid image of Esther Maine.

Mildred stared, horrified. "What's that?"

"Nothing," said Trevor quickly. He tried to shove it back, but the others were too quick.

Forrest twisted around in his seat. "Gimme that."

Irene reached over and snatched the print. "Watch the road, Forrest! For gosh sakes!"

She studied it intently. "Lordy."

Forrest snatched it with his right hand, keeping the other on the wheel. He looked back and forth between the road and the print, the car weaving all the while. "Christ. Whoever it was really did a number on her. Look at those eyes."

Irene leaned over. "There aren't any. Just sockets. Blood-filled sockets."

Mildred put her hands to her ears. "Stop. Just stop!"

Irene tried to reassure her. "Don't worry, Millie. You'll be all right once you get to Raven's Wing."

Forrest was thinking about those eyes. Why would someone kill her then obliterate her eyes? Because of rage? Or was it done deliberately, perhaps to hide something. Or perhaps it was something subconscious. Perhaps . . .

"Millie, you got to calm down." Irene turned around in her seatbelt. "Hold Walter. Stroking a cat lowers the blood pres—"

"No, Irene! No—"

But Irene had already dumped the unsuspecting feline into Mildred's protesting arms. Winston, who had been sleeping peacefully behind Mildred's feet on the floor, opened a wary eye. He lifted his head and sniffed.

"Irene, no . . . oh God!"

Something flashed through Winston's old brain. Perhaps it was the spirit of the hunt. Perhaps it was an electric surge of jealousy. In any case, he moved with vigor that belied his years. Defying arthritis and a weak heart, he put two paws on Mildred's knees and saw the unthinkable. A hated cat. An interloper. In his mistress's lap. He sprang into action, jaws frothing with anticipation.

"Ahhhhhhhhh!" screamed Mildred. Trevor scrambled to help, to hold, to subdue the two animals, but already they were a blurred ying and yang, spinning uncontrollably, snarling and hissing, spewing flecks of fur and foam.

"Stop the car!" cried Irene. "Stop the car! We're gonna crash! Stop—"

"It's the Bronx!" bellowed Forrest. "I can't stop. Look where we are for God's sake."

At that, Walter hurled himself forward. He cleared the front seat, flew over Forrest and Irene, and mashed into the windshield. Irene reached out to snag him. Forrest slammed on the brake. And Walter slid over the steering wheel and into Forrest's crotch, where needle-sharp claws sought stability.

"Aieeeeeee!" howled Forrest.

The car screeched to a halt. Irene managed to grab hold of the terrified feline. Breathlessly, she clutched him to her chest. "There, there," she murmured. "There, there."

"Lord in heaven and mother of God," groaned Forrest. He covered his prickled privates with his hands.

Someone tapped on the glass. "Are you folks all right?"

It was a state trooper.

Forrest managed a feeble smile. "We're all right, officer. Thanks for asking. Things got a little crazy, but everything's jake now."

No one agreed.

"I'm trying to find Route Ninety-five."

"Heading to Connecticut?"

"Yeah."

"Just follow me."

They followed the obliging trooper to the point of access, where he waved them off.

"You know," said Trevor after a while, "I've been thinking."

"About what?" asked Mildred.

"About what Dr. Blaustein told us and what Freddy Townsend told you. About how they both said Esther Maine thought she was having affairs with them. Not that she was. That she thought she was."

"So?" said Forrest. "Maybe they were lying."

"I don't think so. It seems too coincidental that both men would say the same thing when they don't even know each other."

"There was this thing on *Oprah*," said Irene.

"Give me a break!" groaned Forrest.

"Well there was! An episode. On *Oprah*. They had a doctor on the show. It was about figments. About folks who imagine they have girlfriends or boyfriends. Folks who really believe it. They had a name for it even, I forget what."

"Erotomania," said Trevor.

"That was it!"

"What on earth," said Mildred, "is erotomania?"

"It's a little known disorder," replied Trevor, "that was first described by a French psychiatrist, Gaetan De Clerambault, in 1921. According to today's experts, the condition manifests itself in people like Esther. People who live quiet lives of desperation. Lonely people. The person afflicted imagines being loved by someone in a position of higher status—a movie star, a politician, someone like that. Remember John Hinckley, Junior? He tried to impress a young actress—Jodie Foster, if memory serves—by assassinating President Reagan. He suffered from erotomania."

"Just a devious legal ploy," said Forrest, "to get him off the hook."

"Oh no," protested Trevor. "It was real. A delusion."

"A deadly delusion," said Irene darkly.

"So," said Mildred, "you think Esther Maine imagined these things?"

"It's a good possibility. There's nothing erotic about erotomania. The victims are withdrawn. Most haven't had a sexual encounter for years. According to psychiatry's diagnostic manual, the delusion always involves idealized romantic love."

"She called them suitors," said Mildred.

"Exactly. Suitors. Not lovers."

"I still think it's a crock," said Forrest, but he sounded less certain.

"Wouldn't you think," said Mildred, "that Dr. Blaustein would have picked up on it?"

"Not necessarily," said Trevor. "Her delusions could have seemed very real to her. And to him."

"And to whoever killed her," murmured Forrest.

41 When they arrived, an old woman, her face twisted in a smile that looked like a grimace, sat perched in a white wicker rocker on Mildred's front porch. She spied them and hobbled down the steps like a drunken marionette, clutching her cane in one hand and a plate of pastel petit fours in the other.

"Here," she said, thrusting the plate in their faces. "I baked them this morning." The pink and green pastries sweated under Saran Wrap.

Mildred's stomach rolled over. She was in no mood for food and in no mood for this disagreeable-looking woman either, whoever she was. She was tired and sick at heart. More than anything she wanted to go draw the shades and lie down. Nevertheless she forced herself to be cordial and accepted the plate.

"Thank you, Mrs. . . . ?"

"This here's Lucille Jamison," said Forrest. "Esther's mom."

The wicked witch herself. The plate slipped from Mildred's fingers and smashed on the flagstone walk. "Oh," she blurted, "I'm sorry," and promptly burst into tears.

Lucille hunched down, scooping up bits of broken china and smashed petit fours, placing them into a handful of wrap. "Never mind," she said. "No use crying over spilt milk."

"She isn't herself," whispered Irene as she knelt down to help her. "We've had a bad time."

Lucille stood up. "Jonathan said you were coming." Her mouth smiled, revealing perfect plastic teeth, but her eyes were hard as ice picks. "To the party."

"Yes," repeated Mildred numbly. "The party." *People are dropping like flies and we're going to a party.*

Forrest nudged Trevor. "Why don't you take Millie inside. Make her some tea or something. Reenie and I'll set a bit with Mrs. Jamison."

"Good idea," said Trevor.

Once Trevor and Mildred were gone, Forrest smiled broadly at Lucille. "I've been wanting to have a little chat with you, Lucille. May I call you Lucille?"

"Of course." Her smile turned almost coy. "Forrest."

He positioned three wicker chairs in a tight little semicircle. Lucille perched forward stiffly in hers, the uppermost button of her respectable navy blue mourning dress fastened securely despite ninety-degree heat. The only adornments on her gaunt body were a strand of cheap plastic pop-it beads looped around her ropey neck and a black Swatch watch that hung loosely on her wrist. Sensible black lace-up shoes stood like sentinels beneath tightly pressed knees. She pursed her lips and clutched bifocals in her lap with clawlike fingers.

Forrest tried to put her at ease. "It's good you came by," he said. "Some thoughts keep gnawing away at me. You know how it is."

"Indeed I do," said Lucille. "I haven't had a moment's peace since poor Esther passed."

Forrest patted Lucille's hand sympathetically, and Irene felt a jolt of jealousy. *Why, he was sweet-talking her, the old coot!*

"It was a tragic loss," Forrest said sympathetically, "a most tragic loss. I'd like to bounce a few things off you, hope you can give us some insights. You being her mother and all."

Lucille beamed. They were taking her into their confidence. Treating her with the respect she was due.

"There are a few questions too," said Forrest, "that I'd like to ask."

"I'm happy to help any way I can, Forrest. I told you that before."

"I wanted to talk a bit again about Esther's childhood."

Lucille frowned. "Again? I don't see why. I already told you everything there is to tell."

Forrest had struck a nerve, and Irene decided to join in. She reached out and patted Lucille's other hand. "Just bear with him, pumpkin. We know it's tough."

Pumpkin! Lucille snatched her hand away and flared her nostrils.

"Now about Esther's childhood . . ." began Forrest, ignoring Lucille's sour expression. "Seeing as how we're going to be completely honest—for poor Esther's sake—I ought to tell you straight out that certain facts have come to light."

"Facts? What sort of facts?" Lucille's voice jockeyed between a squawk and a screech. She pulled her hand away from Forrest and eyed him suspiciously.

"Well, for one, we found out that Claudia wasn't Jonathan's child."

Lucille shut her eyes and pinched her temples with a bony thumb and forefinger. "That was a long time ago," she said.

"I was hoping you might tell us who the father was."

The hand fell from her eyes. She blinked twice as though unable to understand the question. "The father?"

"Yes," said Forrest. "The father. The one who impregnated her." He enunciated each syllable, making his request as clear as possible.

"Why on earth would you want to know that?"

"Because it may be important."

"No," she said quickly. "Believe me, it doesn't matter."

"Now, Lucille," replied Forrest guilelessly, "if you think on it a moment I'm sure you'll see that it does. Because if Esther maintained a relationship with the father over the years, if she saw him, you know, on the sly, well, the father might have been the one—"

"That's quite impossible."

Forrest's eyebrows shot up. "Oh? And why is that?"

Lucille look away. "I—well—I don't know. I mean it was a long time ago. The father is long gone, I'm sure."

"You say it like you know," blurted Irene. "Like he's dead or something."

Forrest motioned for Irene to be quiet. "That's because he is dead, Lucille, isn't he."

"You're trapping me with your words. I neither know nor care if the father is dead or alive. It doesn't matter anymore," Lucille moved to get up from her chair, but Forrest gently pushed her back down.

As she pitched back into the chair her tone escalated to outrage. "Take your hand off me!"

"Now, Lucille, calm down."

"Who the father was is none of your concern!"

"Ah, Lucille . . ." Forrest shook his head, smiling all friendly like. "I think it is. Because the way I see it this all ties together. Esther was a woman with troubles, see? Troubles that started way back then when she had that baby. Troubles that started *before* then even."

"I'm sure I don't know what you're talking about."

"Surely you must, Lucille. You were her mother, after all. The one who knew her best."

"Her adoptive mother," Lucille corrected.

"Whatever." Forrest eyed her keenly. "Whatever kind of *mother*"—he sneered the word—"you were, I think Esther's troubles started back when she was a small child."

"That's nonsense."

"I think they started the day she had the bad luck to land on your doorstep. The day she was welcomed into that fine God-fearing house you speak so highly of. With fine upstanding parents. Fine *loving* parents—"

"That's enough!" screamed Lucille.

"Who was it, Lucille? Who was the one that gave her a poke?"

"Stop with your filth! Just stop! You don't know what you're talking about! My husband brought her into the house! You with your talk of childhood. With your talk of trouble. She brought trouble on us! *She* did! We were just fine, Connie and Evan and me. Fine. Until she came along. Just fine!"

"It was Evan, wasn't it. He was the father."

Irene was unable to contain herself. "Forrest, you don't know what you're saying!"

But Forrest didn't stop. "The father was the father, isn't that right, Lucille?" He repeated the words, turning them into a sing-song chant. "The father was the father. The father was the father."

"Yes!" screamed Lucille. "Yes!" She lurched from her chair and tottered to the porch railing. When she spoke, she spoke through clenched teeth, spoke to the trees around them, the weeping willows, the sugar maples, the shagbark hickories.

"So you know. I don't care anymore. I protected her long enough. From the day she came she was nothing but a disgusting little tramp."

Irene bolted up and grabbed Lucille's bony elbow. "Hush! How can you say you protected her? You call what you did protecting? It was your job to protect her and you didn't. No. If all this is true, you let her get raped by her own daddy."

Lucille turned around and looked at Irene with crazed, almost gleeful eyes. "Rape? You think it was rape?" She laughed. "I never saw her run. Never heard her cry. She wanted it, Mrs. Purdy. She was a bastard child and a vixen. From the day she came, she drove a wedge between Evan and me. I could see what was happening. You think I'm blind? The way she'd crawl all over him, give him hugs and such. It was shameful. Her own father."

"That's right," said Forrest. "Her own father. Her real father. Evan Jamison."

"That's a lie!"

"Is it? I don't think so, Lucille. I think Evan brought Esther home, brought her home because she was his and because the mother, whoever she was, was abusing her. Or maybe the woman died. Or ran away. Who knows? Anyway, he brought her home. To you."

"That's ridiculous."

"We can find out, you know. We'll go through the old records. Talk to the child welfare people. You'd be amazed what people will remember with a little encouragement. After all, how many times do they hand a baby over to a man?"

Lucille's shoulders slumped. "Never mind," she said wearily. "Don't bother."

Lucille moved back to her rocker and sat down. When she spoke, her voice was tired and defeated.

"I tried to do right. I took the child in, didn't I? Evan's bastard child. Not many women would have done the same. And when I detected . . ." She gulped and forced herself to go on. "When I realized he was, you know, diddling with her, I forced him to leave. My own husband."

"But the abuse didn't stop," said Forrest.

Lucille smiled grimly. "Abuse? That's what folks call it these days, I suppose. Back then it seemed like two willing participants to me. They ganged up against me. They conspired. She never tried to run from him, that was for sure."

"Maybe," said Irene, "she didn't run because he was the only affection she ever got. She was little when it started. She didn't know."

Lucille grunted skeptically. "There was nothing I could do."

"You could have called the police," said Irene. "Or the welfare people. You could have got a restraining order.

You could have moved away. You could have done a lot of things."

"Oh sure," replied Lucille. "I could have told the police—and faced scandal in this town. Or I could have moved—from the only home place I'd ever known. I could have turned my life—and my Connie's life—upside down. For her."

There it was, thought Forrest grimly. Esther Maine was a doomed child from the day she arrived at Evan and Lucille Jamison's home. No, doomed from the day she was conceived. She was worse than nothing to them. For Lucille she was the target of relentless jealousy and vengeance. For Evan, the object of perverted gratification.

"So she had Evan's baby," he said. "A brown-eyed baby. Just like she was."

"Yes." Lucille spat out the word: "Claudia. And look how she turned out. A drug addict. A mental defective. The fruit doesn't fall far from the tree."

"How much did Jonathan know?"

Lucille's eyes narrowed speculatively. "He knew Claudia wasn't his. Esther couldn't fool him on that. He was a virgin when they got married." She turned a thought over in her mind. "But he didn't know about Evan, I'm sure. Esther wouldn't have told him. It was too shameful."

Forrest wasn't so sure. Someone killed Evan. Someone skilled with a knife. And years later someone—maybe the same someone—killed Esther.

But Jonathan loved Esther. He was her rescuer, her knight in shining armor. He rescued her from Lucille and rescued her from Evan too, maybe even killed Evan for her sake.

Then Forrest remembered long-forgotten words he'd read about apparently generous people who mask evil motives under the guise of goodness. At the time, he paid the words no mind, but now they came back with chilling clarity . . . *Behind rescue lies control. Underneath affection, conquest. Underneath sacrifice, domination.*

And on the heels of that he remembered a child's nursery rhyme. *He put her in a pumpkin shell. And there he kept her, very well.*

He felt Irene grab his hand.

"Forrest, what's wrong?"

"Nothing."

"You look awful."

"I'm fine," he lied.

He forced himself to go on. "One last question, Lucille."

"What? What more do you want!"

"Was Esther color-blind?"

"For heaven's sake, what's that got to do with anything?"

"You talked about how she couldn't dress herself—how she wore crazy combinations of colors." And there was that business Trevor told him about the barrettes. Red or green, and she didn't know which.

"Yes. As a matter of fact she was. The school told us. They were surprised. Said it was extremely rare in girls. Now, are you quite through?"

"Yes," he said. "Go on, get along." The last words were but a whisper. "Get out of my sight."

42 "You got that look."

"What look?"

"The look that says you're figuring things out."

"I do not."

"Oh yes you do! I know you like a book. You're solving

the case, and I want you to tell me."

"Irene, just leave me be! I don't know anything. I've got to do some research."

"Research? You mean like book research? Research about what?"

"Genetics."

"Why?"

"Never mind. Go on along. *Now* Reenie." Gently but firmly, Forrest propelled Irene out of their bedroom.

"But I want to help!"

"You can help me best by leaving me be. Just for a little while. I've got to think. I've got to plan." He closed the door in her face and leaned against it wearily.

He stood there for some moments, considering. Finally he went to the phone and dialed.

"Lenny?" he said.

"Hey, Forrest, you're back! That's great. Tell Irene the thing with George Sparkes has blown over. She can come out from hiding. Heh, heh."

"That's good. She'll be relieved." Forrest decided to get right to the point. "Listen Lenny, I'm calling for a favor."

"Oh? What kind of favor?"

"I need you to bring me a gun."

Lenny Pulaski's voice turned nervous. "What's going on, Forrest?"

"Nothing, Lenny. Well, probably nothing. Mildred just thought she saw a prowler, is all. You know how women are. It was probably just a raccoon looking for a handout, but she's a modest woman and it scared the bejesus out of her. So she'd feel better if we had a little artillery around, that's all."

"Don't give me that, Forrest. I know Mildred Bennett, and she'd throw a fit if you brought a gun into her place."

Shit, thought Forrest.

"There was a prowler, I tell you! A man has a right to defend his place! And his women!"

"Okay, okay. So there was a prowler. Why don't I just

send a patrol car around? Check the place out? Tell you what, I'll station a car at the driveway for the night. How's that?"

"It stinks," snapped Forrest. "Look, Lenny, what I'm dealing with . . . well, it's probably nothing, and we don't want to look like idiots, do we?"

This Lenny could appreciate. "No," he said.

"So give me the goddamned gun."

"You know I can't do that, Forrest."

"Thanks, Lenny. Thanks a lot."

"You in some kind of trouble?"

"I don't know. Maybe."

"Well for God's sake tell me what's going on! I'll help you proper. Give me the details, and I'll send the whole damn force up there. Hell, I'll bring the SRT."

"No!" cried Forrest. God, he thought, not the SRT. Anything but that. Lenny's Special Reaction Team was a joke. It all started a year or so ago when Lenny was appointed chief. Marcel Wintermute, Raven's Wing's wealthiest resident and inveterate benefactor, donated a former Brink's armored truck to the town as a gesture of congratulations to the new Chief Pulaski. A gesture of madness was more like it. Raven's Wing didn't have much crime and certainly nothing that called for a half-assed SWAT team, a half-assed, totally *untrained* SWAT team.

But no one was about to look a gift horse in the mouth, least of all Lenny Pulaski and his team of officers, whose visions of explosive gunfire, automatic weapons, and bulletproof vests helped get them through boring days of interminable pinochle games. Hell no. They reacted with unbridled enthusiasm and the firemen joined in to boot. The heavy metal bulletproof truck had been given a tune-up by the Department of Public Works, then painted bright yellow with an eye-catching SRT logo: an upraised black sword split by a streak of red lightning.

Now the hulk sat in the firehouse at the ready where the crew revved its engine endlessly, changed the oil weekly, and polished the exterior to a high gloss. Lenny had been itching for a chance to use the vehicle. Forrest pictured policemen and firemen messing up Mildred's property. Tramping through flower beds. Letting loose with machine gun fire, shredding prize tulips and daffodils, killing themselves in the process.

"No," he repeated, more reasonably this time. "Forget it. It's not worth all that," he added quickly. "Just forget it. Forget I ever asked you."

"Don't go being like that, Forrest. You know I can't give you a gun."

"They never should have taken mine when I retired."

Lenny knew it was a sore point with Forrest. "Yeah," he commiserated. "I know." He thought for a moment. "But they didn't take your shotgun."

Forrest had forgotten all about his shotgun. It was stashed in the attic somewhere with a bunch of other junk he brought when he moved in. It hadn't been fired in years.

"A shotgun's too unwieldy for what I have in mind," said Forrest. And too heavy for me, but he didn't say that.

Lenny tried to be kind. He knew Forrest had arthritis. Worse than that, Forrest had tremors. He'd never hit anything with a handgun.

"Well," said Lenny carefully, "I know what I'd do if it was me that needed protection."

"Oh yeah?" said Forrest. "What's that?"

"This is all hypothetical, of course."

"Of course," agreed Forrest.

"I mean, you didn't hear this from me."

"All right, Lenny, I didn't hear it from me. Now will you kindly spit it out?"

"Okay." Lenny drew a breath. "If'n it was me, if'n I was worried about someone breaking in my place . . ."

"Yeah?" said Forrest.

". . . and, like you say, suppose it's someone experienced doing the breaking. Suppose it's someone armed himself. Someone you can't afford to miss . . ."

"Right," said Forrest.

"I'd saw off my shotgun, that's what I'd do. Can't miss a target that way. 'Course you'd have to let him get close. That's the down side."

"And it would make one helluva mess," reflected Forrest, "if you let fly inside the house."

"There are worse things in life than redecorating," said Lenny simply.

Yeah, thought Forrest. Worse things. Like dying.

43 "What the hell is going on?" said Irene. "The sound of that sawing is driving me nuts. Wa-wa, wa-wa, wa-wa! Jeesum!"

"What do you suppose he's doing down there?" asked Mildred.

"I don't know," said Trevor. "He's not saying."

"I don't like it," said Mildred. "He's got a plan, but he won't tell us what. We're supposed to do as he says, but he won't tell us why. I thought we were supposed to be a team."

"Yes," said Trevor. "But he's the boss. The one with the experience."

"After what happened to Higgins and Winkler and Cora, I'm packing my own protection," said Irene. She reached within the folds of her plaid culottes and extracted an item fashioned in mother of pearl. "This here."

Mildred studied the vaguely familiar object. A straight razor.

"Irene!" She snatched it from her hands. "Where did you find this?"

"In a box in one of the closets."

"It's my father's! You've been snooping!"

"I was not! I was looking for a roll of toilet paper and I found this. Besides, the man's dead. I'm sure he won't mind."

Mildred was too agitated to argue. "Oh all right. Have it your way." She looked around distractedly. "Lord, I'm going crazy in this house. I feel like a caged animal. We're like those little Indians waiting to be slaughtered."

"I saw that movie," said Irene, "and what a movie it was! The house was sort of like this one, now that I think on it. Only it was on an island. And one by one they died, all of them."

"I remember the story, Irene."

"One went and chopped himself. One went and stung himself. One went and crushed himself. One went and drowned himself. One went and hung himself—"

"Stop it!" Mildred decided to retreat to a quiet corner upstairs to read. When she got to her favorite nook, Trevor was there too, with his own book.

"Take it easy, Mildred. Don't let this get to you."

She flung the book down and was about to snap at him too when something crumpled inside her. "I—I—oh God, Trevor, I'm really frightened."

He stood up. He knew for her sake he should be strong, but his mouth was dry and his voice shook slightly. "So am I," he said.

"And that relentless sawing. He's like a man possessed. Sawing something by hand. In my father's old workshop. What on earth—"

"A shotgun."

Mildred froze. "What did you say?"

"I'm not supposed to tell."

Mildred's hand flew to her heart. "Why is Forrest sawing a shotgun?"

"So he can deal with anyone who might try to hurt us."

"So he can kill, that's what you mean."

Trevor closed his eyes momentarily. "Yes. Forrest's getting on in years. His aim is lousy, Mildred. If someone did kill Higgins and Winkler and Cora, he's very dangerous. Forrest can't afford to miss."

Mildred burst into tears.

Trevor took her gently in his arms. She put her cheek against his.

They stood there, locked in one another's arms, like survivors lost at sea. Trevor lost track of time. Somewhere in the cavernous house a grandfather clock chimed softly. And from the basement the relentless back-and-forth whine of the hacksaw continued.

Absently he massaged her back through her starched white blouse. His hand brushed against her neck. Without thinking, he reached for a white pearl button.

"Trevor," she said in a whisper.

He dropped his hands in embarrassment. "Forgive me, Mildred. I don't know what got into me."

"No, Trevor. I didn't mean . . . Oh, Trevor, I need you so badly." To his surprise, she placed his hands back where they had been.

"Take me to my room, Trevor."

He looked at her in amazement. "You're sure?"

"Very sure."

He took her hand and led her down the hall. Quietly they entered her bedroom. The shades were drawn and the light was dim, but he detected soothing shades of mauve and mint green, a queen-size bed covered with an embroidered white coverlet, a bureau with an old family picture . . . Mildred, her son, her daughter, her husband. Happier times.

Gently but firmly she placed the picture face down.

His heart thumped in his chest. It had been so long since he'd been with a woman. Mary Margaret had died a year ago, but their sex life had died long before that.

"Mildred—"

"We don't have to do anything, Trevor. If you don't want to. I mean, you can just hold me."

"Oh no, Mildred. I want to . . . I want . . . you."

Carefully, almost reverently, he took off her white leather pumps. One by one he unfastened the pearl buttons on her blouse. Slowly and with infinite care, as though opening fragile petals of a rosebud, he peeled the blouse away from her shoulders, exposing a filmy cream-colored camisole underneath. When he spoke, his voice was husky.

"You're beautiful, Mildred. So very beautiful."

I'm a New York matron, she replied in her mind. Fifty-eight with stretch marks and blue veins on my legs and hair that needs to be touched up every month. No matter how much I starve myself and ride my exercise bike, my weight will never redistribute itself to the right places. Maybe I was pretty once, but that was a long time ago.

She said none of these things. To her astonishment, Trevor was looking at her as though she were beautiful. His eyes held her and caressed her. She looked away, embarrassed.

"It's the dim light," she said, trying to laugh.

"No," he said. "It's you. You really are beautiful."

She stepped out of her skirt and left it lying on the Aubusson carpet. Scarcely daring to look at him, she removed the rest of her clothes herself . . . the lacy camisole, the silk half-slip, the tight constricting tube of a girdle, the sheer nylon stockings, and the stiff wire-cupped brassiere. With trembling fingers she fumbled her way through hooks and snaps and Spandex.

She wondered if she would be responsive. Achieving fulfillment in Connor's arms had been like a tortuous quest for the Holy Grail. Connor used to say "go with the flow," as if they were travelers on some erotic canoe trip, all of it paddling upstream. Or worse yet, he would suggest that she make herself "loose." Mildred thought if he wanted something loose he should have married a tub of Jell-O.

I am by nature a tight person, she told herself. I was born

tight and I'll die tight. It's the way I am. She winced inside, remembering what Connor had called her. A tightass.

Suddenly Mildred realized what she was doing. She was compulsively cataloging negative thoughts to sabotage any possibility of enjoyment. That much she had learned from those expensive sessions with the sausage-fingered therapist. What's more, she was now standing in the middle of her bedroom stark raving naked. This realization drove her under the covers and into Trevor Bradford's waiting arms.

"Oh," she gasped. "Goodness."

He didn't feel seventy-three years old. He felt strong and virile. And he smelled nice too, like Lavoris and pine trees. And he had nice hands. Soft, gentle hands.

"This is nice," she said.

Trevor's hands skimmed across her body, touching her hair, caressing her breasts, stroking her thighs.

"Mmmmm hmmmmm."

He spent much longer touching her than Connor ever had. In fact, he seemed to enjoy the touching part, seemed to be discovering her body just as she was . . . discovering . . . Without thinking, she reached out and played her hand along his back. She stroked his hip and circled his smooth backside with the palm of her hand. Never before had her hand seemed so exquisitely sensitive, so electric, to the touch. Every line, every fingerprint, devoured the sensation of his skin against hers.

When his hand moved to her most sensitive place she rolled over on her back, allowing him to continue, wanting him to continue.

"Oh," she gasped. "Oh my."

44 A long time ago Forrest had learned you can't run away from someone who means to harm you.

He tried to walk faster. Tried not to look at the pimply-faced twelve-year-old with twitchy hands and copperhead eyes who danced by his side.

"Where you think you're going, boy? Ain't no place you can run. Ain't no place you can hide."

The boy was tall for his age, but weakened from a bout of scarlet fever. Sweat soaked through his plaid flannel shirt, a shirt too warm for September in Tennessee but not, as his mother had reminded him, too warm for a boy who'd had the fever.

Without warning the blunt tip of a manure-crusted work-boot lashed out and scraped the boy's Achilles tendon, sending him sprawling. He flew forward, nearly dropping the bucket of precious eggs. He fell full force, tearing his one pair of decent pants, skinning his knees on the cindered road, reaching out frantically, catching the flying bucket at the last possible instant.

He knelt there dazed. Tears stung his eyes, but he did not let them spill either.

"Crybaby, crybaby, crybaby!" Lester Renfew whirled around him, kicking up road dust.

The boy ran the back of a dirty hand across his nose.

"Leave me alone, Lester. What'd I ever do to you?"

"Mama's boy." Lester hitched up the side of his lip into a sneer that hid brown-spotted teeth. The freckles

on the bridge of his nose stood out sharp as fleas against a porcelain plate. He swiped clots of greasy bangs from his eyes.

The boy tried to remind himself that Lester was dirt poor. That he had a mother who was crazy and a father who beat him. That he lived in a moldy sharecropper shack with a dirt floor, a place even niggers turned their noses up at. But instead of making him feel sympathetic, these thoughts made him more afraid. Because all these things joined forces to make Lester Renfew mean as a rattlesnake.

Buying time, the boy set the bucket down in the dirt, switched to a sitting position, removed his shoe, straightened his sock, put the shoe back on, and retied it securely. It seemed to take forever.

"Nice batcha eggs you got there, you little faggot." In the blink of an eye, Lester reached down and grabbed one.

"Come on," said the boy, standing up. "Give it back, Lester."

"Collect these for your grammaw, didja?"

"Give it back." Please, Lester, give it back. Pawpaw counts those eggs. I get whupped ifn' there's too few. Give it back!

Lester hefted the brown egg in his hand.

"Say please, peckerwood."

He would make him beg. "Please."

"Here." Lester slammed the egg into the boy's face.

Shards of shell stung his cheeks. His nose filled with slime. He could scarcely breathe. Something inside him snapped and a sound ripped from his throat. A bloodcurdling Rebel yell that would have made Pawpaw proud.

Lester Renfew stepped back a pace.

In a blind rage the boy hoisted the bucket from his feet, lifted it overhead, upended it, and rammed it over Lester Renfew's head. He felt a satisfying series of crunches as three dozen eggs cracked in succession over his tormentor's lice-ridden scalp. Then, his outrage yet unspent, he pulled down hard on the bucket, wedging the slimy container securely over Lester's square head.

"You son of a bitch!"

The words were muted and tinny. The handle dangled under Lester's face like a chin strap.

The boy stood there staring at the screaming bucket, unable to believe he had done this. But tendrils of yellow muck and goo that dripped from the bully's shoulders served as irrefutable proof that he had.

"I'll kill you, you miserable little peckerwood! I'll break your fucking ass!"

The boy kicked the bucketed bully in the shins, hard.

He turned and walked away.

It was worth every bit of the licking Pawpaw gave him that night . . .

Forrest lifted his head from the rolltop desk and rubbed his eyes. Lord, he must have dozed off. He was bone tired. Books lay strewn across the floor of Mildred's study . . . a volume of the *Encyclopedia Britannica* opened to a full-page diagram of the human eye . . . an issue dated June 1978 of the *Journal of the American Society of Ophthalmic Surgeons* . . . plus an entire stack of medical books Trevor had gotten for him from the library at Yale University. He glanced at his watch. Here it was after midnight and he hadn't even gotten to them yet.

The sawed-off shotgun, along with Winston, lay by his feet.

"Want to go for a walk, boy? Call it a night?"

The dog struggled to his feet and panted enthusiastically. He wagged his stump of a tail, and his whole butt swayed from side to side.

"Okay, Winnie. Come on."

Suddenly the dog's ears perked up. He whined apprehensively.

Forrest reached for the gun. "What is it, boy? You hear something?"

Winston moved slowly. He ambled toward the back of the house and Forrest followed. They walked through the darkened hallway and were almost to the kitchen when Forrest smelled something. He cocked his head and sniffed again. His hands clutched the gun. It was . . . smelled like . . . like gas.

"Oh, Christ. Reenie left one of the burners on, that's all. She's so damned forgetful sometimes."

He pressed through the swinging door into the kitchen. He groped for the light switch, but never made it. A hand lashed out in the darkness. Something blunt and heavy crashed down on his skull. He groaned and sank to his knees.

The object came down again. Fighting waves of dizziness and nausea, Forrest waved the gun blindly, trying to shield himself with the small barrel. He heard a sharp metallic clink as the barrel of the gun deflected the weapon. But as he tried to struggle to his feet, the hand swept down again. He felt an agonizing bolt of pain, saw spinning pinwheels of fire and light, and felt his knees buckle. Somewhere he heard Winston growl. He slumped to the floor.

Sometime later—it was but moments, although it seemed longer—Forrest regained consciousness. The smell of gas was now overpowering. The pain on the right side of his head throbbed relentlessly. The tile floor under his cheek was slick with blood. Amazingly, the gun was still locked in his hands.

He opened one eye and then the other, staring into blackness. Something scraped and he turned his throbbing head toward the sound. A shape moved toward the back door.

He rose to his knees and pointed the gun in the direction of the black form. "Hold it right there, mister."

The shape moved toward him. The smell of methane was more powerful. Forrest staggered to his feet. "Where's the dog? I'll kill you, if you hurt that dog!"

Forrest tried to remain clearheaded, but his head was throbbing from the concussion and the effect of the gas.

The gun weighed in his hands, heavy as a cinderblock. His movements were dull and lethargic. His eyes bulged from their sockets.

No, he told himself. No.

There was a flash of metal, a blur of motion as the weapon descended yet again.

He pulled the trigger.

The muzzle flash was a ball of fire.

"Reenie!" he screamed. "Help me!"

Numbed by methane gas, his mind kicked into a progression of jerky slow-motion stills, frame after frame of images framed in hell. Images he would never forget.

The last thing he felt for sure was the resistance of the trigger against his finger. The vision of the flash burned in his brain. In a fraction of an instant, he saw a face. It was pretty. A woman's face.

There was a mighty roar, coupled with an inhuman cry. A woman's cry.

No! Dear God, I've shot a woman.

He wanted to reach out to her but the kick of the shotgun pushed him back.

The pretty face exploded into bits of brain and facial tissue that splattered across the ceiling of Mildred's modern kitchen.

I cannot be seeing this, I cannot.

For an everlasting moment the room around him looked like a grisly cave, festooned with dripping flesh stalactites.

Forrest's hands locked around the gun. He felt searing heat from a second, far more powerful explosion and his frail body was hurled back even further, hurled back into a cold dark void.

This is what it's like, he realized. To die alone. Beyond pain. Beyond imagining. Beyond help.

He saw three more faces. Angels. They had white blond hair and looked at him with turquoise blue eyes.

"Yes!" he cried. "Yes!"

And then they were gone.

45 "He looks dead."

"No. His chest—see? He's breathing."

"He's got bubbles all over his face."

"Blisters. Burns."

"And his eyebrows are gone."

"I can't believe they just left him here. We've got to get help."

Forrest managed to open an eye that had crusted closed and propped himself up on one elbow in the wet grass. There they were, leaning over him, his three angels in the flesh.

"They left me here because that's what I wanted. I don't want any help."

Cameron and Lauren stepped back a pace. Timmy squirmed in Lauren's arms.

"Are you okay, Mr. Haggarty?" Cameron looked at him with worried eyes.

"I've felt better." Weakly he rose from the wet grass where he'd been resting. He touched the bandage on his head and winced. He flexed his fingers, then shook each leg. Everything seemed to be in working order. He hitched up his torn khakis and brushed them off with bloody hands.

"What about the others?" asked the boy. "Mrs. Purdy, Mrs. Bennett, and Dr. Bradford?"

"Safe," Forrest managed to say. "Shook up pretty bad, but safe. They'll be okay." He'd sent them over to The Elms early the night before. Thank God he'd convinced them. They'd be safe there, he told them. He would follow, don't worry. When he hadn't, when night had turned to early morning, they'd been frantic. They hurried back in night clothes, chasing the sound of fire engines.

"Mr. Haggarty," said Lauren, "you look bad. Your face, it's all bubbly."

Forrest leaned against the frame of the gazebo. He doubled over in a coughing fit and waved a hand crusted with scabs at the children, shooing them away. When he recovered, he wiped the back of his hand across his blackened face, leaving a gray streak through the soot. . . .

The events of the previous night were hazy in his mind, like a dream that won't be remembered. From what the Raven's Wing Fire Department had been able to determine afterward, the force of the methane explosion blew Forrest Haggarty and his gun clear through the cellar door and down the stairs. In his weakened, unconscious state, he'd fallen limply, a condition that, quite possibly, saved his life. He'd landed in a heap, senseless, at the foot of the stairs.

Vaguely, he remembered something wet on his face. Wet and warm. Licking. An animal, it was.

The animal turned out to be Winston. The dog had become disoriented during the explosion and cowered under an old card table. Then a familiar scent tickled his nose. He found Forrest in the rubble and licked his scorched face.

He saved my life, thought Forrest, that damn dog saved my life. Indeed the old dog with the bad bladder and rheumatoid joints had done exactly that, for it was Winston who led the way surely as Forrest crawled under timbers and over household debris, the gun still clutched in his hands. Together they traversed the gritty cement floor to the bulkhead. Together they crawled up, step by agonizing step. Together they emerged and collapsed on grass drenched by fire fighters. Forrest remembered pressing his face into a muddy puddle.

Mildred, Irene, and Trevor were waiting, praying, as

close to the bulkhead as the intense heat would allow. When they saw Forrest and Winston emerge, they let out whoops of joy and dragged man and beast away from the heat. They had to pry the gun from his hands. . . .

Yes. It was all coming back.

"Just a bad sunburn," he said. "That's all."

"Someone died in there." Cameron gestured to the blackened hole that had been Mildred's house. He seemed taller, sturdier, somehow. "I saw firemen bring out a body. It looked like a twisted black cinder."

The boy didn't know who it was.

"The police weren't to your place yet?"

"They talked to my father. But he hasn't told us anything."

"Go get him."

"Was that body the person who killed my mother?"

"No." Then Forrest remembered who had and shuddered inside. How could he ever tell them the truth? "Well maybe. In a way."

"In what way?"

"In a way you won't understand. A lot of people killed your mother. A lot of people could have done something. But no one did. Let's just say it was one of those people."

"I don't get it."

"Never mind. Just get your father."

"Why?"

" 'Cause I want to talk to him, that's why!" He looked numbly at bloodied hands crisscrossed with cuts and splinters. Two fingernails had been ripped off entirely. He was tired and now he was angry. Why didn't children mind anymore? He raised his hand as if to strike. "Don't stand there gaping! Go get him! The lot of you!"

They turned and ran. Cameron looked back once, confusion and fear etched on his face.

46 "Forrest! Forrest!"
Forrest turned to face Jonathan Maine.

He came running to the gazebo, out of breath, gasping. "I came as soon as the children told me . . . I thought they'd taken you to the hospital . . . God, you look terrible."

"I'll live."

"The police . . . they showed us her wedding ring . . . Freddy, he recognized it . . . Is it true, what they said? That she tried to kill you?"

"That she did."

His breathing came easier, but he shook his head in disbelief. "I never dreamed it would be Constance, never dreamed she hated Esther so much."

"It wasn't Constance," said Forrest quietly.

"I mean, I knew she was jealous, knew she always resented Esther, but—"

"I said it wasn't Constance!"

Jonathan stopped short. "I don't understand. The police showed us her ring. If she tried to kill you—"

"Oh, Constance tried to kill me all right. She won't get to tell us why exactly." He gestured at the smoldering rubble that had once been Mildred's grand house. "But I can pretty well guess. She killed a lot of people. Anyone who posed a threat to Freddy."

Jonathan blinked. "You mean Freddy . . . ?"

"She thought Freddy did it, and she did everything she could to protect him. But Freddy didn't kill Esther. It was someone else."

"Who for God's sake?"

"You."

"What the hell are you saying?"

"You're the one who killed her. It was you all the time."

Jonathan Maine stepped back. "You're crazy."

"Oh yeah?" He gazed past Jonathan as he spoke. He couldn't even stand to look at the man. "I guess you thought it wouldn't do no harm having a bunch of old fools look into Esther's death. I guess you figured there was no risk. That it would put a stop to Cameron's inconvenient questions and Lucille's demands for an investigation."

"That's ridiculous."

"Oh yeah?" Forrest shook his head in quiet amazement. "I've got to hand it to you. You had me running in circles. First I figured it was Claudia who killed Esther. For money. To support her baby. After all, she's crazy. Who better to blame?"

"She's not crazy," protested Jonathan weakly.

"You wanted us to think so! You planned on it. You knew I'd find out about her. Knew Trevor would tell me. About your 'crazy' daughter. A daughter who could kill her own mother."

"You're wrong, wrong about everything."

"Oh, there were a lot of things you didn't tell me. Some you knew I'd find out, like about Claudia's craziness, and others, well, on others maybe I just got lucky. A lot of things happened, Jonathan, things that sealed Esther's fate way before she died. Things that happened years ago. But they all add up, see? And that's what it's all about. Adding up."

Jonathan looked at him sharply now. "What things?"

"Things like the fact that Claudia wasn't your child."

He flinched as though slapped. "She *is* my child," he said quietly. "In any sense that means anything. She's always been my child, from the moment I first held her in my arms."

When Forrest allowed himself to speak again his own words were so soft, so cold, that Jonathan Maine had to strain to hear.

"You didn't tell me a lot of things. You didn't tell me about the deal you made. How you married Esther when she was in trouble. In return for money to start your practice. Her lottery money."

"I loved her!"

"And you didn't tell me how you killed Claudia's real father. How it was you that killed Evan Jamison."

Jonathan Maine paled and sank to the planked bench. "My God." He put his face in his hands. When he spoke, it was into the folds of his fingers. "I did what I had to do."

"You committed murder."

Jonathan Maine looked up with eyes suddenly cold. "You can't prove it."

"Maybe I can and maybe I can't. But since the murder was never solved, it's still on the books. I'll get the police over in Norwalk to reopen the case."

Neither spoke for some moments.

"Don't," said Jonathan wearily. "You don't understand. He was an animal. Worse than an animal. Animals don't abuse their young. He'd been abusing her for years, Forrest. Ever since she was four years old. She couldn't get over it. Couldn't forget. Couldn't lead a normal life, a married life, with me. She wouldn't let me touch her. She had nightmares."

"Yeah, I'll bet."

"And then he wanted money. Her money. Her 'lucky lottery money,' he called it. He wanted a share. Said he deserved it for adopting her. Deserved it for caring for her all those years." He paused. "She would have given it to him, too."

"But you killed him instead." Forrest's lip curled. "For her sake."

The answer was the barest whisper. "Yes." He mopped his face with a handkerchief. "It was for a worthy cause.

The money was supposed to be our stake. Not mine. *Ours.* It was supposed to help me get started in my practice, that's true. But that wasn't the only reason I killed him. He didn't deserve to live, of course. But I killed him because I thought it would help her. I thought it would set her free."

"But it didn't."

"No. She never got better. She got worse. She retreated into a world of her own, a fantasy world. She never let me . . . well, twenty years of marriage and she always recoiled at my touch."

"Must have been hard when you discovered she was having affairs with other men."

Jonathan shot to his feet. "I discovered no such thing!"

"Oh yes you did. You found letters. Poems. You tracked her. Followed her. Stalked her. You thought she was having affairs with Freddy. And with her shrink. You've got a twisted kind of morality, Jonathan. As long as she was the dutiful wife, as long as she didn't stray, you left her alone. But the moment you thought she was playing around, well, then it was another kettle of fish entirely."

"That's a lie."

Forrest paused, considering his words. "The hell of it is, she wasn't fooling around, Jonathan. She recoiled at your touch, but no one else touched her either."

Jonathan looked at Forrest in disbelief.

"You hear me? There *were* no affairs! She imagined the whole damned thing. It was all in her mind, Jonathan. All of it! You said it yourself. Said she lived 'in a world of her own. A fantasy world.'"

Jonathan gripped the railing. "No! I followed her. She was seeing some man named Blaustein! And her own brother-in-law too!"

"Freddy's story matched Blaustein's, matched it exactly. They both said she was deluded. That she believed they loved her. Believed they were lovers even. But they weren't. She had more than a delusion, she had an illness. An illness where a lonely person creates imaginary lovers.

Lovers that don't really exist. They've even got a name for it. It's called erotomania."

"You're lying." The words were a plea.

"No I'm not. You thought she was seeing someone else. You thought she would leave you. And if she did, well, divorce wouldn't be very profitable, would it? Seems to me, divorce would take a mighty big chunk out of your finances. Seeing as how it was her money that got your practice started."

Jonathan staggered backward down the steps to the sodden grass. He swung his head from side to side like a wounded animal, refusing to believe what he heard.

"You killed her for nothing, Jonathan. Nothing."

He pressed his hands to his ears. "No!"

But Forrest wasn't finished. "Then again, maybe it wasn't for nothing. Because with Esther out of the way you could have the life you wanted. The money you have. Plus insurance money on her life. We haven't checked into that, but I wager it's a pretty penny."

"I have money of my own! I don't need any of that. Don't you understand?"

"But best of all, you could have the woman you love. The woman you've loved for a long time. The real mother of your children."

"Shut up!" Jonathan screeched.

"It took me a while to figure that part. Took me a while to figure why Helga would back you up with such a solid alibi. Then I remembered a few things. I remembered the two glasses you had on the patio that night. Force of habit, you explained, one being for Esther. It was a lie, of course, but I believed it. I'd been through grief of my own and it clouded by judgment."

"This is crazy. All of it. No one will believe—"

"Then I remembered what she said when Timmy almost ran into the pool. What she said and the way she said it too. *The child wants his mother.* Fierce, she was. Protective. Like a mother would be, Jonathan. Of course, the child wanted her. But the clincher came later. When I remembered the faces of your children. There it was. Your secret. Written on their faces and in their eyes. Their blue eyes."

"You can't prove any of this."

"I think I can. The eyes were what tipped me off. I don't know why you bludgeoned Esther's eyes exactly, but they got me to thinking. First about colors. You have blue eyes. Esther's were brown. I didn't know a lot about genetics, but I knew brown tends to dominate over blue. Curious, I thought, how Cameron and Lauren and Timmy's eyes turned out blue. 'Course it happens sometimes. Otherwise we'd all have brown eyes."

"What the hell are you driving at?"

"But something else doesn't happen. A color-blind woman can't give birth to a male who's not color-blind. A color-blind woman can only bear a color-blind son."

"That's not . . ." Jonathan stopped himself.

"True? Sure it is. You should know, being a doctor and all. Esther was color-blind. Her old school records so state. But Cameron's not. I saw Cameron pick out red M and Ms the first day I met him. He did it easy as you please."

Jonathan said nothing.

"Cameron's not Esther's boy, that much is plain. I figure he's Helga's child. Just like Lauren and Timmy. They're Helga's children too."

"That's sheer speculation. It will never stand up."

"There are genetic tests—"

"I'd never give permission."

"Permission or no, I don't need fancy lab work to tell me what's plain as day. They got her features too. Her hair. Her nose. Her smile. Anyone with eyes of their own can tell. And I bet Esther could too."

"She accepted it. I wanted children. I wanted my blood walking this earth."

"You bastard."

"It's not too much to ask, wanting children. Not too much!"

"First you turned Esther into a recluse, making her hide in the house during pregnancies that never were—"

"She wanted to hide! She hated to go outside!"

"Sure, and you made the most of it, didn't you? And then, later, much later, you brought Helga into your home. With your family, Jonathan! Right under Esther's nose!"

"I know, I know. But Timmy was too much for Esther. She didn't want him. She backslid even deeper into psychosis. I had to turn somewhere. And Helga needed a place. I thought it would work out."

"Great!" roared Forrest.

"It would have worked out," insisted Jonathan doggedly, "except for Esther's delusions. They got worse and worse. And then she insisted on going to the city. To visit Claudia. I tried to dissuade her, begged her not to go."

"Your little world was crumbling."

"For her sake, I begged her. The city is a dangerous place. There are traps. Temptations. I tried to tell her, but she wouldn't listen. When I saw she wouldn't listen, I still tried to protect her. I followed her. Every week."

"Until you killed her."

"You'll never prove it."

"Oh yeah? Why not?"

"Because there's another story. A more likely one. One people will believe."

47 Forrest turned away. "Save it for the courtroom."

"I think you better listen, Forrest. You'll be sorry if you don't."

"Okay, tell your little story. But it won't make a damn bit of difference."

"You'll change your mind. It's the story of a boy, you see. A boy who has always been overly sensitive. Highstrung and impressionable. A nice boy by appearances, but—"

"You're talking about Cameron, aren't you?"

"—perhaps slightly unbalanced."

"You bastard."

"It's the story of a boy who's always been wrapped up in thoughts. Deep thoughts. Thoughts a child has no business thinking. As his father, I took it for a sign of specialness. Of sensitivity. And for a while maybe it was. But somewhere along the line those thoughts turned alarmingly judgmental, and the boy started to focus on sin. On retribution."

"For God's sake, he's your son."

"The boy developed very rigid ideas about right and wrong. He became very righteous. And on top of that, he saw himself as keeper of the flame. As the protector of the family. As caretaker. Written psychiatric evaluations bear this out."

Forrest felt a stone drop in his stomach. He had forgotten that Jonathan was not a stupid man, but a smart one. A cunning one. He would not have killed Esther on the spur of the moment. He would have planned it. Planned it for years.

"The tragedy is that the boy found the letters. And the poems. He didn't know, couldn't know, they were products of his mother's own vivid imagination. To him they were evidence of a monstrous betrayal. And so, you see, the boy followed his mother to the St. James that night with a hammer hidden in his jacket. I saw him, stationed as I was across the street, trying as best I could to guard and protect my wife. But the boy was too quick. And by the time I got there she was dead. He had battered—"

"You monster!"

"—battered his mother. Crushed her eyes in the sockets. Dragged her to the tub. Impaled her face on the faucets. Turned on the shower. To cleanse her. To purify."

Forrest eyed Jonathan with disgust.

"The weapon bears the boy's prints," Jonathan went on. "I kept it for safekeeping. A souvenir of sorts. You can retrieve it, if you wish. It's in the old well in the meadow. Wrapped in a plastic bag."

"You'll never get away with this."

Jonathan looked at him and didn't blink. "Oh, but I will."

"Cameron won't lie for you. Not about this. He'll tell."

"How can he tell what he can't remember?" He saw confusion on Forrest's face and pressed on. "You yourself said he was vague about that night. It's no accident. He was with me."

"But how—"

"I administered a drug. An amnesiatic."

"You mean he saw what happened?"

"He saw and he didn't see. He was in a trancelike state. He doesn't remember a single moment of that night."

"Fragments will come back," challenged Forrest. "You said already he was having nightmares."

"Yes. It's a risk I have to take. But our relationship is quite good—indeed, it's better than ever. If unpleasant memories start to surface, he'll come to me. He'll believe whatever I tell him. And even if he suspects the truth, I don't believe he'll betray me. It would mean destroying the family, you see. And, no matter what, Cameron has always seen himself as its protector."

"You'd play with your son's sanity to save your own neck?"

"If you choose to put it that way, yes."

Forrest considered this well-constructed crime. Somewhere there had to be a weakness. His eyes opened wide. "Catholics don't cremate," he said.

"What?"

"You're Catholic. You didn't cremate this body. It's in the ground."

"Yes . . . ?"

"So we can prove it wasn't Cameron who committed the crime. We'll do another autopsy. Pathologists can tell the height of the killer from the angle of the blows. They can tell the weight too. They'll know it wasn't Cameron. They'll know it was you!"

Jonathan almost smiled. "No they won't. I reconstructed her face, remember? She was quite presentable when she was interred, both inside and out."

48 "So what are you going to do?" asked Mildred. Forrest's shoulders slumped. "I'll be damned if I know."

It was two days after the fire and Forrest's confrontation with Jonathan. The four friends sat in the gazebo trying to make sense out of events that seemed to have none.

The sun was setting. Along the edge of the gaping black hole that had once been Mildred's house two representatives from Prudential scurried about, notebooks in hand. Mildred couldn't see the point. She'd never get a dime for replacing the house, considering the circumstances of its destruction.

"I was kind of hoping you guys could give me some advice," said Forrest glumly.

Irene looked at him in surprise. "Jeesum, Forrest, you never asked us before. I mean we help you on these investigations, but you never ask us about stuff like this. You always just do the right thing."

"Well this time I don't know what's right."

"It's a terrible dilemma," agreed Trevor. "Jonathan seems to have covered his tracks very well."

"I'm not sure we can win this one," said Forrest. "That miserable son of a bitch."

"What about Cameron?" asked Mildred. "We should consider him, you know. And the other children. How can we leave them in the care of a murderer—and his mistress?"

"That's another thing," said Forrest. "If Jonathan falls, who else is there? To care for them, I mean. Claudia?"

"Maybe," said Trevor carefully.

"Aw come on, Trevor. Claudia's a little off the wall."

"Not anymore," countered Irene. "She's doing a whole lot better."

"A baby could put a strain on her equilibrium," said Trevor, "that much is true. But then again she may rally. She's a smart girl and she has grit."

"Isn't it all a moot point," said Mildred, "if we can't prove Jonathan murdered his wife?"

They sat there gloomily for some moments.

"Funny," said Forrest.

"What's funny?" asked Mildred.

"Oh nothing. Just that Cameron was so insistent when we started. He said he wanted to know the truth no matter what. Said he could take it."

"Maybe we should take him at his word," said Trevor.

"I don't know about that," said Mildred. "This kind of truth is more than a healthy adult could bear, never mind a vulnerable child."

"Telling him may be the most responsible thing to do," Trevor went on. "Forrest was right about fragments coming back. It's more than a possibility. It's likely. Without support, without people who care for him and believe in him, people who know the truth and don't flinch, the boy may think he's going crazy."

"Like his sister," blurted Irene.

"Exactly. There's no telling what might happen."

"You mean," said Mildred in alarm, "he might kill himself?"

"I don't know," said Trevor. "But it would be a hard thing to face. By himself."

"It's settled then," said Forrest flatly. "Cameron has to know the truth."

"And who's going to tell him?" asked Irene, already knowing the answer.

Forrest looked at this hands. "Me," he said quietly. "Who else?"

49 Days passed. Forrest, Mildred, and Irene moved into Trevor's white gingerbread Victorian on Main Street, a walkable distance from Mildred's property several blocks away. She wanted to be near the reconstruction once it started. She also wanted to be near Trevor. Very near. Forrest and Irene smiled knowingly among themselves but gracefully kept their mouths shut when Mildred unpacked her things in Trevor's bedroom. And, for once in her life, Mildred didn't offer any embarrassed excuses.

They all went on long walks, took turns cooking (except Forrest, who refused to engage in domestic tasks), watched videos on the TV, and generally avoided speaking about their failure, for that was how they came to see it. True, they had succeeded in solving the murder. But what good did it do when the killer went on with his life as though nothing had happened? The others waited and hoped that Forrest would do what had to be done. In his own good time. Yet as each day passed, they feared he might, indeed, simply do nothing at all.

Then one day Trevor came back from a trip to New Haven with another load of books under his arm and a sly expression on his face.

"What're you so damned happy about?" said Forrest.

"I'm not happy. Just thinking."

"What're those?" Forrest eyed the books suspiciously.

"Books."

"I *know* that, for Christ's sake. What're they about? And why're you looking like the cat that swallowed the canary?"

"They're books from the library at Yale Medical School. My alma mater."

Forrest couldn't help but remember the books on genetics, lost in the fire. "They let you have more? You never returned the last stack you borrowed."

"My credit's still good."

"So what're they about."

"Hypnosis."

"Oh. Gonna perform at some Vegas nightclub? Or go on the *Ed Sullivan Show?*"

"Ed Sullivan's dead."

"Joan Rivers then. You could do her show. She takes anybody."

"No," said Trevor shortly. "If you must know, they're for Cameron."

"Huh?" Forrest perked up.

"If Jonathan administered an amnesiatic, there's no telling how long it may take for his memories to surface—or if they will at all. And if we tell him what happened, he probably won't believe us."

"I guess," said Forrest.

"So I thought I'd hypnotize him. He may not be a good subject. Who knows? But I figured I'd—"

"You're gonna hypnotize him, and *he's* gonna tell *us* what happened!"

"Exactly. At least I hope he will." He frowned. "But don't get yourself in a lather. It may not work. Even if he turns out to be a good subject, the drug may have eliminated the impressions we're looking for."

"That's okay," said Forrest excitedly. "At least we're gonna try. It's better than giving up, for God's sake. I think it's a great idea."

"You do?"

"Yeah." He bolted to his feet. "I'll call Cameron right now."

"No!" blurted Trevor. "I've got to brush up. I haven't hypnotized anyone in years and years. Not since medical school, and then it was no more than a dormitory demonstration for a young lady I was trying to impress." And seduce, but he didn't say that. "I've got to read up."

"Okay, okay," sighed Forrest. "But read quick. I'm not long on patience."

"Don't I know it. . . ."

The very next day Trevor was ready. He assembled his friends in the family room. Everything was set up according to Trevor's instructions. In the center of the room stood a close circle of five chairs, the focal point being a plaid Stratolounger recliner. Mildred hated recliners, especially plaid ones. Once she looked through a book called the *Encyclopedia of Tasteless Culture* at Books on the Common and wasn't surprised to find an entire chapter devoted to recliners. This time, however, she was glad Trevor had one, because it appeared quite comfortable, at least if one's eyes were closed.

"Now this is what we do," said Trevor. "I'll sit here to his left. Mildred, you sit there to his right. We'll both hold his hand."

"I thought I'd sit there," said Forrest, "so I can hear what he has to say. Sometimes folks speak softly in séances."

"This isn't a séance," said Trevor. "I plan to induce a trance. And I want him to have a woman's touch. I want him to be reassured, to feel safe. Hence, Mildred."

"What am I?" demanded Irene. "Chopped liver?"

"No, Irene, of course not. It's just that you can be, well, a trifle spontaneous in your reactions and it might intimidate—"

"I am not! If anyone's intimidating it's Millie."

"I beg your pardon!" said Mildred.

"Well you are, Millie, let's be frank here. Sometimes it's like you got a ramrod up your—"

"I resent that remark and you better not finish it!"

"Ladies, ladies!" said Trevor. "Please!" He glared at Mildred and Irene. "Kindly sit where you're told without bickering. Irene, I want Mildred next to Cameron because she had a son."

"Oh." Irene felt truly miserable now because she never had a son, or a daughter for that matter, while Mildred had one of each.

"She had a son who had troubles," Trevor went on. A son who died, but he didn't say that.

"I see," said Irene, feeling even worse now, remembering Mildred's loss.

"Tell you what, Irene," said Mildred, "why don't you sit next to me? Then you can hold my hand."

"I'd like that."

"I really didn't have that in mind," began Trevor.

"Does that mean I'm holding Trevor's hand?" barked Forrest.

"Yes," snapped Mildred, "it does."

"I don't hold any man's hand."

"For gosh sakes, Forrest, if you're gonna be so per-snickety, I'll sit in your place." Irene plunked herself down. "Now you can hold Millie's and my hands. Okay?"

"Okay," he muttered.

Which, thought Trevor in exasperation, is exactly the seating arrangement I had in mind in the first place.

"Anybody home?"

"It's him!" whispered Irene.

"Down here, Cameron!" called Trevor.

Cameron Maine bounded down the stairs. He seemed to have sprouted three inches in the last three weeks. His face was flushed and his body muscular.

"Why Cameron," exclaimed Irene, "you're getting to be right handsome."

He grinned. "I've been running every day. This fall I'm going out for track. Dad says I can go to Raven's Wing High instead of Canterbury."

"That's nice," said Forrest, feeling a pang of despair.

"You said you had something to tell me?" said Cameron.

"Not exactly," said Trevor. "We thought you might have something to tell *us*."

Cameron looked at him quizzically.

"You know how you can't remember anything that happened the night your mother died?" said Mildred gently.

"Sure," said Cameron. "But it's nothing to worry about. It happens once in a while. Dad says my circuits get overloaded."

Trevor looked at him intently. "Does it happen when you're home or when you're away at school?"

Cameron thought a moment. "When I'm home," he said at last, "never at school. Funny, I never thought about that. It's kind of spooky, but my folks took me to a doctor—a neurologist—and he ran a bunch of tests. He said it's nothing to worry about. I just go into a real deep sleep sometimes. Because I'm so hyper when I'm awake. It's a way of recharging my batteries, he said."

"Of course," said Trevor. "But now we've questioned everyone else connected who knew your mother, and you, young man, happen to be a loose end."

"A very nice loose end," amended Mildred.

"Yes. And we'd like to help you remember on the off chance that there might be something—anything at all—that would help give us a clue."

"I see," said Cameron gravely. "But I don't think it will help. When I'm sleeping like that I never remember anything. It's like I'm in a trance or something."

"Exactly," said Trevor. "So we want to put you into a trance again."

"Pardon?"

"He wants to hypnotize you," said Irene.

"If you agree," said Trevor.

"But you'll be all right," Mildred offered quickly. "We'll all be right here with you."

"Yeah," said Irene, trying to sound enthusiastic. "It'd be like you were going on a trip or something." She gestured to the recliner. "That there's your spaceship."

Forrest slapped Cameron on the back. "What do you say, young fella?"

"I don't know . . ."

"You said you wanted to know the truth," pressed Forrest. "Remember?"

"Yes. Okay. I guess it can't do any harm."

Forrest looked down at his feet, feeling guilty.

"Okay," said Trevor. "Now everyone get comfortable." He watched while they got situated and dimmed the lights. Then he sat down next to Cameron. "Everyone join hands."

"This *is* like one of them séances," giggled Irene, "and I can't wait to have a word with Earl."

Trevor shot her a glance. "Irene."

"Sorry."

"Now, Cameron, I want you to relax. Relax your feet . . . your toes . . . your ankles. You feel very calm. You're floating, floating on a soft white cloud . . . The world is far below. Receding . . . receding. Relax your legs . . . your stomach. That's a good boy. You're feeling very comfortable. Very safe . . ."

The drone of Trevor's voice continued soothingly. Soon Cameron's face slackened. He looked very peaceful indeed.

"I think he's under," whispered Forrest.

"Cameron," said Trevor softly, "can you hear me?"

The reply seemed to come from deep inside the boy. The voice was small and childlike. "Yes."

"Good. Now listen to me closely. I want you to know that if you become upset, you can wake up. You can stop this any time."

Forrest nearly fell off his chair. "What the hell are you telling him, Trevor?"

Trevor pointedly ignored him. He would not be responsible for causing this boy to break down. If that meant Jonathan Maine went free, so be it. "Do you understand, Cameron?"

"Yes. I can wake up. Any time."

"You have the power."

"I have the power."

"Good. Now we're going to go back in time. Just a little ways. Back to July. Do you remember July?"

"Yes. School vacation."

"Right. You were home from school. I want you to remember one day in particular. July eighteenth. A Wednesday."

"Swimming," said Cameron.

"Tell me about July eighteenth, Cameron. Tell me."

"I went to Bedient's Hardware and bought a humongous pair of wire cutters," said another voice.

Everyone but Cameron turned to Irene, whose chin rested on her chest.

"Jesus," said Forrest under his breath, "I don't believe this."

"Then I went and bought a sack of Purina to lure the critters out. Even black bears like Purina."

"What on earth is she talking about?" asked Mildred.

"Irene!" Trevor nudged her sharply. "Irene!"

"Yes?"

"Wake up. Wake up *now*."

Irene opened her eyes and surveyed her ample bosom. Her head snapped up. "Must have dozed off," she said sheepishly.

"Well don't do it again," said Forrest. "Please."

"Keep your wits about you," said Mildred.

"Now where was I," muttered Trevor. "Oh yes. July eighteenth, Cameron. Tell me about July eighteenth . . ."

"Great Pond. Lauren and I went. Swimming."

"Good. Tell me about Great Pond."

"Crowded. Float was sinking. Lots of kids. Girls. Pretty. Lifeguard made me leave."

"Oh?" said Trevor. "Why?"

"I do breathing exercises. For my asthma. Can hold my breath. Longer than anyone. They were scared. The girls. Thought I died."

"I see. You showed the girls how long you could stay under and they thought you drowned."

"Lifeguard too. She was crying when I finally came up."

"Scared her pretty bad, huh?"

"Yeah. Bad."

"So she sent you home." He kept his voice casual. "Tell me what happened at home."

"What happened? Well . . ."

"Cameron, mind if I come in?"

He looked up in surprise and put the book aside. "Sure, Dad."

"Your mother's in the city, Lauren's sleeping over at a girlfriend's. Looks like it's ladies' night out."

"Yeah."

"What say we make it boys' night out too? How'd you like to go out to dinner with me?"

"No kidding?"

"No kidding. Go wash up. Put on a clean shirt. I'll give you an allergy shot, and we'll be on our way."

"Dad, I haven't had allergies all summer. I'm fine. Really."

His father held up his hand like a traffic cop. "Because of the shots you're fine. Better safe than sorry, I always say. Besides, I happen to know you were swimming at Great Pond today. You know how your sinuses react afterwards. I don't want you to get an asthma attack in the middle of the best steak dinner the Palm has to offer."

"We're having dinner in the city?"

His father laughed. "Yes! Now hop to."

"What happened next, Cameron?"

The mumbled words were barely understandable. "Don't remember."

"Try. Do you remember getting your allergy shot?"

"Uh huh."

"Then what?"

"Sleep. In the car. Stopping for tolls."

"Okay. You're in the car, going to the city on the Saw Mill River Parkway . . ."

"Cameron, wake up! Come on!"

He felt gentle slaps on his face. Slowly he opened eyes that felt glued together. He looked at his father through slits.

"Atta boy. Come on, we have to hurry. Come along now."

He felt one arm being grabbed, felt himself being hoisted from the car, then heard a door slam. He was aware of the acrid stench of exhaust, the sound of grinding gears and city traffic.

His mouth wouldn't form words. "We're here?" he tried to say.

"Yes."

He moved as though through water. His feet felt encased in concrete. The pavement under his shoes was soft and mushy. Half walking, half staggering, he tried to keep up with the man who gripped his arm. His father. Hurting.

"Dad, you're hurting me."

Suddenly they stopped. It was not a good neighborhood. It was a bad place. Dangerous. He wanted to go home.

"Move, Cameron. Now. Come along."

They pressed through a doorway, into a vestibule that smelled of urine and ammonia.

Not a good place. A bad place. A very bad place. Want to go home. Let me—

"Quickly, Cameron!"

Up a zigzag stairway. So many stairs. Up and up and up the dimly lit vertical tunnel.

Tired. Want to sleep. Let me go, please. Let me go.

A whispered command. "Stand here."

"But—"

"Right here. I want her to see you . . . want her to see the people she hurts."

He nodded and felt his eyes start to close.

His ears were filled with the sound of knuckles rapping sharply on wood. Again and again. Insistent. Demanding.

A voice behind the door. Female. Breathless. Sing-song. "Just a minute!"

"Open up. Hotel Security."

A whimper. "I'm not ready."

Please, I want to go. Let me. I want to—

The door opened and he stood face to face with a clown. A clown with penciled eyebrows and livid red lips and a white porcelain face. A clown in a tilted red wig. His mother.

Her face broke into a fragmented smile. "Oh baby—"

There was a blur of motion, like a bat. The bat flew forward and into the white china face. The bat ripped savagely, biting not into porcelain but soft powdered flesh.

Blood! Oh God, so much blood! The china face tilted back, spewing red rain. She reached out, tried to touch him.

"Oh baby!"
He fell forward into her arms.

"No!"
Cameron jerked the recliner forward and shot up from the chair.
"No!"
"Cameron, it's okay."
He stared at them, breathing hard, fists clenched at his sides.
"What did you see?" demanded Forrest. "Tell us what you saw."
"Nothing!" he screamed. "I saw nothing at all!"
Blindly he bolted from the room.

50 Mildred jumped up. "We've got to go after him."
"Not so fast," said Forrest.
"What?" She looked at him, ready to do battle.
"Give him time."
"Time to do what? Time to kill himself? Like my son? Trevor, reason with him. Please."
"I think Forrest's right," said Trevor. "The boy's distraught. We don't know how much he remembered. Or if he remembered anything at all, for that matter. He needs time to sort it out. Without us poking and prying. I'm afraid we've done too much already."
Mildred was unconvinced. "No. He may have remembered everything. He may confront his father."
"Yeah," said Irene. "And he might get hurt. Think about that."

"All right," replied Forrest. "We'll take a walk up to the Maine house and see how the boy's doing."

But they were old. They were slow. And they would be too late.

Cameron ran up King Lane. As he ran, he breathed very deeply, forcing air hard into his lungs. It was a trick. A trick he'd learned to help him relax. He turned onto High Ridge Avenue and sprinted up the driveway.

The house was empty.

"Dad!"

"Back here, son."

He continued to force air into his lungs as he walked across the sun-scorched grass to the back of the house.

There he was, floating in the pool on a Styrofoam lounger, a glass of lemonade in his hand. He peered at his son through mirrored sunglasses.

"Cameron, are you all right?"

Cameron looked down into the blue water.

"Fine."

His father eyed him sharply. "Why are you looking at me like that?"

"Because," he said, "I'm going to kill you."

"What?"

"Where are the others?"

"Out. What the hell did you say?" His father cocked his head and made it sound like a joke. "You're going to kill me?"

Slowly, methodically, Cameron untied his Nikes. He removed them and placed them on the hot flagstones.

"Cameron? For God's sake—"

He dove into the cool blue water, cutting off his father's words. He swam down deep and looked up. He could see his father's body, floating against the cloudless sky.

51 Forrest, Irene, Trevor, and Mildred were already on High Ridge when they heard the screams.

Claudia ran toward them, arms outstretched. "Help!" she screamed. "Somebody call an ambulance!"

Irene grabbed the girl's shoulders and shook her gently. "What's happened?"

"The pool," she gasped. "There's been an accident at the pool. My father . . . Oh God, I think he's dead."

Forrest and Trevor raced up the long driveway and rounded the house.

They found Cameron at the side of the pool, his wet clothes clinging to his body like bubbled skin, single-mindedly performing CPR on his father's inert body.

Trevor knelt and felt for a pulse. He looked up at Forrest for a moment and shook his head almost imperceptibly.

"Let him be, son."

The boy seemed not to hear. He pressed his face to his father's and forced air through the cold blue lips. He pounded frantically on the motionless chest.

"He's gone, Cameron. You've done all you can do."

Trevor held him close. The boy closed his eyes and a sob tore from his throat.

52 "I try to tell myself it was for the best," sighed Mildred almost a year later.

Forrest grunted. "Jonathan got what he deserved."

"Besides," said Irene, "it was an accident. The coroner said so."

"Right." Forrest shifted in his chair and looked at Trevor, whose eyes locked on his own. "An accident."

Irene, who had no lingering doubts, grinned at the baby in her arms. "Hey there, little fella!"

Forrest sighed. He hadn't been able to let it rest so easily. For months he tossed and turned at night, remembering about Cameron's breathing exercises. Remembering how he could hold his breath longer than anyone. Remembering how he scared the lifeguard at Great Pond.

One morning not many months after Jonathan's death, Forrest could stand it no longer. He had gotten up early, put on his heavy L. L. Bean lumberjack shirt and Yorkshire cords, and left Irene snoring under the down comforter. It was round about Thanksgiving and an early frost crunched under his feet. He walked all the way to the old high school up on the ridge overlooking the village. To watch the sun rise, he told himself. Only he went for another reason too, though he wouldn't admit it, even to himself.

He saw the boy in the distance, running at the far end of the old cinder track, his hair ablaze in the early morning light. Forrest picked a place in the peeling bleachers and watched, thinking the boy hadn't noticed him. But the boy was aware and nodded as he came around, legs pummelling, muscles straining, breath condensing in front of him.

The boy made two more laps before he loped over to Forrest and sat down next to him.

"I thought you'd come to see me," he said, "sooner or later."

"I want to know why," said Forrest without preamble, "you were doing CPR. When it was you who killed him."

His head jerked back. "I didn't—"

"Don't lie to me, boy. You of all people."

Cameron looked down at his hands, then out over the field at a stand of sugar maples, their branches naked and brittle. "Okay," he said, "but it's not like you think. I tried to save him."

Forrest said nothing. The boy had put on a good show then and was doing the same now.

"I admit I wanted to kill him when I jumped in the water. I wanted to drag him down. I wanted to see the same terror on his face that had been on hers. . . ."

He rose to the surface under the pontooned chaise, and dumped his father over. Ice cubes flew and the plastic glass bobbed, half full, at the surface. Cameron grabbed hold of his father's shoulders and pulled him down.

It was so easy, so very easy.

An expression of horror blossomed on Jonathan Maine's face. His arms flailed desperately. He clawed at his son, struggling to free himself.

His screams were silent ones. Then he rose to the surface. "Stop! You've got to listen. You've got to—"

Cameron dragged him under a second time and looked at his father's contorted face. For a moment he almost felt a pang of pity. But only for a moment.

By the time Jonathan Maine came up for air the second time he realized he would die. Yet he continued to hope, continued to struggle. "Lies!" he cried. "They told you lies!"

He felt himself going under again, felt Cameron drag him down. In his panic he thought he heard his son say something.

Cameron looked at him with crazed eyes. "I remember!" he screamed. "I remember!"

Jonathan's face pleaded, then bargained, then begged. He would do anything, anything at all to escape his son's final, most intimate embrace.

Then suddenly Cameron lost his resolve. He loosened his grip. He let his father go.

With lungs bursting, Jonathan exploded from the surface. He gulped air convulsively, but although Cameron had released him, the panic would not. And in the clutch of that panic, in the depths of instinctive animal response, Jonathan lunged at his son. He clawed and ripped and kicked, driving the boy beneath him, striving for a foothold.

Terrified himself now, Cameron tried to flee, but his father's hands clutched at his arms, his ankles, his neck. The boy managed to surface for one last breath, then dove deep, dragging his frightened father behind him. And in his panic, in his moment of tragic disorientation, Jonathan Maine gasped, forcing water into his lungs.

His body convulsed. His eyes rolled back in their sockets. And his heart stopped. He went limp in his son's arms. And all too suddenly he was dead.

"I tried to save him," repeated Cameron softly. "I changed my mind. I decided he should live. Living with what he did would have been the worst punishment of all."

"You decided? You changed your mind?" Forrest looked at him in disbelief. "You think life's loaded with second chances? Jesus night! Didn't you know there's no changing your mind about a thing like that?"

"No!"

"Death waits, boy. It bides its time. And when the right moment comes, death doesn't hesitate. There is no second chance. You don't get to *decide*."

"I know," said Cameron. "I know that now." Tears glistened in the corners of his eyes, but he made no move to wipe them away.

"And now," said Forrest angrily, "you're the one who has to live with it." He got up.

"What are you going to do?"

"Not a damned thing. The question is, what are you doing to do?"

Forrest turned and walked away.

Irene ignored Forrest's faraway expression. Sometimes he could be moody, but it would pass. It always did. She rocked the baby back and forth in the rocker. When she spoke her tone was wistful. "You know, I was taken aback when Cameron up and left Raven's Wing."

"He always said he wanted to be a priest," reminded Mildred.

"I know, but I can't get used to it. The seminary at his age? It seems so drastic. Like prison or something."

Forrest said nothing. He wondered if Cameron Maine would ever find the absolution he so desperately sought. Somehow he thought not.

"He'll be okay," said Trevor. "The boy's smart as a whip."

"Too smart. And too quiet. He needs mothering, just like this little fella."

"That baby gets plenty of mothering," said Forrest. "What with you and Lauren jumping at every opportunity to babysit, Claudia has it made."

"And so do we," said Mildred. She surveyed the living room. "I can't believe I'm back in this house. It's amazing. Everything's the same right to the last detail. I keep pinching myself."

"If anyone pinched you," said Forrest sourly, "it was those contractors in town. They took you to the cleaners' rebuilding it."

"Fiddlesticks. What else was I going to do with the

money? You know, this living room is perfect. Except for one thing."

"Oh yeah?" said Forrest. "What's that?"

Mildred cocked her head toward the mantel. "That gun. Unloaded or not, I don't want it up there."

"That gun saved my life," protested Forrest.

"I don't care. It killed poor Constance."

"Poor Constance? Christ on a crutch, she wanted to kill me! She wanted to kill all of us! That's what she wanted."

"Never mind. I hate guns. And think about Ramon. He'll be a toddler before you know it, and when he is he'll toddle straight for that gun. They all do."

Trevor agreed. "She's got a point, Forrest."

"Oh all right." Reluctantly he removed the gun from the mantel. "Now my life's being run by a baby. When it comes to children, I'm with W. C. Fields. I like them fine, if they're properly cooked."

"That's disgusting," said Irene, "and you don't mean it, either." She proceeded to rock faster. "Don't listen to him, honey. He doesn't mean it. He's all bluff."

"Irene's really taken with that tyke, isn't she?" said Trevor.

Forrest grunted. "Got a peculiar color, that baby."

"Why, Forrest," said Mildred, "he's a lovely color. He's olive-skinned. Ever so much nicer than plain boring white."

"Humph." Forrest was unimpressed. He eyed the baby sideways. The little fella was sort of cute. In his way. Even with that color. "I'll say one thing. He's got an amazing set of balls."

"Forrest!"

"Well, he does. I was changing him this afternoon—"

"You?" hooted Mildred.

"Irene was," he amended quickly. "I was only supervising."

"Yeah," said Irene. "Ramon'll be calling him granddaddy before you know it."

"He better not," muttered Forrest.

Trevor and Mildred laughed.

"I betcha Claudia knows who the father is," Forrest persisted. "What with that color, she's got to know, don't you think? Unless she bedded down with all of Spanish Harlem."

Irene covered Ramon's ears. "Shut your mouth!"

"Your problem," said Trevor, "is that you have to know everything about everybody. Let it go, for gosh sakes. No one cares. Let Claudia have her privacy."

"Well he sure doesn't look like a Maine."

Irene looked at Ramon as though he were a jewel of extraordinary value. "That's all to the good. The Maine family can use some new blood. Right, Ramon? A little Spanish spice won't do no harm. Personally, I'm a little tired of dried-up old WASPs. No offense, Millie."

"No offense taken," said Mildred. "Besides, the Maines are Catholic. And as for me, I may be a WASP but I'm certainly not dried up." She winked at Trevor.

"I wonder," said Forrest, "if we'll ever hear from Helga again."

"There you go again," said Mildred, "stewing and worrying. Leave it lie, Forrest. Helga's long gone, and I for one feel sorry for her."

"She was a damned liar."

"Yes," said Trevor, "but she loved Jonathan. She gave up everything for him. Now she's given up her children. To them, she'll never be anything more than just another housekeeper who left."

"Funny how things turned out, isn't it," said Mildred almost to herself.

"How's that?" asked Forrest.

"We thought Jonathan Maine would get away with murder. But he didn't."

Forrest looked out the window at the bird feeder, where two squirrels were devouring their weight in sunflower seeds. As far as he was concerned, the case was closed. He not only knew what happened, he knew why. Sometimes it was better to leave well enough alone. Sometimes it was better to forget the dead and get on with the business of living.

But in spite of these thoughts, his mind turned to Esther Maine. Had anyone ever really known her? He thought not. Long ago a small child named Esther gave up on reality and created her own world. A safer place, or so she thought.

And Cameron? What about him? He wondered what the boy was doing now . . . Picking apples in some seminary orchard? Studying his lessons in a classroom full of fresh young faces? Or maybe he was on his knees, head bowed, hands folded, thinking about things. Worse things. One thing was certain, the truth had not set Cameron Maine free.

The boy had shaken Forrest's hand when he left. "Don't worry," he said, "this is what I want."

"What are you going to do?" asked Forrest a mite too gruffly. "Study the Commandments?"

"Yes," replied Cameron. He tried to smile. "I never thought I'd trip up on the first one."

Forrest didn't know what to say. Suddenly his eyes stung. He pulled Cameron to him and spoke into his white blond hair.

"Don't forget us, boy."

"Never," replied Cameron into the folds of Forrest's shirt. "Never."

Forrest could feel tears against his chest and choked back his own. Someday, he thought to himself . . . yes, someday the boy will learn to do that too.